CITY OF A GREAT KING
BOOK TWO

SEVENTY-FIVE DAYS TO THE RED LAND

Y.G. SHORESH

DPSM
PUBLISHING

City of a Great King Book Two
SEVENTY-FIVE DAYS TO THE RED LAND
Y. G. Shoresh
Cover Art: Avi Blyer
Published July 2022
Copyright © 2022
Gary I. Wurtzel
All Rights Reserved under International and Pan-American Copyright
Conventions

Library of Congress Control Number: 2021925675

ISBN 979-8-9855066–4-8 (Hardcover edition)
ISBN 979-8-9855066–2-4 (Paperback edition)
ISBN 979-8-9855066–6-2 (Ebook edition)

CONTENTS

IN THIS PART OF THE TALE

House of Hesera
Hesera, Sorcerer of the Two Kingdoms
Mereyamun, his former apprentice, now a scribe in the service of Harkuhotep
Nebamun, Steward of Hesera's House (deceased)
Sartuma, widow of Nebamun, Mistress of the House
Adjedaa, a serving maid
Kheruef, a manservant

House of Harkuhotep
Harkuhotep, Seal Bearer of the King of Kehmeht
The Princess Esemkhebe Ta-Sherit, his wife (deceased)
Okpara Ir-en Harkuhotep, their son
Neferet, daughter to Harkuhotep and Esemkhebe Ta-Sherit, now married to Setka
Herit, Okpara's wife.
Inyotef, a Herald and Harkuhotep's illegitimate son

House of Djedhor Hordedef

Djedhor Hordedef, General of the Army of the
UpperKingdom
Setka, his son

In Gohshen

Amenakhte, an Administrator of Overseers in Rahmessu
(deceased)
Mayati, his daughter
Bakenmut An Overseer in Rahmessu
Senwosret An Overseer in Rahmessu

Iebiru of the Nation of The Dahnii

Avishamah
Shuvina, wife of Avishamah
Aelinahtan, their son
Baht-Tikvi, his wife
Geula, his sister
Amikhai, her husband

WEEKS AND MONTHS IN THE BLACK LAND

In the Black Land, at the time of this tale, the year was divided into three seasons, each one lasting four months, each month counted in three weeks of ten days each.

So, when Mereyamun counts seven and a half "weeks," he means weeks of ten days each. That would be two and a half months, which to him is seven and a half "weeks," or exactly seventy-five days.

The tale resumes on the first day of the first week of Hnsw, First Month of Shemu, Season of The River Running Low, day one of the Seventy-Five Days.

The year, in our reckoning, is 1313 BCE.

CHAPTER I
THE FIRST WEEK OF HNSW, FIRST MONTH OF SHEMU, SEASON OF THE RIVER RUNNING LOW
DAY ONE OF THE SEVENTY-FIVE DAYS

The moon had just risen and I had barely gotten a start on the flagon of wine I had stashed in my room when Adjedaa came to tell me that-a Lord was waiting downstairs.

"What Lord, Adjedaa? What is his name?"

"He did not say. But he seems very lordly." She was a simple girl.

The "lord" I found in the vestibule was a servant, but of a very high house, dressed well, jeweled, and with both a torchbearer and a man-at-arms. Adjedaa's error was understandable.

"Your Honor," he droned, "my Master Setka, son of Djedhor Hordedef, General of the Army of the Upper Kingdom, begs your pardon for this late invitation, and asks you to do him the kindness of attending dinner at his home."

"Now?"

"Yes, now," he smiled in an irksome way. "At your convenience."

Such airs from the house of Setka and Neferet! I

wondered if, penned-up in the Great House during the siege of the animals, they had finally succumbed to Okpara's instruction on acting as rank required. But then, this was only the second evening since Neferet's mother had died. Was this some sort of mourning meal? Being in honor of The Princess Esemkhebe Ta-Sherit could explain the formality of it all.

This would not be a comfortable visit. It would have been awkward enough with Setka and Neferet before this family tragedy. Did they think I felt nothing about their putting the friendship of our childhood behind them, ignoring me these last two months? What pleasure could there be now for them, or me, in trying to reconnect under the shadow of death and mourning? It seemed a poor alternative to going back to that flagon of wine in my room.

But what if they really did crave my company now, when death had come so close? It would be unkind to refuse. It would be a betrayal of loyalty or of whatever it was that still bound us. So I nodded and stepped out into the night without changing my clothing or oiling my wig. That would express my cool disdain for their fancy new style. But my words would be of friendship and solidarity in a sad time.

The lordly servant fell into step with me, though at a respectful distance. The torchbearer led our way, with the man-at-arms following behind. Upon approaching Setka's house I could see another figure in the shadows outside the door. He showed no weapon, but his bearing said he was a soldier.

The torchbearer and the man-at-arms fell out of step and remained outside with the soldier while the servant walked me in, opening the doors himself, as none of Setka's and Neferet's household servants were in sight. From inside

I heard a number of voices chatting very amiably. "Mereyamun is here," someone said.

I entered the great room, a colorful and warmly lit blur of small tables with grapes and nuts on them, surrounded by couches and chairs thick with people. Setka and Neferet were there, of course, she looking very much with child now and dressed in a blue garment of mourning. But there also was Ankhuemhesut, his hand re-bandaged quite nicely I noticed, and some other sorcerers I recognized but whose names I did not remember.

There was the old scribe who had ventured to speak when we were taken to see the sculpture of the Iebiri Mother deep in the palace. There were others who I did not know, though they all looked noble enough, or were at least dressed as only those high in the Service of The Throne of the Two Kingdoms would be. The wave of a hand turned my vision toward the end of the room and there was Inyotef, arm raised in greeting, and next to him, Harkuhotep.

I had never spoken to Harkuhotep outside of the Great House. I could hardly imagine him anywhere else, least of all in a gathering like this. This was more like what you might see in the common room of an inn, though one for the very rich and at a mournful time. I had no idea what you're supposed to do in such a situation. It seemed silly to prostrate myself before him, but I didn't think a wave of the hand and a simple "hello" would be right either. I made a sort of half bow from the waste, and, fortunately, he spoke first.

"No need for that here, Mereyamun," he said. "How are you feeling?"

How was *I* feeling? This man had just lost his wife in a most horrible way. More, his personal loss was also a public humiliation to him, for if his policies had prevailed the Iebiru would have gone on their religious excursion and there would have been no need for the Plague of Soot (that's what people were calling it now) and his wife would have lived.

But I had seen this before; I knew what it was. People who have been dealt a harsh blow suffering an irretrievable loss, turn away from their grandeur and became something else, at least for a while. Like a sand snake shedding its skin, their honor and position is shuffled off and left behind and they go forward in a sad simplicity marked by empathy for all the little sufferings that everyone else bears. So, then, how was I feeling?

"I am well," I said.

Harkuhotep raised his eyebrows a bit as if to say "Really? How can that be?"

"I mean," I stumbled onwards, "that with all that has happened to so many, to yourself... I was lucky, I think. I have no right to complain. I am sorry for your loss."

"I have no right to complain either, Mereyamun," he said. "So many of our people have died. We must think now of the living."

His voice was strong, but mild. It was "blue" somehow, the blue of his mourning tunic and robe. It was no time to respond in fancy words, but I could find no plain ones.

"You have nothing to fear here Mereyamun," he said. "And nothing to prove either. You are among friends, true friends, who know your worth and who love you for it. And I count myself among them."

I must have looked stunned as a clubbed calf.

"True, I do not show you this favor publicly, but that is calculated. I want no one thinking you are in special favor with me, though you most assuredly are, as is everyone in this room. What we discuss here requires discretion, even secrecy. That's why you were called so late and without preparation, so no prying eyes would take special note of your coming. And that's why you were called to this house. Even if it became known that I have come here of an evening, what is unusual about a father visiting his daughter and her husband at a time like this? You understand?" he said, with some sympathy.

"Very little," I said quite honestly.

Harkuhotep actually laughed a bit.

"You will leave with a great deal more understanding before we adjourn tonight. Please, take a seat. Drink something."

Inyotef got up from his stool and moved over one, tapping the one he had vacated, so I found myself at Harkuhotep's right hand. He gave me a light pat on the shoulder as I settled in. Then the meeting –for that is what this really was– began in earnest.

"Pahroh is wise," Harkuhotep said. "But much has been hidden from him by advisors who are mostly false and all quite stupid." The fire was in Harkuhotep still.

"Our task is to bring Pahroh that which has been concealed, whether by ignorance or perfidy." He took in the room and rested his eyes on Ankhuemhesut.

"Ankhuemhesut, you have spoken with Aaharohn and Mohsheh." It was a statement, not a question.

"I have been to see them," Ankhuemhesut confirmed. "Several times. But never by myself, always with Yiyahnohs and Yahmbrohs. I spoke little during those visits. But they acknowledged me."

"Can you bring me to them?" Harkuhotep asked with a whisper of uncertainty I never heard in him before. "Will they receive me?"

"They receive everyone who comes to them," Ankhuemhesut said. "They receive the high born and the lowly, the wise and the simple, all courteously. Even cheerfully, I would say."

"Then I will go to them," Harkuhotep resolved. "And I will bring my own report to Our Father Pahroh. And he who holds the Crook and the Flail of the Two Kingdoms will believe me again. He will understand, and this senseless suicidal contest will come to an end. I am certain of it."

And that would be that, I thought. Harkuhotep believed in this destiny and, at that moment, I believed in Harkuhotep. I shared in the warm *maat* that went through each of us in that room chosen to witness this decision. So that was why I was invited here, I thought. To witness this. To write of it, perhaps, in some future scroll that would tell how, after this turning point, Kehmeht was saved.

"You are to come with us, Mereyamun," Harkuhotep said. "We leave at dawn."

When I was seven years old and Neferet was eight, her Mother would sometimes send a maidservant to break up our games by calling Neferet to dance lessons. The servant always oozed servile distaste for me, as if her little princess was being rescued from playing with some contemptible slimy thing newly slithered out of The River mud.

And I, being too young to have the good sense to show noble disdain for the servant (and her mistress) used to just tag along anyhow. I usually had nothing better to do and often hadn't had my fill of Neferet for that day. So there I would be, sprawled in the empty gallery of the hall used to instruct young princesses in sacred dances.

There were always about a dozen girls there lined up to face the dancing master. He was a tall man of some minor nobility who wielded a long staff that he sometimes tapped on the marble floor to rebuke the musicians for flagging rhythms and other times extended to jostle the girls into place. The gallery was cool in the hot afternoons, and I would slump on the empty stone benches and smirk at the performance.

I would make sure to let out a breath of sophisticated exasperation every once in a while, when the girls did something especially awkward. Neferet, I noted, showed no sign at all of the grace and talent that had made her grandmother a legend in her day. But Neferet surpassed all the princesses in *belief*.

When the dance called for the girls to behave as sacred herons, she would bob her head and set her eyes downward and out to some middle distance, like a heron stalking fish. At first you'd have to snigger at how she looked, but after a few seconds the snigger would fade and you would see how the spirit of the heron was in her. Or at least she made it look that way, which is pretty much the same thing.

Near the end of the lessons, the princesses had to put on capes of starched linen, stiffly folded and strapped to their arms to represent wings. The sacred birds would form up facing one another in two lines and the otherwise bored musicians would perk up at the sight of it. The drums became very rhythmic and insistent and the lyre player would beat his strings as much as pluck them, adding more percussion at a higher pitch. The flutes would soar and two singers, little older than girls themselves but very skilled, would soar even higher.

The princesses would swoop and pass each other, one wing folded and one wing extended, and then turn and swoop and pass each other again so that the two lines would merge and part, over and over. And the patterns they made were so beautiful that I would feel a lump in my throat and I was glad that I was alone and well hidden in the shade of the gallery.

And that was what I thought of now, this morning, as I stood on the bank of The River watching six boats with lateen sails looking for all the world like the unfolded wings of sacred herons gliding past one another as they ferried Harkuhotep's train across the water.

When Harkuhotep told me I was to go with him to Gohshen, I assumed we would travel north on a great ship with a hundred oarsmen, and then be escorted by a force of mounted soldiers and charioteers to the village of the Leyvie where Mohsheh and Aaharohn lived. When the servant who was sent to fetch me at dawn told me that the trip was to be in wagons, I assumed that Harkuhotep had decided to dispense with a military escort and, instead, enter the area quietly, disguising us as wayfarers or merchants. It was only when I got to the assembly point that I understood that neither of my assumptions was even close to what Harkuhotep had in mind. Our journey was to be neither a show of power by the Throne, nor a secret infiltration. It was to be a parade.

I counted fourteen covered wagons draped with pennants, some with six horses in harness, matched for their colors. There were another twenty or so open wagons, some pulled by donkeys, others by tall horses with bells on their bridles. It was to be a gesture, a grand one. Harkuhotep would come to Gohshen as a benefactor in rich wagons laden with all the good things of the Black Land. It was to be a sign of the new policy Harkuhotep advocated toward the Iebiru, returning them to their original status of welcomed and trusted citizens of Kehmeht.

Our pace was bright but not rushed. It took a good quarter of an hour from the time the locals first heard us coming until we vanished down their stretch of road. We wound our way around the villages of the floodplain where farmers would down tools for a while, wave to us, and shout greetings in praise of Our Father Pahroh and, sometimes, of The Lord Harkuhotep himself.

Children would run out to see the sight of us and scamper alongside for as long as their parents might allow. Harkuhotep instructed Setka and the others riding up next to the drovers to toss things to the crowd: figs, dates, and small satchels of nuts and raisins. Sometimes they would scatter copper coins too.

Word of it travelled faster than we did, so that at each succeeding village more and more men, women, and children were there to greet us and to receive the gifts Harkuhotep bestowed upon them. It was hours then, mid-morning, when we finally paused to turn right and cross over to the east bank of The River. And that was where the six boats met us, each of them with a lateen sail and a crew that understood how to capture the wind even if it was against them.

Whether headed east laden with wagons and animals, or turned back west to take on another load, applying oars sometimes but always gracefully, they glided past one another, never veering in their course but never touching, each with a sail extended like the single wing of the sacred heron.

"This is who we are," I thought to myself. "This is what we, the children of the Black Land, *do*. We make paths in flowing waters. We build roads and cities and bind water and sky, animals and men, wood and bronze into a sacred dance. And we are happy in this."

True, we were in the middle of a crisis just now. A force, a Power we were helpless to resist, was toying with us like a cat with a captive songbird. But it might yet all be turned to good, Harkuhotep told us. If only we would embrace the Iebiru again as we once had. Unless it was, as Okpara fretted and Hesera said, an evil trick of the Iebiru brothers to humiliate and destroy us? Who could tell for sure?

But just look at those ships! Look at the wooden ramps bound with strips of bronze notched perfectly into hewn stone on each bank of The River so that the wagons are driven right up and onto the barges, their teams still in harness. Listen to the sounds of the drummers on the ships, beating in perfect unity the sacred dance on the sun-sparkled water. This was Kehmeht, this was The Land That Makes Her Children Happy. Surely all would still be well. Somehow.

∼

After the crossing, a half-hour's ride east brought us into Gohshen. Here the spectators were Iebiru and more circumspect. They were curious, to be sure. But they were not quite certain what our parade might mean. There was no cheering, but a number of them bowed from the waist and murmured some sort of salutation in our language, badly accented. Some watched impassively, their faces impossible to read. Some smiled. Some gave looks that bordered, to my mind, on treason.

The children seemed glad enough. They scampered around, snatching up the gifts tossed in their general direction. The adults however, out of awe, respect, suspicion, contempt or some admixture of them all, mostly ignored us.

Around this time Inyotef cantered down the line on a white stallion to tell me that it was my turn to go up and ride for a while with Harkuhotep himself.

"Give me a lift up to him?"

It was no big feat for me to get up on the stallion behind Inyotef. The wagon bed was half as high as the stallion's withers, and Inyotef just about yanked me up with one strong arm. As we cantered back up the line I realized I should dismount and appear before Harkuhotep's wagon from the ground, a position of more deference for the Unique Friend of Pahroh, Trusted of All His House.

"Inyotef," I said from behind his back and into the general direction of his ear, "slow down. Let me off."

"Why?" he laughed.

We cantered until we were alongside Harkuhotep's wagon. Inyotef reined-in hard, slowing us just enough to match the wagon's pace, then stuck the reins in his teeth, turned in his saddle and just about yanked me off the horse's back and onto the wagon bench next to Harkuhotep. Very dignified.

Harkuhotep didn't seem to mind. I think he actually smiled. Well, why not? This was a prank of his beloved son, the one with the strong arms and the light in his eyes, embers of the love that once burned in Harkuhotep's heart for Inyotef's mother. And besides, hadn't Harkuhotep, just last night, said that he loved me, loved me for my worth? Or something like that?

"What do you think we will find, Mereyamun?" Harkuhotep mused. "I know, of course, that we are not the first to meet with the Iebiru brothers. But there has never been a delegation of our rank before, has there?"

I didn't know, but I imagined he was correct in this. So I nodded.

"Yes, men of fine intellect have been to speak with them," he continued. "But these brothers, they are princes, Mereyamun. The older one is the high prince of the Leyvie, and respected and loved by all the Iebiru nations from what I hear."

I nodded again, and this time it was because I knew it to be so. I heard Iebiru express suspicions, complaints and even accusations about Mohsheh. But never about Aaharohn.

"And as for Mohsheh, well, Aaharohn himself defers to him. Before the Throne he acts as Mohsheh's herald, he has clearly made himself second to his younger brother. Do you know why, Mereyamun?"

"I do not," I confessed.

"I have a notion about it," Harkuhotep said. "The brothers defy the Throne of the Two Kingdoms. They contest the will of Our Father Pahroh himself. But they always do it most respectfully. They are adamant in their claims, but they are courtly in how they phrase them. So I wonder if Aaharohn, the elder and most loved of the two, defers to his younger brother because he was, once, a great prince of Kehmeht?"

This was strange and disturbing to me. True, Senwosret had told me that his grandfather served in the army under Mohsheh's command. And there were references to Mohsheh's military victories in the archives, and brief entries in which he approved something or ordered one thing or another for the work in Rahmessu. But to see this wooly man of the Iebiru as a young prince of the Black Land was near unimaginable. And now Harkuhotep, whose speech always held layers upon layers of meaning, was challenging me to imagine it.

"Does he want the Throne, then?" I blurted out. "Is that why they preserve its dignity? Is that why they haven't killed us all?"

"It could be thought so," Harkuhotep said. "It is, by some. But could it not be that they simply want the Iebiru to be again what they once were: loyal citizens of Kehmeht? I feel I will know when I speak with him, Mereyamun. I am confident about this."

We fell into a companionable silence. The wagon jostled along. I drifted into sweet thoughts about how I would play a role, however humble, in this historic encounter that would come before the day was done. Kehmeht would be released from her sufferings as the Iebiru were released from theirs. A new epoch would be born, and I would be there, in its service.

"Ho!" the postilion rider on Harkuhotep's matched team called, his right arm raised. I could not tell if the gesture was meant to signal "Halt!" to our driver or "Hail!" to the delegation that was coming down the road to meet us. Both maybe.

Their wagons and teams, stood respectfully off in the distance as they approached on foot. They were Iebiru, but men of wealth and of some rank, for they were dressed very well (too many layers of cloaks and scarves, of course, but of fine fabrics). "Rehuveyni," I thought to myself and said so to Harkuhotep to show how clever and indispensable I was.

As they drew closer, I recognized among them the three associates of Amenakhte I had seen at his home. I looked at them and, as happens always when I take a good look at anyone, their heads swiveled and their eyes locked instantly on mine. So right there, in the middle of their effusive greetings to the lord Harkuhotep, Seal Bearer of the King of Upper and Lower Kehmeht, Unique Friend of Pahroh, Trusted of All His House, all three were grinning with pleasure at finding *me*. They welcomed me expansively by name. They rejoiced in their good fortune at my coming. They explained to Harkuhotep how they "for *months* now," have had the pleasure of my acquaintance.

That they would spin this tale so long and so far puzzled me. But it shouldn't have. Like Amenakhte, they thirsted for favor from the Great Ones of The City. And there I was, riding next to the Great Man himself. Surely it looked like fortune smiling on them.

What was truly strange though, was how pleased Harkuhotep seemed to be with the whole encounter. The Harkuhotep of old, the one I thought I knew, would have shunned this from wealthy Iebiru. It was overly familiar, a breech of the fear and respect due one so near the Throne. But Harkuhotep today was perfectly gracious.

He regretted, he said, that his business was pressing and would not allow him to accept their generous offer of hospitality. I almost believed him.

"But," Harkuhotep continued to the Iebiru, "let young Mereyamun attend in my place. Those of you who know him have some sense of the esteem in which he is held in the Chamber of Judgments. His attendance will be like my own, for he has my trust and carries my command. His word to you is my word."

And that was that. My wagon was called up the line, laden with extra supplies that could double as gifts for my visit. My driver was told to follow as I was seated on the finest wagon of the Iebiru, along with the three who "knew" me and one who seemed to want to.

Failing to net the big fish, they contended now to get hold of the smaller one. So off we went, down a track that turned aside from Harkuhotep's route to the village of Mohsheh. The new epoch would begin without me.

∾

We arrived at an estate nestled among several others in a grassy, pleasing part of Gohshen. It was cool but well-lit inside, with ivory furnishings and woodwork of acacia and oak and stone carving that would rival that found in the fine houses of The City.

A small army of Iebiri house slaves stood at the ready with crafted copper washbasins, perfumed linen towels, silver platters of beverages, and extra pillows to be offered once we ascended the embroidered couches. It was clearly The Lord Harkuhotep, Seal Bearer of the King of Upper and Lower Kehmeht, Unique Friend of Pahroh, Trusted of All His House that they had prepared for. But they were stuck with me.

Well, I was stuck with them, wasn't I? The more they lavished on me, the more annoyed I became at them, and at Harkuhotep, and at the strange decree of the gods that I must always miss everything!

History was going to be made in the next few hours, the uncrowned king of the Iebiri nations would meet with the Strong Hand of the Throne of the Two Kingdoms. An understanding would be forged, promises would be exchanged, the Power of the Iebiru would bless The Black Land and Kehmeht's star would rise again, higher than before. And I had been an hour's ride, two at most, from being there, from seeing it, from playing some part in it.

The physicians of the Black Land have ointments that make the flesh as unfeeling as stone. This they apply gently and wait a few moments until the patient agrees that the feeling is pleasant and then, a few moments later admits to no feeling at all. Then they cut, they draw blood, they do what they will, and the patient is insensible to pain. That's what Harkuhotep's words, back on the road, were to me.

Who had ever praised me like that? I was held in "the esteem of the Chamber of Judgments," my attending this reception would "be like Harkuhotep himself," for I have "his trust and carry his command, my word is his word!" How good those utterances felt when he first applied them. How numb I became as I was carried away to this pointless feast of Iebiru-owning Iebiru. And now the ointment had worn off and I felt the ache of my amputation from everything that mattered.

Smack! One of the Iebiri house slaves was reeling from a slap administered by the master of the house. I had no idea what imperfection Meishav ben Amiel (for that was his name, if I was remembering correctly) found in his slave, or why it required this blow.

Of the Iebiru who professed to know me, this Meishav was the one I liked least. He was always servile towards me and unctuous to an extreme, but verbally cruel to his Iebiri servants. Now I guess he wanted to show me that he was capable of actual violence towards them too.

He had learned somewhere along the way in his thirty odd years that Sons of Kehmeht liked watching Iebiru afflicting other Iebiru. He was right about that. In my days under the pavilion in Rahmessu, Amenakhte, Bakenmut, and Senwosret enjoyed nothing so much as watching Iebiri task-captains torment the Iebiru under them. This happened rarely enough, for most of the time the Iebiri task-captains defended their Iebiru, even took blows for them. But that just made the occasional exception a spectacle not to be missed. I, however, was in no mood for such games.

So I remained impassive. I could feel them wondering what had gone wrong? Why had I not offered a cruel but witty quip, or at least a guffaw? Everyone snuck glances at me to see why I was not pleased. A silence fell on the room, one that went those few seconds too long so that my hosts were getting uncomfortable.

"We're starved, Ben Amiel!" one of the other Iebiru finally joked, in fake good-fellowship. It was forced, but still a decent way to break the awkward silence.

"Yes, let's get on it with it, shall we?" another said, settling onto his couch.

The house slaves took it as a cue to begin presentation of the meal. Two of them took up lyre and flute and their music smoothed over any lingering discomfort. Meishav ben Amiel understood that his gambit at impressing me had failed colossally, but that was behind us.

We drank, we dined. I saw not a trace of the lamb, beef and poultry these Iebiru no doubt would have loved to eat. And we talked. And we drank. We ate and drank, and talked some more.

"What message will the Lord Harkuhotep convey to Ben Ahmrahm?" one of the Iebiru asked me.

Well, that was an impertinent question for an Iebiri slave, no matter how wealthy, no matter how many Iebiri slaves he himself owned. But we were into our fourth cup by then, this one being a very decent grape wine spiced with something I could neither recognize nor resist. And besides, I was feeling a little impertinent myself. If Harkuhotep was making me miss the meeting with Mohsheh, was I to be barred from speaking about it too?

"My Master Harkuhotep," I said, "is well-disposed toward Mohsheh and his brother. He looks with favor upon the request that the Iebiru be sent on the pilgrimage out into the Red Land to worship their Power."

This was met with grunts of affirmation, even admiration. Only the grunt of our host Ben Amiel seemed tinged with derision. It's amazing how expressive grunts can be. I finished my cup. An Iebiru house-slave appeared instantly to refill it.

"Meishav is no lover of Ben Ahmrahm," the Iebiri on the couch to my right offered, as if that last grunt required exegesis.

"I guessed that," I said as I reached for my revived cup.

"No one knows who he really is," Meishav said in his own defense.

"Or what he is," the fellow on the couch to my left joined in.

"He is beloved of the Eternal, isn't he?" the fellow on my right said. "He does wonders in the name of The Most High, doesn't he?"

"The Most High does as The Most High wishes," Meishav said. "What need does He have of Ben Ahmrahm? I wonder if Ben Ahmrahm is really doing anything at all. I too can stand at a window and decree that a storm come, once it's already blowing."

There was another round of grunts, pro and con. Meishav seemed to decide that the preponderance of grunts was moving in his favor, so he went on.

"This man is not one of us. He was forty years a Prince of Kehmeht, then disappeared into the East for another forty. Now he just strolls back into our lives and speaks for us?"

"He was raised among us," Right Couch said. "The Princess who plucked him from The River sent him back to his natural mother for a wet-nurse."

"And he was returned to the Great House when he was two. What part of a man is formed before he is two?" Left Couch said. "Does a man even remember those years? If memories make us who we are, he is not one of us."

"He brought victories to The Black Land," I inserted at that point, just because I thought I should say something. The scrolls in the archive were clear on this, and on some role he played in the building work at Pi-Thohm and Rahmessu.

"He was *destined* to bring victories," Right Couch said a little dreamily. The man was twice my weight but you could see he could not handle his cups.

"Destiny whispering her secrets to you now, Tzuriel?" Left Couch said. Meishav grunted an affirmation to this retort.

"They say when he was born, the house filled with light," Tzuriel declared, as if this would win everyone over to admire Mohsheh.

"Enough, Tzuriel," one of them said, gently but firmly, as one might speak to a child. Or a drunk. But it didn't stop Tzuriel.

"They called him Tuviyah, the Good One, and Yedidiyah, The Beloved of the Eternal One."

"And with all that he still goes by the name he was given by a Princess of The Great House," Meishav retorted. "Does that not tell you something?"

Tzuriel sat up on his couch and inclined his head in thought for a moment. Then he raised his eyes and looked straight at me. You could hear the collective intake of breath by the others, wondering what new embarrassment was to come from their tipsy colleague now.

"*You* understand, Your Honor," He said. "You *understand*."

I didn't understand. Not really. But I couldn't miss that, alone among his brethren, Tzuriel sensed that some great thing was unfolding. I liked him for that.

"You will go with him then?" I said to Tzuriel. "To the worship in the Red Land?"

"Me?" he answered, smiling as if I had said something of great wit. "*Me*, Your Honor? No, no. I cannot go."

My face must have asked "But why?"

"Mohsheh wants to make us all priests of The Most High! He wants us to live in worship, to live for The Most High. As he himself does. But we are just men. We like to eat. We like to drink. We like to work and trade, too. Maybe the nation of Leyvie is suited for this pilgrimage into the Red Land. But not us, Your Honor. Not us."

"Please, My Lord. Forgive me, My Lord,"

The title was not correct, but it was the best the Iebiri servant could think of as he contrived to rouse me from outside the room in which I slept without waking the rest of the house.

"Forgive me, but it is an officer who says his message will not wait. An officer of The Chamber of Judgments, he says to tell you."

So! Harkuhotep wanted me back with him after all! I was half undressed but I bolted from the room and followed the Iebiru to the entranceway where, under a flickering torch, the messenger waited for me. The man was dusty and had apparently traveled through the night. To reach *me*. I was to be a witness to history after all.

"What does my Lord Harkuhotep need?" I said courteously. "I am ready for his command."

"I do not know, Your Honor" the messenger said to me, clearly puzzled, perhaps by my age, but also by my question.

"I am sent from the Chamber of Judgments," he went on.

Then, slower and louder, realizing I must be an idiot, he patiently explained.

"Not from the Lord Harkuhotep, Your Honor. From his son, the Lord Okpara, who sits on the Seat of Judgment in his father's stead, while the Lord Harkuhotep mourns his wife, The Princess Esemkhebe Ta-Sherit who is in the days of her preparation for her journey to The Happy Land of Reeds."

So that's what people thought Harkuhotep was doing these days. He wore the blue of the mourner, he left the affairs of the Chamber of Judgments to Okpara, he went out on excursions to see into this or that. It was all because of his "mourning." Clever.

But what could Okpara have to tell me that was worth sending a rider after his father's train, only to learn that I was at this Iebiru house, and then to make his way to me here by moonlight?

"My Lord Okpara says to tell you that there is a treasure for you to seek, and it will be found in the house that was Amenakhte's. You are to go there, and take it."

"That's it?" I asked.

"That is the message I was told to bring to you, and to you alone."

~

My driver had wisely avoided any offer of drinking with the Iebiru, so he was rested and uncomplaining about taking off at dawn down the tracks of Gohshen to Amenakhte's abandoned estate. I surprised myself with my memory of the way, and by the time the sun was well up, we were there. I had only to deal with one question: "Why?"

I am in the service of the Chamber of Judgments, so harkening to Okpara was, in fact, obeying Harkuhotep who had posted him as his deputy. There was no question that I would go, though I resented that it took me further from the great things that Harkuhotep was doing at the house of Mohsheh.

But I had no idea what I was supposed to be seeking. Treasure? I was not in need of money, and neither was the Chamber of Judgments, though that never stopped Harkuhotep from collecting a tax or two. Or a fine. Or a "gift" for that matter.

No, if there was a literal treasure in coin or precious stones, Okpara could have sent anyone to grab it for him. This "treasure" had to be valued in some other way, and the only commodity of value I dealt in was information. There must be information, then, left at Amenakhte's estate, papyri that would tell something the Chamber of Judgments would want to know.

But what could fat, foolish, ignorant Amenakhte have known that would be of any interest at all? This I asked myself as I left my driver and the wagon at the gate of Amenakhte's courtyard and walked toward the silent buildings.

"Why, his own crimes, of course!" a voice inside my

head responded. The only thing of interest that Amenakhte could possibly have known is how he contrived to keep for himself some of the livestock he was charged with delivering in sale to the Iebiru. This had got him killed when those unsold animals caught the plague, spread it to him and choked out his life. But apparently that wasn't enough of a punishment. With written proof of the transgression, the Chamber of Judgments could confiscate his entire estate.

It made me angry. I was being sent here just to rummage through the estate, abandoned in haste as it was through fear of the plague which took the life of its owner and his sole heir. There was no great task for me to do here. All I was good for was low-grade entertainment with rich Iebiru, and fetching papyri so that Okpara could show his father that disloyalty was punished and coffers filled.

I was so lost in thinking these things that I almost missed a new structure, halfway across the courtyard, off to my right. It was more an earthen mound than a building, though when I reached it I could see it rose taller than I was, and had hewn stone about waist high wrapped around it.

A slab of smoothed rock inscribed (not very well) in the sacred image-language of Kehmeht declared that this was the tomb of Amenakhte, Sixth of That Name in His Line, Servant of the Throne of the Two Kingdoms. Given my mission here, I wondered, maliciously, if I should amend the part about his serving the Throne.

And then my eyes filled with wet and I felt impossibly sad. Mayati must have seen to the building of this tomb, who else was there to care? I imagined her, already ill, the fever chilling her, supporting herself against the wall in the hot sun while she ordered and cajoled frightened workers into staying long enough to finish it, so that her father's journey to the Happy Land of Reeds would go well.

Who had seen to a tomb for *her?* Was she completely alone when the end came? I lifted my eyes to the main house just ahead of me and had the macabre thought that if she was, indeed, alone at the end, then this house was her tomb.

How sad and stupid everything was. What did it matter if Harkuhotep would never include me in his great deeds or if his son used me as an errand boy? Mayati was dead for no reason other than that Kehmeht had offended a Power who choked us on blood, sent frogs into our stomachs, loosed animals to bloody us, and diseases to rack us until no one knew if death wasn't better than life. So what did it matter what I did or did not do?

I stood still, a statue in the courtyard, feeling like nothing so much as Hesera cackling in his madness that the Power did not care about any of us. It made no difference to Him whether I was brave or cowardly, loyal or treacherous, kind or cruel, smart of stupid. I would do nothing of any consequence because nothing had any. I would walk into this abandoned house now and stumble upon the fever-wasted corpse of Mayati and it would mean nothing, for there was nothing for it to mean. Except, perhaps, a hint that I might as well end my own life too in this house of a fat fool, for I was no better.

It was cool inside. And quiet, of course. But not hastily abandoned. There was no disorder, things were either where they should be or else bundled in neat wraps of leather or burlap, lined up, waiting to be carried off. The shutters were open to air and light, but there was no accumulation of sand or dust. There was no odor of decay, and a peek into all the chambers revealed nothing more than empty beds, some still laden with ticking, others bared to their leather webs. No corpse on any of them. And no papyri, incriminating or otherwise.

There was a sound then, faint but clear, like the clink of metal on ceramic. It was an everyday sound, an unremarkable sound, except that it was the only sound I had heard since entering this place. A breeze maybe, nudging some hanging utensil ever so gently against a vessel? The kitchens, then.

I made my way around the furnishings of the great room and out the door onto the portico. It led back around the side of the house to the small kitchen building. I strained to listen and heard another clink confirming that I was headed the right way. But I didn't require it, for I remembered having visited this out-kitchen before, the day I discovered Amenakhte's house-Iebiru boiling meat for him.

The clink sounded again softly as I rounded the corner of the portico. The light streamed in under the roof, bright, white, and blinding after the cool semi-darkness of the house. My sun-blasted eyes could make out the open doorway of the squat kitchen building only as a rectangle of black. I heard the clink again and went into that black to see what it told. There was someone there.

A form, the shape of a person seated at the table, leaning over a bowl. My eyes could not adjust fast enough from the bright sun to the dark shadow, but sounds in rapid succession told me that a copper spoon was put down in haste on the wooden plank table. A bench was pushed back on the packed earthen floor. Someone rose from seated to standing and turned fully toward me.

"Hello, Merey," she said.

It is not true that I thought she was a ghost or a demon-spirit, though that poor joke was made by people so many times afterwards. But what then did I think? The truth is, for perhaps the first time in my life, I didn't think anything at all. There was nothing to think. And even if there was, I could not think it. I took a step forward and she took a step forward and without remembering choosing to do it, my arms were around her, and hers around me.

I do not know how long we remained that way, a blink of an eye, maybe five blinks. Then we snapped apart as if a sparking eel of the Crescent had sent a shock between us. My eyes adjusted to the dim of the room punctuated by thin shafts of sunlight where the shutters did not properly meet the window frames, and I looked at her. Thought rushed back in. "Say something! Anything!" my brain whispered urgently. "If only to show you are not struck dumb."

"You didn't die," I said. Not brilliant. But true, and all that really mattered.

"No," she said. "I didn't."

"Senwosret came to me in The City and told me that you were surely dead."

"It was the day after you and Inyotef left," she confirmed. "My father fell to his bed in the evening and by noon the next day he was on his journey to the Happy Land of Reeds. It was months since we had any Iebiru working, and the Sons of Kehmeht who we employed wanted to flee. They were terrified Merey, afraid the plague would take them too. Senwosret and Bakenmut forced them to stay and see to my father's wrapping and the building of a tomb. It took two days, and it was all I could do to stay out of their sight, because anyone could see that I also had the fever."

Mayati folded back down onto the bench, as if the memory of her illness had made her weak all over again. Or maybe she still was ill. Her face was not so full as it once was, her cheeks were more sculpted, and she seemed thinned all over.

"Are you alright?" I asked helplessly.

"I am," she said with a single firm nod of her head to assure that she really meant it. "I'm getting stronger every day."

"Good," I said. What a banal thing to say! But it *was* good, wasn't it? And it made her smile a little.

"Anyhow, I was in my bed, soaked with fever, half in this world and half in the next. I remember hearing Bakenmut tell Senwosret to go ahead to The City, that he would stay with me until the end, which could not be long. Were you able to help him, Mereyamun?"

"I got him into the charioteers," I boasted. "It's what he wanted."

"Good," Mayati said. "He stuck by us, he deserves it."

"He told me that Bakenmut wanted to join the army too, but I have not seen him."

"He never left! When he saw that I lived, he brought his wife to care for me. He even brought the children for a while. They were fearless. About catching the disease."

"Where is he then?"

"He has gone to his own house to help his wife pack their things. He'll be back with the wagon for mine and then we'll go to The City. The Lord Okpara has promised him a place in the Great House Guard."

Of course. Someone had to report Amenakhte's demise to the Chamber of Judgments. Bakenmut went there. Okpara guessed how upset I was about Mayati's death, maybe I said more than I remember at our talk in the archive. He saw a chance to do a kindness with me, so he rewarded Bakenmut with a better life away from Gohshen and me with something he knew I wanted more than I knew myself.

I had greatly misjudged Okpara. True, all the accusations I had made against him were made in the privacy of my heart. But I felt ashamed, as if I had hurled them to his face. I resolved to show him gratitude, if only there would be an opportunity.

"So you're going to The City?" I asked, with more hope than I meant to betray in my voice.

"There's nothing for me in Gohshen anymore," Mayati said, mostly to the tabletop. "The Lord Okpara invited me to stay in his household until I'm fully better..." She looked up at me and went on, "... in memory of the service of my father. That's what he said, Merey."

She watched my face for a long time, and then she burst out laughing. It was bitter laughing, but sustained and uncontrollable. Well, it *was* funny. I had to push some words out through my own mouth before I started laughing too.

"I have a driver here, and plenty of room in the wagon. We can take our route by way of Bakenmut's house and tell him there's no need to come out here," I offered, "if you can tell my driver the way."

CHAPTER 2
THE SECOND WEEK OF HNSW, FIRST MONTH OF SHEMU, SEASON OF THE RIVER RUNNING LOW
THE ELEVENTH OF THE SEVENTY-FIVE DAYS

Does it thunder in the Black Land? Sometimes. A few days a year maybe. When Neferet and I were very small we'd wait for those days when clouds rolled in from the Great Green.

The room would turn gray and we'd scramble up onto a high window seat and settle-in to watch for a flash on the horizon. We'd investigate each other's faces in delicious unbearable tension until the clap of thunder. Then we'd scream and fall to the floor and laugh until we couldn't anymore. Then we would climb back up for another wonderful round of terror.

It's the bearded merchants from beyond the Two Rivers of the East who spread the error that there is no thunder – or even rain– in Kehmeht. Coming and going in the dry seasons which favor their caravans, they miss the few days of storms. So they tell a tale of how the Land That Makes Her Children Happy does so without rain, since its black earth suckles from The River, a wet-nurse who never disappoints. And in this they speak truly. Kehmeht *needs* no storms. But it still gets some.

So when Mohsheh and Aaharohn first warned that the Power was going to send a storm of hail, most Children of Kehmeht thought "Ha! So what? Why, everyone knows that in the desert to the west, beyond the floodplain where the nights are cold, there are years in which hail is more common than rain!" What lesson, then, could be taught by sending more of what we already had? Or so people thought.

But we who had thrown in our lot with Harkuhotep were schooled now and knew better. Hail is natural in Kehmeht, yes. But so are frogs and lice and sickness in livestock. What mattered was the precision with which these came.

Mohsheh warned that if Pahroh would not send the Iebiru to their days of worship in the Red Land, hail would come. This did not impress the Court, who found the threat trivial and unimaginative.

Mohsheh insisted, however, that this hail would be something strange and fearful, something the world had never seen. It would utterly ruin the harvests. It would slay animals. It would destroy men and the works of men. But it would come with such precision that, this time, there was to be a way for each and every Son of the Black Land to save himself, his family, even his animals. How? Simply by bringing them inside.

It was this offer that so galled the Court. Were the People of Kehmeht weaklings and cowards who would fear the word of the Iebiru brothers where Our Father Pahroh did not? Were their crops and herds so dear to them that they would dishonor the Throne by accepting the Iebiri threat?

～

Harkuhotep returned from his encounter with Mohsheh serene and optimistic as I had never seen him before. Back in The City he assembled us again at Setka's and Neferet's home. I knew most everyone who attended, yet I felt like a stranger among them because I was the only one who missed that fateful meeting with the Iebiri brothers in Goshen. I was like a deaf man amidst people enchanted by a melody only they could hear.

They were all friendly, of course. They told me everything, every word of their meeting with Mohsheh in great detail. But as they spoke to me they would glance at each other, as if to confirm with someone else who had "been there" that, "yes, this really was how it was," and "yes, it really did feel like that," and "yes, all will be well, even if neither the Court nor our countrymen can yet understand." It was like being with friends who had started drinking an hour before you arrive. You never really catch up.

But in addition to all this shared good feeling I could not share, there was a practical and urgent aspect to the meeting. It had to do with the task of getting simple people to go ahead and take their families and animals indoors, even if Pahroh's advisors would later call them weaklings, cowards, and traitors.

This did not have to be difficult. The very appearance in a village of messengers who spoke in the name of Harkuhotep, Seal Bearer of the King of Upper and Kehmeht, Unique Friend of Pahroh, Trusted of All His House would still suffice to instill obedience in the lowborn. And even if Harkuhotep was not quite so "Trusted of All His House" right now, how would the villagers know that?

The more difficult part of the mission would be to convince the villagers that it was possible to do what Harkuhotep was telling them to do. Why, just squeezing their wives, sons, and daughters, into their squalid mud huts for a full week with food and water enough to save them from venturing outdoors, seemed insurmountable. And where in the world could they possibly find shelter for their animals?

There were not enough sheds and stables in all of the Black Land for her plough oxen, donkeys, camels, cows, and sacred herds of sheep. There were not even enough lodgings for her horses. Might we transfer them again to the Iebiru, as had been done before the curse on the animals? Driving all these to Gohshen in time to sell to Iebiru would be near impossible.

Maybe written contracts would be enough to transfer ownership to Iebiru, even if the animals were never moved at all? Didn't that work for Inyotef's horses during the curse on the animals?

But for Harkuhotep to arrange it would mean acting against the direct will of the Throne. Chariots and cavalry are the pride of Kehmeht, and Harkuhotep could not afford to give the Court an opportunity to charge that he had broken in fear of an Iebiri threat. Not this time.

S o we came to our first village. The arrival of a royal chariot with two outriders and a wagon full of men and equipment was enough to gather all the villagers around us. Inyotef addressed the crowd and he spoke well enough to make a dent in the laconic villager mind. Having been raised in a hamlet as squalid as this, he understood his audience. He took their inevitable quips in stride.

A few of the jokes were about what it would be like to stay indoors with your wife for a week. Some wives gave back as good as they got, for the women of The Black Land have plenty of spirit, even in the villages. One young man, newly married, suffered bawdy catcalls about how his week would be all right for him. Someone else reminded everyone that, along with food and water, they'd better have plenty of chamber pots with well-fitted lids, and everyone seemed to think this was extremely comic.

But, with patience, Inyotef won at least mild agreement that the threat was real. Or, in true villager fashion, that it was best to just do the task rather than later regret leaving it undone. But *how* was it to be done?

There were more animals in and around the villages than there were sheds, barns, and houses. Were they expected to build massive new shelters for their animals? Shelters strong enough to stand up to a hailstorm of seven days?

It was at this point that Inyotef tried to explain the solution, though it was inexplicable. For he had learned it in Gohshen from Iebiru close to Mohsheh, and he believed it to be true, strange though it was. It went like this:

The Power, Mohsheh and his brother had taught, is not a tyrant who asks for the impossible. He wants only the heart of a person. He wants only their good will. So, Inyotef explained, it would be enough for the villagers, herdsmen, and shepherds to simply build a pen with a few posts at the sides reaching up to the height of where a roof would be.

And for that roof, they were to simply extend strings of

hemp or flax where sturdy roof planks would have been. If there would be no more than three handbreadths of space between the strings, then the Power would count it as if they had built a roof of thickest oak. It would show the desire of their heart to believe the Power. And that would be enough. The hailstones would not enter there and all the animals below such a "roof" would be safe.

In the Court the notion of making any gesture toward belief in the Power was never thought worthy of consideration. And you would think that simple villagers too, would conclude that Inyotef had been bitten by a mad dog. But villagers fear gods and those who speak in their names. So after the men in the supply wagon set up a few poles and ran a few lines of flax rope, the villagers joined in, built the pen, and the job was done. I took out our survey map, located the next village (that was my job) and off we went.

We did this for several days, and the results varied. Sometimes there would be flat refusals with much patriotic cursing of the Iebiru and violent condemnation of anyone who would bend to their threats. Sometimes there would be some irreverent humor, mild acceptance, and a shrug of "why not?"

Other times there would be a wave of fear and awe and the villagers would hurry to prepare as we bid them. We could not enforce our advice. We had few men at arms, the Court was against us, and there was no time left, for the hailstorm would soon be upon us. So we did not force. But we did persuade. Or I should say, Inyotef did.

Inyotef was always charming. He was handsome and fun, women adored him and men followed him. But you would have to be something more than all that for people to embrace a belief in the new and strange Iebiri Power. You would have to be a little strange and new yourself. Like Inyotef.

This was most obvious in, of all things, his hair. The highborn of Kehmeht love cleanliness. We bathe often, we scrape and oil our skin, and, most of all, we remove our hair.

When I was younger I could barely wait for the day when my childish topknot would be lopped off and my full head shaved smooth as is the way of all the Great of the Black Land. Since then there had never been a normal day in which a servant or, if necessary, I myself, have not put a razor to my head, my cheeks, my chin.

Yes, it is true that a neat and well-braided beard is an ancient symbol of greatness in The Land That Makes Her Children Happy. That is why Pahroh, when he sits upon the Throne of The Two Kingdoms with the crook and flail folded across his chest, wears a "beard" of pure gold, strapped to his ears by cords coated in the same. It is not unlike the wigs we all wear. It is the *idea* of hair, neat, sculpted, perfumed, and removed at will.

But now Inyotef had departed from this way of the Black Land. He had not shaved since his return from Goshen and I had never seen him the way he appeared now. Of course you could think that it was just this mission we were on, rushing from village to village, sleeping rough to keep on schedule and make it back to The City before the hailstorm came. But I could see it was something more.

With his short growth of beard and still minimal but emerging head of hair, he did not yet look like an Iebiri. But neither did he look anymore like one of the great of Kehmeht. He appeared to me something between the two, and so he sounded when he talked in the villages about what was coming and what he had heard from Mohsheh in Gohshen. It made him convincing. But I did not like it.

It was new and strange to me. And a stark reminder that, if you had been at that meeting in Gohshen, if you had met Mohsheh and Aaharohn, it changed you. And I was left out of all that. I was not changed.

CHAPTER 3
THE THIRD WEEK OF HNSW, FIRST MONTH OF SHEMU, SEASON OF THE RIVER RUNNING LOW
TWENTY-FIRST OF THE SEVENTY-FIVE DAYS

"Feeling stupid? You should. You are."

This from Hesera, addressed to me as he came down into the great room where I had gathered the household. Only Sartuma continued to keep her eyes on this encounter, as she still possessed Hesera's respect, even in his madness, for her long years with us. Adjedaa, who was next to her with the serving-maids and Kheruef among the manservants suddenly discovered that their toes were exceptionally interesting.

"Got everyone up before dawn, did you?" Hesera went on. "Hurried back from your villages, got the windows shuttered up, got everyone indoors, safe and accounted for. As if you are master in this house."

He wheeled and shouted into the startled faces of the entire household.

"Which he is not! You are not to take instruction in your duties from him. Do you understand?"

All the serving girls and working men nodded vigorously. Hesera was still a sorcerer, and who knew if a crazy sorcerer wasn't more dangerous than a sane one?

Then he made his way to the last of the newly shuttered windows, and, as he wrapped his bony hand around the shutter cord, spoke again to me.

"You got everyone up and gathered them here because you thought you knew what was coming and look, there's nothing."

Hesera yanked the cord and the wooden shutter fell off its leather hinge and clattered noisily onto the floor stone.

Whether the falling to the floor part was for effect or because in his frailty he couldn't yank the cord properly wasn't clear. He certainly was no picture of health. All of us still bore scars from the soot boils and maybe a few spots that weren't really healed. But he still had oozing lesions on his face, neck, arms and legs, and for all I could tell, under his kilt and robe, too. He would have been a horror to look at if he just stood there and smiled. Muttering invectives made it worse.

He looked out into the fresh blue of the sky. We all did. The pink of the dawn was almost gone and the sky was clear. There was no storm. There was no hail. It was the twenty-first day since Mohsheh and Aaharohn had warned that hail was coming. All the other curses happened on the twenty-first day after their announcement, always at dawn.

"Ha!," Hesera barked."Ha, ha! You are puzzled, are you not? Admit it."

"I'm puzzled," I admitted, but in toneless voice to give him as little satisfaction as possible.

"The Iebiru brothers appeared before the Throne yesterday," Hesera related."But not at dawn. Pahroh does not hold court at dawn!"

Hesera cackled at this, as if it was a very witty observation.

"It was hours into the morning," he went on."I still have

friends at Court, you know. And I still have the farsight, too. Do you deny this?"

"No," I said truthfully. Hesera was insane but since when did that stop anyone from being both well-connected and skilled in sorcery?

"In the midst of his appearance before Our Father Pahroh, Mohsheh scratched a mark on the wall of the throne room. Insolent, was it not? But they are becoming insolent, those two. Mohsheh made the scratch and said: 'When the sun reaches this point tomorrow, the hailstones will begin. And all those who do not fear the Power and remain out of doors will die'."

Adjedaa began to cry. It was all too much for her, the things that were happening to Kehmeht and the things that had befallen our household. We had seen hardship together here, we had seen pain here, and death, but none of it so frightening as when recalled for us by this crazed old man who used to be our Master. It was too much to remember that he had been, once, kindly and wise, and so she wept and some part of me wished to join her.

"That time has not yet come," Hesera continued as if voicing the simple solution to a problem in arithmetic. "It will though," he said. "Any moment now."

This was followed by several long uncomfortable moments in which Hesera neither dismissed us nor addressed us. So we looked from window to toes to stolen glances at each other and back to toes again.

And there we saw sunlight disappear from the floor as quickly as the light vanishes upon the snuffing of a candle. This was no slow darkening of the sky, no warning of a few gentle drops to tell those still outside to flee for cover.

Lightening flashed in a dozen places at once, thunder shook the earth, rolled and echoed and shook the earth again. And again. For it did not cease, there was no break between the peals and crashes, as if some giant was relentlessly hammering a drum bigger than the world.

"It is, then," Hesera said, "the..." and I could see his lips moving but his weak voice was no match for the thunder and it was impossible to hear him even if I wanted to. And none of us could peel our eyes away from what was happening outside.

The sky was full of spheres hurtling towards the earth. About half were clear ice, with flames flickering inside. They were quite beautiful in their way, until they made impact. The ice hit with the force of rock, cracked open, and released the flames, which ignited whatever they touched. Other ice spheres were encased in flame on their outside, like meteors streaming smoke and fire behind them, slamming in with the same effect.

We watched in horror as the restored gates to the garden orchard came down in shards and splinters and then went up in flames. They burned hot and bright, the ice having no effect on the fire. Neither did the fire have any effect on the ice, building up to heaps of great height where the gates used to be.

The trees of the orchard that survived the Curse of the Animals now collapsed in piteous wreck and conflagration. We awoke from our shocked stupor and hurried to put the shutter back, for what would be our fate if one of these spheres of ice and fire sped into our great room through the open window?

But as the shutter was being resealed I was certain that I glimpsed a man, a gentleman I knew by sight who lived not far from us, turning and running back and forth, anywhere to get away from this death. Next thing I knew there was a pounding on our door and Kheruef turned to me and I nodded and he leapt to the door, for whatever the risk of opening it, we could not leave that poor man out there to die.

Kheruef pulled the door inwards but there was no opening there, for a wall of clear ice had filled it and through it I could make out the silhouette of our neighbor. He pounded on the ice wall but it would not give way. I ran to Kheruef's side and we beat at the ice with our fists and a stool that was close at hand but we barely chipped it. And through it I saw the silhouette convulse as hail beat the life from him. He slid down in a smear of red blood on the ice face. Then his body ignited in flames and we shut the door on the sight of it.

I have seen beasts of burden beaten so often that they no longer flinch at the swish of a whip or the stab of a cattle prod. Their instincts are broken by relentless blows. And so it was with us. Fright thrives on surprise. There is no fright when assaults are regular and unrelenting. There is only pain, horror, and despair. And so it was with us.

For the first day and night of the hailstorm, and well into the afternoon of the second day, we remained, all of us, in the great room. Only Hesera had returned upstairs to his chamber, which being under the roof was certainly a more dangerous place. Perhaps he was so frustrated about being unable to make himself heard that he preferred the dignity of that perilous location. We, who were able to shout to be heard, found ourselves yelling all the time. Even when we would speak of everyday things, it was done in shouts like sailors in the midst of a storm on the Great Green.

"We should eat something now," I would shout and bid some of the girls run into the kitchens and fetch flatbreads and some flagons of watered-down wine. "Make your resting places away from the shutters," I would yell to them when it was time to sleep, in case an incoming hailstone shattered them.

Sartuma shouted and used hand signals to me whenever she left the great room, which was often, to bring something of value or beauty to offer at the alter of Behs. "Behs will protect us," she would call out each time to anyone who would listen, a mother comforting her children from a nightmare.

"Adjedaa, I have forgotten cardamon for Behs," Sartuma would call out urging the girl to go back into the kitchen and bring it. Or, "Adjedaa, bring some new coals for Behs," she would coax, "some nice red ones for him."

Sartuma looked upon Adjedaa as a daughter and she wished to bring blessings upon her by giving her things to do in service of the god. And it was Adjedaa, wasn't it, who was happiest when I first set up the altar to the golden Behs? Wasn't it she who was so joyful, telling me how her parents always had an image of Behs, though a poor one of clay, still, always had one in their village home? But now whenever Sartuma asked her to do anything for the god, Adjedaa made excuses.

She needed to uncake the salt, which was lumping due to the humidity. She needed to shake out the linens that we had used to soften our sleeping on the floor or dust would set in them. She needed to check that she had banked the fire in the small indoor oven. She needed to ready some more oil lamps, for we used them all day now in the indoor darkness of the storm. She needed to do anything but what Sartuma asked of her. But that, only when what was asked of her was in the service of Behs.

It had become exhausting to shout against the relentless thundering. Still, Adjedaa asked me several times in a single day, "Do you think that Inyotef made it home before the storm?" I assured her that he surely did. Her brow would unwrinkle and grave concern would leave her face. But a few hours later she was back at it again. Was I certain Inyotef was safe?

"He is surely safe," I said as gently as I could while shouting over the booming. "His house is of cut stone, and is as strong as ours. Stronger maybe."

"But he is so adventurous," she said back to me, using a term I didn't think she knew. "He does not fear dangerous things, maybe he went out in the storm?" she pleaded.

"No, no," I assured her. "Inyotef is too smart for that. Why, he's the one who convinced the villagers that they would be all right if they did as Mohsheh said! Surely he would heed his own instruction?"

This seemed to assuage her, and she returned to her tasks, busying herself with any housework that could still be done. Unless it was in the service of Behs.

Kheruef, who was god-fearing as most of the people of the Black Land are, drank more than his ration of date beer, day after day, night after night. I had no heart to stop him because he needed it, he was so afraid. But locked-in together as we were, his piety became tiresome.

"It is Sutekh, the Evil One who has brought this upon us!" he would shout, though there was no way to tell if the shouting part was from righteous zeal or just the only way he could make himself heard over the storm of thunder. "It is because we have offended Sutekh!"

So we all just nodded "yes, fine, you're right" because there was nothing to gain by arguing with him, though he made no sense. Mohsheh said this would come. It came. Mohsheh said it would be from the Power of the Iebiru. And so it was, for the Iebiru were not being broken and frozen and burned by these hailstones as we were.

Then, on the fourth dark afternoon, Kheruef stood up, shaking with righteous indignation. His mouth moved but he could not get any words out, he was so visibly shaken. He raised his right arm slowly and pointed a finger of accusation at Adjedaa. "It's her!" he finally managed to say. "She is bringing this down on us! Don't you see it? Can't you see it?"

"Sit down, Kheruef," I said.

He folded in on himself and sat down. No one spoke. What can you say to a man who is doubly drunk on date beer and terror? We all just sat there and let the thunder roll over us, our only version of silence during these days of dread.

I stole a glance at Adjedaa expecting to see her reduced to sobbing and falling into Sartuma's maternal arms. But she sat upright and unmoved, a little red rising in her cheeks maybe, but her eyes steady. This was not the girl she was, and I wondered about it, though not for long. Kheruef was up and at it again.

"She despises Behs, Your Honor," he shouted to me. "You've seen it, I know you have. Every time Sartuma asks her to fetch or do for the god, she makes an excuse, right in front of Behs himself, she turns her back on him and dishonors him!"

Kheruef pivoted a little, unsteady on his feet, and gave a quick bow to our golden Behs. Just to make clear, I suppose, that he had nothing to do with the little village girl full of rebellion against the Way of Kehmeht.

At this point, Adjedaa of old, Adjedaa of even last week, would have had tears rolling down her cheeks. She would have begged me to "make him stop." But the Adjedaa of last week was gone, and the one of today barely turned from where she sat regarding Kheruef with disdain fit for a queen. And then she spoke.

It had to be shouted, of course, or else she would not have been heard at all. But it had no feel of shouting, her words were spoken with simple conviction and some pity for anyone who could not grasp her meaning.

"Behs, is a lie," she said. "There is no Behs. That thing is a statue, an image of a lie. I spit on Behs."

Everyone in the room was stunned, but each in a different way. Kheruef's face was a mask of horror, his ears burned at so brazen a confession of the very crime he had "discovered."

Sartuma's eyes grew moist in grief, seeing her almost-daughter, sweet young innocent of the villages, so corrupted. The other serving girls edged away from Adjedaa, for who knew? Maybe this dark madness would lay its icy dark fingers on them, too.

The men in service looked around to see what all this required of them, settling their glances on me as the only authority available, Kheruef being apoplectic and Hesera hidden in his chambers.

And I? I tumbled from thought to thought, pieces of the puzzle falling into place but never enough to form the whole. Where in the world did Adjedaa learn to talk like this? She came to us from her village, a pretty maiden, smelling vaguely of manure and with a vocabulary of maybe two hundred words. She cleaned, she fetched, she helped where told to help.

With whom did she discuss things like the existence of the gods or what honor was or wasn't due them? Where did she even find language to think such things, let alone pronounce them defiantly? She had no lessons in philosophy or logic. She had no tutor...

Oh! She has a tutor, I realized. And probably a lover.

Inyotef on the roof speaking with her in the small hours before dawn. Inyotef entering our household through the kitchens in the back, spending hours there before I even knew he had come. Inyotef.

For years Adjedaa gazed upon him with wide-eyed admiration, but all the young women did. It never meant anything to Inyotef, who could have had any Lady of Kehmeht in marriage if he wanted.

And if he had set his eyes above his station, the besotted lady would surely have had her father use influence to make the match possible. Titles would have been heaped upon Inyotef and he would have been raised high enough. But Inyotef had changed.

He had been changing since the beginning of all this, since Mohsheh and his brother first appeared. I didn't catch it then, the quips and the remarks, the things he said and the things he was careful not to say. It was just my big brother Inyotef being Inyotef, solely for my enjoyment.

But one thing led to another and change welled up within him and his soul, no doubt, needed someone with whom he could share it. He needed an apt pupil, but one who could accept who he really was. For in his heart, Inyotef was still a boy from a village too small to have a name, a youth who liked to speak plainly and truly. And he wanted a companion who could hear what was in his heart in the simple and direct way villagers share such things.

I felt jealous of Adjedaa. I felt annoyed at Inyotef. I felt very much alone. Then I felt ridiculous and ashamed for feeling those things, especially in front of our household. But they probably thought I was simply being reflective and wise, so the shame in me died down. I firmly bid everyone return to their chores, though there were hardly any to do. It was the right thing to say.

~

What good would wooden shutters do against this hail? The impact of a single hailstone could smash a good-sized chunk out of a limestone building. Trees and all things men fashioned from them were exploded into splinters. The fire that enveloped the ice spheres or blazed within them could incinerate wooden shutters within twenty breaths. So why did I have us shuttered in? Because Mohsheh said it would work.

How did he know? I had no idea. Or too many. Was it sorcery he used? Or was Mohsheh simply capable of uncanny prediction of natural events? Or was it Beings of Ka acting in concert with him? Or was it, as Hesera insisted, Mohsheh exerting his will on forces that the Most High left behind in a world He abandoned, forces that anyone could use if they would but find the will? Or was it, as Mohsheh taught that this Power cared deeply about Iebiru slaves and would fight for them?

And if that were so, if the Power did care about Iebiru slaves, then why? What had they ever done to earn such protection? And why did the Power care only now, after centuries of allowing the Iebiru to be tortured?

Iebiri children had been burned alive on altars in Kehmeht yet the Power never sent fires of retribution before. Why now? And were all of us in Kehmeht equally guilty? Of course not. So why did all of Kehmeht have to go through seven months of suffering?

And what good did all this do the Iebiru? Their Power

could have taken them out to worship at any moment if He wanted to. But no, the Power was waiting for Pahroh's agreement! Pahroh could not simply *let* the Iebiru slip away to their holiday of worship. No, Pahroh had to *send* them! But why in the world did the Power crave this?

All gods are strange, there was little wonder that a god of the Iebiru would be strange too. This Power had clearly wanted to remain hidden for a long time, and even now, what had He revealed of Himself? There was no image of this Power. No one had ever seen Him. Mohsheh said the Power spoke to him on several occasions. But even that was only in Mohsheh's mind. Others standing right next to him at those times never heard a thing.

What was hardest to swallow was Mohsheh insisting that this Power was not the god of only the Iebiru, but of everyone. And everything.

This Power held lordship over water, for He could turn water to blood in rivers, cisterns, and cups. And the Power also held sway over frogs and reptiles making them slither up from water onto land at His command. And the Power also had control over tiny lice insects but also over animals of every size and origin. The Power wielded disease against our livestock, then a month later, sent painful sickness against the flesh of men. Now the Power was hurling ice and fire from the heavens. So what did this Power *not* command? What was left for any other god?

Some resolved the problem by suggesting that other gods were quite real, but subordinate to this Power, like warlords who serve a mighty King. This seemed reasonable enough. Didn't Iebiru themselves keep images of other gods in their homes, Astarte or the Baalim, powers out of the lands from which their ancestors came?

The Iebiru I knew, Avishamah and his family, kept

images of Attar of the Morning Star and Shapshu Lord of the Setting Sun. They found no inconsistency in treasuring these while believing in the Power that Mohsheh proclaimed.

Mohsheh, however, told anyone who would listen that this was a mistake. Mohsheh's nation, the Leyvie, would not tolerate even the mention of gods, let alone images of them. The most generous of the Leyvie might concede that each of the "gods" was simply a name for one or another aspect of their Most High.

It was as if someone were called by one name when he planted, and another when he reaped, and another when he walked, and another when he sang until, over time, people would think you were talking about several different people. But that was just a way of explaining an error, not a way of justifying it.

The Leyvie were adamant that the other "gods" were no gods at all. Just as Adjedaa said. Just as Inyotef had instructed her. Just as all those near Harkuhotep had come to believe.

I, however, was not among these enlightened ones. I was puzzled, tired, and near crazy from being pent up in this house smothered in endless thunder. I had no idea what Mohsheh was really doing. But still I had the shutters put in, and comforted myself with the certainty that if we would keep inside, we would be safe. Because Mohsheh said so. Because he knew what he was saying.

Never was this clearer than at the moment the storm of ice and fire ended. Our Father Pahroh called for the Iebiru brothers, though how his messengers were able to go outdoors without being bashed to death, frozen, and incinerated was never clear to me. Maybe Pahroh had Iebiru within the Great House to send, for the Iebiru were immune to this destruction. Or maybe he sent sons of Kehmeht who were protected for the length of their mission by the Power itself?

Whatever the means of their summons, Mohsheh and Aaharohn did come before the Throne. Pahroh appeased them, it seems, with promises to send the Iebiru to their days of worship. Mohsheh agreed to ask the Power to stop the hailstones, though he would only do this after leaving The City. He was not willing to make such a request in a place that was full of images of gods, an affront to The Most High. All we knew was that, quite suddenly, with no warning at all, the thunder stopped.

I cannot describe the relief and strangeness of that moment, or the delicious quiet that filled it. We could hear the scrape of leather sandals on floor stones again, the click of a copper cup replaced gently on a tabletop, the swish and release of breath. I pulled away the shutter from the nearest window and beheld what I would not have believed but for the fact that we all saw it.

Hailstones, ones with fire flickering within, and ones with flames enveloping, stood motionless in the air. From a hand's-breadth above the earth all the way up to the highest vault of the sky they floated, suspended. They were no longer commanded to fall upon us. So they stood in silent obedience to the Power that sent them. And then, they were gone.

We opened the door and the ice that had sealed it gave way to our chopping and to the warm sun that now radiated from a reborn blue sky. Then I got my first real look at what had befallen us.

The bloody remains of our neighbor who had been slain on our doorstep seven days earlier was a horror. Part of his torso was frozen so that the rivers of blood that had poured from his wounds were now pooled as red ice. But parts of his legs were savagely burned. And he was not alone.

I had never seen a battlefield after combat, but I was sure it could not be worse than the streetscape I walked into now. There were bodies here and there, some frozen, some charred to blackness, some opened in gaping red wounds, some showing signs of all of these.

Piles of ice began to sweat meltwater under the now sunny sky. Fires still smoked and flared in what was left of things that burn. Wagons, remnants of trees, scattered bits of broken implements, laundry, papyri, strewn everywhere.

A rigidly dead pack animal here, a frozen and bloody corpse there, smoke everywhere. "This is the end," I thought to myself. "This was the last stand, the war is surely over now."

Kehmeht could lose men and animals and still not surrender. What rang of finality was rather what had happened to our orchard and to all gardens that graced The City. They were no more.

No district of The City had more trees than ours, and not a single one was left standing. They were all fallen, all splintered or turned to charcoal and ashes.

Yes, a city can survive without orchards. A city needs no gardens save for their beauty and a few delicacies. But it took but a particle of imagination to realize that if the tall, strong, and bountiful trees in The City were annihilated, what must have been the fate of the fragile barley that was just about to be harvested up and down our floodplain? What would the Children of the Black Land eat?

The flax harvest, which comes each year with the barley, would be gone too. How would the People of The Land That Makes Its Children Happy weave clothing and blankets? What would weavers exchange now for other goods?

There would still be food for households such as ours. We were wealthy and could, at need, pay the exorbitant price of grain shipped in by the Sea Peoples from over the Great Green. But the millions of simple Children of Kehmeht?

Even if Pahroh would buy imports for them, there could never be enough to feed them all. Kehmeht had been the source of bread for many lands, always a seller, never a buyer, and certainly never a beggar. And now we would need a miracle greater than the one that just destroyed us if were to survive at all.

Surely Our Father Pahroh had this conversation with Mohsheh by now. Surely something was being worked out. Surely the seven-day pilgrimage of the Iebiru into the Red Land would begin any day and Mohsheh would request his Power to bring succor to the defeated children of The Black Land. These were my thoughts as I picked my way around the wreckage and bloody broken bodies.

Neighbors emerged from their shelters in ones and twos to learn what had become of their city. We passed one another without so much as a nod, for we were pale and near-dead ourselves, wraiths floating through a necropolis. It was fitting, then, that upon stepping back over the threshold of our home I was greeted by our own resident wraith.

"You're wrong," he said.

This alone was no proof that Hesera could read my mind. He had already decided that anything I would think would be wrong. But he did get more specific.

"Kehmeht will not starve," he said. "And so our Father Pahroh need not surrender."

I knew this game by now. Hesera would make a cryptic statement of little apparent sense, so that he could then pounce on my "stupidity" in not grasping his subtlety. There was no way around it, so I gave him the quizzical look he was just about asking for, and he went on.

"Forgotten the wheat and the spelt, have you?"

I had not forgotten the wheat and the spelt because I had never given them a thought.

"Their harvest is weeks away," he cackled. "They're soft now. They're short and small and green, too moist for the fires to have done much harm. They'll have bent easily under the hail. They'll spring back. They'll ripen. Then we'll harvest them. Then we'll eat them. Who but animals would care to eat barely anyhow?"

~

It wasn't until late afternoon that I learned Adjedaa had left our household and found Inyotef not only safe, but willing –no *insisting*– that they marry that very hour.

"Why should we wait?" he said. "We're alive, we love one another, what are we waiting for?"

Adjedaa needed no convincing, though she dutifully returned to our house and quickly gathered the few things that were hers, avoiding everyone as much as possible. This was for the best because who knows what violent fit would have seized Kheruef if he encountered her?

Worse, Sartuma was in bereavement, for she had witnessed the downfall of her "daughter" in the very same room which a few months earlier saw her husband ripped open by a lioness (who Sartuma was now certain was the god Sakhmet who takes a lion's form).

Had Adjedaa lingered, I don't doubt that Sartuma would have run to Hesera and begged him to cast out the demon that had taken possession of her girl. And though Hesera had some gratitude and maybe even affection for faithful Sartuma, still, in his madness he might have hurt Adjedaa as easily as healed her.

Poor Sartuma! Her loss was pitiable and none could help her. It took no time at all for her to fix the blame on Mohsheh and his brother and on all the Iebiru.

They were the reason for the rampage of the animals that took her husband. They were behind the ordeal of the hailstorm that took her daughter. It was the accursed Iebiru, they had no pity, no humanity, and Kehmeht would never know peace until they were put back in their place. No, until they were wiped off the face of the world! This Sartuma muttered to no one in particular and to anyone who would listen.

Adjedaa did manage the courtesy of coming to my chamber and telling me that she was leaving and why. It was the proper thing to do, though I had little hold on her. It occurred to me that I could rightfully claim she had not served long enough to pay off her indenture. But that would have been base of me, and besides, hadn't Hesera already made clear that I held no authority in this house? If he wanted something for the remainder of Adjedaa's indenture, let him deal with it himself.

I felt so dirtied by these thoughts that I told Adjedaa I would personally come to Inyotef's home within the hour and bring coins to serve for her side in the marriage. She brightened at this, thanked me, took up her small bundle and sprinted off to her beloved.

∾

Weddings in the Black Land were simple and easy. And why not? In the Land That Makes Her Children Happy all kinds of pairings were considered natural, everyday things, not worthy of fuss or too many rules. If a couple decided that their delight in one another was great enough to last a lifetime, they simply came into a common home and in doing so, were married.

If after days or years they saw unhappiness, they could part and this was accomplished with nothing more than a scribe to write out how their property would be divided. But at the beginning at least, all who married hoped and believed that they would find enough happiness together in this life to carry with them into their second life in eternity.

The only real formality in starting off a marriage was the agreement between the families about an exchange of wealth, usually gifts from the family of the bride to the family of the groom. Adjedaa was virtually an orphan, her villager parents having all but sold her into service in The City and they certainly weren't showing up for this wedding. That's why I offered to stand in their place for her.

Not that Inyotef wanted or needed anything from his bride other than herself. Certainly Inyotef's father had no need of gifts from the distaff side. But I felt it would make Adjedaa and Inyotef happy to have their wedding go as weddings went.

When I got to Inyotef's house I was surprised to hear a flute and see about a dozen people on the portico chatting, snacking on raisin and nut cakes, hoisting cups while Harkuhotep himself, seated at a small table, wrote out a brief betrothal contract in his own hand.

He looked up and greeted me warmly but quietly, for the death and destruction of the hailstorm was still all around us. No one could have arrived at this wedding without picking their way around the wreckage and corpses. But I believe he was happy for his son, though he did not name that relationship in the contract. I produced my coins for Adjedaa's side, Harkuhotep accepted them for Inyotef's side, and all was done.

At this point the flute played louder and more joyously and I couldn't help but think that this was a custom better fitted to a marriage of Iebiru. For they, being so particular about their pairings and obsessed with all kinds of dull limitations on them, treated weddings as public celebrations instead of the simple and natural thing the Children of Kehmeht knew them to be. Was this flute Inyotef's idea, I wondered? Another way to be a little more Iebiri?

~

The next morning I decided to walk over to Inyotef's house and bid him and Adjedaa a good morning. It was a clumsy way of telling myself, and perhaps Inyotef too, that I was not jealous of his happiness.

In this I would still be his younger brother. I would remain his friend, always. And I smiled in admitting to myself that I wouldn't mind being invited in for a bit of second breakfast. Not for the food, but for the joy of being with my big brother and his bride at the peak of their happiness.

But when I got there I was met by a servant, a man about the same age as Inyotef. I knew him to be a stable hand, for he groomed horses well and knew his way around bridles and chariot gear. But he also wore a large dagger at his waist and always seemed to be looking around at several things at once even as he spoke with you.

The truth is, I had no idea what he really was. The man told me that Inyotef and his bride had gone away earlier that morning. They had? Where? I asked him.

"Gohshen," he said flatly.

Gohshen? What errand could be so urgent on this first morning after Inyotef's marriage that Harkuhotep would send him there?

CHAPTER 4

THE FIRST WEEK OF ḤNT-ḤTJ, SECOND MONTH OF SHEMU, SEASON OF THE RIVER RUNNING LOW

THIRTY-FIRST OF THE SEVENTY-FIVE DAYS

The better part of a week passed, and then I was called, once more, to a gathering of those in Harkuhotep's service. It was, again, meant only for those who shared his views —whatever those views were, exactly. Because if you kept track, you couldn't miss that they were shifting.

A few weeks ago I had taken Harkuhotep at his word: Our Father Pahroh had to be saved from the evil counsel of the Court. Our Father Pahroh had to be supported in making amiable concessions to the Iebiru. In that way alone, Harkuhotep said, the Black Land would become again a place of safety and happiness.

But then Harkuhotep took himself and those who served him (with the notable exception of myself) to meet Mohsheh and Aaharohn. And you could plainly see that they came back changed.

Outwardly, Harkuhotep was the least transformed. At ease in the home of his beloved daughter and her husband, he wore no wig and didn't bother with powder or paint for his eyes. His clothes were still the blue of mourning, as the seventy days in the House of the Dead for The Princess Esemkhebe Ta-Sherit were only about half done.

But if you knew Harkuhotep as he had been only a few months ago, you would see that he was much changed. He was kind and careful not to use any authority on us. Where he used to deal in crisp commands, he now relied on persuasion to get us to think as he was thinking.

And if you looked closer, you might notice that the linen of his blue mourning tunic was now of a thicker weave, something that no longer showed off the lines of his powerful body, but actually obscured them. Almost like something Iebiru would wear, using cloth to hide their form, as is their way.

The most striking change in the room sat four chairs away from Harkuhotep. An Iebiri, full-bearded and dressed in wool, and I looked hard at him, wondering, who is he to be invited into this intimate gathering of children of The Black Land? Only his shy grin at my gawking revealed to me that this was no Iebiri at all, but Ankhuemhesut.

No one in the room had been to Mohsheh and Aaharohn so often as Ankhuemhesut. And it showed. He no longer studied sorcery, for the Iebiru brothers did not favor sorcery. But he still loved secret wisdom and so he went to Gohshen regularly and stayed long to drink his fill of the teachings the Iebiru brothers. Harkuhotep greatly valued Ankhuemhesut's reports of the things he learned in this way.

Then there was Inyotef, returned from his own mysterious visit to Gohshen, with Adjedaa his bride standing against a wall behind him. Her cheeks and forehead were seared by sun and blasted by fine sand from fast riding. Her eyes were afire with... what? Love, for starters. You could see how she rested her adoration on

Inyotef, who turned around in his chair regularly to return a smile.

But the shine in Adjedaa's eyes spoke of something more. It reminded me of the strange look I used to see in Setka's eyes when I was still a boy and he would tell us that his father was taking him off to war, real war. It was the light of something new and powerful, something coming that would change you forever.

Harkuhotep opened the gathering with the tale of what he witnessed at Court. Though excused from regular appearances in these days of his mourning, he had chosen, upon his return from Gohshen, to attend Court.

It was during the hailstorm and Harkuhotep believed in Mohsheh's warning that no Son of Kehmeht could step out into the ice and fire and avoid paying with his life. But the walk from his apartments to the Throne room could be accomplished without venturing outdoors. So, on the seventh day of the storm, when Mohsheh and Aaharohn were called back before the Throne, Harkuhotep was there. And this is what he described.

"Our Father Pahroh said to the Iebiru brothers: 'This time, I have sinned.' He said: 'The Eternal One is right, and I and my People are the evil ones, doing wrong.' He said: 'Beseech The Eternal One. Enough of the thunders, the voices of the Power and the hail! And I will send them,' (meaning the Iebiru). 'And I won't hold them back anymore'."

Had report of such words come a week ago it would have been cause for relief, even celebration. But by now we all knew that this admission had been rescinded. The Iebiru were not being sent to worship in the Red Lands. So why did Harkuhotep feel a need to bring this up all over again?

"You see it, my friends?" Harkuhotep continued.

We all tried hard to see whatever "it" was.

"You see it, don't you?"

He looked earnestly into our faces. I felt worried that he was about to ask me if I saw "it" and to say what "it" was. But he didn't.

"You see it in these words," Harkuhotep explained with some warmth, "that which is really and truly in our beloved Father Pahroh's heart. It is as we said. He *wants* to embrace the Iebiru. He *wants* to send them to their worship and return them to their place as citizens in our Land."

"It's the Court, then. They ruined it."

This from Neferet, the only person in the room who could not be accused of trying to curry favor from Harkuhotep by parroting back his own position. It was a sincere outburst and cherished by her father whose affection for his daughter was great, as always. She was, after all, a fellow seeker into the ways of the Iebiri Power. And she was also extremely pregnant with what would be Harkuhotep's newest grandson. (It *had* to be a boy.)

"Yes, yes," Harkuhotep said ruefully, shaking his head a little. "They ruined it. The weak and foolish ones, cowed by the plotting ones. And no help to be found from the King's Great Wife and the Sister Wives. Most of them, anyway."

He paused here to rouse himself from pessimism. He looked up at us again, his face shining with new courage and shimmering hope.

"*This* is why what you do is so important! The change we seek was at the tipping point, just one week ago. It was a very close thing! So, now we redouble our efforts. Bring me facts. Bring me lore. Bring me stories, proofs, precedents, and I will pile them on the scales of judgment until it dips in favor of the truth and Kehmeht is saved."

I would have sworn at that moment that every single

one of us was ready to rush out and claw the earth with our bare hands if only we knew where those facts, lore, stories, and proofs Harkuhotep needed were buried. I went off into a daydream of being the one who brings back the words that would tip the scale. And in my reverie, I missed hearing Harkuhotep move on to the next item on his agenda. Ankhuemhesut was to share something he had learned in Gohshen.

"These Beings of Ka," Ankhuemhesut was saying. "The ones the Iebiru call Emissaries. There are among them greater and lesser ones. There are some that come into being to do a single thing, and then, when their task is done, cease to exist!"

I tried to imagine what that would be like. Did they dissolve like smoke into air?

"But the greatest among them live beyond the lifetimes of men. I believe they are actually immortal," Ankhuemhesut went on. "I am not absolutely certain on this point. But what I did learn is that they have names, names that state their power. And I think... I think I will share them with you," he said, with some trepidation in his voice.

"You see, to speak their names," he went on, "is the way of evoking them and, possibly, *commanding* them. But they do not wish to be commanded by men. And they can be terrible in their might, as all of us have seen. For they will only be commanded by men who have found favor with the Power, men who are beloved by The Eternal One."

"Such as Mohsheh and his brother," Harkuhotep said to encourage Ankhuemhesut.

"Yes, exactly. And I believe that even they must proceed carefully with these Beings," he continued. "This is what I understand from talking with men of Leyvie who, more than all the other nations of the Iebiru, preserve this lore."

"Can we not learn the names of these great Beings without provoking them?" Harkuhotep asked.

"I believe so," Ankhuemhesut said. "It is in pronouncing them that there is peril. So, I will relate their names in parts," he said, sharing a trick he had learned in Gohshen, "and you may assemble them in your minds and know what we must not pronounce."

This was getting interesting. I like learning secrets. Who doesn't? And this was no idle gossip about some noble or another. This was touching on the terror that had all Kehmeht in its grip.

"There are two Beings whose names I know now. The first rules over water, and his name has three parts. The first part is said as 'Mee.' The second part is pronounced 'Kah.' And the last part is said as 'Aale.'"

"Who Is Like the Power" I said softly to myself, parsing out the meaning of those syllables in the Iebiri language.

"That is correct Mereyamun," Harkuhotep said to me. I reddened at realizing everyone heard me sounding out the meaning. But I was happy that Harkuhotep acknowledged me for it.

"The second Being commands fire," Ankhuemhesut said. "And his name is pronounced first "Gahvrie" and then there is a second syllable that is, again, "Aale."

That would be "My Strength" is "the Power." Or maybe, better, "The Strength of the Power." Only this time I sounded it out from my lips inward, though I couldn't resist stealing a glance to see if Harkuhotep noticed. Someone else spoke out the meaning.

"But it's puzzling," Harkuhotep said, the only one in the room who would easily admit to being puzzled. "Mohsheh tells us that there is only The Eternal One, that He alone is the Power of the Iebiru and of all the world. Yet these Beings live perhaps forever, and they have power over water and fire! Are they not gods, too?"

More than a few foreheads wrinkled at this.

"They have no will of their own," Ankhuemhesut explained. "They are purely emissaries, and they may do only the will of their master, the Power. You can see it in their names."

"This is deep wisdom, Ankhuemhesut, and requires study," Harkuhotep said. "Thank you."

Then Harkuhotep asked Inyotef to make a report about something *he* had learned in Gohshen. So now I would learn what was urgent enough to dispatch a man there just hours after his wedding. Inyotef rose to his feet.

"There was no hail in Gohshen. No ice, no fire. As we would expect." Inyotef paused for effect, looking around the room. "But there *was* thunder. Just like in the rest of Kehmeht. Constant, rolling, relentless thunder!"

Inyotef resumed his seat and the room erupted. How did he know? some asked. Was he in Gohshen during the hail? Surely that would not have protected him, for though no hail fell there, we heard accounts of sons of the Black Land who fled over the boundary into Gohshen and were pursued by the spheres of ice and fire until they were overtaken, brought down, and killed.

Now, it would have been possible for one of us to survive in Gohshen if he got himself indoors and stayed there all week. That is exactly what Mohsheh had instructed the Children of Kehmeht to do. But Inyotef did that in his own home in The City the entire time. I was certain.

Hadn't I been with him on our journey to the villages

and hadn't we returned the evening before the onset of the hailstorm? And hadn't I seen him in his home the day the hailstones stopped? And wasn't that true for all of us who attended his wedding to Adjedaa? So how could Inyotef know anything of thunder in Gohshen during the seven days?

"I sent Inyotef to Gohshen the day after the hail ended," Harkuhotep explained. "We needed to confirm that the fire and ice did not trouble that place of the Iebiru, as Mohsheh had said it would not. I was certain that all would be untouched there, so certain that I thought it a pleasant wedding gift for Inyotef and Adjedaa to get out of our bloodied and battered City to a place of peace for a few days.

"And it was untouched," Inyotef confirmed. "But it was not untroubled. The vault of the heavens thundered for them, too. For all of them. This is what they told me. No hail fell, no one came to bodily harm. But every crooked heart was straightened out in fear and awe, as only thunder can do."

This was amazing. In many tales, gods may be protectors and fierce partisans of those who serve them. Or they may be bitter enemies of those who deny them. Or the gods may be indifferent to the affairs of men. But never, ever, had I heard of a god who will champion a people to the point of slaying their oppressors, but at the same time, frighten those people with a week of terror to "straighten out their crooked hearts."

"I'll tell you how the Iebiru understand it," Inyotef said. I heard this from old Avishamah, the head of a household of the Dahnii. Merey introduced them to me when we were in Gohshen after the disease of the livestock. I remembered them as simple folk, from one of the lesser Iebiri nations who, having met me already, would be willing to speak frankly with me."

I basked in the fleeting admiration the room had for me for supplying Inyotef with his source. But something about it was bothering me, a vague itch of a feeling I could not scratch.

"Avishamah admitted that he was surprised by the thunder," Inyotef went on. "Surprised, then frightened, and dismayed. For hadn't the Power shielded them until now? Hadn't He fought for them? For seven months Mohsheh said that The Most High calls the Iebiru 'His Firstborn Children.' Does a loving father rage and thunder at his own firstborn? Did He not love them anymore?"

"I am no philosopher," Inyotef quipped and the room chuckled a little with him, for he was wildly popular just for being handsome and in the flush of love with a pretty wife and now he was going to be a hero of Harkuhotep's too.

"And I do not think that old Avishamah is much of one either, having spent his life knee-deep in the muck of the brickyards. But if only you could have seen how his face shone as he reasoned it out to me.

"'No,' Avishamah said as the realization dawned upon him, 'the thunder in Gohshen was their Father gently rebuking them for the false and foolish things they needed to cast away.' It meant, he said, that they have *grown* in their Father's eyes. He can correct them now. For He loves them, and means to bring them closer to Him, closer than they have ever been. Those," Inyotef said, "were his words."

Inyotef turned to Adjedaa for confirmation that his account was correct, and she nodded enthusiastically. Her eyes were wet and glistened in the candlelight and I believe everyone else's eyes were moist too. Except mine.

~

There is a secret place where The River is born. It is far to the South, they say, beyond the far border of Koush, beyond the great reed-choked swamps no boat can navigate. A wall of mountains rises up there, coated in trees with vines wrapped so thickly that no man can enter.

Somewhere, inside that secret place, there is a patch of moist dark soil where a tiny spring bubbles up. A slim tendril of cool water rolls away from it, slowly over the ground, unremarkable. Unbothered by leaves fallen in its path, it skips over rotting twigs and small stones, and finds its way down the slightest inclines.

After a time, days maybe, as it goes on its way it calls to other waters. Raindrops that fall on those green lands join it. New waters from subterranean springs emerge from the earth, give birth to rivulets and they join into the flow too.

They fill a great lake, it is said, high in mountains touching clouds. Then The River –for that is what it is now, young but worthy of that name– spills out to the north. It hurries, leaping down rocky slopes, crying out as it goes. It crashes off great precipices and thunders over the First Cataract from which it comes to us, triumphant.

Well, that was me. That was the tale of my own thoughts from the time I left Neferet and Setka's house that night and set out for home.

At first my thoughts were a bubbling spring, light speculations. Curious, I thought, that such important things were learned from a visit of Inyotef and Adjedaa to my Iebiru in Gohshen. *My* Iebiru. For they were mine, weren't they?

I'm the one who first came to know them. And it was

through the pain and terror of being buried alive and then held captive in their attic while they plotted to kill me. Didn't that count for something? Did anyone admiring Inyotef for his great report consider what it had cost *me* for him to have "his" sources?

My thoughts were a rivulet now, rushing downstream: And wasn't it I who saved their lives when Senwosret was about to club them to oblivion? Hadn't I taken them back to The City to preserve them? So who would Inyotef have had to talk with had I not saved them?

The thoughts were leaping and clamoring over rocks now: And hadn't Nebamun meant to use my Iebiru for lion combats on the Feast of Tekh? Hadn't I, alone, preserved them that night?

We were coming to the First Cataract now: Inyotef only met them because *I* brought him to their home in the village of the Dahnii. And that was because of *my* idea about how to prove the true nature of the Plague on the Livestock!

Crash! Thunder! Mighty waters sweeping everything from before them: And now Inyotef was the hero of day, and I was an unnoticed thing! The River of my thoughts was mighty in anger. I think my head might have burst were it not for two surprises.

The first was that I had found myself at the threshold of home, though I had only walked for what seemed a few moments and had never noticed a single thing in my line of sight the entire way.

The second was Mayati, waiting in the moonshadows by the door. The thundering river of thought came to a quiet halt in deference to this new situation.

"They did not admit you, Mayati?" I asked.

"Well, a servant started to," she said. "But then your

Master Hesera appeared and started ranting that I was not welcome."

"You *are* welcome," I said, "as long as I live here."

"Which you don't anymore," Mayati said.

"What?"

"That's what your Master said. He's crazy. You know that, right?"

"I know that."

"But actually, I'm the one who doesn't live anywhere anymore, Merey."

"Surely Okpara would never turn you out," I said. "Did you have some sort of argument with Herit?"

"No, no arguments. They're both very nice to me. So nice."

"I'm listening."

"They're relentless, Merey. They want to punish my father and take his estate as penalty. They have nothing that proves anything about him dealing in livestock or anything that belonged to the Throne. But they have me.

"So they won't stop feeding me and dressing me up and entertaining me until sooner or later I say something they want to hear. Then my words will be written, the judgment will be sealed, and they'll take everything. They'll take everything Father left me, and his good name too."

That River in my thoughts, the one that had suddenly been silenced thundered again. "Is no one in this world to be trusted?" it roared. Must betrayal fester under every friendship or courtesy?

Inyotef had as good as betrayed me, and all the people in the room thought nothing of it, so in love they all were with this handsome lover and so lovesick themselves for their new Iebiri philosophy. And now Okpara, who sent me to the house of Amenakhte for what I thought was my own happiness, was simply using me to bring a little more wealth into the Chamber of Judgments. I could not bear for this to be.

"Are you sure, Mayati?" I just about pleaded. "How do you know?"

"They ask questions all the time, as if that's the way the great people of The City chat," she said. 'Your father was a great administrator, dealing with so many men of so many kinds! You must have lots of droll stories, no? Tell us some!' Sooner or later the talk always gets around to 'the wealthy Iebiru.' Surely there were some good stories there, no?' Relentless, Merey."

"Alright. Come with me. If we hurry we can still catch Harkuhotep at Neferet's house," I said. "We'll tell him everything!" That's how much faith I still had in the wisdom and goodness of the Seal Bearer of the King of Upper and Lower Kehmeht, Unique Friend of Pahroh, Trusted of All His House.

"Have you lost your mind?" Mayati said. "It's his Office that is doing this, his treasury that will be filled."

"He is beyond such things now," I said with a certainty I didn't have.

"Is he so far beyond it that he'd trip up his own son who he's left in charge of the shop? He'll just talk smoothly to us, and by dawn I'll be right back in Okpara's house for another day of honeyed interrogation."

"Honeyed interrogation?" I was impressed by the simile. Or was it a metaphor?

"I'm not going back to Okpara, and not to his father. If you can't help me Merey, I'll find somewhere else to go."

Where would that be? The City was dark and probably dangerous for Mayati to wander alone. And she was so alone, for who did she have in the world now but me?

"Come inside then," I said and started for the door. "Hesera can rant all he wants, we'll stick flax wads in our ears and try to get some sleep."

"He'll send for Okpara, Merey. Or Okpara will send his men here as soon as he realizes I'm gone. It's no good."

She was right. And the injustice of it made be mad. Mayati, who had never harmed anyone in this City and had never been part of her father's crimes, was now to become a fugitive? Mayati, who sickened and nearly died because of the policies of contending courtiers, now was to search for refuge in the shadows of night?

They say that up in those southern highlands there are two streams that nurse the newly born River. One is called The White River for it beats and foams over rocks. The other is called The Blue River, for its waters are deep and quiet but mighty and implacable. It is when the two join that The River of Kehmeht truly forms. And so it was in my thoughts.

The foaming white anger at Inyotef and Okpara and all who honored them, met deep blue counsel for both Mayati and myself, the only two people I actually cared about anymore. And so, a path forward opened up for us. We would simply vanish from the plots and plans of those who cared nothing for us.

Without a word to anyone, we would disappear from The City and find our way to the least remarkable home in a barely noticed village in a most insignificant region of Gohshen. We would pay a visit to my Iebiru.

No one would look for Mayati there, for who could connect her with that obscure place? Senwosret and Bakenmut might remember that she came there once, with them, looking for me. It was her father's interrogations that led terrified Iebiru to name that village of the Dahnii as a place where I might have been taken after the cave-in. But she had been in tens of other places searching for me, and no one would think that simply having been somewhere once in your life made it a hideout.

Avishamah and his family would welcome us if I just framed the story in the right way. Mayati was an orphan now from both parents, I would say, and still recovering from the illness that nearly took her life. Her home had been abandoned as a house of the sick and the dead and she could not remain alone there, not in her present condition.

I would not mention that she had been in The City since before the Hailstorm, and so I would let Avishamah come to the understanding that we were arriving fresh from Amenakhte's estate, right there in Gohshen. No harm in his seeing it that way, and the rest of what I planned to say would actually be true. The Iebiru revere kindness as a virtue. Taking Mayati in would simply be virtuous for them.

Of course I could have told the same story to any innkeeper or householder with a room to rent in any part of the Two Kingdoms. But innkeepers and householders are routinely asked about new tenants. And they love to comply with requests from officers sent by the Chamber of Judgments, especially when it is understood that there is a generous reward for useful information, and a painful penalty for obstruction.

But who would ask such questions of an obscure Iebiri family deep in a village of the Dahnii? And, truthfully, who among the Officers would want to risk antagonizing a throng of Iebiru right now? It would be enough, they would say among themselves, if the Iebiri Power didn't seek them out and slay them in their own beds. Why go into a hornet's nest? But it would be no hornet's nest for me.

The relationship I had with Avishamah and his family, especially with Aelinahtan, was odd to be sure. But it was dependable. They were very agreeable to me, even cordial, something Inyotef understood and took to his good advantage in using them as the source for his report. Just recalling it made me angry again.

Inyotef had traded horses in Gohshen countless times, he must have known many Iebiru through that. He had met Meishav ben Amiel and other wealthy Iebiru at Amenakhte's dinner and could have easily turned to them if he needed Iebiru to talk to. And he had been to the house of Mohsheh himself in a village of the Leyvie. He met Mohsheh and Aaharohn and who knows how many others of their nation. He could have easily called on any of them, leaders of their People, certainly the most reliable sources of information possible.

I, alone, had been excluded from those meetings. Avishamah and his family were all I had among the Iebiru. Now Inyotef had to go and pluck that fruit, my only one, and take credit for it in front of everybody?

Oh yes, he made a short remark, a quip almost, acknowledging that I had made these Iebiru known to him. That just made it worse! It was as if to say that was all I had to offer in the service of Harkuhotep. But now, in finding a way to protect Mayati, I might also have found a way of wining back some honor for myself.

I would talk long and deeply with Avishamah and his family. I would learn their lore and bring it back on rolls and rolls of papyri, all that Harkuhotep could desire. It would put Inyotef to shame and amaze the others.

I led Mayati by backstreets to the Temple of Djehuti who takes the form of a man with the head of an ibis, and is believed to have domain over the moon, magic, and words, both spoken and written. Or maybe he had domain over none of these, since the Most High of the Iebiru was claiming everything. But his temple did have domain over one thing: The valuables I placed there for safekeeping.

Every month I paid the priests of Djehuti silver and occasional sundry gifts to carefully guard whatever I deposited with them. For if wealth were not secure in those sacred precincts, where else could it be?

Many of the great people of The City made use of temples this way. I became serious about it when it was certain that Hesera had lost his mind. I still kept a good number of valuables in the house too, as I was sure that neither Hesera or any of the servants knew most of my hiding places. But with the unrest of the last seven months, it made sense to move half of my gold, silver, and precious gems, along with deeds of my landholdings, to the security of a temple.

Mayati and I sat down on a stone bench in its garden and waited for the stirring of dawn. At first light I banged, flat-palmed, on the great bronze doors until a sleepy priest admitted me. I withdrew the money we could need and gave the priest a generous coin for his trouble. He seemed happy with it.

We went into the upper market where the stalls had just opened. I bought a traveling cloak for myself and one for Mayati, some papyrus and ink, a leather satchel for our things and some fresh cakes made of last year's barley (since the hailstones and fire had seen to it that none of this year's existed). They were scarce, those cakes, so their price was high. I wondered what the common people who keep no treasure in temples would be eating this day.

We traced a quiet path down to the pier and took passage on a boat headed north to Gohshen. It cast off and, once certain that we had made our escape, let our heavy eyelids close in the morning sun, neither of us having had a wink of rest the entire night.

As sleep took me, I thought of Okpara and Herit sending servants to call Mayati for breakfast and learning that she was, mysteriously, gone.

I thought of Inyotef, arriving in a clatter of hooves with some errand from Harkuhotep and finding that I had not been seen since the previous evening. And, no, he would be told, none of the servants had any idea where I could be found.

I pictured Hesera cackling with satisfaction that I was finally, really, gone from his household. None of them would know where we were. It was a pleasant way to slide into a sunny nap of the morning.

CHAPTER 5
THE SECOND WEEK OF HNT-HTJ, SECOND MONTH OF SHEMU, SEASON OF THE RIVER RUNNING LOW

FORTY-FIRST OF THE SEVENTY-FIVE DAYS

The first time I saw this village of the Dahnii it was through a single functioning eye in a fog of pain on a shattered leg as I leaned through the window of the attic that was my prison. It was all dust and filth piled up against cracked mudbrick walls, hovels built too close and too high, cloaked in the stench of too many bodies exuding too much sweat and too much fear.

The second time I came here, some six months later, it was a thriving place populated by Iebiru who were slaves in name only. Their village had become a place of commerce and industry, with herding, shepherding, and farming at its edges. Its homes were made comfortable and, to some degree, happy. But now, this third time, I was to find it something else again.

Mayati and I hired a wagon and driver off the dock where we landed. And I told him, in agreeing to his price, that it was only because he would have difficulty navigating the narrow streets of the Dahnii village.

These had become crowded marketplaces, I told him, with workshops under awnings spilled out into the traffic.

There would be deliveries coming and going in all directions, and impossibly large bands of children at breathless play everywhere. But no. We arrived and found the village strangely quiet.

The children were still out at their games, but they had the run of the place. Except for their play, the streets were almost empty. Here and there a few housefront stalls offered fruits and nuts, fresh or parched. One wine merchant was ladling from barrels into a clay jug presented by a lone customer. There were a few stalls with wool, cuts of leather, firewood and charcoal, some pots, some utensils. But their owners hardly needed to have bothered, so few were the buyers.

There was no ring of hammers on anvils, no roaring of forges or hiss of kilns, no echoes of axes on cedar beams, no shouts of wagoners and porters scuffling for right of way. Even the bleats of sheep and lowing of cattle out at the edges of the village were sparse, the sounds of animals at rest in calm pastures, not the driving of flocks and herds to auction.

The driver chuckled to himself as he made his way easily, pointing out to me that a deal is a deal and I, as a gentleman, didn't want to challenge the *maat* of the world, did I, by reducing the fee we had agreed upon, right?

I assured him he'd get his money. He, trying to smooth over any bad feelings, recounted a long anecdote about how strange and unpredictable the Iebiru were. I paid him no attention. I was listening, instead, to the strange quiet of the place.

"You take that street to the left," Mayati said to the driver, seeing that he was uncertain and I was inattentive.

"You remember that?"

She shrugged.

"You were here only once. And at night. And it was different then."

"If something's important, you remember it."

"But you couldn't have known then that it would be important now."

"It was important then."

There was no need to knock. In the uncanny serenity of the street, the clatter of our wagon and commentary from our horse were enough. The door of the house opened inwards at the hand of a curious child. Avishamah and all his family were revealed, reclined in a circle at a meal spread over several small tables. Aelinahtan was the first to rise from his place and offer greeting.

"What a surprise," he said. "A *welcome* surprise," he quickly corrected himself.

This made the others smile. I thought I noticed Amikhai suppress a laugh. Avishamah came to his feet to show hospitality in the more traditional way of the Iebiru.

"A blessing on those who have come!" he said. Or maybe the words meant "those who have come to us are a blessing." I wasn't sure of the translation.

I had slid into being less adept at the Iebiri language, having had little contact with them lately. I resolved that I would use this visit to become as fluent as possible. So naturally at that very moment, Aelinahtan blurted out something that was too fast and too slurred by the wine they had been drinking for me to catch. But it was met with laughter by children and adults alike, and only when the merriment died down was it explained to us.

Aelinahtan had pointed out that, apparently, from time to time, a young Lord of Kehmeht would show up at their door with a bride. It took me a minute to get it, and then I did see how it might have been funny to them. Inyotef had recently showed up with Adjedaa and now here I was with my "bride." Mayati thought it was funny too, but I corrected it right away.

This dampened their merriment. I could see actual disappointment in the women's faces. People love to see people in love, so that was the story they wove around Mayati and me. Add to that their strange prejudice against a man and woman engaging in anything but marriage, and you had a room of dismayed Iebiru.

I told them the story we had prepared, about Mayati being alone now and still recovering from being ill and they quickly redirected their thoughts to hospitality, healing, and modesty. That last factor was expressed in the idea that Mayati would stay in the attic, which was now accessed by a steep but nicely crafted staircase. I was to stay in a small room they had added in the rear.

This displaced no less than three small boys and their sister who all danced with delight to learn that they would be allowed to take their straw ticking and wool blankets and sleep right there in the common room.

It was barely afternoon and no one was going to sleep anytime soon, but getting all this worked out seemed a priority for them. Now they were content. They sat us within their circle and offered bowls of the courses we had missed while they brought out the next one.

This was surely a celebratory meal, so I asked what the occasion was. Avishamah replied it was a weekly feast (which meant every seven days to Iebiru who do not understand that a week is ten days). They called it their Day of Resting. I had never seen the Iebiru observe such a day all my time in Gohshen. But the Iebiru were still building the store-city at Rahmessu then.

"Even if the Overseers had allowed it," Aelinahtan said darkly, "there was the straw."

That was a discrete way of reminding me that barely half a year ago, Iebiri families that could not meet their quota of four hundred bricks per day would have one of their babies bricked-up alive in a wall. Compelled to forage for their own straw and still make that quota, the Day of Resting was lost. A silence fell on our little celebration. It was uncomfortable.

Amikhai seemed to find it awkward too. He volunteered something about the custom of the Day going back to their nomadic ancestor Avraham. That was, he pointed out, some four centuries ago, long before the Iebiru were in servitude to any throne. The Day fell into disuse in later generations here in the Black Land, he said. Though the nation of Leyvie had clung to it.

"In their villages," he added, "They always kept it up, one way or another. Until Mohsheh restored it for everyone." He exchanged a little nod of confirmation with Aelinahtan.

"Once the slaving began," Aelinahtan joined in, "there was no such thing as taking a rest, not for a day, and not for any part of a day. That was until about sixty years ago when Mohsheh took over the supervision. He would have been about twenty at that time, out surveying the worksites and reporting to the Throne.

"He tells Pahroh that the slaves will work better if they have periods of rest. The Throne entrusts him with the work, and tells him to do what he thinks best. So Mohsheh decrees that there's to be a day's rest every seven days. And it just so happens that the day he chooses is the very day that his own nation, the Leyvie, have been keeping as the Day of Resting all along!"

Amikhai and Aelinahtan exchanged quick nods of triumph. It was not so long ago that Aelinahtan told me he had neither affection nor respect for the "Son of Ahmrahm" who he considered a pampered traitor. Now he was taking pains to claim that when Mohsheh Ben Ahmrahm was a prince of Kehmeht, he had actually been working in secret for the wellbeing of his Iebiri brothers all along. Interesting.

Conversation turned to praise of the soft breads before us, newly pulled from the oven out back, and laced with both the honey of dates and crushed leaves of zaatar. There was a stew of root vegetables with dumplings made of dough but also other things floating in it, things I suspected were chunks of flesh from dead sheep and, perhaps, parts of pigeons or doves.

I avoided it politely, and tried not to gag when I saw Mayati happily digging into her bowl. Mayati even went so far as to ask how the stew was made. I think she really meant it too.

The women warmed to the conversation and there began much free exchange between them. Aelinahtan's wife, Baht-Tikvi, laughed easily with Mayati. The older Shuvina who, as wife of Avishamah, was matriarch of this family joined in as well.

The young Geula spoke little, preoccupied as she was with cycles of nursing, rocking, and entertaining the new baby she and Amikhai had just had. But she made small comments here and there just to let Mayati know that she also welcomed her.

And Mayati, for her part, surprised me with twin abilities to speak easily in Iebiri and remain unfazed by their customs. True, she had grown up in Gohshen as a mistress of Iebiri slaves and the daughter of an Overseer. Could that have prepared her to be so comfortable with them?

Whatever the reason, it seemed to work. Talk of servitude and terror was politely forgotten. And so it would have remained, were it not for one other custom of the Iebiru.

The Iebiru believe that every man, woman, and child should be able to read their language and have at least rudimentary skill in writing it. This is of great importance to them.

It is said among them that their forefathers, the sons of the twelve brothers who were the progenitors of their nations, made a pact that they would not learn the language of Kehmeht or teach it to their children. They would, instead, keep their families proficient in their own tongue, both spoken and written. And even though, over the generations, some Iebiru born in The Black Land and aspiring to a portion in its glory gained mastery of our language, they never abandoned their own. They spoke in it, read it, and even wrote it.

This was extremely perverse in the eyes of the Sons of Kehmeht. The Speaking In Images of our most sacred written language is secret. It is taught only to young men selected to become priests, scribes, sorcerers or lords of The Two Kingdoms. It is no wonder that it alone is the writing we carve into stone and carefully color with rare pigments dissolved in melted beeswax.

Even the diminished form of that writing, used by scribes on papyri to record our affairs, is sacred and not to be shared lightly. It's true that a simplified writing taken from that papyrus-form might be scratched now and then on a tablet of wax or a scrap of wood by some merchant recording a short list for himself. But the men and women of Kehmeht as a whole need no writing and do not learn to read it. And that, we believe, is the natural *maat* of the world.

The Iebiru, however, were great disrupters of the natural *maat* of the world. So now, perhaps more than ever, they carried on instructing their children in reading and writing. And apparently it was one of the customs of their Day of Resting that a child would demonstrate his progress in this. Today it was to be Aelinahtan's oldest boy.

His name was Yashiiv and he looked like a beardless miniature of his father. I took him to be a sort of ringleader of his brothers and sister, organizing them in giggling mischief. But all the while he had one eye on the adults, watching for his moment.

When he saw signs of the celebration winding down, he reminded his grandfather that he had not yet been tested on his reading. Avishamah nodded indulgently and the boy sprang onto a bench to reach down a small chest from a hollow space, high up in the mudbrick wall. From within it, he withdrew an old yellowed parchment.

Now, parchment is made by peeling layers of tissue from the hides of beasts, sometimes even sheep, which are sacred in Kehmeht. The smell of the animal never really leaves it, at least not for those of us who will not eat animals. If the Iebiru insisted upon writing, could they not at least use papyrus, which is made of plants and is clean?

But parchment holds its ink very well, far better than papyrus, and for several lifetimes of men. Of course we in the realm of the Two Kingdoms accomplish permanence by hewing our most important words into limestone and granite, which last forever. But that was never an option for nomadic Iebiri herdsmen.

Yashiiv unrolled the short parchment, which I gathered was the only written text his family possessed. And if it was all they had, and if they read from it every seven days, then I imagined we wouldn't be able to tell if Yashiiv was reading or simply reciting from memory. But he showed a certain eight-year-old confidence and couldn't resist a couple of sidelong glances at me and Mayati to see if we were paying full attention. Then he set his eyes to the short scroll and read aloud.

It was a poem of sorts, handed down in Iebiri families for centuries. It had maybe fifteen or sixteen lines, I couldn't be sure since Yashiiv made a few starts and stops that may have owed more to reading difficulties than versification. And, to be honest, I can't say I understood all of it. But I understood enough to know it was disturbing, dark, and in opposition to the peaceful *maat* of The Black Land.

It began with happy statements about how good it is to thank The Eternal One, and to sing praises to Him with lyres and other stringed instruments and to rejoice in His works. This was fine. It wasn't so different from what we might sing to Wsir or Iset or their son, Haruw.

Then the verses darkened, for they spoke quite openly of a problem only an Iebiri could think of: How is it that their Power allowed the wicked to do evil to the innocent?

Now this would never be a problem for a Son of Kehmeht. We knew of the existence of many gods, and some were simply evil. Being evil meant, of course, that they did evil or aided men in doing evil. So what surprise was it that innocents suffered?

You could try to appease the evil god. Or you could

appeal to a beneficent one to protect you. That was life. But Mohsheh was teaching that there is but one single Power and that He is good. Well, if He is so good, why does he let wicked people harm innocent ones?

Yashiiv read out the answer with some eight-year-old emotion in the verses that followed. These "wicked," Yashiiv intoned, "spring up like grass," these "men of violence thrive," true. But it is only the plan of the Eternal to expose them and "destroy them forever."

I have never in my life heard a prayer like that in any temple of any god of Kehmeht! There are prayers for victory in war, of course. There are prayers for the annihilation of our enemies. But never have I heard it asked "why does the god allow evil?" followed by the reply that He wishes to leave men free to choose their path but then, if they choose an evil one, brings down terrible retribution upon them! And could I doubt for a moment who my Iebiri hosts were identifying as these "wicked men" soon to be destroyed forever?

To watch slaves absorb such words was frightening. Baht-Tikvi closed her eyes as if to lose herself in the narrative. Aelinahtan's eyes remained quite open and burned with fervor, though he was thankfully glancing at some point off in space and not looking at me.

Geula was looking down at her baby with admiration for whatever destiny she was imagining these verses would bestow upon her child. A future warrior of a newly arisen Iebiri nation perhaps? Living in our cities and holding sway over us until we "surely perish" and were "scattered?"

The recital concluded. Yashiiv went to his grandfather Avishamah to receive a kiss on the forehead and a small coin in reward for his progress. Everyone got up from the meal, contented, and a little drowsy. No one reached for a weapon or cried out for an uprising of the Iebiru. No one even looked at Mayati or me with anything less than friendly hospitality. The moment had passed. But it could not be forgotten.

~

I woke the next morning to the sounds of the village reborn from its Day of Resting. Vendors were crying out praises of their wares over the bleats of sheep driven to auction or shearing. Somewhere out there, cows were being milked, donkeys loaded. Hammers rang from metal crafts, saws were shaping logs into beams. Whatever people were doing, there seemed to be a great deal of calling out and talking about it.

I had not meant to be the last to rise. It was an outcome of my laying sleeplessly until just before dawn in the small room vacated for my comfort by Yashiiv and his siblings. I could forgive myself for this, since the last time I had spent a night in this house it was waiting for Aelinahtan to come and slit my throat.

Maybe that's why I reacted so strongly, *too* strongly I suppose, to their verses. But it was always that way with the Iebiru, wasn't it? You think you know them, you think you know where you stand. But there's always something else, some other layer of things, just waiting to be revealed.

I emerged into their common room to find the women of the house with Mayati finishing a breakfast of bread and what looked to me like the yellow that emerges from the egg of a bird if it is cracked and dried before the chick can take form. It was not how I would have preferred to start the day.

There was also a noticeable absence of men.

Aelinahtan, his son Yashiiv, and Amikhai, were off to whatever it was that occupied them (flocks, I think). Only old Avishamah was there, and he seemed anxious to get out to whatever business he had. But he would not leave without me.

I thought he was being kind and I wished to reciprocate by telling him that he could go ahead and not worry about me, I'd be fine, right here. But he said he would wait for me. I begged off again, not wanting to so inconvenience him because of my late sleep. He thanked me but insisted on waiting. After a few more rounds of this I realized that he had something unspoken on his mind.

It was that bizarre Iebiri fetish about the blending of men and women who are not united in marriage. His daughter and his daughter-in-law and, of course, his own wife were married women so it would not be proper for me to fraternize with them when no other man was around. And as for Mayati, yes, she was a daughter of Kehmeht and could do as is the custom of her own people. But she was also within his house, and there is no house with two customs. So either I had to go out or he had to stay home, though he didn't want to say so outright.

"May I walk with you, Avishamah?" I said, finally getting it.

"Why of course," he answered gratefully.

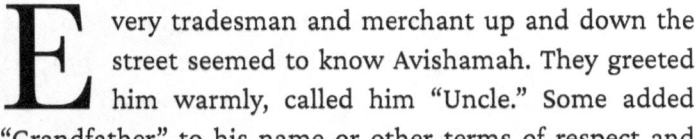

Every tradesman and merchant up and down the street seemed to know Avishamah. They greeted him warmly, called him "Uncle." Some added "Grandfather" to his name or other terms of respect and affection.

Many stole extra glances at us, attempts to parse out the meaning of an Iebiri elder walking in conversation with a young lord of the Mitzriim (as the Iebiru called the sons of Kehmeht). I think it was mostly shrugged off as just some business between a "master" who no longer had any mastery and a "slave" who was no longer bound to do anything other than he pleased. For this was what we had come to.

The Iebiri on that street knew there was nothing to stop them from walking out into the eastern wilderness and holding a festival to their Power –if their Power wished that to be. But their Power did not wish that, not at all. He did not want them to seize any opportunity on their own. And He did not want to take them out by force. No, the Power wanted our Father Pahroh to *send* the Iebiru to Him. Were the Iebiru as puzzled about this as I was?

"It is strange, isn't it, Avishamah," I mused as we walked, "that The Eternal insists on Pahroh not just *allowing* you Iebiru to worship in the desert, but rather requires that Pahroh *send* you?"

"It is as Mohsheh says," Avishamah agreed. "The Most High wants very much for the Throne to send us to His worship."

"In doing that," I conjectured, "Pahroh himself would play a part in that worship too then, wouldn't he?"

"Perhaps," Avishamah acknowledged with a small smile. The idea was new to him and he liked it as it grew on him.

"The Most High wants Pahroh to recognize Him," he agreed. "He doesn't trouble Pahroh to trek out into the wilderness to take part in the worship. But Pahroh must at least send us. That will be his part."

We walked on in companionable silence until we

cleared the edge of the village. From there we started through the pastures to look for Aelinahtan, Yashiiv, and Amikhai with the flocks.

"You know," I said as we made our way into the grass, "that I serve the Lord Harkuhotep, Seal Bearer of the King of Upper and Lower Kehmeht, Unique Friend of Pahroh, Trusted of All His House."

"Yes. Of course."

"But you may not have heard, Avishamah," I went on, "that my Master Harkuhotep is much in favor of Mohsheh's request. He has even spoken with Mohsheh about it. And he urges the Throne to agree."

"Does he then?" Avishamah said.

Was this sincere surprise? Or insolence? I couldn't tell. I could rarely tell with Iebiru. But I didn't want to spoil my chance of getting this old man to share his lore with me. That was half the reason I came to Gohshen. So I counted it sincere surprise and plunged on.

"He does," I said evenly. "And he relies on me and all who are in his service to bring him information. He needs information he can use to turn the Throne away from those at Court who counsel Pahroh to forbid the Iebiri pilgrimage into the Deshret."

"What information could I have?" Avishamah responded. "I am not part of high councils, even within my own nation of the Dahnii. And none of the Leyvie or any of the Twelve Nations seek advice from me."

This last point came with a self-deprecating chuckle.

"But you are an elder of your nation nevertheless," I reasoned. "You preserve chronicles of what was. You know a great deal of the lore of your people."

By now we could make out Yashiiv and his herding dog with the flock dotting the next hill. But Avishamah halted in his steps and took a long appraising look at me. It was disconcerting. So I talked. A lot.

"My master Harkuhotep values your lore because it helps him put the lie to the whisperings of the evil courtiers who are against Mohsheh," I went on. "Already he has reminded the Throne of the true history of the Iebiru in Kehmeht, how your fathers came as honored guests. And how they served the Black Land so well for so long, and were not always slaves. This history is very important to us. Lord Harkuhotep and those who agree with him are locked in a dispute with those highborn counselors who hate Mohsheh. The fate of both your people and mine hangs in the balance."

Avishamah took another appraising look. And then he laughed.

"So that's the way it is, then," he chuckled. "That's how it started, you see. And now it seems that's how it will end."

I didn't understand what he was talking about. But some dam had burst in him and he started us walking again as if he could hold back neither his strides nor his story.

"It was back in the days of the father of my great grandfather," he said. A century and a decade and a half a decade ago. Leyvie, the last of the founders of the Twelve Nations, had just passed away. He was, I believe, also the last to inspire respect from the Children of the Black Land. For they looked at my People differently after his passing."

"Differently?" I asked, just to show I was listening.

"Oh yes. Where there was once friendship, there was now suspicion. Where there was once respect, there was now derision. We were too numerous, it was said. We were too powerful in government, too conspicuous in the arts, too successful in business. We were too strange in our language, and too foreign in our dress."

Far off on the slope of the distant hill Yashiiv had spotted us and was waving. Avishamah smiled, waved back, and then returned to his tale.

"'What if Kehmeht is invaded?' they said. 'What will be our fate if these Iebiru rise up and join the invaders? Will that not be the end of us?' That's how people were speaking then. But Pahroh, the Pahroh who was King in those days, he did not agree with any of this!"

Avishamah said that with some feeling. I wondered if it wasn't the voice of all the Iebiru of those times who loved their life in this country and would believe only good about its King.

"It is strange to you, I think." he said. "You wonder why you have never heard of this. You wonder why it is not written in any of your chronicles. But your chronicles were written by those who wanted to see my People enslaved."

"And the Pahroh of that day was not among them?" I was skeptical of this tale.

"It was the courtiers of that time," he continued. "Most of them, anyway. There were great lords among them, some with large estates in both Kingdoms who never forgot that their families were as highborn as Pahroh's and could also produce men who might sit quite capably upon the Throne. And so they looked for allies."

"'Was it not so,' they inquired of the Generals, 'that a population as foreign as the Iebiru would pose a threat in a time of invasion? Especially one that came out of the Land of Kahnahn, whose language and gods were so much like those of the Iebiru?'

"'Was it not so,' they asked of the Priests of Ohn, 'that the Iebiru were less than whole-hearted toward the gods of Kehmeht? Will that not surely bring the disfavor of our gods down upon The Black Land?'

"And, most of all, they asked the lowborn in the villages. 'Are you not frightened for your wives and children? What will they suffer if the large and ugly Iebiru rise higher above you? Are you not outraged?'"

"But Pahroh did not agree," I pointed out. "That's what you said, that Pahroh did not accept any of this. So what did it matter?"

"Pahroh remembered the deliverance that came to Kehmeht when Yoseyf ruled," Avishamah said. "He remembered how this land was blessed when Yaakov and his sons arrived. No, he was not going to be swayed by jealous lords. He would not enslave my People. So, they deposed him," Avishamah said simply.

"What!?"

"They deposed him," Avishamah repeated. "Dismissed him from being king," he added, thinking I did not know what the term "deposed" meant. "For three months. Until he agreed."

"That cannot be!" I protested. "There is no record of any such thing in all the chronicles of Kehmeht! And I have never, ever, heard such a thing spoken. It is a tale, Avishamah. It is a made-up tale!"

"It is a tale," Avishamah agreed. "But it is a tale that is true."

I did not like this tale. But I also knew there could be a simple reason for such a story to remain untold and yet be true. For to tell it would bring dishonor upon the Throne of the Two Kingdoms. And nothing Kehmeht engraves in stone or even inks onto papyrus may bring dishonor upon the Throne.

I knew of narratives inscribed on a monument for a time, only to disappear later under the chisels of stonecutters dispatched to remove them. Then they would carve tales of greater honor in their place. Still, to bring a ruler down off the Throne of the Two Kingdoms, even for just a few months, that would have had to been a bloody affair. How could it be forgotten?

"There was no bloodshed," Avishamah said. "The common people, in dread of the rumors about the Iebiru, mobbed the streets of The City shouting for something to be done. The Lords, glad of the unrest, counseled Pahroh that there was no choice but to heed the popular voice.

Pahroh resolved at first to ignore such demagoguery. But he soon found that he had no Lords before whom he could demonstrate that resolve. The Lords left The City, or pretended to, and advised all who served The Throne to do the same."

"No king can be taken down from his throne in such a manner," I argued.

"There is no king without a people. And soon there were no people presenting themselves at court to take orders from the king. He may have remained seated in his usual place in the Great House, I do not know. But the thing he sat on was no longer the Throne of the Two Kingdoms. With no one to harken to him, it was just a pretty chair."

"And this went on for three months?" I asked, all of it hard to imagine.

"It did. Until Pahroh agreed to do what those who hated my People desired."

I tried to picture what that day at the end of the three months would have looked like. But I could not. Men are not naturally slaves. Only those born into slavery accept it easily. It takes defeat in a war or the sudden violence of gangs of slavers to turn a free man into a slave. So how could Pahroh simply decree slavery one morning on hundreds of thousands of free Iebiru with any hope of their submitting to it? This I put to Avishamah.

"He made no war on my People. He didn't even make a decree, not at first. He proposed, rather, a great task for the salvation of Kehmeht against any future siege or famine. He...oh!"

Avishamah was all but knocked off his feet by Yashiiv who, bounding down the hillside, miscalculated the impact his flying embrace would have on his grandfather. His herding dog ran happy circles around us as Yashiiv bid Avishamah a "good morning" that would have sufficed if they had not seen each other for years.

Yashiiv followed up with a polite nod to me, and led us over the ridge to where Aelinahtan and Amikhai were shearing ewes. They were filthy from the work, and glistening with sweat though it was still early in the day. But they seemed happy with their efforts.

"Best to do it on a hot day, right Your Honor?" Aelinahtan said to me as if I had any idea of why that would be true. "Because it chills them, you know. When we take their wool. You need a good strong sun to warm them up."

I nodded agreement. Why not? It made sense.

"His Honor was asking me about what things were like in the days of the father of my great grandfather," Avishamah told them. "How the Tax of Labor began."

"A trick," Aelinahtan said laconically. "And a lie. But a good one. We were fooled."

Avishamah motioned us to sit in the shade of a lone fig tree where he took up the reins of the conversation again.

"Pahroh proclaimed a great national project. Store cities were to be built, massive in scale. In them, food and fuel would be put aside as in the days of Yoseyf who your people call Tzaphnaht Pahnayakh. It would mean security in any famine that might come, and surety if there should ever be a prolonged siege or warfare on the Two Kingdoms," Avishamah said.

"Men, women, children were all to join in this great undertaking. Pahroh himself appeared at the worksite on the day it was inaugurated. Around his neck he wore a braided chain with a small trowel crafted from the finest silver. You could see it flash and glisten in the morning sunshine. My great grandfather saw this."

"He was a tall man," Aelinahtan interjected. "That Pahroh, he was tall. That's why everyone could see it, shining around his neck, when he addressed the assembled. Because he was tall. Nothing like the Pahroh of our times."

Amikhai shot a look of horrified amazement at his brother-in-law and then snuck sidelong glance at me to see if I was offended by this reference to our beloved Father of Kehmeht. The ignorant Iebiru never understood how wonderful our Pahroh's closeness to the sacred earth was in our eyes.

"Well, who among our People would stand aside from this great effort?" Avishamah went on. "Especially when all the people of Kehmeht were accepting this Tax of Labor upon themselves for the great good it would bring? So, we would also put our shoulders to the task, like all the other citizens of the Two Kingdoms. And in this way, we would put to rest, once and for all, the question of our loyalty."

"Except for the Leyvieiim," Amikhai said. "They stayed away."

"And how the other nations criticized them for that," Avishamah related. "'You will bring shame on us,' they said. 'You will bring suspicion on us, too. You will be putting a sword into the hands of those who accuse us!' they said."

"But the Nation of Leyvie stayed in their villages that day," Amikhai said.

"My great grandfather's father, and all who were there, took up the work with enthusiasm," Avishamah went on. "There was no pay, and the work was hard. Yet they rejoiced in the chance to prove themselves.

"But as days went by, it became clear that it would be hard to sustain the effort. The workshops and fields was being neglected. Soon the question of how to provide for themselves while spending their days on the Tax of Labor began to trouble them."

"People sold off some of their herds and inventory just to keep their families going," Aelinahtan added. I think he wanted me to see that he too was well versed in this history.

"And most troubling of all," Avishamah said, "was that, day by day, there were fewer Sons of Kehmeht at the work sites. Until there were none at all. Only Iebiru remained at the labor."

"And Mitzri taskmasters," Aelinahtan added. "Some appointed, originally, just to keep a record of how many clay bricks a family could make in those first days of enthusiasm."

"Four hundred per family," Amikhai said. "Every family. It didn't matter if they were large or small, blessed with strong sons or having only daughters, houses full of provisions or near starvation, all of them alike had to deliver four hundred bricks every day."

"And if not," Aelinahtan said darkly, "there were... punishments. But you know about that."

Was he blaming *me* for a decree made long before my own grandfather was born?

"The Nation of Efrahyiim was also exempted from the

Tax of Labor," Avishamah related, "because they were descended from Tzaphnaht Pahnayakh himself, and so had some royal status. And many wealthy of the Rehuveyni and other nations were allowed to pay Iebiri bondsmen to do their work."

"To be slaves who owned slaves, to put it plainly," Aelinahtan said, and not with kindness.

"And the Nation of Leyvie," Avishamah went on, "they were allowed to remain free of the Tax of Labor, as they were regarded as lore-masters and priests of all the twelve nations, and in Kehmeht priests are free of taxation."

"But the Leyvieiim did not stand aloof," Amikhai said. "The Throne demanded a layer of our own people to serve as supervisors who would report to the Task Masters of Kehmeht. The Leyvie stepped into that role, taking many beatings and blows to protect their brothers, crushed under the labor."

"And if you wonder" Aelinahtan said, "why the Throne extended relief to parts of our people, then consider how easy it is to take the ewes and lambs from a flock while you feed and water the rams."

I had no idea how easy that would be, having never spent time with a flock of anything until this morning. All I knew was that Harkuhotep would be very pleased with this history. It showed that the original enslavement of the Iebiru was a lowly thing, conceived by conniving counselors inciting the basest mobs to manipulate the Pahroh of that day.

So our Pahroh could accede to the request of the Iebiru with no betrayal of Kehmeht's greatness. It would be, rather, a return to the original wisdom of The Father of The River. It would be the restoration of the tranquil and happy *maat* of the Black Land.

The only problem was, who would believe such a tale? I had trouble believing it at first, and it was only the ardor of Avishamah and his family that persuaded me. But it was still just a story told by some obscure Iebiru. I would need proof. But I knew where to get it.

All I had to do was return to the archives and look for documents dated during the three months that Pahroh was made helpless to command. If suddenly, during those ninety days, there were no royal decrees, no acts of the Throne, no agreements or pacts sealed by the Father of The River, then their very absence would show the tale of the old King's temporary deposition to be true.

It made me laugh a little to think that the most boring part of the archive would yield its richest prize. I was light-headed with excitement. I had to return to The City. I wished I could fly there.

∼

"Have you lost your mind?" Mayati said. She was saying that quite a bit lately. "What did they give you to drink out there with the sheep today?"

"Shhh," I whispered. "You'll wake up the whole street."

The street was where we went to have this conversation, as Avishamah's family was well asleep.

"Alright," she whispered. "You're tired. You got too much sun. Let's talk about it tomorrow."

"It's urgent," I whispered back. "Harkuhotep needs this lore. I need to bring it to him."

"So, bring it to him. But I can't go back there."

"You'll have nothing to fear," I said. "Harkuhotep will be so pleased with this, he'll tell Okpara to leave you alone.

He'll write a judgment assuring you of your father's property. I'm sure of it."

"I'm not."

"We can't stay here forever, Mayati."

"Maybe you can't. I can. If I have to."

"And do what? Make believe you're Iebiri?"

She let out a hoarse whispered laugh that had no mirth in it, turned on her heels and went back inside and up to her attic. So that was that for this night.

I would not renew our discussion in front of Avishamah's household. There was nothing exactly shameful in it, but it felt personal, private, like the secrets of my own kin, which, in a way, the Lords of Kehmeht are. Did Iebiru really need to hear about one of us trying to take the property of another by defaming her father?

As a result, the entire day passed without me ever having a chance at a private moment with Mayati. We were together at breakfast, but the entire household was with us.

So I ate fresh bread with a dip of sesame seeds ground into a paste and mixed with date honey, washed down with cool cups of very new, very diluted grape wine. We were through it quickly enough, but before I could take Mayati aside, Avishamah asked me if I would walk with him on his errands, for which he was already late. Considering the prudish customs of his house, what could I say? So we went.

❧

This day we did not head out to the pastures but, instead, visited particular places within the village, all of them having something to do with the manufacture of copper or tin. I wondered if, when he was younger, Avishamah had been among those who worked with forges and metal crafts, for he seemed to know everything about them.

He would exchange a few sentences of trade talk with each craftsman we passed. Many sought his opinion on the quality of some sheets of burnished copper or the tricky repair of a tin vessel they would hand over for his examination.

I forgot myself and almost made the mistake of asking him to tell me of his years in this craft, since most people like to be asked about their skills. But Avishamah was not most people. He was an Iebiri who would have had to abandon his trade to help his family make their quota of four hundred clay bricks a day. Either that, or see his loved ones beaten to death or maimed into a crippled life, or be forced to watch their most helpless bricked-up alive into walls or drowned in the dark ooze of a clay pit.

So the day passed in small talk and small transactions with tradesmen in copper and bronze, punctuated by offers to rest a while in the shade of this one's awning or that one's home, and refresh ourselves with nuts and date-water. I had become less of a curiosity than on the previous day. The village was getting used to the idea that Avishamah was visited from time to time by wealthy Sons of Kehmeht, perhaps doing better business than he let on.

It was near evening when we returned home, and soon found ourselves together with the entire household at the second meal. I could not wait again for them all to go to their beds, so I simply asked Mayati if she would take a walk with me to see the sunset. This seemed mildly romantic to some of Avishamah's family, but in a proper way. So we were easily excused, encouraged even.

"I didn't mean anything," I said as we walked. "About you pretending to be Iebiri."

"Then why did you say it?"

"I mean it wasn't an insult. It was just a way of saying that sooner or later you're going to have to go back to The City. But that it would be safe now."

"How? Just days ago we had to leave without a trace. What suddenly makes it so good to return now?"

"I told you. The lore I have for Harkuhotep, it changes everything. He will be so pleased, it will be his smallest token of gratitude to clear your Father of any accusations and assure that your property remains yours."

"Why should he bother?"

"Because he is a man of honor," I said.

"Ha ha ha," Mayati said in more mirthless laughter. She was getting good at that.

"He's changed, Mayati. He really has. Maybe it was the death of his wife. And all the other deaths, and everything that's happened to us these last ten months, we've all changed, haven't we?"

"What? He loves the Iebiru now? That's it? That's how he's changed?"

"He respects them now, yes. He's spoken with Mohsheh and has the greatest regard for him. He understands Mohsheh to be a teacher of kindness, and, in his own way, he wants to be more like him. And he's surrounded himself with those who feel the same."

"He's scared, Merey. No, not scared. Scared out of his mind. They all are. All these new friends of the Iebiri from the great ones of The City. They're too ashamed to admit it, so they talk about a return to the days when the Iebiru were honored among us. They talk great policies and philosophies. But they're all just frightened near to death.

Because the Eternal One of the Iebiru will not be patient forever. And soon, very soon, He is going to bring them all down in blood. And they know it."

"Of course people are scared, Mayati. Who could not be frightened by what we've been through this year? It doesn't mean that frightened is all they are. What about you? Aren't you scared of all this, just like everyone else?"

"No."

I sputtered something but it wasn't quite a sentence. How could Mayati claim that all the Black Land was in panic over what was befalling us and she, alone, remained unafraid? She understood the sputter. And she answered.

"Because I already died, Merey. I died of the cattle fever that took my father. I was dead."

"What are you talking about? You're here, you're alive."

"Yes, I am alive now. But I was dead. I left the shell of myself on my sickbed, I looked down on her, singed with fever and cold with death.

"I pitied her greatly and I would have stayed and wept over it, and worried about who would purify it for the journey to the Happy Land of Reeds. But I could do nothing for her. I was Ka, not substance. I was separated, helpless and sad.

"Then I was drawn upwards, and I could see our entire house from above, my father's tomb, the out-buildings, the walls, everything. It was unspeakably sad to see, and I felt pity for all of it, for the date palms and stones, and slate tiles of the roof below me. And most of all I felt pity for the me that was on that bed, still and dead.

"Then a voice called me, and I found myself rushing towards a brightness. It was brighter than the sun, but sweet and golden and I could bear to look at it. And the voice told me that He loved me, but that I could remain in the world if I wanted to. It was Him, Merey. It was the Eternal One of the Iebiru."

"What did He look like?" I asked, half suspicious but half in sincerity, for it seemed to me that Mayati was speaking strangely, but true.

"I never saw Him," she said. "Just the bright. Just the voice."

We walked on in silence down the village path painted in the sunset.

"So I do not fear Him," she said, "though He is fearful. For He is also full of love for us, Merey. Love and pity. And I *know* this. I don't need any great ones of The City to tell me philosophy or secret lore. He has given me life and He asks only that I trust Him. That's what I know."

"So you really do mean to stay here and live as an Iebiri," I said.

"I'm still just me, Merey. I'm just Mayati. But I do mean to keep faith with The Eternal One. Whoever He is. Whatever He is.

"I'm going to stay here until the Iebiru are sent away to the seven days in the Red Land. And I will go with them, if they will have me. And I will worship Him there, in whatever way we are told to worship. It won't be long now. You know it. Everyone knows it."

CHAPTER 6
THE THIRD WEEK OF ḤNT-ḤTJ, THIRD MONTH OF SHEMU, SEASON OF THE RIVER RUNNING LOW
FIFTY-FIRST OF THE SEVENTY-FIVE DAYS

When we were small, Neferet and I shared a pet locust. Neferet caught it but we agreed that if her mother found it she would surely crunch it under her finely sewn papyrus sandal. So it lived in my room, in a small wooden box lined with sweet grasses. We'd take it out to see the sun and play with us whenever Neferet came.

It was young and solitary and wingless when she found it near The River. But it changed under our unseeing eyes until one day, when we took it out for its daily race around the arena formed by our legs spread out on the floor, a notion of freedom came into it. It sprang up to the sill of my window. It looked out onto the orchard. It took in the abundance of green, then spread its four folded wings and flew away on a sunbeam of the late afternoon.

Locusts, back then, were amusing and harmless in our eyes. Yes, we knew that at times those solitary little creatures, so common in the grasses along The River, might combine into a swarm.

Then they would be a pestilence to the Children of The

Black Land, eating the crops up and down the floodplain throughout the Two Kingdoms. But that happened rarely enough, and besides, what did we, two children of wealth, know or care about such things?

But now locusts were to come, and in swarms that had no precedent in numbers or kind unless Our Father Pahroh would send the Iebiru to their worship in the Red Land. Mohsheh announced this before the Throne and it was already known to us when Mayati and I decided to disappear from The City and leave our two sets of troubles behind. Locusts, that evening, didn't seem to count as anything I needed to think about.

I was no farmer, and the orchard that used to be the grace and charm of our house in The City was ruined by the plague of the Animals, then destroyed beyond repair by the Hailstorm. Besides, as far as Hesera was concerned, it was no longer my house anyway.

I figured that when it came, Mayati and I could withstand this new curse in Gohshen as well as anywhere (perhaps better, since the Iebiri Power protected Gohshen in all that had come before). But now that I had Avishamah's tale to tell, I wanted to fly back to The City, gather the proofs from the archive, and present it before Harkuhotep and all the others who thought so little of me as Inyotef stole my glory.

The journey back should have been simple enough. But I wasted days poking around for a suitable cart and driver. My pickiness was, in part, a way of giving Mayati time to reconsider. Did she really want to remain in this village of the Dahnii without me? She did.

Next morning I looked for a cart in earnest and discovered that every driver in this village was absolutely unwilling to take me to The River landing, and not at any price. They knew very well what day the Hailstorm ended, as the thunder of it had been in Gohshen too. And they could count twenty-one days from the New Moon and know that the Locust Swarm, whatever it would turn out to be, would arrive the day after tomorrow. And who wanted to be out and about during that?

Not that they doubted their Power would protect them from the Swarm. The Dahnii now embraced whatever Mohsheh told them. I could not help but notice that in Avishamah's household his small clay images of Attar of the Morning Star and Shapshu Lord of the Setting Sun were dusty with neglect. I never saw any of his family offer so much as a drop of olive oil or a pinch of incense or even a quick muttered prayer to those poor neglected gods.

Avishamah had been faithful to them once. But Mohsheh taught that these gods were no gods at all, and that their images were displeasing to The Eternal. And though Avishamah and his family may have felt some longing for these old familiar deities, they believed that the deliverance being wrought for them was from The Eternal One of Mohsheh alone.

In any case, Avishamah and all the Iebiri in his village found it politic to avoid mentioning the coming Swarm in conversation with me. It was to be another blow to my People, how could they speak of it to my face?

And so, I let their awkward reticence lull me into waiting too long.

~

The journey to the landing needed only a few hours, and I still had a full day until the Swarm would come. So there was nothing to worry about. As long as all went as it should. But it had been a long time since all went as it should, and there was so much that could go wrong.

What if it took the whole day to find a carter? What if an axle broke on the way? What if it took an afternoon to find a wheelwright who could make the repair? And what if, as the hours closed in, the carter's resolve would melt in his wife's tears begging "what will I do alone with the children if the Swarm turns out to be as deadly as the Hailstorm and you are taken from us?"

It wasn't until an hour before sunset that I found, quite by chance, an Iebiri with a small donkey cart returning to his home in another village not far from the landing. He agreed to take me along since he was trying to get home anyway.

And so I reached the dock not long after dark and found, to my luck, three boats tied up for the night. Two of them were of a good size but not crafted well enough for voyages on the Great Green. So they would surely be turning back up The River in the morning.

I found the master of one of them, and he agreed to give me passage at dawn. I left a coin with him to seal the agreement and went to the inn to spend the night, confident that luck was now with me and I would be in The City before the next morning was out.

I handed the watchman at the lodging a silver coin and told him there would be two others like it for him if he would wake me an hour before first light. He was happy with the arrangement, and I felt that with an hour set aside for both waking and the brief walk to the dock, there would be time for unforeseen delays. All would still be well.

But all was not well. Something more than the Sun rose out of the East that morning. Storm winds. Dust dervishes swirled around me as I made my way to the dock, eyes closed to slits and my traveling cloak wrapped around my mouth and nose against the fine sand. It was a strange wind, for the sky was clear and blue, no storm clouds to be seen. Yet the warm wind blew as if storm sent. Stranger still, The River continued to sparkle in sunlight even while it churned in choppy waves.

The wild sparkling water rocked the ships and made them strain at the halters binding them to the dock. Timbers creaked and the boards of the dock groaned as wind and water slammed the ships into the piers again and again.

The masters of all three boats were shouting orders, straining to be heard over the wind. One ship let out rope to distance itself from the dock, while another angled inward, the crew trying to bind it closely with multiple lines to keep it from banging into the dock repeatedly. I ran down the planks to jump onto my ship before it departed without me, but its master waved me off.

"We'll have to wait this out," he shouted over the wind.

"But I have to be in The City today," I cried back.

"It cannot be done, Your Honor," he shouted.

"I'll pay you triple the cost," I shouted back.

"I could not do it for all the gold in Kehmeht, Your Honor," he replied. "The River will not allow."

He was right, of course. The journey back to The City was upstream and required help from a friendly wind out of the north into the sail. But here, now, this east wind blew *across* the water, making it splash and explode in foam against the western bank. If the ships were let loose they could only be thrown up against that shore.

I turned to make my way back up the long dock and caught the east wind full in my face. Was this the evil god Sutekh who causes storm winds and chaos and all manner of confusion? Or was Sutekh just another Being of Ka, doing this at the command of the Power of the Iebiru? Or was it as Adjedaa (and now Mayati) would say: "There is no Sutekh, he is not and he never was! His name is just a word the ignorant call the Power of the Iebiru when he sends the storm."

A gust caught my cloak and threw me off balance. I was almost edged off the planks and into the water, but I bent forward and managed to push my way to the end of the dock and back onto land. And there I saw my last desperate hope. Down the path back to the inn, just before it turns away from The River, a man struggled mightily to pull his small fishing craft up onto the land.

"Wait," I called as I ran to him.

He looked up at me quizzically but without daring to leave hold of his boat, it being tugged fiercely by The River and the wind.

"Ferry me across," I called to him. "I'll pay you more than you earn in a month of fishing."

I had no idea what he earned in a month of fishing, but it could not have been equal to the purse of coins I pulled out of the travel pouch on my belt. I was prepared to spend it all. He stood there, still holding his boat half-extracted from the water and blinked at me. He must have thought me insane.

"Here," I said as I thrust the purse towards him. He wanted to at least examine it but had no hand free to do so, fearing his small boat would be swept away.

"Look," I said and untied the purse strings for him and held its mouth open so he could see the coins inside.

"It's dangerous," he said.

"I don't care," I shouted back over the wind.

"Come then," he said and lowered the craft back into the water, wading in up to his knees to steady it. I climbed in, he followed, seating himself on the bench that bridged the boat's middle so that he faced backwards towards me where I sat in the stern. Wet nets were piled carelessly at my feet and the thing stank of fish, but we were launched.

His arms were corded in muscle and they strained hard at the oars. Those efforts were not needed to propel us across, the east wind was doing a fine job of pushing us in that direction. But The River was still rushing north towards the Great Green and it meant to take us with it if it could, east wind or not. Pulling at the oars was about keeping us on a straight westerly course for the far bank.

He struggled mightily, but the current was strong. So instead of moving straight west before the wind, or due north before the current, we were traveling somewhere between the two.

This was making the crossing much longer than usual and much harder on the boatman. He fought as best he could, but his right arm was surely stronger than his left and the uneven power of the oars allowed the current to turn the boat a bit. That was all the wind needed.

It found the side of the craft, took hold of it, and spun us around. We turned around again and again as we hurtled downriver, rocking as we went and taking on water. I wanted to bail the water with my hands, but I needed them to hold onto the sides of the craft or be thrown into the angry flow.

We rocked and spun and took water as the current and

the wind pushed us at cross-purposes, north against west. They were rivals struggling against one another, yet allied to make a bad end for us.

The boatman finally surrendered his left oar to the current and placed both hands tightly on the right, no longer pulling at it but holding it locked and steady as a rudder. It was well done, for in doing it he forced the water to join with the wind in pushing us, finally, against the western shore.

Had our landing been against rocks or even earth, I believe the craft would have been smashed and our bones with it. But we plowed into tall reeds, thick clumps of them towering out of the water and so we came to a soft stop. The reeds scratched our faces and we had to ignore a dozen tiny cuts and fight through the stalks to wade onto the land. But we were alive.

The boatman was breathing heavily and fell to his knees in exhaustion. I handed him the purse, soaked but intact, and a word of thanks with it. Too winded to speak, he nodded and I scrambled up the bank until I found the road and headed left, meaning south, to The City.

I was soaked to my hips so the wind-blasted sand began to adhere to me. My sandals, my feet, my legs, and my tunic, soon bore a coat of sand. From my belt and up I was still a lord of Kehmeht with a golden collar. But my lower half was rough brown, neither flesh nor cloth. I looked like a satyr newly emerged from one of the tales of the Sea Peoples.

I wondered if this would deter any fearful carters from stopping to give me a ride, but the issue never came to the test. There was no one on the road and after an hour of walking in the morning sun (which still shone hot, despite the windstorm) I slowed to a sweating, panting, halt. The pumping of my heart and my gasping breaths quieted, and the voice in my head, always ready with a bad word, began its accusation.

"Why did you let the time slip through your fingers?" it said. "You knew there would be twenty-one days until the next Curse. Can't you count? Couldn't you have made a plan?"

"I had a plan," I protested. "I was going to wait it out in Gohshen with Mayati at Avishamah's."

"So?" the voice challenged.

"I discovered something important," I said, "something that Harkuhotep needs to know."

"If it was so important, why didn't you leave days ago? You would have been in The City by now. You would have accomplished something. You would have had honor."

There was no answer to this. Or there was an answer but it disgusted me: "Because I am stupid, and without honor, and everyone knows it."

I think I might have just sat down right there, wrapped in my traveling cloak and thoughts of my own unworthiness, bathed in sweaty resentment of everyone who knew the ugly truth about me. But another voice, a real one, outside my head, intruded.

"Over here, Your Honor," it called.

"Come in, Your Honor," another said.

Two voices then. Squinting through the swirls of dust and leaves and twigs and fine sand borne on the wind, I saw two men in the shadow of a squat structure visible just beyond the rise up ahead. In twenty paces I recognized it for what it was: A soldier's fort.

The two men opened the thick double doors for me and then shut them behind us against the wind once we were inside. This was the first moment of something like quiet since I woke to the roar of the windstorm that morning. It was a great relief and I found the sound of natural speaking voices a delight.

"No day for traveling, this," said one of the soldiers who seemed not much older than me.

"A thirsty day too, with sand down your throat," the older and larger soldier added as he handed me a cup. It was watered-down wine of the worst quality. It was delicious.

As I drained the cup, my eyes adjusted to the darkness of the place. They had blocked up the windows with wooden shutters against the sand, and were making do with small shafts of sunlight that came through cracks between the boards and a few oil lamps.

The twelve men in the place all turned to look at me. I nodded to them and they returned to their naps, their dice, their games of mandala, their stitching of a tunic, or their oiling of a sword.

"Make a place for His Honor," the older soldier said to the room.

He must have been their commander, for everyone got up and moved things until a corner was vacated. It was quickly furnished with a bed-stand padded with linen blankets, a stool, and a lamp of oil.

"It's soldier's accommodations," he said to me while he ignited the lamp, "but it's the best we have. And better than the windstorm."

It didn't take long for the general interest in me to die down. The men returned to their tasks and pastimes. I really wasn't that interesting, sitting there on the edge of the rough bed trying to think through my next step.

They must have been curious about why a young lord would be out alone in the windstorm without a servant, a driver, and a wagon pulled by a decent team. But none of them were of rank sufficient to ask, though the one in charge floated a few polite hints.

"Would you like to wash up, Your Honor?" he said presenting me with a basin and full pitcher and what passed for a clean towel in this place. "Looks like you had a hard road..."

I nodded my thanks but didn't reward him with my tale.

"I am on urgent business for the Chamber of Judgments," was all I gave him. It served as both the title of my untold story and a warning to aid me in any way I might request. It did the trick.

The hum of banter by the other eleven men stuttered for a moment, betraying that they were all listening to what was going on in my corner. Good. It meant they would help me if I demanded it. But what exactly was I going to demand? They had no horses in their small stable, their duty being only to keep it readied with water and provisions should a royal messenger or a troop of cavalry arrive.

I could require them to escort me on foot until we came upon a place with suitable transportation. But how far were we from a village? I raised the question later as we shared the afternoon meal.

"Oh there are villages near enough, Your Honor," the older soldier said. "But how can we get to them in this windstorm? And even if we could, the horses would be spooked beyond usefulness, seems to me."

The others nodded or grunted agreement. They were used to handling horses and knew what you could expect of them.

"Well, we're lucky it's wind and sand this time,"

another of the soldiers said. "Compared to balls of ice and fire, it's a walk in a field of flowers, isn't it?"

This was followed by general agreement. Did they think the windstorm was what the Power of the Iebiru was sending this time? Didn't they know that it was to be locusts, a great swarm of them? Mohsheh warned of it publicly before the throne for twenty-one days now, everyone knew about it. Well, no, not everyone. These men, isolated by their duties or by their ignorance, thought that the windstorm was it.

"The windstorm is not what is coming," I said to them between mouthfuls of spelt with boiled leeks. "The windstorm is just what brings what's coming."

They downed spoons, stopped in mid-chew, and looked at me with puzzled and concerned faces.

"It's locusts," I said. "This east wind will bring them. It is carrying them through the skies of the Red Land even now."

"When will they come, Your Honor?" one of them asked.

"Soon. Tomorrow is the twenty-second day since the New Moon after the Hailstorm, they will come no later than tomorrow."

They didn't grasp what the span of twenty-one days or new moons had to do with locusts. They just assumed that I was gifted with farsight and I allowed them to believe it. The day was ending anyhow, all would be better understood in the morning.

～

T hey posted a gate sentry for the first watch of the night, but allowed him to stay inside the double doors, opening them just a crack every now and then to see what might be going on. The other sentry, who usually ascended to the roof, was allowed to sit at the top of the ladder and open the hatch every half hour or so. Second and third watches were assigned, the lamps extinguished, and we all went to bed.

Moonlight penetrated the cracks in the boards shuttering the windows. And with the moonbeams, a soft but constant chant of the east wind found its way in to us. Outside it was blustering and loud, but here it made a not disagreeable sound.

I let it lull me to sleep. The men of the three watches were carefully quiet. I slept through their changes until what should have been dawn. But there was no dawn.

No rays of light came through the boards, neither the light of the moon nor that of a rising sun. It wasn't exactly black, but a murky grey, as if there was light out there somewhere, but unable to reach us. Then, waking a bit more, I sensed the muffled rush of the east wind suddenly fall absolutely still.

There is nothing so loud as a sudden silence. I made my way around the sleeping men and joined the sentry of the third watch at the doors. He was as curious as I was about the sudden silence and the strange grey darkness where daylight should have been. He parted the doors a handbreadth and we both looked outside.

The sky above was black and undulating, a monstrous dark thing that extended up from the far horizon and over the dome of the world, shutting out the light that was meant for this day. But it was no giant creature blotting out the sun. It was, rather, an uncountable number of very tiny ones. The locusts had come.

This enormous pulsating thing, this new dark mass under the sky, began to descend upon us. The brief moments of silence after the east wind stopped gave way to a thunderous buzzing of innumerable wings beating the warm and now stagnant air.

It was this great noise that woke the others. They joined us at the open door, faces turned upwards towards the doom that was coming.

We should have rushed to slam the doors shut. We should have leapt to find rags and stuffed them into the cracks in the window shutters. We should have grabbed shovels and burlap sacks and anything that could be used to beat these invaders to death. And, in time, we did all of that. But first we stood still as stone, faces upward at the thing that was coming down upon us. We could not look away. Not until the first wave of locusts smashed into our faces and woke us to action.

How many of them managed to get inside until we stirred from our shocked stupor? A few hundred? A thousand? No matter. These men were soldiers and though their duty of late was storing feed for cavalry horses and grease for chariot axels, they were, in the end, men whose craft is killing. In a few moments' exertion wielding empty sacks, flat shovels, and bare hands they dispatched the first wave of locusts and blocked up all the places where others might enter.

The floor was thick with the dead insects and it was growing uncomfortably warm, now that the places that air could have entered was sealed against more invaders. The smell of sweat and surprise mingled with the mass of tiny corpses. A kind of order was restored.

Outside the locusts had settled down. They roosted in the trees, perched on rocks, and covered the earth. And then did absolutely nothing.

"That's queer," one of the soldiers muttered. His comrades grunted assent, worried. When locusts swarm they are relentless, they never pause in their onslaught. But these were at rest.

It occurred to me that this day was the Day of Resting of the Iebiru. But the idea that their holiday was somehow being observed by swarms of insects was too insane to consider. Besides, the lice and the rampaging animals didn't take a rest on any of the seven days they afflicted us, why would the Power of the Iebiru make His locusts act differently?

Or was that the point? To make creatures that never rest, rest at His command? I had the remainder of the day and the night that followed to consider this. But I didn't. It was too unnerving and I had to put my thoughts to finding a way back to The City. I resolved that at first light I would take some of these men with me and get moving. But first light brought new troubles.

It may seem hard to imagine the mandibles of a mostly soft insect making an audible noise while it eats. If the world held its breath and all was absolutely quiet then, maybe, you could put your ear next to a locust and hear it dining on a blade of grass. Maybe. But the sound we began to hear at dawn was hundreds of thousands of the creatures eating at the same time. Eating everything.

They chewed at the ropes that held the window shutters in place and at the rags stuffed into the cracks. They chewed at the wood itself. They chewed at anything that grew, tree, stalk or stem and at things that sprouted in the cracks between the wall stones wherever mortar was lacking. They chewed voraciously at the leather tackle and harnesses out in the stable. They entered the storehouse and chewed at the seals on the large clay jugs of grain and olives. And when those seals were gone, they rushed headlong down into the contents and gorged themselves.

Soon there were a dozen breaches where locusts could enter our room at will and so it became, again, a battleground. The soldiers whacked the insects in mid-flight, slapped them out of the air with empty sacks and blankets, stomped them underfoot, squashed them against the walls. I was soon exhausted and retreated to my corner, figuring I would save my strength to kill just the ones attacking my body.

At first this disgusted me. The crunch of the insects under my sandal, the smashing of them with a flat cooking paddle I picked up and wielded. When they landed on me I slapped at them with my bare hands. But in time disgust became annoyance and a strange kind of boredom. "Was this it, then?" I wondered as I sat on my bed, back up against the wall, legs folded under me to offer a smaller target.

At that instant a locust slammed into my face and began to make its way into my nose. It could not fit but it made it impossible to breathe through that nostril. Another landed next to it and another after that, pressing into the gap between my lips. Others were upon my eyes. I could not breathe or see.

I panicked, scratching at my face with both hands until I could get air again. I dared to open one eye and saw that all of the men were being assaulted in this way. It was a bizarre dance of madmen, everyone slapping at their own faces and pulling at their own flesh.

One soldier let out a fearsome scream and fell to his

knees. A locust had somehow pierced his open eye. The soldier grabbed the locust in his hand and threw it hard to the floor, rocking back and forth on his knees in pain. There was only a very small trickle of blood from that eye and I thought it strange that he seemed more like one who had been stung by a desert hornet than irritated by a locust.

But his screams were pitiful. We went to see if we could aid him but before anyone could help him up, he fell sideways onto the floor. He convulsed, his legs shot out from under him and his arms flailed in the air. He made choking sounds and gasped for breath as one being strangled. His mouth opened wide and he twitched a few times and he was dead.

I noticed the locust he had hurled to the floor laying broken at my feet. It was strange in appearance and I prodded it a little with the edge of my cooking paddle. Its antennae were not soft and pliable but stiff and hardened like the horns of a tiny ox. I knelt down to get a closer look.

"Don't touch it!" the older soldier said and kicked it away from me. "There's venom still on those stingers."

Stingers? None of us had ever heard of a locust that could sting, let alone with venom that could kill a man in fifty breaths like a desert viper. But this soldier had died just such a death right before our eyes. I was not the only one frozen in confusion and fear.

The older soldier was worthy of command, for he instantly gave orders and got us moving again. Six men were detailed to a quick burial out back for their fallen comrade. Three were to dig while the other three fought off locusts.

Four others were dispatched to unlock the small armory and take what they could of copper or bronze. They found shields there, mostly of wood and leather but a few had coverings of metal. These were stripped off and banged into window shutters the locusts could not breach.

We continued to destroy locusts all the while, but now with one eye always on the kill to see what strange new species we were up against. The swarm was mostly the familiar grey green but now that we looked we found all manner of sinister mutations.

Some of them had teeth, tiny but sharp enough to draw blood. Some had claws. Some had wide powerful wings like birds of prey. Some resembled flying reptiles. Some dripped saliva that burned the skin on contact. And we could only wonder which of these strange species might be venomous.

The burial was a battle all its own. Locusts blanketing the ground marched towards the place where the grave was being dug. To reach it they had to get over an irrigation channel that brought water to the stables. That channel had at least three handbreadths of water in it and locusts cannot swim. But they can die.

And so they came, falling into the water, drowning in heaps that grew higher as more advanced. Soon the dead filled the channel completely and the living marched over the bridge of their corpses. A moment later they were plunging into the grave itself.

Now it was a contest of which would fill the excavated grave first: The shovelfuls of earth the diggers were pushing back upon the body of their comrade? Or the horde of locusts pouring in?

I did not ask aloud what all of us had to be wondering. Would these creatures eat the flesh of this fallen man? The diggers labored hard to fill the grave with earth not just to close it but to suffocate and kill, if they could, the thousands of locusts who had gone down upon the still warm body.

By the time the burial was done the windows of the fort had been closed-up anew by metal from the shields and a quick mix of mortar sealed them in place. It made everything more manageable.

Men were assigned to watches, three at a time on duty to kill any locust that might yet find its way in, while the others were given leave to rest as best they could. I laid flat on my back and looked up at the ceiling beams and wondered what would be. Was there even a number to tell the tale of what we were seeing?

There are images in the sacred writing of Kehmeht to express all the numbers anyone would ever need. There are images for one, for ten, for a hundred, for a thousand, for ten thousand, for a hundred thousand, and for a million. What tally of things could not be told by combining these in the proper way?

But even if I inked the signs for "a million" to be multiplied by "a million" who would be able to imagine the number that would result? We had no word for it. It was darkly comic to remember that in Kehmeht, when inscriptions needed to describe, say, the massive number of warriors in an historic battle, the term used was always "like locusts."

It occurred to me then that Avishamah and his family must have seen this swarm in the air yesterday. It had been their Day of Resting, they would all have been at home. They would have felt the darkness at dawn as I did. The children would have roused the household and they would have all emerged, sleepy and barefoot into the narrow street to see the blotting out of the sky.

It had to be so, for the east wind that brought the swarm to the Lower Kingdom had to pass over Gohshen. I imagined Mayati there, looking up at it in a mix of fear and joy, longing to give herself over to the Power that sent it.

Did the Power create all these creatures from nothing just for this assault on the stubbornness of our Court? If that were so, why would He need a full day's blowing of an east wind to bring them? He might as easily have made them here in Kehmeht.

These were surely born far in the east, in the land between the Two Rivers, for locusts need wet soil. Their eggs must have been sleeping there under the earth for years. Then, at a time none could foresee, they hatched.

They fought their way through the dark earth to the surface. They dried in the warm sunlight. They unfolded their four wings. Then, at a signal that no man can hear, they rose up into the sky and swarmed. And then a mighty east wind carried them a full day's journey to bring destruction down on the Black Land.

Mohsheh knew, at least twenty-two days ago, that this would be. He warned of their coming from that time. But these creatures were not created in twenty-one days. They were sleeping in the mud on the banks of the Two Rivers for years, as is the way of locust swarms. So did the Power put them there, years and years ago, knowing in farsight that He would need them this day?

But then, if He did know years ago when the millions upon millions of eggs were first laid, that they would attack Kehmeht on this day far in the future, then what did all that we did until this day matter? If years ago all this was already destined to be, what difference did it make what Pahroh or his Court did or did not do?

What if, a few months ago, Pahroh had agreed to send

the Iebiru to their seven-day worship? What then would have happened to these locusts? Would their eggs have rotted in the soil and never hatched? Or would they have been born into the land between the Two Rivers without an east wind, swarming and devouring the crops of that far off land instead of ours?

And what, then, about me? If I had been just a little bit smarter, a little faster, a little more alert? What if I had acted the very day I heard Avishamah's history of how the Pahroh of old had been forced from his throne by wicked courtiers and unruly mobs until he agreed to enslave the Iebiru? What if I had brought that tale home and Harkuhotep and taken it to The Throne of the Two Kingdoms that very day?

What if Our Father Pahroh, upon hearing it, awoke to the treachery of his false counselors? Might he have handed his ring to Harkuhotep and told him to go and bring Mohsheh and Aaharohn before him? Would he have given his kingly command that the Iebiru should be sent immediately to their pilgrimage in the Red Land?

Would the locusts have died then in the distant land between the Two Rivers? Or swarmed, but far, far away from us? Would the villagers of The Black Land still have a harvest of spelt ripening in their fields? Would young mothers in the cities of the Two Kingdoms this evening smile lovingly at their children, knowing that, even after the depravations of the Hailstorm, there would still be food to sustain them this year?

Would the young soldier who died so horribly this day be alive among us now? Would he be right here, drinking the bad wine with us, laughing at his bad luck as he gambled away his wages on too many games of Senet?

∼

It's strange that no matter how disgusted a person becomes with himself, he will still seek to tell the tale to another. It is the hope, maybe, that the other will listen and then tell us that we are not so contemptible after all. So I rolled over to face the room and find someone to talk to. But the room was in a tumult again, everyone up and doing –but quite happy with themselves. They were pickling locusts.

I knew that Iebiru would eat locusts. Villagers of our people would too, though I never witnessed anyone dining on them. But here were these men now, busying themselves with what they decided was a harvest.

Some were mixing salt and water in large clay jugs, arguing about how to get the brine just right. Others were in and out the doors for quick sorties to gather dead locusts into a basket if they could find one, or simply into the skirts of their tunics pulled out from under the restraint of their belts.

"Even an evil wind, Your Honor, must blow some fruit," one of them quipped to me as he delivered his basketful.

It was madness, these men finding something to laugh about when their Land was being destroyed and the smell of their dead comrade was wafting up from his shallow grave. But what else should they do?

By the third day there was not a vessel of either clay or copper left for the pickling. The salt was used up too. Happiness gave way to boredom. The heat of the day weighed heavily on men with no work to do. Nothing to do but think, and as is the way with the lowborn, out loud.

"Why don't we just slay them?" someone said to no one in particular, with no particular anger either.

"You can't slay them you dung encrusted idiot," his comrade in the next bed replied. "Want to drink blood again? Or scratch your ugly skin off with boils?"

"Be an improvement to his looks," someone else offered.

"I don't mean the Iebiru," the first man said. "I mean the traitors around our Father on the Throne. Slit some throats, shut their lying mouths, and let Pahroh do what he has to do."

There were general grunts of agreement.

The older soldier flicked his eyes in my direction, a reminder to his men. He might as well as rebuked them at the top of his voice, for all realized that I was awake and that I heard every word. What would this boy who was somehow an agent of The Chamber of Judgments do now?

I let the silence linger long enough to be uncomfortable. This looked like authority to them, but it was really because I didn't know how to respond.

My first thought was that I had just heard treason spoken openly. Openly and dangerously, coming from soldiers of The Throne while Kehmeht was under attack. That was the first thought of my mind. But not of my heart.

Why, after all, was I so taken with the history that Avishamah had told me? Why did I risk my life on The River to rush back to Harkuhotep with it? And now these coarse and simple soldiers spoke what my heart knew but could not say: We must rise up.

As simple as that. We must rise up. That is what we were destined to do. That is what the Power of the Iebiru wanted of us.

Just as the locusts sleeping in the mud of the Two Rivers could not know that their destiny was to rise on a great wind and despoil Kehmeht, so we, Kehmeht's people, her best people, had been sleeping too. Until now. Now everything made perfect sense.

The Power could have slayed us all, the first day Mohsheh and his brother appeared at Court. So why eight months of assaults, any one of them capable of killing all of us? Yet each time there was a reprieve and we were allowed to live. Why?

Because before this is done we too have a part to play. If the Power is waiting for Pahroh to send the Iebiru to worship Him, then He is waiting for us to make it so.

"I will tell you a tale," I finally said.

After all that silence it must have come as a strange and frightening thing to say. It was as if I were first going to chasten them with a parable about loyalty and then send to The City for a squadron of executioners to avenge their perfidy against the Court.

But the story I did tell was a great relief to them. It was the tale that Avishamah told me, simplified so they would understand what happened over a century ago and what was happening now.

The Pahroh of that day had been good and wise, but was betrayed by the courtiers and the mob they manipulated. And the Pahroh of our day is good and wise, too. He wants to let the Iebiru go to their worship, he wants to reach a truce with their angered Power and end the suffering of Kehmeht. But he cannot do it, for no king rules but by the loyal courage of his people.

Pahroh *needs* us to push away the plotting courtiers, I told them. Pahroh *wants* us to do it. He is only waiting for us to act.

I became lost in my own telling, so that when I fell silent I was as moved by my words as if another had said them. I had never spoken like that before. No one made a sound for a long moment. Then:

"Let it be as His Honor says!" one man said.

"Let it be so," other voices agreed, and others added "Let's make it so!"

And they were all talking at once and they rose to their feet and their eyes were shining and their speech became louder and bolder.

"They won't fool us again, your Honor!" someone said. "They won't fool us this time!

"The good folks of the villages will join us," another said and repeated it several times.

"The plain folk in The City too," another insisted. "They won't be putting up with this either. Not anymore."

"Our Father Pahroh will thank you all," I said to them, though they were making such a noise, I'm not sure any of them heard me. It took a third of the night for the storm of feeling in our small sweltering fortress to ebb and allow us to fall into sleep.

Even then, as my eyelids finally grew heavy, I was pulsing with purpose. I could not stop thoughts racing with plans of how best to get back to The City and to the revolution that must break out there. An hour into the morning and I was shown a way.

A wind out the west began to blow. It was a cold wind, the very opposite of what carried the locusts to us from the east. The relentless noise of their swarming and eating diminished and died. I looked outside and saw fingers of this cool west wind touch a hillock here, a treetop there, and gently, gingerly, lift locusts off of our land.

Soldiers joined me at the open doorway. They started exchanging backslaps and cheers as they realized that what they were seeing was the first step in the salvation of Kehmeht. There was still an insurrection to be fought and won. But we accepted this gift of a cold west wind as a first omen of our good fortune for the fight to come.

It blew everywhere, this west wind, so that any locust who so much as spread a wing found itself lifted up and away from the fallen carcass of our Black Land upon which it had been feeding. Some of the happy soldiers near me were already greedily eyeing the thousands of dead locusts who could not take wing. These would make good eating for the men and what else did they have left in their stores? But then these dead locusts also began to swirl upward into the wind, out of reach of any man.

This was strange, dead locusts tossed high up on the wind along with the living ones. And stranger still, some locusts managed to swoop down for one last pass at our earth and then rose up again carrying a dead comrade on their backs. The soldiers blinked at this, doubting their eyesight or, if not that, their sanity.

A crash from inside the fort turned our attention to where the clay vessels of pickled locusts had been carefully stacked against an inner wall. But not carefully enough it seemed. The wind which blew through our open doors toppled the vessels.

Some cracked, though most stayed intact. But their seals fell open, every one, and the strange wind reached into them and pulled out the salted locusts. Up they flew, swirling above our heads, out the door and into the sky.

There they merged into the great dark swarm of locusts, living and dead, blown back into the east.

A few of the men who could still think, bemoaned the loss of the only food left to them. Most were too confused to manage even that. But I, I was barely surprised.

Of course, I thought. These locusts were never just creatures. They were works of the not-sorcery of Mohsheh and Aaharohn. They were the armies commanded by Beings of Ka sent to punish Kehmeht. They were the unknowable will of the Power of the Iebiru. Unknowable in what He would do. But understandable, finally, in what He wanted.

He wanted us to rise up. He wanted us to overthrow the court and free Pahroh to send His Iebiru to their worship. He wanted us to mount an insurrection.

～

I have long known that what will amaze one person will pass without comment by another, all according to what each has been trained to see. I was raised to note the smallest inflection of wording in an incantation, and I guess I will always admire any text that is well crafted. Or any event that can be read as if it were a well-crafted text.

But the four soldiers who were sent to see me on my way back to The City? I doubt they saw a page of writing as anything more than ink shapes crowding a piece of perfectly good papyrus that might have been better used to seal a decent bottle of wine.

These four were still bewildered at the way the locusts left us. It made no sense to them because they could not read it any better than they could a papyrus. But I could read it.

I could go back now and read all those texts sent to us, the ones written in locusts, or in water turned to blood, or in beasts and pestilence, or ice and fire. They were all so clear to me now that it made me smile. It took the sidelong glances of these men who were walking with me to make me realize how insane I must have appeared to them.

We were passing through a landscape of terrible destruction and that was a text they *could* read. It cried out the doom of a lingering death by starvation for themselves and their families and our People.

Well, I was a lord, they were probably thinking, and lords will always get what they need. Caravans would come out of the east bearing grains that only we could afford. The ships of the Sea Peoples would come out of the north with olives and wine and produce for us who could send servants with coin to snatch it up at the docks. But the plain people of Kehmeht? What would they do now?

The Hailstorm had utterly destroyed the barley and flax. Both had been ripe on their tall stalks and easily broken and burned. Yes, the wheat and spelt, barely sprouted, were soft, moist, and pliant enough to survive the ice and fire. So the hope of people was to live off of them. But now the locusts had taken the wheat and spelt too. The good Children of the Black Land would starve. So what was I smiling about?

I regretted that they had come with me into this landscape of devastation. We had set out that morning just to reach a nearby village to acquire a wagon and some horses. But the horses we found were weak and starving. What little was left of their feed was now coveted by the hungry villagers for themselves. So we pushed on.

After passing through two more unlucky villages it was clear that the best way back to The City would be on a boat up The River. Both the windstorm out of the east that brought the locusts, and the cool wind out of the west that swept them away, were gone now. The prevailing wind of Kehmeht, the one that blew out of the north to the south was back. This was a wind of kindness that filled the sails of her ships so they could travel upriver easily.

But we found that the locusts had eaten through the rigging of the large sailing ships. Even the hemp that bound the oars to their sockets was ruined and the stores of flaxen rope were likewise chewed, shredded and useless.

There were still skiffs on the water and I suppose I could have hired one of them. But after the windstorm crossing in that fisherman's boat, I had enough of skiffs for a lifetime.

If this was cowardice it was tempered by a not totally crazy concern: What if the locusts, in their stings and bites and devouring of river grasses, had somehow provoked the hippos in The River? What if they were especially hungry now or angry?

And what about the crocodiles, in all this disruption? Were they not starved and emboldened? Face them now, in a skiff? No. Though I needed to speed my way to The City and to Harkuhotep and to my mission, I needed to get there in one piece and not as the remains of a hippo's rage or a crocodile's dinner.

So, to lighten the long walk I spoke to the men of our mission. I reminded them that if we held our purpose, all this doom would soon be over. And, I told them, there were, no doubt, hidden stores of food in the control of the Court. Soon these could be shared out to the Children of the Black Land.

I did not know for sure if this was true, but I wished it to be so and did not feel that I was lying. It heartened the men and gave them hope and quickened our steps.

The road became ever straighter as we went south until we could see into the distance and there a cloud of dust rose up. We saw it before we heard the hoofbeats of the riders that were causing it, coming up towards us at speed. Sunlight glistened on bits of metal in both their mounts' tackle and their own uniforms. They were fresh and clean and as polished as the copper tips of their spears.

My rank should have demanded some deference from them. But at the rate they were coming and the way I looked, unbathed, caked in grime, making my way on foot with four lowly troops, they would not realize what I am. So the wisest thing was to step aside and allow them to pass on their errand, whatever it was. But their errand, it turned out, was me.

They came to a much too sudden halt, their commander almost passing us by until he considered the possibility that the filthy and sweating boy with his four peasant-soldier companions could be the object of his ride. Unsure of himself and not wanting to seem a fool in front of his men, he asked not impolitely but without any real respect, if we had seen a scribe in the service of the Chamber of Judgements on this road, one named Mereyamun?

"I am Mereyamun, comrade of Harkuhotep, Seal Bearer of the King of Upper and Lower Kehmeht, Unique Friend of Pahroh, Trusted of All His House."

I don't know where I got the idea to call myself *comrade* of Harkuhotep rather than, say, "scribe," or "agent," or simply "on a mission for." But I was annoyed at the attitude of this Royal Guard and I think, in some intuitive way, I realized that he and others like him could be our enemies soon. Did he serve Our Father Pahroh as we did? Or was he in the service of the courtiers who we would have to fight? Some voice within me told me that if I did not stand up to him now, I would never do the thing I had resolved to do when I got to The City.

In any case, it worked. He dismounted and actually handed his horse's bridle to another before he dared approach me. This impressed my four soldiers and heartened them very much. I thanked them and dismissed them and told them that I would very likely see them again when all would be made right. They smiled knowingly at this and I enjoyed the perplexity it created on the face of the Guard commander.

He walked with me. He could have offered me one of his horses but I guess he sensed, correctly, that I had no training or skill as a horseman. So his mounted men stayed respectfully back and we walked onward in silence. But not for too long. We came to a place where there were more troops and a fine wagon with a decent team and near it a Royal Guardsman by his uniform but an old friend by his face.

"Hello, Young Sir," he said with a toothy grin.

"Greetings, Bakenmut," I returned.

So Okpara really had rewarded him with a position in the Guard.

"This is the Scribe Mereyamun then?" the Commander of the Guardsmen said to Bakenmut, who nodded minimally.

"Is my own word not good enough for you?" I said to the Commander in the lowest and most deadly voice I could find. He did seem at least a little uncomfortable.

"I was instructed to verify your identity with this man, who was said to know your face," the Commander said. Then, quick as he could, he touched his heart in something that looked vaguely like a gesture of deference and mumbled "Respects." And with that he was mounted and gone up the line.

Bakenmut helped me into the carriage, joined me there and off we went, Royal Guard escort and all, ordered to stop nowhere until I was delivered safely to the Great House.

~

"Well, hello, Mereyamun," Okpara said rising from the Chair of Judgments. "How are you?"

Did I really think it was Harkuhotep I would find seated on that chair? His heart was elsewhere and so was the rest of him. Still, it was jarring to find Okpara in his father's place. It was one thing to leave an apprentice in charge of the shop while the master was away, but another thing entirely for the apprentice to take his master's status.

Okpara was still wearing the blue of mourning for his mother. Her seventy days in the House of the Dead would surely be completed soon but Okpara was taking no shortcuts with this duty. Why then was I thinking of him in such an unfair way? If his father left him in charge then what was he to do but take charge? I decided I would honor that.

"I am well," I said, "and if you are well and your family is well then I am happy."

Okpara smiled just a little at my addressing him this way. Did he think I was making fun of him? He cleared the room with a simple gesture of a single arm and scribes and officials scurried for the exits just as they would have done in the presence of Harkuhotep himself. The old Harkuhotep at least.

"No need for formality between us," Okpara said and gestured for me to sit on a small couch while he took a place on its facing twin. "Thirsty? Hungry?"

I'm fine," I said. "The escort you sent had a wagon loaded with whatever I could think of."

"Except a bath," he said.

"They told me they were not to stop until I was delivered here," I said.

"It is true, I requested that. You're trying to figure out why."

"I have some thoughts on the subject," I said.

"Such as?"

"Well," I said, "who gets escorts? Important people get escorts."

"They do!" Okpara agreed.

"But prisoners also have escorts, don't they?"

"And you think I have taken you prisoner?"

"I think someone seeing me brought here could read it that way."

"Ha! Very good! You are clever, Mereyamun! You always were."

"Not clever enough to know what you want."

"I'd wager you'd figure it out soon enough. And it would be lots of fun, a delight really, watching you do it. But we have a lot to discuss so let's get right down to it."

"Mayati."

"*Mayati?* You think I sent a detachment of Royal Guards to bring you here over Mayati's inheritance?"

"It crossed my mind."

"Not the cleverest part of it, that's for sure. You must be awfully fond of her to be so addlebrained about her affairs."

"She's a friend."

"At the very least! Why else would you sneak through

backstreets before dawn to withdraw money from the Temple of Djehuti, then purchase traveling cloaks and run away with her to a village of the Dahnii in Gohshen? And please don't ask how I know this. I can't think you clever if you're going to act dumb as a mud-peasant."

"It's your duty here, in the Chamber of Judgements," I said resignedly, annoyed that I foolishly thought my secrets would be my own, "to know everything that happens in the Lower Kingdom."

"It is! It really is! That's why your suspicions about me are so comically wrong. If I wanted to disinherit Mayati it would have been done. If I wanted to disinter her faithless fool of a father and feed his corpse to the jackals, why that would have been done in heartbeat too. I don't believe that there is a soul in the Lower Kingdom who could stand up against any desire of this Chamber."

"Then why did you send me to find documents in Amenakhte's house?"

"But I never did that. If I needed documents I could have had them drafted to say anything I needed them to say. We certainly have enough scribes! And if I needed testimony, I could have bought it. Or demanded it. No, I never meant for you to find evidence of anything at Amenakhte's house. I meant for you to find Mayati."

"Why?"

"Ha! I enjoy it so much when I can perplex you. You were always so much more clever than me, you and my sister. It's fun to perplex clever people."

"Fine. I'm perplexed."

"Well, now you're not. You're annoyed."

I said nothing to that, as there was no sense rewarding it. Okpara let out a breath to signal that the first part of this comedy was over.

"Alright. I could see that you cared for Mayati. You couldn't talk about the stubbornness of the court without bringing in the sad case of her fate. So when I learned that her fate was not so sad after all, I thought it kind of me to let you rescue her from the tomb her father's house had become."

"So her fleeing your house and our vanishing from The City and the trip to Gohshen was for nothing."

"Nothing is for *nothing*," Okpara said more thoughtfully than I would have given him credit for. "It was for things other than what you originally assumed."

"Like?"

"Like learning lore about how our history with the Iebiru began with a revolt of the Courtiers and the Mob against Pahroh."

"I told that only to Mayati, I never spoke of it to anyone else."

"You also mentioned it in one of your inspirational talks to some soldiers while you were their guest during the locusts."

So. One of those men must have been tasked with reporting things to someone who reported things to someone who reported to the Chamber of Judgements. Foolish of me to not remember that there was always such a man (or woman, or child) in every corner of the Two Kingdoms. It was how Harkuhotep protected the Throne.

"Don't feel too badly about it. It is history that is known to my Father. He would have been pleased to have your report, simply because he likes diligence in those who serve him. But he would not have been surprised."

"So I nearly drowned and suffered a week with the locusts for nothing."

"We've already covered that. Not for *nothing*. But for something other than you originally imagined."

I was getting truly sick of Okpara's game.

"Can I go now?" I asked evenly. "Or am I actually your prisoner?"

Okpara assumed that hurt expression he used when he felt misunderstood. Fine with me, since he was the biggest contributor to that misunderstanding.

"No, Mereyamun, you are not my prisoner. But yes, it certainly could have looked that way to any who knew of you being brought here and that was highly intentional. Because no one must know of your mission or my role in it."

"I'm not sure *I* know of my mission."

"I need you to go to my father and persuade him that we must overthrow the courtiers and free Our Pahroh to send the Iebiru to their worship. We cannot succeed without my father, people will be too fearful to act without him. Or worse, against him."

"Why don't you go yourself?"

"Because he will not listen to me. He does not trust me."

"He's put the entire Chamber of Judgements in your hands, Okpara. There's no bigger trust than that!"

"He trusts me with the Chamber of Judgements, yes, because he trusts me with the world as it was. But he does not trust me with the new world he believes is being born. I have had no part in that. You have."

"He has plenty of servants who have taken a much greater part than me. Ankhuemhesut is practically Iebiri now. He goes to Gohshen regularly and speaks with Mohsheh or Aaharohn. Inyotef and Adjedaa are halfway to being Iebiru in their own way, and Inyotef is his own s..."

I caught the word "son" too late to really swallow it. But Okpara took it in stride.

"Yes, my half-brother Inyotef. I know. And there are many others like them and that's why they cannot do what must be done. They have forgotten that they are Children of Kehmeht, they have given up all interest in her policies or power. They dream only of the day when the Power of the Iebiru will reveal Himself to them in the Deshret. They are intoxicated with this, nothing else interests them. But not you, Mereyamun. Your feet are still firmly on the ground of the Black Land."

"And there is no one closer to your Father than I to do this?"

"There is one closer in his affections than you. But he cannot yet speak."

Who was Okpara talking about?

"I mean his new grandson. My nephew."

"Neferet had her baby?

"Obviously. The day before the locusts came. The timing was fortuitous. Father insisted that a confinement-pavilion be built on the roof where the air would cool my sister in her labor. It was quite traditional actually, papyrus-stalk columns, covered with grape vines, you know, the whole thing."

I didn't know actually, at least not very much, about customs in birthing.

"Well, as you can imagine," Okpara went on, "the timing really was critical. The locusts arrived the day after the birth and devoured it all. But you know what strikes me most about the whole thing Mereyamun?"

"That Neferet and her baby were safe inside the house when that happened," I offered.

"Well that was good fortune, yes. But what strikes me most about the whole thing is that the birthing pavilion on the roof was the only traditional thing they did. I mean they knew it was to be a boy. They had placed the barley seeds and hulled-wheat in two bags and had my sister moisten them with her urine daily. The barley sprouted, it was clearly to be a boy-child, there was no doubt. My Father's excitement knew no bounds. And yet, except for the pavilion on the roof, what else did they do?"

"I'm sure they did everything they could to assure it would go well."

"Did they? My sister dismissed Djedmutesankh, clearly the most experienced midwife in The City! Just told her and her assistants to leave, go home. Setka and Father pleaded with my sister about this, but she actually persuaded them, and this was once it was clear the baby was coming that very day. And do you know why she did this?"

"No idea."

"The birthing chair that Djedmutesankh brought was decorated, beautifully decorated actually, with images of Hathor who watches over women, Behs to vanquish evil, Taweret who protects in childbirth, Meskhenet in the shape of a birthing brick to give strength in the labor, Khnum who gives health to the newborn, and Amun to sooth labor pains with a northern breeze. All quite traditional, wholly appropriate, done for the daughter of every caring family – and my sister would have none of it!

"She would not have the *names* of those gods mentioned let alone their images present when she would give birth to her new son of the new age. Djedmutesankh was asked if she didn't have a plainer birthing chair and she simply left, quite scandalized, though Father paid her."

"Neferet had no midwife then?" I asked, actually frightened for her though this was all safely in the past.

"Ha! She had two, for she had, on her own, sent for two

midwives of the Iebiru. And they had a very plain birthing stone to offer."

I had to smile. This was so like Neferet. But I dared not say so because Okpara was going somewhere with this tale.

"My wife heard of it and was beside herself with worry. She went up to the their roof and sat with Neferet and held her hand and then, ever so quietly, tried to murmur the spell that is required: 'Come down, placenta, come down! I am Horus...' surely you were taught this in your lessons with Hesera?"

"Come down, placenta, come down." I recited mechanically from a memory that was at years unused. "'I am Horus who conjures in order that she who is giving birth becomes better than she was, as if she was already delivered. Look, Hathor will lay her hand on her with an amulet of health! I am Horus who saves her!' It is repeated four times over an amulet of Behs placed on the brow of the woman in labor."

"We never forget our childhood lessons, do we?" Okpara smiled. "But Neferet has pulled them out by the roots! She told Herit to stop murmuring...or leave. Neferet would call only on the Power of the Iebiru, who she named The Eternal One. As if she was not a daughter of Kehmeht. As if she had been born to some Leyvieiim in Gohshen.

"I was downstairs with Father and Setka as all this was unfolding. You should have seen them Mereyamun. Father was fierce with pride about it all! And Setka, where a man in his right mind would have worried for his wife's safety, Setka's eyes were ablaze with enthusiasm for... for what? For this Power which has come to replace all our gods and all our ways. So you see, Mereyamun, I cannot really communicate with them anymore."

"But you want the same thing that they want," I

reasoned. "You want the court to relent and let Father Pahroh send the Iebiru to this worship. So do they."

"That we agree about this is just a coincidence now," Okpara said, rather sadly I thought. "I want it to happen so Kehmeht can return to peace and safety. They want it so Kehmeht will be changed forever and we will all become servants of their Eternal One."

"I understand," I said unhappily, for I did not want the task Okpara was handing me.

"It won't be so hard," Okpara said. "All you need to do is tell them that many of us desire to act against the court so that Pahroh will be able to do the thing we all know he must do. We ask of my Father to change nothing of his new beliefs, only to let it be known that he sides with us and wishes this thing to be done, and that he will protect those who help us. That's all."

"You sound more persuasive than I'll be able to be."

"Maybe. But they are intoxicated with their Eternal One and I am quite sober. So they cannot listen to me. But you Mereyamun, you have drunk some of that wine. They will listen to you."

I emerged out of the Great House compound into the night, alone, unbathed, and smelling rank from the days in the fort and the journey back to The City. But Okpara was right, this was as it needed to be so that no one would associate with Okpara the things I would say in the morning to Harkuhotep.

When the time came (and it would be very soon) Okpara would need to take the courtiers by surprise. No one knew which of the Great House Guards might leap to the defense of the court and which of them would obey Okpara. Surprise mattered.

But I wasn't going to show up in front of Harkuhotep in the morning smelling like this and looking much as I smelled. So I headed home for a bath, a few hours' sleep, and a change of clothing.

I hoped that didn't also mean fending off motherly questions from Sartuma about where in the world I had been these weeks or, much worse, an inquisition from Hesera in his suspicious madness. One slip on my part and either of them could become the first link in a chain of gossip that would end with Okpara's plan revealed to our enemies. I was playing with lives here and I would be careful.

I knew from long experience how to grip the front door so that it would open silently without even the squeak of a hinge. But it was already latched and barred for the night. I considered climbing the thick fig tree in the orchard, Neferet's entrance of choice throughout our childhood. This was not a natural option for me, I was never a climber like Neferet. I was always afraid of falling and breaking my neck.

But this thing we meant to do would need courage, and if I was afraid to climb a tree what use would I be in the Great House coup? But then I remembered that there was no tree to climb anymore. It had been split and half uprooted by the animals and then broken and burned in the Hailstorm. I suppose the locusts had feasted on its carcass too, so there was nothing left to climb on.

I went around to the rear of the house, scrambled over the wall, lowered myself onto one of the outdoor ovens and from there to the ground. From that point it was just nine or ten quiet steps to the door of the kitchen.

There were voices in there. Well someone would have to know I was home, better it be a scullery maid. I knocked on the door softly. The voices fell silent as if the speakers inside were listening to be certain that they really had heard someone.

"Open the door," I said in a very loud whisper. "It is Mereyamun."

A scrapping of chairs, clumsy footsteps, and the door was whipped open by Kheruef.

"It is Mereyamun," he exclaimed, way too noisily and with no particular brilliance. Hadn't I just announced as much?

Sartuma rose from the other chair at the table where, apparently, she and Kheruef had been drinking some sort of hot infusion of peaches and cinnamon. The aroma was very pleasant and must have come from some dried provisions stored in a metal box that escaped the locusts.

"Come in Mereyamun," Sartuma said, "come in out of the night!"

"No, do not come in," another voice called from beyond the kitchen, "do not come in under any circumstances whatsoever. He is not to be allowed in!" In this way Hesera appeared from inside the house and faced me at the doorway.

Poor Kheruef was at complete paralysis, the door half opened in his hand but unable to either open it completely or close it in my face.

"Step away from the door," Hesera insisted and a frightened Kheruef did just that leaving it in mid-swing on its hinges, though the command was never meant for him. It was meant for me.

"You shall not enter my house," Hesera continued, giving more heat to his rant. Sartuma, perhaps the only member of the household who could still get away with such things, protested gently.

"But it is Mereyamun's home too, is it not?"

"It is not!" Hesera said, as much like an obstinate child as a demented sorcerer.

I surprised myself with how little any of this meant to me. Just a few weeks ago I felt wronged, indignant, hurt and angry at such a display. But the whole world had turned since then and this was at most an inconvenience.

Tomorrow morning I was going to conspire in an armed insurrection. Who cared for the insane nullities of a burned-out shell of an old sorcerer? So I said nothing. He did not like that.

"Why don't you speak?" he said. "Do you think your silence makes you appear wise?"

"No," I said. "I do not think it makes me appear wise."

"Then why don't you speak to what I have said?"

"There is little to say about it."

"There is much to say about it, you obstinate ingrate!" he rasped in what had to pass for a shout now. "Say that it is so! Say that it is true!"

"It is true," I said evenly, in the hope that it would calm him down.

"What is true? What do you admit is true?"

I was about to say 'whatever you want' but realized that this would only set him off even more. He really did have some sort of aim in his rambling insanity, but I couldn't quite grasp it.

"Admit that you have no portion in this household," he said. "Admit that you are no owner here, nor master."

"I have no portion in this household," I said trying to sound like I meant it. "I am no owner, nor master."

He seemed to like these statements but his eyes were still wild so I improvised what I thought might calm him.

"I may give no commands here to any of the servants of the house, nor make any claims to possession of any part of it."

"And you have no honor here," he added. "No respect or honor or glory pertains to you here or on the part of any who serve in my household."

"No," I agreed. "No honor, no respect."

"And you shall inherit none of these," he added rather calmly. "You have no inheritance here."

"No inheritance," I agreed. "I have no inheritance here."

He took this in and seemed satisfied. He turned to leave the kitchen by way of the hallway through which he had arrived. But as he did, he spoke one last instruction.

"Sartuma," he said. "You may accommodate this young vagabond as a guest. And lend him fresh clothing, he smells."

CHAPTER 7
THE FIRST WEEK OF IPT-HMT, THE THIRD MONTH OF SHEMU, SEASON OF THE RIVER RUNNING LOW

SIXTY-FIRST OF THE SEVENTY-FIVE DAYS

I woke the next morning with the light of clear dawn streaming through the window of what I still believed was my room. I had a fine warm bath the night before and a good sleep in what I still felt to be my own bed.

The air was fresh as it is only in this third Month of Shemu when it is not yet too hot and the floods, though gone, still satisfy the thirst of the Black Land.

I needed a fine day like this, for I was uneasy about what words I would find to convince Harkuhotep that we must rise up and that we cannot do so without him. I wondered if he would be surprised and pleased that Okpara was in the thick of this. I was not sure how to speak of it, but I knew that if I hesitated, I might not go at all.

This day demanded courage more than diplomacy. Harkuhotep always liked me best when I spoke plainly. Neither flattery or scheming ever worked with him, and of late he had heaped praise on me and others for simply trying to live true to what we thought the truth to be.

So with that I would go to Setka and Neferet's home

where he was staying. I would find him, no doubt, in a good mood, delighted in equal measure by his new grandson and by his new belief. Both had been conceived and born into the world at just about the same time.

I was too nervous to eat any breakfast, but I did drink what was left of a jar of sweet date beer sent to my room after my bath. I wiped my mouth and picked up the polished brass mirror to check my appearance one last time before I made my way to Harkuhotep.

The sunlight pouring through the window was bright and I had to angle the mirror so that it did not reflect its glare into my eyes. But before I could find the proper angle, the light was gone. Not diminished, as it might have been later in the day when the sun had moved in the sky. It was gone. Truly and actually gone.

There are no words to easily describe what was instead. I want to say 'darkness' but that word does not suffice. 'Dark' is what we say when there is no light. When light leaves we say what's left is 'darkness,' meaning, simply, that the light has gone. But the light that had lit up the world a few heartbeats ago wasn't diminished, and what was around me was not just the absence of light. It was a thing, a dark thing in its own right, filling every space where light used to be.

My first thought was that I had been struck blind and I was filled with denial and dread. It couldn't be! How could my sight just cease? I was not ill, I had suffered no blow. Could this be evil sorcery? Did Hesera really hate me that much? Was he that crazy? If this was his work, surely he could reverse it. I just needed to get to him, and beg him in whatever way would satisfy his insanity.

I groped my way around the furniture and felt along the wall until I reached the door. I would have to be careful moving down the hallway so as not to fall down the stairway. I took slow shuffling steps, so that my forward foot would feel the opening to the stairs before I committed my balance to it. This took a few moments and as I made my way I heard voices from downstairs.

"I am struck blind," Sartuma was saying, over and over again in a piteous voice, small as that of a little girl.

"No, no," Kheruef was saying, "it is me too, it is all of us, it is a darkness. You can feel it, can't you? You can touch it. Touch it, Sartuma."

And so I learned that I was not alone in my blindness and that it was not blindness at all. It was some dark material, something thick that had taken the place of wherever air used to be. I pressed my finger against it, then my palms and it was as Kheruef said. It was a nameless dark material, thick to the touch, thick against my skin. And thick in my mouth, and throat, and lungs.

Suddenly I could not breathe this dark thing. Fresh panic ran through me. I turned back in the direction I hoped was away from the steps and pawed my way frantically along the wall until I found my room again.

I crashed against my bed which was not where I imagined it to be, but that was for the best because it brought a linen sheet to hand. I ripped it into a long strip and tied it as a mask around my mouth and nose. It eased my ability to breathe this acrid dark material.

I stood there for a moment just taking breaths, one hand on the wall now that touching took the place of seeing. As my breathing calmed, so did my thoughts. We were not blind then, just deprived of light. So we must seek light.

I let my hand guide me by never leaving the wall as I made my way to the hallway and then to what I thought would be the top of the stairs. From there I called out into the nothingness.

"Sartuma," I called. "Kheruef?"

"Mereyamun..." Sartuma's voice.

"Are there no coals in the ovens?" I asked. "Can you not light a lamp from them?"

"Nothing burns in the ovens, Your Honor," Kheruef said.

It was against Hesera's orders for him to call me by that title, but with the world gone dark who could think of such things?

"The tinderbox is extinguished," Sartuma's voice added though it sounded like she was speaking to herself and wheezing at it. I understood. Light comes from fire and fire needs air. Normal air, good air. Not this thick black material that we could barely draw into our nostrils. I needed to think but all I could think was: Why?

I didn't mean what justification was there for this torment. For over a century we had darkened the days of the Iebiru, we made their lives one long hopeless night. We made Iebiru labor beyond the setting of the sun with neither a torch nor a moon to illuminate the blackness.

We tortured Iebiru by imprisoning them in sunless dark cells. We made Iebiru illuminate our feasts by balancing lamps on their heads, and when those lamps were inevitably extinguished, we hewed off their heads and posted them on stakes dripping blood. I saw this in Gohshen. I saw this.

And we worshipped the sun god. We worshipped Amun who gave light and goodness but who would not recognize Iebiru as his children or have us take any mercy on them. My very name was a tribute to that god. So why wouldn't the Power of the Iebiru take retribution upon me by removing light from my world? It was just.

But did it make sense?

Here we were finally going to do what the Power desired. We were going to rise up and enable Father Pahroh to pay his homage to The Eternal by sending the Iebiru to worship just as Mohsheh had requested. So why make it impossible for us now?

If I had a thousand days to grope through the streets of The City, I still would not be able to find my way to Harkuhotep in this dark thing wrapped around us. And even if I found Harkuhotep, and even if he and every good Son of Kehmeht agreed to rise up and rid Pahroh of those who hindered him from sending the Iebiru to their Eternal One, still, what could we do about it now?

Did the Power want to mock us by making it impossible to do the very thing He wished us to do? But there was no answer. Only Darkness.

And so it was and so it went for who knows how long? Hunger and thirst were my only clock, for what other way did we have of telling time without being able to see?

All the finely crafted sundials of the Two Kingdoms were bitter jokes now. They could not mark time without rays of sunlight and even if they could, no one could see to read them.

There was the water clock in Hesera's chambers. I struggled to remember if the calibration lines in the upper bowl were merely painted within the smooth glaze, or if the potter had actually made them indented or perhaps bumped-out a little. Then running my fingertips over them would give me some notion of how much time was passing.

But this would mean almost certainly bumping into Hesera, and that would bring with it whole new worlds of unpleasantness. Hearing his disembodied voice when I couldn't read the insane face that produced it was more than I was willing to bear. And he was just as likely to remain silent in the darkness, simply to unnerve me.

There was more than a little cowardice in my decision. But who felt brave in this thick and utter dark? And besides, it took hours just getting downstairs without breaking my neck or slashing my veins on a blade as I groped through the kitchen for something to eat.

At least it seemed like hours, who could say for sure? Time was gone from us. Or rested on us so heavily that it would crush us.

~

After three cycles of hunger, thirst, sleepiness, needing the chamber pot (which on one occasion I could not find and so ended up soiling the floor) I estimated that three days had passed. So it seemed.

I was weakening. Or the dark material was thickening. Because every footstep I took, every reach of my hand, was more and more difficult. A walk of twenty steps exhausted me as a hike of twenty furlongs. Just extending my finger to touch the wall took the will of lifting lead weights.

I thought to take to my bed for a rest, but I could not complete the journey. I slid down onto the floor with my back to the wall. I was very near to where that wall met my bed, but I could go no further.

My arms and legs were useless things now. I desired to move them but they would not move. My head, my neck, my torso, all ceased to obey my will. This was not numbness, quite the opposite: Every itch, every cramp, every pressure, every pain was felt acutely. What I lost was the ability to remedy any of it. I was locked-in upon myself and could not move.

Once again I thought I must surely die of suffocation, for if my chest could not rise and fall, how could I breathe? And yet, somehow, I did breathe shallow breaths, enough to keep me alive.

You would think this a relief, but it was a horror. For it meant I was being kept alive by the Power of the Iebiru only to suffer this locked-in death. And who knew for how long? Would there be hours of this? Days? Could we survive that? Or was this, itself, our death? Were we already dead now? Was this our doom for all eternity?

Long before this terrible year, back when I was still Hesera's bright little child-student lapping up the wisdom of Kehmeht as fast as it could be dished out to me, I memorized whole chapters of The Book of Going Forth By Day. I was only six years old when I could recite the entire one-hundred and twenty-fifth spell at Hesera's request to amuse and delight the Great Ones of the Court.

"Well this one certainly has nothing to fear when he meets Wsir and the Forty-Two Judges," some Lord or great Sorcerer would say and pat me on the head or slip me a sweet of honey and sesame. But I was just a little kid and though I liked the approval, it frightened me.

How could adults speak so lightly about my death? So I would plunge back into the recital all over again, making everyone laugh at how adorable that was. I alone knew in that this was not adorable. This was terror and the only relief was to make myself very, very, certain that I had the spell down perfectly.

I would imagine Wsir standing before me, flanked by

Inpu and Djehuti and the Forty-Two Judges, blocking my path to eternal life. I knew that if I hesitated before Wsir, the terror would overwhelm me. So I would hurry my recital in a desperate singsong:

"Hail to you, great god, Lord of Justice! I have come to you, my lord, that you may bring me so that I may see your beauty for I know you and I know your name and I know the names of the forty-two gods of those who are with you in this Hall of Justice, who live on those who cherish evil and who gulp down their blood on that day of the reckoning of characters in the presence of Wennefer."

What did all that mean? At age six I could not know. But I did not care. All that mattered was that this is what you say when you meet Wsir on the path of the dead. Failure to recite it perfectly meant suffering beyond imagining. But I *could* recite it. I would be alright.

It made me angry now, this memory. They had lied to me. I was just a child of six, what satisfaction could they take in tricking me? But they did trick me. There was no Wsir here, there was no path. No spell could help me. And no one would see me and pity me. Except, perhaps, the Power of the Iebiru.

But the Power of the Iebiru did not show himself and would allow no image of Himself to be made in paint or stone or even gold. Hidden from us, but the author of everything, of this terrible story I was in now, was he watching me from His hiding place?

I was dead, or very near to it, and no one came to offer me a way forward into the Happy Land of Reeds. I was stuck here, my life having ended but my way to the happy land of the dead impassable.

I tried to say the spell, and my immovable lips made my voice a thought instead. But the spell is to be uttered, the

Book says quite clearly, and only by one who is bathed and anointed with myrrh, in white garments and with black eye-paint.

And there must be offerings of incense and bread and beer, all presented on a clean floor powdered with ochre. And I was filthy and twisted in pain, dwelling in darkness.

~

My arm ached, my back was shot with pains like sharpened points of spears pushed and twisted and twisted some more. I wanted to cry out in agony but I could not. For sounds are made of air and there was no air, just this dark, dark thing that took its place and extinguished voices like it did flame.

If only I had stretched my aching legs before I was locked into the position I was in. If only I had sat back a little closer to the wall and not slumped on my lower spine that now shot with hurt down my legs and up my back. If only my left hand had not been caught mid-gesture, torqued into a painful claw.

Thirst burned my throat, my lips were cracked, but I was locked into myself and could do nothing about it. I grew dizzy and faint and I must have fallen into some sort of dream, for slowly but relentlessly I began to grasp where I was and what I was.

This darkness all around me, thick and growing thicker, solid and pressing against every part of me, it was mortar, wasn't it? It was thick mortar, cold and hardening into rock, burying me alive.

"But I cannot breathe," I wanted to cry out, "I have done nothing, release me, I cannot breathe!" And then I knew.

I was in a wall, in Rahmessu.

Or, I was newly birthed, torn from my mother, tossed into The River, sucked down into the muck at the bottom.

Or I had just been born into a clay pit with no midwife to catch me and I am falling, falling, falling into the wet clay and it is growing hard around me.

My mother, exhausted and bleeding out is feeling for me frantically in the wet clay. But she cannot not find me.

❧

I woke from that dream, but what did "waking" mean now? I could not move. I could not speak or even take a deep breath. I only woke from one nightmare into another.

Still, I counted myself better off that I could feel actual pain and clawing hunger and burning thirst. These were tortures but at least they were real, not sudden frights of my mind to terrify and confuse me.

But there were plenty of those terrors of mind too, all the more frightening because I could not expect them or know if they were real. I saw demons moving about the room, and other creatures, neither man nor animal, monstrous things that seemed to be eyeing me. If I had been bound in taut chains I could not be more defenseless against whatever they might decide to do to me.

I imagined any one of them tormenting me with a single claw for days and days rather than simply ripping me apart and making an end of it. And who could say that even with my limbs finally severed and torn from me, that I would find an end? Perhaps even then I would continue to suffer in the immovable shackles of this dark matter.

If I had been rational I would have concluded that if I could "see" something it could not be real. Nothing could be seen in this dark, so "seeing" something should have been excellent proof that it was a thought, not a thing. But then I did see something. I saw Iebiru enter my room.

Two men, a woman, and a girl-child. They were not paralyzed as we were. They did not even grope their way as we had during the first three days of the thinner darkness. They moved naturally and easily through the thick dark material that was encasing me.

How did I know this if there was no light and I could see nothing? The answer is that they had a light of their own. I do not mean they carried any lamp or torch, for they did not. They simply possessed a light that was with them or maybe *of* them. Where they went, there was light for them. But not for me.

Their light did not illuminate anything else in the room, I could not see anything by it. Their light belonged to them and was with them, it illuminated whatever they cared to look at. It was a light that would not serve my eyes —except that I could see that they possessed it and I could see some of what they chose to look at.

This was beyond any sorcery I had ever heard of. It was simply a gift from their Power, I guessed. I felt then how great was His anger upon us for what we had done to His Iebiru.

Now my death would come, I realized. Not by the hand of demons, not by the fright of monsters, but by the vengeance of these Iebiri. They moved about my room with such ease because they could see that I was as helpless as a fly trussed up in a spider's web, alive and waiting in terror to be killed. But they gave me no more than a passing glance before returning their attention to, of all things, the wall.

"Over here, behind this one," one of the Iebiri men said

as he kneeled at a spot on the lower third of the wall. There the stones were not covered with whitewash. They were beautiful and cut and fitted with precision that made a fine contrast with the smooth white area above. But the Iebiri was not admiring the craft work.

"I see it too," the girl child said, which was strange because there was nothing for anyone to see –unless they knew that this stone was the removable seal of my secret vault. They knew because that strange light of theirs was focused on that stone alone and, somehow, gave them knowledge of what lay behind it.

The other man produced a broad knife and worked it around the stone until it was edged out just enough to grab hold of and remove it. They then reached in to the small vault and pulled out the two bronze chests that had been hidden within. The woman opened the smaller one and the two men worked on the larger so that both were opened at the same moment, revealing a good part of my personal fortune.

There was jewelry here that had been in my family for generations, fine gold inlaid with precious stones and filigrees of silver. There were bracelets, nose rings, earrings, necklaces, all of the finest work and all worth a fortune had they been no more than the lumps of the precious materials from which they were wrought.

There were coins, too, well-minted ones with precise weights and firm shapes. So that was the way it was going to be then. The Iebiri were going to rob me first and then get around to killing me as an afterthought.

But, no. They went through my things, each of my treasures one by one, all that was in the chests and the everyday jewelry on my shelves too. Then they replaced what had come from the shelves back on the shelves and what came from the chests back in the chests.

These they closed with care, then lifted them back into the hidden vault. They replaced the stone that covered it, edging it carefully into place so that the wall seemed perfect and whole again. They took nothing.

Without so much as a parting glance, they left. And when they had gone, their light was gone with them.

I was alone once more in my dark encasement, wondering what had just happened? Why had they come? Was this some strange instruction of Mohsheh, to enter into our homes, use a miraculous light to find our possessions, and then leave the things they found precisely where they found them? Why?

Finally, the Sun found me! Shafts of it made my face warm and my eyes hurt. I squinted and moved. I moved! The dark material that had entombed me was gone!

I was free to move –as much as one burned by thirst and bound into painful positions could be free to do anything. I was like a prisoner in a torture chamber, suddenly released from his chains and collapsed on the floor, but happy for it. It was good to be in the land of the living.

It hurt to unbend my legs but they would have to unbend if I was to get water, without which I would surely die. So I managed to stand myself up, using the bed and the wall. I inched over to the water that was in the washing bowl from days ago. It was putrid, but I drank it. It made me feel sick in my innards, but it also made me more awake. With that, I made my way down to the kitchens.

I passed Kheruef sprawled on the floor of the great room but stirring a little. And from the corner of my eye I noted Sartuma stumbling out of her room. None of us could produce any words, we were wraiths moving slowly, silently, intently.

I found water in the cistern and drank of it with a shaking hand, spilling half of it on myself. But even this was for the best since I had sweat, filth, and my own waste caked on my body, and no one was going to draw a bath for me just now.

I collapsed onto a kitchen bench in front of what must have been the remnants of the servants' meal of days ago. I ate from what was there, dried remains of a wheat porridge, some crusty barley cakes, some leeks. I ate too much and retched it all back out again, right there onto the table where it didn't look all that different from the remains of that last meal itself.

But at least I was fully awake now and I remembered Harkuhotep and how I had to convey Okpara's plans for a coup and convince him, if I could, that he would have to at least not oppose it. But then, after all that had happened these past days, could there be any argument?

I was heartened and felt some strength return to me. I stripped off my tunic and pulled buckets of water from the cistern to bathe myself. I poured them over my head and torso and used a ladle and some rags to wash my arms and legs.

I was leaving a great mess for Sartuma, Kheruef and the others to clean up, but what else was I to do? Today was a day of insurrection, a day of blood perhaps, and all of our lives were at stake. So what did some extra housework matter?

I returned to my room, took clean clothes and make-up

and added jewelry appropriate to an audience with Harkuhotep. Jewelry that the Iebiru who entered my room had picked up and fingered and examined and then returned to its place. The strangeness of that troubled me. But everything was strange now.

～

I n the street, making my way to Setka and Neferet's house where I was sure Harkuhotep would be, I heard snatches of conversations.

"There's fighting going on in the Lower Market," someone breathlessly reported, though it was not clear who was fighting.

"They're there now," someone said, "right now in the Great House. They're both there."

It was just a snatch of words but "they're both" could only mean Mohsheh and Aaharohn. Maybe the whole issue was being settled between the Iebiru and The Throne this very moment. Maybe by the time I got to Harkuhotep everything would be resolved and we would be at peace again?

A hundred steps later I paused to speak with two neighbors and my good mood turned darker. It was certain, they told me, that the entire curse of the Darkness lasted only six days. This was known, they said, because of Pahroh's own water clock kept in The Great House.

Its reservoir held water for ten days and it was filled promptly at the beginning of each week. The astrologers in charge of it were diligent and relied on it when there was no sunlight for their calculations. There could be no mistake. The Darkness lasted six days. Not seven.

Why did this trouble me? Well, everything we had

suffered at the hands of the Iebiru brothers had lasted seven days. The Blood Curse, the Infestation of Frogs, the Lice, the Invasion of Animals, the Death on the Herds, the Soot Boils, The Firestorm of Ice, the Locusts, all were fully seven days, an Iebiri week. Yet we had lived through only six days of Dark.

The ending of it in six days was too soon. We would pay for this. I had no idea how that would be, but I just *knew* that this gift of a seventh day without Darkness would be a debt we would have to pay.

Then, as Setka's and Neferet's house came into view, I had to laugh at myself. I realized just how much I sounded like Hesera: cranky, pronouncing doom out of my own madness. And I did not want to be anything like Hesera, not now when I had finally found out where I fit into the great thing that was unfolding.

No, I decided, I would be optimistic and fulfill my mission to Harkuhotep and be part of the great salvation that was at hand.

I passed a knot of tradesmen who fell silent as I went by and eyed me a little. Well, who cared about whatever pettiness was on their minds now? History was being made and I would be part of it. I ignored them and strode up to Setka's door.

"He is not here, Your Honor," said the servant who greeted me. "The Lord Harkuhotep has been called to the Great House to serve before the Throne."

I felt relief at this news, and not just because it exempted me from trying to persuade the least persuadable man I knew. Harkuhotep being called to the Court was likely better than the best I could have hoped for.

The plague of Darkness must surely have convinced Our Father Pahroh to put aside the venal courtiers and to harken to his true and trusted servants, Harkuhotep being chief among them. No doubt Mohsheh and Aaharohn were there too and all was being arranged to send the Iebiru to their worship. There would be no bloodshed and Kehmeht would know peace and happiness again.

"Who is there?" Setka's voice from within inquired of his servant.

"It's me," I called into the house, "Mereyamun."

Calling out like that was rather common in front of a servant, but I was so relieved it just rang out of me. I was not terribly wrong to do it, because it brought a smiling Setka springing to the door to escort me in.

"You don't look so well," he said once he had gotten a good look at me in his great room shaded from the glare of the late morning sun.

I was moving kind of slow and unsteadily. Setka sat me down on a tooled-leather stool and I noticed that he (and, come to think of it, his servant) looked a lot better than me or anyone in my household. It was then I first noticed what would be confirmed later: not all of us experienced the Darkness in the same way.

Setka and his household must have had an easier time of it. Was this a boon of the Iebiru Power to those who were trying to honor him? The thought made me feel a little sick.

"Here," Setka said extending a cup of grape wine that must have been set out for him. I drank it and did feel more myself and then remembered my manners too.

"Fortunate is the New One and good fortune to his parents," I said.

"Thank you, Mereyamun," Setka said and clapped his hand on my shoulder with warmth and a little more strength than I was prepared for. He was so visibly proud.

"His name is Neferhebef," Setka told me. "Ir-en Setka,"

he added with pride, though unnecessarily for he was, of course, "born of Setka." It was his first name that caught me off guard.

Most names in Kehmeht signified a relationship with a god. My own name meant "Beloved of Amun" and it was difficult to think of names that didn't denote something to do with a god's love or spirit or power. All the other names that came easily to mind denoted some trait. Setka's own name meant "I am strong" which is a strange sentiment to attribute to an infant, but I suppose it was a kind of prayer on the part of his parents and they did indeed get what they asked for. But Neferhebef?

It meant "He of the beautiful festival" and would have made sense had he been born during a holiday or at least a happy time. But he was born on the eve of the Locust Curse, when Kehmeht was on its knees before the Iebiru Power, with no festival in sight. Except, perhaps, for one that would be held in the Red Land three days' journey from our borders. A festival to the Eternal One of the Iebiru. Did Neferet and Setka so look forward to being part of it that they named their firstborn child in delight at its imminent arrival?

I looked at Setka more closely, I could not help it. Yes, his hair was grown in somewhat. Not yet so much that he could not wear a wig, but still, grown in. And his tunic was larger, looser, and made of thicker weave than was the style for one of his age and rank. The thin flax he used to wear showed off the sculpted muscles of his torso and legs perhaps even more than his parts that were uncovered. But these lines were all hidden now. This was the custom of the Iebiru.

"He is sleeping now," Setka explained. "Neferet is seizing the chance to sleep along with him, he gives her so little opportunity," he smiled. "My father-in-law arranged a wet-nurse to ease the burden on her," he confided. "But Neferet would not have it, and do you know why?"

I could guess, but Setka so much wanted to share this with me.

"We expect to go along with the Iebiru to their worship in the Red Land," he said. "And Neferet would not have it that any break in nursing be the cause of her becoming short of milk for our son on that journey."

"But you could simply take the wet-nurse along with you."

"No, no, Mereyamun. For that would mean compelling the wet-nurse to come to a worship she has no part in. And who knows if the Power of the Iebiru desires such a thing? Hasn't everything this year been for us to choose The Eternal One of our own free will? Isn't that what Pahroh is being asked to do? To choose, by his own free choice, to send the Iebiru to the worship?"

How the world had been flipped over. Setka, who never put two words together if he could get away with one, was now talking philosophy with me.

"How can you call it free will if it comes at the end of nine beatings and a threat of more?" I countered.

"I have thought about that, Mereyamun," he said with great seriousness, arguments about ideas never having been a sport to him like they were with me. "I have thought about it, and finally I was granted understanding," he said.

"Tell me, then," I encouraged.

"Well, when a great king makes war, he crushes his enemy swiftly. He sacks the enemy's city, he lays waste to all that he does not take for plunder. He removes some of the living for slaves and slays all the rest. The enemy is no more and will never be again. This is the way of war."

I nodded just to speed him up because I got his point (though I didn't know where he was going with it) and he talked rather slowly.

"But what happens when one of the king's own cities rebels against him?" Setka said meaningfully. "It is his own city, he does not wish to destroy it. He wishes it to return to him."

"Of course," I agreed.

"So what is the king to do? To tolerate the rebellion is impossible, especially if there are in The City some who remain loyal to him but are under the thumb of the rebels. But to make all-out war on The City is to destroy the very thing the king wishes returned to him. So what does he do, Mereyamun?"

"He sets up a siege," I replied, and realized that Setka's allegory was better than I had first thought.

"He does," Setka agreed. "The king first sends heralds, they stand before the rebel leader and state the king's demands. That would be the Iebiru brothers, would it not? You were there, Merey."

I was there, yes. It was just about one year ago, though so much had happened since then. And, looking back now, yes, they were heralds of their Power.

"If the rebels defy the message, the king cuts off their water supply, long enough to slay a few and frighten them all, for even with water returned, they know now the king can cut it off at any time."

"The blood," I agreed.

"The frogs were agents of chaos and discomfort inside the besieged city. The lice penetrated skin like arrows shot randomly over the walls. The wild beasts were a sortie into The City itself, a raid, short in duration but deadly. It is the way of sieges, Merey. It is meant to make the populace turn away from the leaders of the rebellion and consider their return to the true king."

"Then the king slays The City's animals, leaving none for work or transport or even food," I volunteered.

Setka nodded in agreement, pleased at my falling in with his narrative.

"The soot that burned and blistered the skin into boils," he continued, "These were the bombardment of slingers and archers against the inhabitants of the rebel city. But when it did not lead to surrender, then the heavy catapults of the Ice and Flames were brought in. Buildings were brought down, trees were laid low, fires erupted everywhere and bodies were smashed."

"The locusts wiped out the remaining food supply," I added needlessly, it was all so clear really.

"But then, Merey, the siege reaches a point of decision for the king. If he continues with new assaults, if he even repeats any of the measures he has already taken, then this long siege will turn into a sacking of The City and its people destroyed. But the king does not wish this. So, what does he do?"

Setka's question was rhetorical but I wanted to offer a real answer, the one that had been my reason for coming to his house this day.

"At this point perhaps the king looks into The City to see if, the people, fed up with the foolish and stubborn leaders of the rebellion, will rise and return The City to him."

"But what need would the king have of that?" Setka asked incredulously. "He needs no help in battle."

"Maybe he needs no help from the people as fighters, but wants to see what is in their hearts," I offered.

"Maybe," Setka conceded. "But the king can read hearts. And he has better ways of having people show their regret and return to him. But first he must remove their false leaders. So he casts all the people in dark dungeons. Is that not where we have all been these past days, Merey? In dark dungeons to await judgement? And now he has issued that judgment. The verdict is given, the date is set, it will be done."

So moved was Setka by this that his voice trailed into a whisper and he fell silent. But I needed to understand what, exactly, he was saying.

"What verdict? On who? On what date?"

"You have not heard, Merey? Oh, but you were away in the north, stuck in a fort during the locusts. You were probably still traveling back when Mohsheh and Aaharohn called the elders of the Iebiru together."

"Mohsheh told them what was to be and the word spread among all the Iebiru that night. We heard of it before dawn. But just then the dungeons of darkness swallowed us for six days, so of course, there was no way for you to have heard the news."

"Which is?"

"It is over, Merey," Setka said with great feeling, placing his hands on both my shoulders. "It is done. In seven days, counting from tonight as the Iebiru do, in seven days The Eternal One will slay the First Born of Kehmeht, from those in the lowliest house to the ones who surround the Throne."

"What?!" I sputtered.

"Perhaps those who have been stubborn will change their minds in the time that remains," Setka offered. "They might still save themselves from this doom, they have seven days. But if they do not, they will surely die. And then

Pahroh will send the Iebiru to their worship. And we will join them. You see now? It is done."

"Your Honor," someone called after me as I crossed the street away from Setka's house, more absorbed in my thoughts than where my feet were taking me.

"Your Honor, forgive me, a question Your Honor."

It was one of the tradesmen from the knot of loiterers who had eyeballed me as I came to the house an hour earlier. The knot had grown considerably. The one who called me broke away from it and came within a few feet of me, giving a quick hint of a bow from his waist.

"Begging your pardon, Your Honor," he said again. "But tell me please, for it is most urgent, is the Lord Harkuhotep, perhaps in this house?"

"Who asks this?" I challenged him.

"I am Donkor," he said bowing a bit again. The name meant "humble" and he tried hard to convince me that he was, but it was getting annoying.

"I am a potter, I have sold some wares to this house."

So? Did that give him the right to know the whereabouts of Harkuhotep, Seal Bearer of the King of Upper and Lower Kehmeht, Unique Friend of Pahroh, Trusted of All His House? But then, was he Pahroh's unique friend anymore? Was he trusted of all his house? If he was, wouldn't Pahroh have heeded his advice and sent the Iebiru to their worship in the desert?

While I considered this, one of the knot of tradesmen watching us with some annoyance, threw up his hands and started for Setka's door. He strode past me, muttering just loud enough so that all could hear:

"Take this talk to Ammit Swallower of the Damned," he said.

This was a vile and insolent curse.

He pounded on the door. Setka's servant appeared with a thick wooden kitchen paddle. He said something, then jabbed the man in the chest with the end of it, making him reel backwards, and closed the door on him. He skulked back to where the others waited, their attention back on me again.

"Do not be angry, Your Honor," Donkor pleaded, "he is a boor and doesn't know what to do with his fear. He is afraid. We all are. We only hope that the Lord Harkuhotep will save us."

"What do you expect him to do?" I said with little patience.

"He is vizier in the Lower Kingdom," Donkor said, "his word is absolute. Can he not send the Iebiru to their worship? At least the ones who live in the Lower Kingdom? That is most of them, surely. Can he not send them to their worship and save us all from death?"

"He serves Our Father Pahroh," I said. "He commands in Pahroh's name and only as Pahroh wishes."

"Does Pahroh wish us all to die, then?" he said. "At least the firstborn among us, must they all die? And how can we stand by idly with the executioner's sword raised over the necks of our sons and daughters, our wives, our brothers and sisters, our mothers and fathers? For everyone is either a firstborn or bound to one by love or family."

I turned my back on him and walked away. Not because he was insolent, for he was most respectful. And not because he spoke falsely, he spoke true. But because I had no answer.

And my feet? Where were they taking me? Back to Okpara? To tell him that my mission had failed? To tell him that I truly had meant to see his father on the morrow after our conversation, I truly had meant to persuade him to join in an uprising against the courtiers? But then I was cast into darkness and then I was chained in dark matter while six days passed and then this doom on the Firstborn had been pronounced?

It was to my home then, that's where my feet were taking me. Or as Hesera would have it in his madness, the place that was not my home but where I was being allowed to stay for a while, a guest. Only now this madness was true.

I was a firstborn, wasn't I? I would be dead in seven days. I would need that bed only seven times more. I would require a washing bowl and some food and a few cups of wine just seven times more. A guest I was, and for a very short stay. Then I would be gone.

❧

The streets were filling with people. Word spread of all that I had learned from Setka and more. The highborn came out of their houses and spoke earnestly with tradesmen, merchants, laborers, each knot of them sifting through rumors. Circles of conversations expanded with the breathless reports of new arrivals fresh from the crowd gathered outside the Great House.

Yes, Mohsheh and Aaharohn had appeared before the Throne this morning. But it ended in Our Father Pahroh ordering them to leave, to leave and never see his face again! Mohsheh turned away in great wrath, it was said, after pronouncing this doom that was upon us.

I cursed the fact that I was a firstborn, it seemed so unfair. Was I worse in the eyes of the Iebiru Power than any other son of the Black Land? Had I ever done any of the cruel murders that would now be remembered in this mass execution? I wondered at the injustice of it. And then I wondered at something else.

What, truly, would this have meant to me if I were not a firstborn? The potter Donkor protested that he could not stand by idly and watch the firstborn of his people die. And now, in my despair, I thought: Really? Why not?

Sometimes at a funeral you hear a father or a son, a wife, or a mother cry out in anguish. "Why?" they wail, over and over. "Why could it not have been me who died instead?" And maybe, at such a moment, some truly wish this. But most of us? Aren't we secretly happy that it is him or her and not me that death has carried away?

So with all this tumult in the streets and cries to "do something," who really wanted something done? Yes, every man loves his son and daughter, wife and brother, sister and parents, any whom could be firstborns.

But to throw away your own life in a bloody insurrection that might not save theirs? When you could save yourself by doing nothing? In the end, wouldn't that be what most of the children of Kehmeht, the vast majority who were not firstborn, would choose?

So there would be no uprising. There would be no hope. There was nothing to be done any more, except to go back to my room and live through the last seven days of my short life.

I would sleep through as much of it as I could, using whatever wines we had. I didn't imagine the market would be very well stocked anymore, but I guessed there was enough within our walls to get by. And if I ran out? If of a night I found myself too sober to sleep, what difference would it make?

I could curse, or weep for myself, it would all be the same. I could as well howl like a jackal at the moon. It would still remain round and full and bright on the last night of my life.

~

"Master Mereyamun," a man-at-arms called to me as I approached my door. He was slouched there in what shade he could find, but stood himself up when he saw me coming.

"You are wanted, Your Honor," he said. "You are called with all possible haste to the Chamber of Judgements."

Okpara was up to something? He was not simply waiting to die as I had just begun to? I felt ashamed and then reassured myself that my thoughts were my own, no one on this street busy with talk and gesticulations could know what shameful despair had passed through my mind.

As far as this man-at-arms knew, I was a paragon of courage as I turned and strode with determination towards the Great House. He had to catch up with me and fall into my pace. I felt hope again.

Maybe Okpara could still succeed in his plan, with or without Harkuhotep. The restless crowd gathering in the street might never work up the resolution to do what had to be done. But Okpara, who was well inside the Great House might, with a small force of picked men, still oust the courtiers.

Alone, and surrounded with these loyal but bitter men

of Okpara's, Our Father Pahroh might decide to send the Iebiru to their worship. It would be a close thing, and desperate. But it could still be.

The crowd outside the Great House had swollen to thousands. The chaotic press of people was hard on me, a reminder of the full recovery I still needed from the days of the Darkness. I didn't see how I could make my way to the gate.

My man-at-arms saw me foundering and got in front of me. He pushed and shoved people of all ranks this way and that, and I followed in his wake. Before we reached the gate our path merged with that of another man-at-arms making way for yet another scribe who I recognized from the Chamber of Judgements. Together we squeezed through the bronze gate opened just enough to allow us to slide in sideways.

The gate clanged closed behind us by four Great House guards pushing hard against the crowd. We hurried down the porticos and into the corridors and found ourselves catching up with no less than three others who I knew by sight or better.

Okpara was apparently calling in every reliable man. And he seemed to have mobilized enough men at arms to fetch and escort each and every one of us. This was itself a bold thing to do. Okpara's dangerous gambit was in play.

The nine or ten of us hurried up to the great bronze doors of the Chamber of Judgments. There the men-at-arms pushed the doors open and stood aside as we five scribes entered.

There must have been two dozen scribes and clerks in the room, all busy comparing papyri, copying some, rolling others into tubes and handing them to runners and riders. And there, in the center of it all, conferring with this one or that, calling for reports and directing dispatches, in his place on the Seat of Judgements, was the true master of this chamber, Seal Bearer of the King of Upper and Lower Kehmeht, Unique Friend of Pahroh, Trusted of All His House, Harkuhotep.

My heart leapt in my chest. He was back where he belonged, back when we so desperately needed him. He must have come to the Chamber directly from the court, for he had exchanged his blue clothes of mourning for white, and wore his eye make-up and a fine wig and a collar of gold. He radiated certainty and this is what we needed most this day when all the old authority had been eclipsed.

He called to us at the door and bade us come up to his Seat. He greeted us warmly and launched into an explanation of the tasks to be done. I was certain that these would include securing with armed men the Great Hall and all the gates to the Great House.

There would have to be arrests, at least of Rhamschosi, Fan Bearer to The Right of the King, and Nofrerenpe, Sandal Bearer to the Divine Pahroh. And all that would be for nothing if the craven butler Tumekhor was allowed to move around freely. Same for most of the courtly Priests. And the King's Great Wife herself? Surely she should be kept apart from Pahroh while the matter of sending away the Iebiru was reconsidered. And her Sister Wives, too. But Harkuhotep spoke of none of these things. He spoke of animals.

"It is not horses or camels we are concerned with today," Harkuhotep began, as if we had all been in some long dull meeting about livestock and he was correcting a flaw in policy.

"It is the herds, the bulls and cows and their calves, and, of course, the flocks, both goats and sheep. We need their numbers, and we must know their locations. And those that tend them must see them fed and watered sufficient for a drive to Rahmessu. And you must calculate the days needed for that, I would not have them exhausted, they must be delivered to Rahmessu rested and fattened sufficient for a three days' drive into the Red Land."

Everyone gave a quick nod of affirmation or a bit of a bow from the waist. Some uttered an "As you wish!" All went purposefully to tables where piles of papyri were waiting for scribes to act upon them.

These were mostly tax rolls, I imagined. That would be where you'd look if you were trying to find wealth in the Lower Kingdom, whether inanimate or the four-legged kind. Only I remained, standing there before Harkuhotep like a clubbed ox. He could have ordered me to get to work with all the others. Instead he looked at me for a good while.

"The days of darkness were hard on you Mereyamun," he said, half question, half statement. I was unable to speak, but I gave a quick nod 'yes.' He came down from his Seat.

"Come," he said. "Come with me."

He guided me toward a door in the far wall of the Chamber. I had never seen it used, for as a rule you entered the Chamber of Judgements to find the Unique Friend of Pahroh already seated on the Seat of Judgements. And when it was time for you to leave, you backed away and never turned you face from him until you were out in the corridor and the great bronze doors were closed before you. But of course Harkuhotep had to go and come through some private entrance or another, and this was it.

But this was no passageway. That was behind a second door on the far wall of this room. This was a place of its own, very well decorated with comfortable couches and tables laden with fruits and drinks, all bathed in soft sunlight from high windows. Harkuhotep sat me down on a couch and poured a goblet of raisin wine for me, diluted for morning consumption but very good. He took a seat on the couch facing.

"Better?

"Yes," I said. "Thank you."

"More?" he asked.

"I'm alright now."

He looked me over to assess that claim. Then he rose and poured a new cup, this one of water from a cool copper flagon and extended it to me. I took it, of course. This was the Vizier and we were in his chambers. I drank.

"You were unable to move those last three days?"

I nodded as I drank down the cup. I did need that water.

"A man may die from such dryness, Mereyamun," he said. "You must be careful to replenish."

As a rule, you don't laugh in the face of the Seal Bearer of the King of Upper and Lower Kehmeht, Unique Friend of Pahroh, Trusted of All His House. But it just welled up in me unbidden, for it seemed the funniest thing I had ever heard. It was like 'Be careful, watch your water intake, you have to be healthy so you can drop dead in seven days."

I think I actually sputtered out the last drops of water, even though I put my hand over my mouth to stifle the spasms of laughter. Didn't work. But it didn't matter either.

What was he going to do? Execute me for my trespass? It was like one of those gambling games the villagers of Kehmeht play, only now the three lots shaken in the cup were "Die of Thirst," "Die by Beheading," or "Die by the Power of the Iebiru." There was no winning.

"It is reasonable to be afraid," Harkuhotep said. "But all

can still be well. We must do our part, that's all. As of this morning, our part is to see that the animals are well-ordered and ready. The Iebiru will not bring offerings from horses or camels. And not from donkeys. Only from cattle and flocks. So those are what we must assemble."

"For their worship? In the Red Land?"

"Yes, of course."

"But why are we supplying animals for their worship? Don't the Iebiru have more than enough animals of their own? Theirs survived both Plague on the Livestock and the Hail of Fire and Ice, too. Their herds have prospered, I've seen them in Gohshen. Their sheep dot the hillsides like a morning frost in the Month of Renwet." I could be very poetic when afraid.

"Now it is my turn to laugh," Harkuhotep said, though he didn't. "For your words echo those spoken by Pahroh to Mohsheh this very morning."

"They spoke about animals?"

"They argued about them," Harkuhotep said. "Oh Mereyamun, we were close. We were very close to ending this. We had come so far.

"When Mohsheh warned of the locusts he asked the Throne to send the Iebiru women and children and all their livestock to the worship. Pahroh was greatly angered, for he argued that worship of a god is for men, not for women, certainly not for children, and surely no place for great quantities of animals. And with that he expelled Mohsheh and his brother from before the throne!"

"But when the locusts did come and ate everything, this meant nothing to Pahroh?"

"Oh, it meant a great deal to him, for everyone could see that The Two Kingdoms were on the precipice of destruction. But before The Throne could decide what to do, came the Darkness with all its terrors. The moment it ended Pahroh called for Mohsheh and Aaharohn and told them he would send the Iebiru to the worship. Not just the men, but the women and children too. After all, if the Iebiru want to worship with women and with children, let them! It would not be the first thing that made them strange in our eyes. But there was one condition."

"The animals," I said.

"Yes, the livestock would have to stay. For even if the Eternal One really did require animal offerings, how many could He possibly need? The flocks and herds of the Iebiru are vast, as you said, Mereyamun. Why should they be allowed to take all that wealth out of the Black Land?"

"And Mohsheh did not agree."

"No, he did not. The Eternal One is everywhere, Mohsheh teaches, and so He is served through everyone and everything. Every man, great or humble has his part. Every woman too, and every little boy and girl. And every animal. For no one knows, Mohsheh argued, how The Eternal One will wish to be served on the day of worship. Those who go must be prepared to serve with all that they have. So not one hoof may be left behind."

"What difference can it make to us now," I said in despair, "if the Iebiru bring their livestock?"

"Not just their livestock," Harkuhotep answered. "Ours, too."

"Mohsheh asked Pahroh for livestock?"

"He did not ask. He predicted. He pronounced what would be. In seven days' time, he said, Pahroh will not only send the Iebiru with all their livestock to the worship, but he and his servants will contribute sheep and cattle too."

"Pahroh has agreed to that?"

"No, he has not agreed to it."

"Then how can the Chamber of Judgments arrange for the cattle to be sent? It is not Pahroh's will!"

"No, not yet. But it will be. In seven days' time. And then it will be too late to do the job well. Better to act now."

"Do we carry out the future will of Pahroh when he himself does not yet know what it will be?"

"We do know what his wishes will be in seven days' time. Mohsheh has told us. How can we avoid acting on that now?"

There had never been such a question in my life and I doubt in anyone else's either. Harkuhotep saw me pale and reached over to swipe the empty cup from my hand. He refilled it from the water flagon and pressed it back upon me, talking all the while.

"Mohsheh has not been wrong yet, Mereyamun. Everything he has predicted so far truly came to pass. This will too. So I am acting now on what will surely happen.

"I could wait until the day itself, but the more we wait the more difficult it will be. Much will be going on in the next few days, great things, and each of us will have much to do."

"But then today, on this day in which we are living, whose will are we carrying out? It is not yet Pahroh's. We are acting on Mohsheh's?"

"I think it is the will of the Eternal One that we are carrying out," Harkuhotep said. "And in a few days it will be Pahroh's will as well."

What was Harkuhotep saying? Was he hinting to me at what I most longed to hear? Was he secretly moving to force the Throne of the Two Kingdoms to accede to Mohsheh's request and save the First Born of Kehmeht from death?

"But will it be too late for me? And the other

firstborns?" I was afraid to speak more plainly to The Vizier of The Lower Kingdom. He was being kind enough, but not entirely open with me.

"No one has to die, Mereyamun," he answered. "No one."

"But Mohsheh said the firstborn will all perish in a single night."

"Not if they join the Iebiru," Harkuhotep said. He leaned forward in his seat so that his eyes leveled with mine.

"I will join them in this worship. So will Setka and Neferet and their little firstborn son. So will Inyotef and Adjedaa and many others who you know. And we will not be alone. Many, many, sons and daughters of Kehmeht will come. And none of us will die. Mohsheh has taught this. And Mohsheh has never been wrong."

"But what about the First Born of Kehmeht who will not join this worship?"

Harkuhotep looked at me but said nothing. And it meant everything. This was to be his way, then. The lives of my brothers and sisters, the Children of The Black Land would depend upon their being accepted by Mohsheh to join the Iebiru in the Deshret.

"What about the Children of Kehmeht who cannot find it in their hearts to do that?" I asked.

"It is their choice," Harkuhotep answered. "Each of us must make this choice for ourselves."

"But what if our Father Pahroh was to be..." I had to choose the next words very carefully. "What if our Father Pahroh *felt* compelled... by... *circumstances*... to send the Iebiru to the worship... before the time for this decree of death is carried out...?"

"You have surely been speaking with Okpara," Harkuhotep said.

"He summoned me," I admitted. "The day after the locusts, the evening before the Darkness."

I realized then that Okpara was strangely absent from all the action in the Chamber of Judgements today.

"He has been avoiding me, I think," Harkuhotep said pensively. Then shook himself loose from whatever thought was engaging him and rose to his feet. This signaled that it was time for me to go. I rose accordingly.

"You must rest today, Mereyamun. Return to your home and be sure to drink as much as you can. And sleep too. Tomorrow there will be much to do."

"As you wish, My Lord," I said with a bit of bow. Harkuhotep sat himself back down on his couch and I backed my way towards the door.

"But think about the things we discussed," he added. "I may require your help in a number of them, and it would be best if you had clarity of mind."

These words were heavy with portent but light on meaning. What "things" was he hinting at? What could my help possibly be? But Harkuhotep had already given a cursory nod of his head and was absorbed in a papyrus he had picked up from a nearby table. I was dismissed.

Then, just as I had backed up to the door and reached behind with my arm to turn its latch, Harkuhotep spoke one more time. With his face still in the papyrus on his lap he said:

"Mereyamun, if you see Okpara..." He paused, then continued haltingly, "I think he may well see you in the coming days..."

Harkuhotep looked up at me.

"Tell him...say that I... I would very much like to see him. Tell him there is still hope."

～

"**W**ake up!" a voice rasped into my dream. "Wake up, young guest. A guest may not overstay his welcome you know."

It was Hesera. At least it was his voice. My eyes stayed shut through a couple of more "Wake ups!" and it was only upon the complete surrender of my sleepiness that I opened them to behold Hesera looming above me.

He found me above my blankets, still in yesterday's clothing. I must have returned from Harkuhotep exhausted, fallen into bed and slept through the sunrise. Fine. But what was Hesera doing in my room, a place he had not entered in years?

"Will you not rise? At least to a sitting position?" Hesera requested.

I would. I swung my feet over the edge of the bed to face him. He grabbed a stool and lowered himself onto it facing me. So it was to be a day begun with a rude awakening and lecture from a madman. I was not pleased.

"Why did you wake me?"

"I wish to know what transpired between you and that ape who sits in the Chamber of Judgments," Hesera answered evenly.

"If you know that I was there, then you surely know what was said."

"A vagabond guest in my house, and yet he answers me discourteously?" Hesera reproached.

There was no profit in stirring up his madness. I should have known better.

"Apologies," I said. "Harkuhotep instructed his scribes to ready the flocks and herds of Our Father Pahroh and his servants, so that they could be delivered into the hands of the Iebiru for use in their worship."

"But he then spoke with you privately, did he not?"

It wasn't necessarily sorcery that allowed Hesera to know this. He could have received a report from anyone who was there. Still, I wondered.

"We spoke about the doom that is coming in seven days. He said that Mohsheh has taught that any firstborn who joins with the Iebiru in loyalty to their Eternal One will not die in the slaying."

"And you believe this?"

"Yes," I shrugged. "All that Mohsheh has said so far has come true. Why not this as well?"

Hesera cackled to himself and shook his head a bit. It meant that he pitied me for being such a feckless idiot, another Son of Kehmeht lost to the tricks of the Iebiru brothers.

"Believe what you wish, young vagabond," Hesera said. "But tell me, is this then the strategy of the Ape Vizier of the Lower Kingdom? Does he plan to betray his nation and his King by sending its sons into the Deshret with the Iebiru to worship their Power? After contributing our own animals?"

"He himself plans to go to the worship," I offered. "As many others are planning to do."

"So he will grow his beard and dance before a barbarian altar in the Red Land? While the firstborn of Kehmeht are slain without even giving battle!?"

I couldn't tell if Hesera really wanted an answer to that, or if he was just spitting out his anger. But it awoke in me a question that had taken root as I left Harkuhotep. Was he actually working to move things so that Pahroh would be forced to send the Iebiru away and, in doing so, avert the slaying of our countrymen?

He never said he would do any such thing. Yet he knew of Okpara's plans, he said as much. And he was marshaling scribes, messengers and men-at-arms to carry out a major surrender to the Iebiru by sending the livestock of Pahroh and his servants to them.

The Chamber of Judgments had every right to audit the livestock of the Lower Kingdom. As long as he did not actually deliver the animals, there was no treason. And yet it was surely a provocation to the courtiers who hated Mohsheh and egged Pahroh on to steadfast refusal.

More, Harkuhotep asked me to be tell Okpara how much he wanted to meet with him. Was this the alliance that Okpara so desired? And didn't Harkuhotep tell me that in these coming days there would be "much to do"? What could there be to do if all he meant was for us to either join the Iebiru or just sit around and wait to die?

"I don't know anything for sure," I answered Hesera. "But there were hints. It may be that Harkuhotep is gathering forces."

"To slay the Iebiru? To stop them from leaving?" Hesera said with some wheezing hope.

"No," I said to his clear disappointment. "The opposite. To compel the Throne to send them to their worship before it is too late."

Hesera's face contorted with rage. But no words came out. It passed. He collapsed back into himself. Then, with some effort of his now spiritless body, he got up.

He appeared older than I had ever seen him, resigned now to give up what was left of his life. That could be seven days, for he was himself a firstborn. But for the first time in many months Hesera appeared something like sane.

"So Harkuhotep might be planning to compel the throne to capitulate to the Iebiru," he mused. "But he might also be preparing to stop the Iebiru from leaving on their pilgrimage. Or he might be doing nothing but defecting to our enemies and urging others to do the same. Those are the three possibilities, then. Correct Mereyamun?"

"Correct."

"Can you not learn which of these it will be?"

He left me. And I realized that, yes, I could learn which of these it would be. I could ask the one person who always understood Harkuhotep. The only person really. His firstborn son. Inyotef.

～

"You."

That servant who was the groom to Inyotef's horses (but also wore a large dagger which said he was something else) was pointing at me. He said "you" as if it was my name and he just recalled it.

"You," he repeated.

Maybe I was gawking a little too much at the hand axe he had added to his belt. Even so, he smoothly ignored it, turning his glance slowly in all directions like a hunter who feels a predator is near.

This habit of his made some sense today, for the street before Inyotef's home was dotted with clusters of unhappy and restless people. They were talking too loudly, too intensely, and casting dark looks every once in a while toward Inyotef's door.

They knew Inyotef had something to do with the Court. So they believed he was in some way part of the terrible doom coming to take their lives. They were frightened. And, as is the way of frightened people, they were angry.

Every man and woman in that street was going to

receive a terrible blow in just six days, counting from the coming evening as the Iebiru do. Either they were first born themselves, and doomed to die. Or else they were going to suffer the loss of a spouse, a child, a parent, a brother, a sister, a friend.

They had to do something. Yet there was nothing to do. Unless, perhaps, they could press the King and his Court to send the Iebiru to their worship. But how could these people ever gain admission to the Court at this time and with this request? They could not. But Inyotef the Herald could.

Their nearest and only hope to reach the court was this Inyotef who none of them knew, really. But he was there neighbor, wasn't he? If only this grim groomer of horses who looked like an assassin wasn't standing very much in their way.

"They're inside," he continued to me with a quick inclination of his head for directions. "You've just caught them. Five more flicks of these horses' tails and you would have missed them."

And so with this permission I went toward the door, much to the envy of the crowd growing in the street. It was uncomfortable to have their eyes on me. It was worse to feel the weight of their dark thoughts about who I might be and what they might try to make me do.

I circumnavigated those horses with the flicking tails and the large wagon to which they were harnessed, laden with things for a journey. Where were Inyotef and Adjedaa going?

Before I could reach the door to knock, it opened from within.

"Come Mereyamun," Adjedaa said brightly.

"Well come!" Inyotef said as I entered where they were

just tying off the last boxes and bundles to be added to their wagon. It gave the impression that they were moving house.

"Where are you going?" I asked. I guessed the answer might be to some place where Inyotef would supervise the audit of livestock Harkuhotep was sending to the Iebiru worship? But I was mistaken.

"To Goshen," Inyotef said. "Want to come?"

"Now?" I said in disbelief. "With all that's going on?" This was no time for Inyotef's jokes.

"Precisely now," he answered seriously enough. "Precisely because of all that's going on."

He walked me to the window, and displaced the wooden shutter just enough to let us peek.

"That crowd out there? Today they're still shy of doing more than grumbling. Tomorrow it will be threats. In two days' time, it'll be storming houses and fighting in the streets. So getting out of The City? Seems like a very good time to me."

"Maybe in four days' time the fighting will move from the streets to the Great House," I said.

I was surprised and a little shocked at my own audacity. But we were all going to be dead in six days, so why not?

"Maybe the fighting will end in the removal of the courtiers surrounding our Father Pahroh," I went on. "Maybe with the courage of his People behind him, Pahroh will break free of the Court and send the Iebiru to the worship. So maybe this mob of angry people will save their own lives and all of our lives with them!"

Inyotef, I believe, was actually surprised by my treasonous speech. He looked at me the way a big brother looks when the kid brother he's practically fathered suddenly grows into a clumsy manhood before his eyes. He exchanged a look with Adjedaa and they sat down and gestured for me to sit down with them.

"You think, Merey, that Pahroh is being held captive by the Court?" Inyotef asked softly.

"Not in his body," I said. "But in the advice he receives, in the information he is allowed to hear, yes, I do."

Inyotef and Adjedaa exchanged looks again. This was getting really annoying. The married people I knew were constantly conferring like two physicians whenever I said anything, as if my ideas were symptoms of some dread disease.

"It is not so," Inyotef said. "Perhaps it was so back before the Curse of the Soot and the Boils. But from that time on, it has been Pahroh who has been obstinate.

"Harkuhotep himself told us it is the Court! He charged us to bring proofs and facts and histories to prove them wrong. You know that Inyotef. You know it better than I do!"

"My father..." Inyotef saw something in my face. I could not have hidden it if I tried. No one ever spoke openly of this before.

"Yes Merey," Inyotef explained, "he is plain-spoken about it now, at least among those who share his belief in the Power of the Iebiru. Harkuhotep, my *father*, used to believe as you describe. But he can not deny what he witnessed when he returned to Court.

"He was there when Mohsheh warned of the locusts. The courtiers, even the worst of them, *begged* Pahroh to accept that The Black Land and her children would be destroyed if he did not relent. But he has not relented."

"Then we must make him relent," I said. "It is our lives at stake!"

"Yes, our lives hang in the balance, but it is base treason to take down a King!"

"It has happened before," I retorted, prepared to tell Avishamah's tale of how the slavery of the Iebiru first began. But there was no need.

"Yes, we have had civil insurrections in our history, Merey. But never against a King like this one."

"What? Is he so powerful? He is a dwarf, he is a bookish scholar, a lover of nature and bound to the life of The River and the moist black earth," I argued. "He is no warrior to dread."

"He is protected, Merey, and not only by soldiers. If the Eternal One wanted Pahroh dead he would be dead. Do you doubt it?"

I could not.

"But He has kept Pahroh alive," Inyotef reasoned. "*He* has made him impervious to the terrible blows that have rained down upon us, well beyond the point where most men would have surrendered. And why? In order that Pahroh choose, of his own free will, to send the Iebiru to the worship. And in doing that, accept the Eternal One as the only Power there is or ever was."

"A whole nation must die because one man refuses to bend to a new belief?"

"Yes, maybe, if that one man is its King."

"How do you know that the Eternal One doesn't want us to rise up and replace this obstinate king with a better one? One who will bend the knee and send the Iebiru to their sacrifice?"

"I don't know. Maybe. But it will not be done in these next six days. Mohsheh has already pronounced what will be. In six days this King will still be King. And he will send the Iebiru to their worship. And this King will command that they should go. And he will send livestock of his own and of his lords to add to the festival."

"Yes, alright, Mohsheh has pronounced this. But is it something that *must* be? Or is something that *can* be... unless we change it?"

"My Father asks the same question."

"Will he do more than ask, Inyotef? Will he use his office and his power to force our King to do what must be done? Will he shape those mobs in the streets? Will he lead them? Or move on their behalf with trained men?"

"I do not know, Merey."

"Then no one knows," I said.

"Whatever happens, he will join us six days from now, on the night of the full moon in Goshen. And in the morning he will go out into the Deshret to the worship with the Iebiru. We are going now to arrange things. Setka and Neferet and their baby will come. As will many others that you know. I wish you would come, too."

"It is unfair," I said. "A few of us go and join the Iebiru at the full moon and save our own lives, while untold thousands of the Children of Kehmeht will be struck dead because of the stubbornness of one man. Is that not cruel?"

"But it is very kind," Adjedaa said. "We have always had to live with the whims of kings, haven't we? It never mattered if the king was wise or foolish, we were always stuck with him."

I still could not get used to the idea that our servant girl from a mudbrick village had learned to speak like a wisewoman whenever the topic of the Eternal One came up.

"But now, in this," Adjedaa warmed to her words, "the Eternal One is doing something new. For if Pahroh will choose correctly and send the Iebiru to the worship, then, good, all the lives of his people will be saved.

"But if Pahroh fails to choose as he should, then each and every one of us may still escape into the protection of the Eternal One. We can turn our backs on this Pahroh and choose the Eternal One to be our king! Has there ever been such a thing before?"

∾

"Your Honor!" people in the street were calling to us as Inyotef drove his wagon slowly through the crowd. Adjedaa sat up beside him, and I sat behind them on one of the larger bundles. I agreed that it would be best for me to take a ride with them for a few streets until the mob was thinned out and I could go my way on foot.

Our path through the crowd was cleared by Inyotef's "groom" who was driving Inyotef's chariot with four horses in harness. This was no way to drive in a city, but Inyotef wanted to bring the horses with him, and it did make it easier to part the crowd.

But once parted, the crowd flowed back around us as we passed, until they were pressing on the wagon, urging us to stop, urging us to please *listen* to them.

"Will you not save us, Your Honor?" one man hanging onto the wagon was pleading to me. "You are a Herald, you will be heard, can you not go to our Father Pahroh and save us?"

The poor man thought I was Inyotef. After all, I was the one dressed in a golden collar and fine linen with eye makeup and an expensive wig. Inyotef was wearing a traveling cloak and had let his own hair grow, and Adjedaa was wearing a shawl of light wool partially hooded over her own long hair. They did not look like people welcomed in the Court. They looked half Iebiru.

I wanted to say something to the poor man and the others with him. But what could I say? "I am not welcome at court either, and it looks like in six days I'm going to be just as dead as you are. So what do you say you all get kitchen knives and axes and we storm the Great House and make Pahroh send the Iebiru?"

What would that have meant to them? They still thought of Pahroh as their beloved Father. How would they react if I told them their Father is too stubborn to care if they all died before the week was out?

It was not long, though, until we left that crowd behind and passed through streets that were less tumultuous. Inyotef and Adjedaa were exchanging looks again, so I knew someone was going to say something. I stood up to thank them for the ride and hop off. But Inyotef just turned his eyes back toward his horses and started talking in the distracted way of drivers making conversation.

"Adjedaa?"

"Uh-huh," she answered.

"Do you have any spare rope from the bundles?"

"Yes."

"Enough to tie up Merey? Then we could just take him with us until he comes to his senses."

Adjedaa giggled.

"Guess it's time for me to get off," I said to Inyotef and climbed down from the still rolling wagon. He slowed it to accommodate me.

"Goodbye, Inyotef," I said from the street. He brought the wagon to a full stop and turned in his seat to look at me.

"Whatever you're thinking, Merey, your life isn't worth it."

"My life isn't worth much now anyway," I said. "Only six days left."

"Come with us and live," he said.

"There's still hope here," I said. "Your own father said so, Inyotef. He said it to me yesterday. We will fight."

~

"Mereyamun?" Sartuma said outside my door careful to avoid calling me "Master" within Hesera's possible hearing. At least she didn't call me "Young Vagabond."

"Mereyamun?"

I climbed off my bed and opened the door to her.

"Good morning, Sartuma," I offered in as much good cheer as I could muster. I had slept badly, even with a belly full of date beer. We were well into the second day of the seven that would bring us to the Slaying, who could sleep? And of those who could, who would want to wake?

After leaving Inyotef I had spent the rest of the day and much of the night waiting for a call to arms. At first I felt sure it would come from Harkuhotep. It had to, there was no one in the Lower Kingdom better situated for what had to be done.

But the hours passed, the day grew dark and my hope darkened with it. Why was I even bothering to withhold drink from myself? No call would come anymore this day. So I drank what I could find in our stores, hoping to pass into sleep.

Then I was woken by noises in the street, strident voices, arguments carried on the still night air from distant houses and courtyards. The City was as restless as I was, so I got up and went to the window to look for a sign of struggle and hope.

Okpara was still out there, I reminded myself. He had hidden from this father and the Court and what could that mean but that he was gathering forces. I felt heartened and watched and waited to be called.

But midnight passed and there was no knock at the door, no whispered call up to my window. I downed what was left of the date beer and passed out on the bed. Until now. Until Sartuma came to wake me. Which was itself strange.

Because being woken by Sartuma of a morning was part of a different life, a life I lived until about one year ago, now vanished into the mists of another Age. Yet here Sartuma was at my door, as if it were still a year ago, as if Kehmeht was still The Land That Makes Her Children Happy.

"A good morning," Sartuma replied. "Sorry to disturb you of your morning, but I thought you would want to know," she went on as if she was herself from those happier times, and unsure of how to use the words of those days now.

"Yes?" I encouraged her.

"The Young Princess is here," she said. "The Young Princess is here to see you."

And so it was. I went downstairs to find Neferet, as if this year and all its confusions and terrors had never happened. As if we were safe again. As if I was still the half-child half-man I had been and Neferet was still my best friend.

"Hello, Merey."

"Fortunate is the New One, and good fortune to his

parents," I said, this being the first I saw of Neferet since the birth of Neferhebef Ir-en Setka.

"Thank you," she smiled. Even in these days of dread, she could not hide her pleasure at being a mother.

"Sit?" I offered. She did and I followed.

"Actually I must get back to him soon, he'll need to nurse."

"I could have come to you," I said.

"But I couldn't have spoken freely there, not with my Father coming in and out and not with everyone believing they must report to him everything they see and hear," she said. "And these are urgent things, Merey, things I need you to understand."

"I'm listening."

"There are just six days left," she began. Did Neferet think that I or anyone else in the Two Kingdoms had forgotten for a minute?

"Everyone knows that."

"Yes, yes of course they do," she hurried. "But they don't grasp what is happening on each of these days."

"What's happening each of these days?" I asked, since she was right, I had no idea what would happen even the rest of this day let alone the five that would follow it. Was I an astrologer or a reader of bones?

"Tomorrow the Iebiru will take lambs," she said. "They will select the best that can be found and keep them until the afternoon before the Full Moon," she continued, as if this was us years ago, Neferet telling strange stories that tested my credulity but held me enthralled.

"And then, between noon and sundown on that day, they will slaughter them, roast them and eat them before midnight when the Slaying of the Firstborn will begin." She looked at me meaningfully to see if I understood. She wasn't certain. "It is an offering to The Eternal One."

"This cannot be," I blurted out.

"Why not? It is as Mohsheh teaches."

"Neferet," I practically pleaded in unassailable logic, "it's barely half a year since the Curse of the Animals and Pahroh offered Mohsheh to let the Iebiru worship their Power right here in the Black Land, and what did Mohsheh answer?"

"That they would be offering sheep and could not do so before the pious Children of Kehmeht who revere the rams as sacred," she agreed as if it was a small matter.

"Isn't the Ram still worshipped as the living god of the constellation that brings the spring harvest?"

"By those who know no better, yes."

"And didn't Mohsheh say that he could not agree for the Iebiru to do such offerings within Kehmeht, as the people would be outraged and rise up against them?"

"That was then," Neferet shrugged. "It's different now."

"Then why do the Iebiru have to go out into the Red Land at all?"

"It is the command of the Most High," she answered. "He wants the worship in the Red Land but before we go out there, He wants this offering here, in six more days. This is what Mohsheh has taught. I thought you might not have heard."

"You're right, I didn't hear this," I admitted. "But so what?"

"The Iebiru cannot offer the animal unless they check it for blemishes a few days before the offering. So they will take the lambs tomorrow. Can you not see it, Merey? They will put ropes on them and lead them from the markets through the streets to their houses, they will tie them to their bedposts. To watch them. To guard over them.

"People will wonder, Merey. They will ask the Iebiru 'What are you doing with that lamb? The Ram is a god, it is sacred to us, especially in this month!' Can you not see that?"

"So people will get upset. Seems like a pretty small thing compared to what we're headed for."

"But when the people challenge them, the Iebiru will answer. They will say 'This lamb is your god? We are going to slit its throat. We are going to paint its blood on the inside of our doorways and we will roast it and eat it as an offering to The Eternal One.'"

"People will not stand for that!" I said. "It's too much, they will snap. There will be bloodshed."

"Yes," Neferet agreed. "But whose blood?"

And that, of course, was the whole point. There were many Sons of Kehmeht who still thought they could fight the Iebiru and win. Hesera did. But there were many others who saw this as the wrong fight. If fighting were to be done, it would have to be Sons of Kehmeht against Sons of Kehmeht until those who still refused to send away the Iebiru would be overthrown.

"I believe that tomorrow my brother will emerge from wherever he is hiding. He will have men who follow him and he will watch what happens when the Iebiru take their lambs through the streets. He will set his tactics according to the mood of the mob. He will gather whoever he can to him, so I am sure that he will contact you Merey."

"I still don't understand," I replied. "First, I need to know, is your Father going to be part of this?"

"I don't believe that he himself knows yet. His heart is torn in many directions. But no matter what he does in these days, he will come with us to the worship in the Red Land. And as that now means first this worship here on the night of the Full Moon, he will join in that too. So it is not my Father that I am worried about. It's my three brothers."

"*Three* brothers?"

"Inyotef is no secret anymore, though I worry about him least, he believes in the Eternal One completely. It's just that he is still wound up in so many errands and intrigues, I fear something will go wrong. If he will just stay put in Goshen once he gets there, it will be alright I guess."

"Inyotef always lands on his feet," I offered.

"He does," Neferet agreed.

"Okpara is my real worry. He is a firstborn, he will surely die unless he comes and joins the Iebiru."

"Or unless he forces the Throne to send the Iebiru to their worship," I said.

"It's Okpara, Merey! You know who we're talking about," Neferet argued. "He's no warrior, he's not particularly strong. He could be killed."

"His heart is strong in this," I said.

"Don't say that! Please don't say things like that, I'm afraid you'll start believing it yourself and help him believe it too. Okpara is no soldier, and the Throne is defended by soldiers! Okpara is no street brawler and the mobs that will fight are made of street brawlers. How will he survive it all?"

"He will have soldiers on his side too," I said. "And desperate men who know how to fight."

"Will they protect him? Even if they want to, will they be able to? Will they protect you, Merey?"

"We're going to be slain in six days anyhow, isn't it better to at least die trying?"

"You know better than that. If you didn't know the

truth already I wouldn't ask you to pretend, even to save your life. But you know better! You know something of the Eternal One now. After all you've been through? It was knowledge hard-won, wasn't it?

"We have come so far from what we were a year ago! Don't you want to be part of what happens next? Don't you want to be there when The Eternal One reveals Himself in the Red Land?"

"I think that sometimes," I admitted. "I don't want to miss it."

"Then have pity on yourself Merey and come with us! And have pity on Okpara. He doesn't understand as you do. But he trusts you and if you try you could bring him along. You could save him."

"It's funny," I almost laughed. "That's just about what Okpara said to me about your Father, that he trusts me and I could persuade him to join Okpara's uprising."

"All I ask is that if Okpara finds you tomorrow, you tell him something of what you know of the Eternal One. Make him understand that no one thinks the worse of him for not yet believing what we have all come to believe. Least of all Father."

"Fair enough."

"And if he doesn't come tomorrow, then you will surely find him the next day when they take my mother from the House of The Dead to her tomb in the Valley of the Kings."

"The seventy days ends day after tomorrow," I realized out loud. "I knew it was about now."

"I will not be there. People will say it's because I have just given birth. But it will be because I'll have no comfort watching my Mother's body treated in a way that is hated by the Most High. Mohsheh has taught this."

"What about your Father?"

"He feels the same way, but he may attend, I do not know what he has decided. But Okpara will surely be there. If my brother doesn't find you tomorrow, find him there the day after. Please."

"I will."

Neferet got up to go. I followed her to the door.

"Thank you, Mereyamun."

"You said you were worried about three brothers," I reminded her. "Who is the third?"

"Who do you think?"

No, I thought, no! I cannot bear another revelation about who I was or who anyone really was, and why should I have to hear such things now when in six days there was every likelihood I'd be dead? It showed on my face and made Neferet, of all things, smile.

"I don't mean 'brother' like that, Merey. We share no blood, not of my father nor my mother. But we share most of the days of our lives growing up, don't we? We share ka, I think. So I am your sister, and you are my brother and always will be. I don't want to lose you. You have to live."

~

The sun passed its apex, the shadows of the afternoon began, and I took up papyrus and ink and sat down to write. I would write all that happened to me from the time I came into the world until this day, one of the last six of my life maybe.

I don't know exactly why I chose to do this. It just felt right that if, after five more sunsets my life was snuffed out, something of me should remain.

I wrote about the days of my childhood in this house. I wrote of those days when Hesera was a kind father and

Sartuma a sweet mother. I was just a little kid, it was normal, for all I knew, to be raised by a sorcerer to the Court and a kindly servant-mistress of the house.

I had been content in my studies and happy believing that I would grow up to be numbered among the great, many of whom already called me by name and loved me. And I had Neferet, the best friend that could be, sharing adventures and new secrets day by day. It was perfect. And then it wasn't.

In a week or so it would be a year since the *maat* of the life I was supposed to have collapsed, and the *maat* of the Black Land with it. A year almost since Mohsheh and his brother appeared and made a small rent in the fabric of the world, just a few threads of destiny tugged loose. But it unraveled and tore until we saw that what we thought was real was just a painted curtain. It had been a beautiful curtain, it portrayed a delightful world. But it was an illusion and ripped open. We could see what was beyond it now. We could see that everything we thought we knew was wrong.

So I wrote how this unfolded, how I had come to be a year older since the beginning of this sad tale but would probably see no other years. Unless I ran away to the Iebiru. Unless I became as one of them. Unless I plunged a dagger into the heart of the desperate and dying idea that I would ever accomplish something great in Kehmeht, something of value.

Maybe Okpara would still send for me? Maybe Harkuhotep would stand beside him and lead us in the uprising that would save everything? Was that not also a way to bow the knee to The Eternal One? Would He not be well-pleased if we won and sent His Iebiru to the worship as He wished?

Wouldn't that be greater service on my part, to play a role in that? Wouldn't that be greater than just running away to the Iebiru and leaving the greatest nation in the world to suffer the slaying of its choicest children in a single night?

But no call came. Not from Okpara. Not from Harkuhotep. I fell asleep at my writing table, then woke and felt angry. I was done with sitting and waiting for the death that would surely find me if we did nothing. I watched for the first light. When it came, I would go out and find whatever destiny held for me.

Finally, the first light out of the east painted my room and I rose to what this day would bring. I tied my sandals, washed my face from the basin, went out into the hallway and closed the door quietly behind me. It was still dark there, having no windows to admit the dawn. But I could see a flicker of lamplight from the great room below and used it to make my way down the stairs. Who in our household would be sitting with a lamp there at this hour?

It was no lamp. It was a small fire of grain soaked in olive oil giving a steady flame upon the altar before the image of Behs. And before it, chanting in his muffled way, knelt Kheruef.

He swayed from his knees and I believe I heard him sob a little. I believe he was crying. That is until he felt my presence and jumped to his feet, startled or embarrassed, I couldn't be sure. Both, maybe.

"Your Honor..." he started to say, then swallowed it, realizing that in calling me this he was violating Hesera's command. Who knew what sorcery would rain down on him if he was caught? He cast around for something else to call me, but could come up with nothing. He would not allow himself to call me by name.

"It is alright, Kheruef," I said. "I didn't mean to interrupt you."

I was making an offering to Behs," he said by way of explanation and apology, though it required neither. Still, it was a bit of presumption for a servant of the house to initiate such a service.

"It is alright," I repeated. But he wanted to say something.

"It is for Sartuma," he offered by way of explanation. "She is firstborn," he went on with tears gathering in his eyes. "I mean she thinks she is, she is not sure, she left her family when she was young and things were never made clear…"

Tears escaped down his cheek. I knew that he and Sartuma had become close after Nebamun's terrible death right here in this room. He was a comfort to Sartuma and I was glad of that, even if their comfort meant mutually assuring each other that anyone involved with the Power of the Iebiru was a miscreant and criminally insane.

"Nebamun took her to wife when she was just a girl, you see, and her father was not at home in those days so there was a lot of confusion. He saved her you know," Kheruef asserted. "Nebamun. He was a nasty one to everyone else, a real piece of work. But he was always good to her."

I had never taken the trouble to learn much about Sartuma's past before she came into our household. I never thought about who she was or what her life had been before it was about baking and cooking and sewing and mothering me.

"I'm afraid," Kheruef said simply in near whisper. "I'm afraid that come this full moon, I will lose her."

Kheruef had always seemed a happy and simple soul.

He did decent work (though never decent enough for our sour steward Nebamun). He was cheerful, and liked by the other workers and serving girls. He enjoyed himself in brothels and wine houses but always rose for duties next morning. He never gave me reason to think very much about him so I never did.

But he was bereft now, utterly lost. He loved Sartuma. He could not bear the death that was coming for her in five nights. He was trembling.

"Come with me, Kheruef," I said.

What else could I do? Leave him paralyzed in anguish over the fact that the woman he had finally found to share his life was going to be ripped away from him? If I couldn't comfort him, at least I might distract him a little. And wasn't this exactly why we needed an uprising? So that the simple but good folk of The Black Land would be saved from this final blow after a year of suffering?

"I have errands to do," I told him. "I could use your help."

And so he came with me. I believe he was grateful. We set out for the Great House to see if I might find Okpara or word of him in the Chamber of Judgements. And as we went I wondered, might Kheruef actually help?

The thought heartened me, because The City was full of simple good-hearted laboring men like him. How hard would it be to mobilize them? With all that had unfolded, maybe there was no longer need for a powerful leader like Harkuhotep. The simple sons of Kehmeht might yet understand on their own what they had to do to save those they loved.

"Tell me Kheruef," I said as we walked out into the street washed by rays of rising sun. "Have you ever been in a fight? A serious one I mean, with weapons?"

His face darkened as he chewed on an answer. He thought I was leading up to an accusation.

"You know me, Your Honor," he said, now that we were out of Hesera's hearing and it was safe to call me that. "Have I ever been one to pick fights with anyone?"

"No, you've always been a cheerful fellow," I said, ignoring the time when we were cooped up in the great room together during the Hailstorm and he was nearly deranged with shock and anger over Adjedaa's renunciation of Behs. But that was an unusually stressful time for all of us. And besides, that was precisely the kind of passion, latent within him, that I needed to rekindle now.

"Sometimes Kheruef," I explained as we walked, "it is necessary to fight. To protect the ones we love. I believe that now we have come to such a time."

His face lit up.

"I would fight, Your Honor. I would fight with all my strength if I could save..." His voice trailed off, not feeling quite sure he should actually name Sartuma in his response, "...if I could save all the poor people who are doomed to die."

"Have you ever wielded a weapon?" I asked him.

"Never had a sword or spear in my hands, if that's what Your Honor is getting at," he said. "But I've swung a hammer or any other heavy tool you can name since I was old enough to hold one. You know that," he added hopefully.

So that is how Kehmeht will find its salvation, I realized. Through armies of plain and good working men who would arm themselves with the tools they had always used to build the Black Land, but now as weapons in the battle to save it. I was moved by this and decided to share with Kheruef a notion of the uprising that would be in the next, few, last days we had.

"You will need your hammer, then, Kheruef. Because any day now those of us who are willing to fight will gather today and make a stand. It could be bloody, I will not hide that from you. I hope not. I hope that the good sense that has always been..."

"Ai!"

Kheruef gave out a yelp and pointed high up the market street we were passing.

"Ai! Look Your Honor! Look!" he said, jabbing his finger several times in the air toward what was happening some twenty paces from us.

It was a small but buzzing knot of early visitors to the market, though there was almost no produce to buy and little reason to trade or sell, with mass death just four days away. Everyone in the knot was talking at once, some shouting towards two figures for whom they had parted and cleared the way, but only just barely. It was a pair of Iebiru, leading by a rope a lamb they had just purchased.

"Sacrilege!" people were shouting at them.

"The lamb is the god himself," someone kept yelling in their faces.

"Stop them," the people cried to one another.

Some picked up rocks, others set down the wares they were carrying to free their fists for action. They closed in on the two Iebiru and their lamb in tow. But none actually stopped them.

"He is sacred," one man shouted at the Iebiru after leaping into their path. "You may not take him, he is sacred!"

The Iebiru slowed a bit, but did not stop walking. There

was some fear on their faces and their eyes scanned left and right to gauge how close they were to harm.

And yet, when the man who had leaped into their path, said to them, "Where are you going with our god? What are you doing with our god!?" the Iebiru answered, and they did not lie.

"We are taking this lamb to our home. We will guard it there for the next four days. And then, on the afternoon before the night of the full moon, we will slaughter it. And roast it. And eat it. It is to be an offering to The Eternal One, the Most High, the Power of Heaven and Earth."

Everyone started shrieking at them and Kheruef joined in, his face distorted in shock and rage. "Filthy Shasu," he cried. "Dirty Iebiri dogs!"

"Kheruef," I said as I touched his shoulder gently. "Kheruef, this is not going to..."

"I understand Your Honor!" he said to me with new hope in his eyes. "I will slay them with my hammer, I will slay them with my bare hands, you can count on me."

It took me a few seconds to unravel the enormity of his failure to understand what fight I was talking about.

"I would rather die than leave them to their evil worship," he said with tears pooling in his eyes. "You can count on me. I will fight."

I parted my lips to tell him that he had misunderstood completely. I put my hands firmly on his shoulders. I wanted to shake him and make him see that the fight that might save us would not be against the Iebiru, but against the Lords of The Black Land who still resisted sending them to their worship. But he looked at me with such gratitude and stupidity that I gave up.

"Alright, then," I told him. "Go back to the house now. Be ready. I'll call you when you are needed."

~

By the time I reached the Great House it was surrounded by agitated crowds, everyone talking at once in a dozen different opinions.

"Snatch the sacred lambs away from the Iebiru," some said. "Won't we be saved by the gods for our righteous deed?"

"That's madness!" others said. "Let the Iebiru just get on with it, do the sacrifice today, and get out into the Deshret to their worship! Push them out to it if we have to!"

"But that's impossible," some said, "Mohsheh will not leave with his Iebiru until they are sent by Pahroh."

"Then let us beg Pahroh to send them before it is too late," others argued.

"We have already *begged*," some said darkly. "We must make him do it."

"This is treason!" others cried.

"Our war is not against the Throne. It's against the Iebiru. Let them lift one foot to leave, on the second foot we will slay them."

And just to complete the madness there were some who had given up on the debates altogether and were just crying out. They were crying out at the top of their lungs, shouting over the gates that would not admit them and up beyond the walls into where they imagined their Father, The Life of The River, would be seated on his Throne of the Two Kingdoms with the crook and flail crossed upon his chest, listening to their pleas. Surely Pahroh would do something? Surely he would save his children?

It would have been madness of my own to press any further into this crowd. I might stumble into a pocket of men who could take me for one of the lords thwarting their will, whichever will it was.

But what if Okpara really was inside? Or what if someone there could tell me where to find him? I had to gain entry. Another gate, then, maybe one less hemmed in by agitated crowds.

I began the long walk around the Great House, made longer still by the fact that the crowds enlarged the circumference of my path. But I hadn't gone far when I remembered the one entrance that no one ever used if they could avoid it. The one Neferet and I used to call "The Corpse Gate."

With all that had happened over this past year, maybe the long passageway it led to had been cleared of the broken and desiccated Iebiru corpses hung from chains its entire length? After all, why would the Throne want to anger the Power of the Iebiru with evidence of crimes against His children?

I found my way to the place where the gate stood locked and silent, no crowd gathered around it, for it was not meant for the use of Sons of Kehmeht, only as a way to intimidate petitioners of the Iebiru. It was so quiet that I wondered if it even had a guard posted at all. But as I came up to it I saw there were a few bored men on duty there.

I should have known that in these stormy days there would be armed guards at every possible entrance to The Great House, no matter how locked and little-used. Two of them looked at me warily through the brass gate bars while an officer listened to my request to be admitted.

He thought about it for a moment but there wasn't much to think about. I wasn't a mob, I was just a young man, more than likely a "boy" to his mind. But whatever I was, I held a rank he could not aspire to and feared to offend. He had the gate opened for me. Now came the tricky part.

I did not want to go through the passageway that might still be hung with tortured and slain Iebiru dangling from clanking chains by torchlight. So I explained that my destination was not the Throne Room, to which this passage led, but rather to the Chamber of Judgements to see the Lord Harkuhotep, Seal Bearer of the King of Upper and Lower Kehmeht, Unique Friend of Pahroh, Trusted of All His House. I asked that I be shown the way there.

Whatever intrigues and defections were going on between Pahroh and Harkuhotep, they were apparently not known to this officer. He responded to the name and title as I hoped, with complete compliance. He directed one of the guards to lead me through a maze of service corridors, so I avoided that fearsome path of the corpses without having to let anyone know that I feared it.

It was a brisk walk of perhaps six or seven winding minutes, until I found myself before the bronze doors of the Chamber of Judgements. I was quite alone. The corridor fell silent as the footsteps of my escort returning to his post receded into the distance.

There were no guards posted here and no flurry of messengers or scribes going in and out. I wondered if I should knock. I pushed on one of the doors gingerly and let myself in. The place was empty, save for Hemptah, the old scribe who sat alone on a small bench.

"Greetings, Young Mereyamun," he said to me.

"Greetings, Hemptah," I replied. "Where is everyone?"

"Out doing their duties, I imagine," he said. "You know, mobilizing the gift of animals. To the Iebiru. Should we be commanded to make such a gift."

"And the Lord Harkuhotep has left none here to respond to... to new issues that may arise?"

"He left me, didn't he?" Hemptah responded shortly.

I hadn't meant any disrespect, and was relieved when his gentle smile returned to his face. He was just having fun with me.

"There were a good number of scribes and messengers here with me yesterday," he explained. "But some of them became quite morose with no new orders to occupy them. Conversation turned to the deaths that were coming. Some went home to be with their families. Some declared that they would join the Iebiru and live in the way of the New Power. Some went out to join the mobs that were set on fighting. Did you not encounter fighting on your way in here today?"

"I saw crowds outside," I responded. "There wasn't any real fighting."

I wondered, did Hemptah know more than he was revealing about plans for an uprising?

"Well, I did not want to abandon my post," Hemptah went on. "But it is easier for me than for some," he continued. "I am not a firstborn. Are you, Young Mereyamun?"

"Yes," I said, swallowing my words. "Yes, I am."

"Pity, then," Hemptah said. "Unlike me, you must do something."

"I am resolved to do something," I said, hinting as much as I dared to Hemptah that if he knew more than he was revealing about an uprising, I was ready to take my place in it.

"Good then," he said. "Good."

He looked at me a moment, considering something. Then he spoke some more.

"Our Master Harkuhotep left a message for you should you arrive here. He says: 'Go to Ankhuemhesut who has information of great importance to share with you'."

"Ankhuemhesut?" I wondered out loud.

He was the last person I would have expected to be part of an armed conspiracy. For months now his life had been mostly in Gohshen sitting at Mohsheh's feet, learning what he could of The Eternal One. True, Harkuhotep relied on him for his understanding of the Power of the Iebiru. Did this mean that The Eternal One desired an uprising?

"Thank you, Hemptah," I said. "I will go to him."

"Wait, Young Mereyamun," he called to me. "You will not find him at his home. You must be led to the place where he is staying these days."

"Will you lead me then, Hemptah?"

"It is a secret to me too," he said. "But if you will be taken there, you must be at the bottom of the Street of the Potters at exactly noon. The one who will lead you to Ankhuemhesut was there yesterday and will be there today and once more tomorrow, at noon. I do not know his name or his identity. But he will find you there. At noon. This is what Our Master Harkuhotep instructed me to tell you."

～

I left the Great House as I would have on any other day, down the corridors and out into the courtyard that culminated in the gate I usually used. But it was closed tight and I found myself added to a number of officials waiting impatiently to be allowed to leave.

The guards were afraid to open even this small side portal for fear that the stormy crowd would surge in. The officials grumbled and threatened the guards, who had their hands full pushing back the crowd when it pressed close. Arms and legs intruded between bronze bars. All I could think of was that if this went on for an hour, it would be too late to get to the Street of the Potters by noon and meet the mysterious man who would guide me to Ankhuemhesut.

Then, for no reason I could understand, the crowd made a great deal of noise and turned away, all of them running at breakneck speed for the First Gate. Had they opened it to these mobs? Or had the mobs broken through? And what were all these people going to do once inside? Plead with Pahroh, I imagined, to do whatever they thought would save them.

They might beg him to send the Iebiru away. Or they might just as likely beg him to let them slaughter the Iebiru. What mattered to me was that our gate was swung open and I was able to leave.

I didn't know the exact hour, but the sun was still high, assuring me that I would easily make it to the meeting place by noon. So I decided to use the extra time to stop by Okpara's house on the chance that it was there he had been hiding all this time.

I turned the corner and saw what was happening at the First Gate. There was no breach, but some young men, well-dressed and clearly of high-birth, were standing up atop the portico where it met the gate and haranguing the crowd.

"We spoke with him, my brothers," one of them was saying. "Only moments ago we appeared before the Throne. We pleaded for our own lives and for yours, my brothers. But he is adamant. He will not send the Iebiru to their worship. He will be our deaths!"

At this the crowd roared like a wounded animal, and

then cried out "No! No, it will not be! No!" I could not tell if this meant "No, our Father Pahroh would never abandon us so!" or "No, no, we will not let him do this to us!" Both, maybe, depending on which part of the crowd you belonged to. The speaker raised his hands in a request for quiet so he might continue.

"My brothers," he said, "my firstborn brothers and those who stand with us, will you not demand that the great of Kehmeht fight for our lives? For if Pahroh could refuse us, can he refuse our fathers and all who are great in the land? If all the lords and honorable men of The Black Land were to come before Pahroh would he refuse them? Could he? Let our fathers answer for this! Let them come before the Throne this day!"

A great roar went up from the crowd. The men on the portico leapt down into it, were caught and hoisted up onto shoulders. The crowd surged, an army with its commanders riding upon its backs, gone to force fathers to act on behalf of the sons.

I had to skip out of the way and back around the corner a bit. It was either that or be carried away in this surge of desperate and angry young men. I felt their heat. I shared it even. But I could not make sense of it.

Did they literally mean that they were going to force their own fathers to pressure Pahroh? Surely not all of them had fathers who were in a position to do that, at least not before the Throne. I supposed that for the low-born, just rioting in the streets was a form of petition.

But the fathers, didn't it seem likely that at least some of them, perhaps quite a few, were firstborn themselves? So why wouldn't they protest Pahroh's intransigence? Or maybe the mob meant "Fathers" in the broader sense of great men, men of influence and stature in Kehmeht?

I wondered for a moment if they would march on my house to recruit Hesera for their cause? Surely they knew that the sorcerers were in disfavor with the Throne? No, it would be very wealthy men. Or more powerful men. Harkuhotep, perhaps. Would he dismiss them? Would he rally to their cause?

There was no time to think about this now, not if I was going to check at Okpara's house and still make it to the noon meeting with the one who was to guide me to Ankhuemhesut. I ran a bit, just to make good time. I was at Okpara's gate before I was even winded.

I was admitted to their great room, and met by Herit with a child of about four years underfoot. He looked very much like Okpara, smiling shyly at me from the safety of having one arm anchored around his mother's leg.

"Can you tell me, Herit," I asked, "where I might find Okpara today?"

"I cannot," she answered. "Not because I do not wish to, Mereyamun. My husband trusts you completely. I just don't know. He has been moving around a great deal."

"You know what he is doing, then?" I asked.

"Yes," she said quietly. "Not all the details, but yes."

"I want to help him," I said. "I want to help him in any way I can."

"I do not doubt it," she said. "If he makes contact with me, I will tell him you were here. But I am sure he will find you, and, if not, there is his mother's procession. From the House of the Dead. Tomorrow."

"Of course," I said.

"One other thing, Mereyamun, if you have a minute?"

"Yes?"

"It's just that I don't know who else to ask," she said. "I mean among those who know about these things…"

I nodded for her to continue.

"Well, it's this: If for some reason everything my husband is trying to do, what you're both trying to do, if for some reason it should…fail," she said and brought her voice down to half its volume.

"If nothing changes with the Throne and we come to the night…five nights from now?" she gestured with her head a bit at the child clinging to her, taking care that he should not guess at any meaning, even from her tone.

"Yes, five nights from now," I offered so that she would know I understood.

"If a child of our people, a firstborn child, were put to sleep that night with a child of the Iebiru… in the home of the Iebiri child, in the same bed…would that…could that save him? Would that make him safe?"

"I don't know," I had to admit.

"Because I know several Iebiri women who would do that for me…for us…" she trailed off, her eyes flicking back and forth across my face searching out any sign of hope.

"I'm on my way now to see Ankhuemhesut," I said. She shook her head, the name meaning nothing to her.

"He is a royal sorcerer," I explained. "Or was, until recently. He understands more about what Mohsheh teaches than anyone I know. Your father-in-law relies on him above all others for these things. I will ask him."

It wasn't the answer she wanted. But it was not the end of all hope. She thanked me gratefully, as if I had just saved her firstborn son. Loaded now with the added burden of her desperate question, I left for the Street of the Potters.

～

I took a short cut through the Old Market, since it ran southwards and I could avoid the streets where mobs were gathering. Ordinarily the Old Market would be the most likely place for a mob to coalesce out of the many who crowded it. But not today.

There was no food to buy there. The locusts finished whatever the Hailstorm left of the new crops, and the panicked populace emptied the stalls of whatever was in stock. The wealthy were eating what they hoarded and everyone else was getting by on whatever they could improvise, glean, or steal. So the market was nearly abandoned.

It was different on the Street of the Potters because there the craftsmen and their families lived above or behind the workshops. Like everyone else in The City this day, they were out of those homes and in the street, angry, frustrated, despairing, conniving, and, underneath it all, frightened. Death was coming.

Death was just five nights away, you could hear its footsteps. And no one could do a thing to stop it. So they fought with one another.

I saw two men locked in a shouting match when one suddenly lunged at the other and they both went down into the dust. A crowd gathered shouting for this one or that one to kill the other, to finish him.

A man realized that the one right next to him was shouting for the wrong combatant and cuffed him hard on the ear. The cuffed man reeled in pain, but regained his balance and sent a fist into the face of the one who cuffed him. Teeth and blood splattered, as if this was the agreed-upon signal for everyone to start punching, kicking, choking everyone else.

Some picked up tools or thick pieces of wood the potters burned for charcoal in their kilns. These fell and rose and fell again, until they tipped red with blood. I ran, having no question that in a few seconds someone would notice me and decide I was an enemy of Kehmeht too.

I ran until I had put most of the street behind me, then weaved through several side alleys just to be sure I was no one's target. I slowed to a walk to catch my breath and circled back to the bottom of the street, the appointed meeting place. I was sweating in the near-noonday sun. It was almost time. But I was there.

I stood back, up against a building, partly to enjoy the cool of its slim shadow, partly to look like I belonged there. I listened to the sounds of the fighting up at the far end of the street and hoped it would not spill down this way as I waited for my guide to find me. But there was no guide.

I saw a beggar go by, I watched three children pass him on their way. I saw several Iebiru along the side street, which was likely enough since so many of them lived in the southwest district whose boundary extended to where I was waiting. I saw a pack of dogs trot by, competing these days with people for scraps of anything you could eat. A man with a nasty bruise on half his face went by, a refugee from the fighting up the street, probably. But no guide.

I checked the sun overhead and I was certain that it had already passed its high point. I wondered what had gone wrong? I wondered how long I should wait. It was by Harkuhotep's word that I was here, and when Harkuhotep made a plan, the pieces fitted together like the pins in the tumbler of a lock on a chamber in the treasury of the Great House. But then, where was my guide?

"Walk after me, Mereyamun," a woman's voice said. She was Iebiri and never broke her stride or even turned to look at me as she passed. But she spoke those words, I was certain. So I did as she said.

She walked briskly for an Iebiri woman, given the length of her wool garment. I kept a good twenty paces behind her and when she turned corners I feared I would not find her again. But she was always there, waiting just beyond each twist in the alley. Soon we were well inside the southwest district.

I heard both the tongue of the Black Land and the speech of the Iebiru from within the mudbrick houses packed so closely together in the narrow alleys. And it occurred to me that this woman I was following had spoken her few words in our language flawlessly, with no trace of an accent. She was no Iebiri woman. The sound of her words betrayed her as a daughter of Kehmeht.

"Do you not know me, Mereyamun?" she said as she turned for me to catch up. "I am Khenut. Ankhuemhesut's wife."

I did recognize her, now that I saw her face. And I realized that this was no disguise. Ankhuemhesut was looking every bit an Iebiri man these last few months, it was likely that his wife was just as smitten with the Power of the Iebiru and also took on their ways. But did that include leaving their home in the finest part of The City to live here among them in these narrow alleys? Even the Iebiru didn't live in this rough part of The City by choice. No one did.

A few more twists and turns and we entered a house of no particular distinction. It was small, mudbrick as its neighbors, bathed in the cooking smells of the poorest Sons of Kehmeht intermingled with those of the Iebiru who crowded among them.

It took a moment for my eyes, narrowed by the

noontime sun, to broaden in the cool darkness of the place. Out of that darkness a rough table emerged and some stools and a stone oven and a clay stove and storage jars and beds, all in the single room. And in one of the beds was Ankhuemhesut, sitting up with his back against the wall.

"You found him, Khenut!" he said. "Thank you."

"It wasn't difficult," she said. "He was the only one not brawling."

"Thank you for coming, Mereyamun," he said. "It's a relief to me."

"You are ill?"

"Not ill, no," he said, and grimaced a little. He certainly looked like he was in pain, though cheerful enough.

"It is the third day after my circumcision," he said. "They say the third day is the most painful. It gets better after that."

"You cut off your own foreskin?!"

"No, I couldn't rely on myself. An elder of the Iebiri did it for me. He lives not far from here. He was very fast, it wasn't bad at all. He dressed the wound nicely, too. As you once dressed another wound, on my arm, remember? I still think you could be a skilled physician, Mereyamun. You have a feel for it."

I was horrified. Why did he do this to himself? Was there no limit to his strange desire to be Iebiri? I tried to conceal my horror with conversation.

"But the Iebiru themselves no longer do this thing, Ankhuemhesut," I said evenly. "Not for a hundred years, now."

"The nation of Leyvie never stopped, they still circumcise on the child's eighth day if he's healthy. But you're right, most of the Iebiru haven't done it for generations. They will now, though."

"Why?"

"Because no one may eat of the sacrifice this coming night of the full moon unless they have removed their foreskins. Mohsheh is teaching this."

This was strange beyond understanding. Why? What did it matter? And what did it mean for all those who thought to join the Iebiru in their worship?

"You mean Harkuhotep and Setka and Inyotef and every other man who is going to the worship will do this?"

"They'll have to. There is no other way."

"What about all the Iebiru who are not circumcised? Sons of the Black Land have to do this and they don't?"

"No, they must do it too. And they will, Mereyamun, you'll see. Many are reluctant right now, but in four days they all will. Some may wait until the last moment, but by sundown four days from now, they will be as their great grandfathers were. As the Leyvie are. As I am now."

"Harkuhotep never said anything about this to me," I said. "Neither did Inyotef. Or Setka."

"But they will do this. Not one of them is willing to be left out of the sacrifice. It is why Inyotef left early for Gohshen, to get it done and see to arrangements for the others. Neferet especially is anxious for her little Neferhebef to be done as soon as possible."

When I was told that Harkuhotep wished me to meet Ankhuemhesut in a secret place I imagined it was about the Uprising. I expected to find him surrounded by armed men, veteran fighters every one of them, waiting upon his instructions about where to storm the Great House, who to seize, and who to slay.

Instead I found him wounded by the removal of his own foreskin, telling me that all the friends I had were doing the same. All to be with the Iebiru four nights from now at the offering of a lamb to the Eternal One. I wanted to laugh, and not from happiness.

I never thought that joining the Iebiru would be a way for most firstborns to save themselves. There were too many barriers to belief, too many turns of the heart that had to be made. But now that I heard all this, I wondered that *anyone* would do it. I let myself collapse onto one of the stools. Was it for this that Harkuhotep sent me here?

"Harkuhotep said that you had information of great importance to share with me. Is this it?"

"There is more," Ankhuemhesut said. "A matter of lore and history that not many know. I heard of it from the Leyvie in Gohshen. I wondered if there was any record in our own annals. I searched the archives of several sorcerers who preserve knowledge that is not generally let out of their keeping. And I found scrolls and scraps of scrolls not known to you or even to Harkuhotep. When I told him what I discovered he was profoundly moved."

"And he wants you to tell me this? This thing that you learned?"

"Yes."

"Why?"

"I imagine because he loves you, Mereyamun. In his way."

"Tell me, then."

"It goes back to the days of the Great Hunger. Everything that was done in those days was at the sole command of Yoseyf the Iebiri. He built the granaries. He laid up food for the famine and seeds for the recovery. He pressed men into service and released them at will. This much you know, I think."

"Yes." There was nothing new to me in this.

"But are you aware that he also moved populations all

over the Black Land? Entire villages were uprooted, whole districts relocated, city dwellers to villages, villagers to cities, southerners to the north and northerners to the south."

I was not aware of this curious detail. But who cared? In ordinary days, histories like this interested me. But these were no ordinary days, why was Ankhuemhesut recounting this now?

"Consider yourself, Mereyamun. You are of the Upper Kingdom aren't you?"

"Yes."

"But do you look like a man of the Upper Kingdom? Aren't they typically men of broad noses and thick lips with dark skin and usually of some height? Like Setka? You have the height. But the tone of your skin, the shape of your features, aren't they more of the Lower Kingdom?"

"Not everyone in the Upper Kingdom has features like Setka," I said.

"Not anymore, no. Because two centuries ago Yoseyf shuffled populations. I have no doubt that your grandfather's grandfather was of the Lower Kingdom and was moved to the Upper."

"So? You just said Yoseyf moved people around. What does it matter?"

"It matters because of *why* he did it."

"He surely did it to put people where they were needed most," I replied. "For the building. And for the sowing and the harvests to save the Two Kingdoms."

"That was the reason given out. But he had another, secret, purpose."

"Which was?"

"Yoseyf was not only a reader of dreams," Ankhuemhesut said. "He was also a reader of souls. He could look into a person's face and know his ka, where it was from, to what other souls it was related, where it was meant to fulfill its destiny. That's why he sat and personally judged every request from every villager of the Black Land. That's why he interrogated each and every purchaser who came from afar. He would look into their faces and learn the journey of their souls, the lives it had lived, and what it was meant to do next."

This was crazy talk.

"Souls don't live again in this world," I protested. "Those who find favor in the eyes of Wsir live in Sekhet-Aaru. They delight in the Field of Reeds and walk among gods forever."

My voice trailed off and this childish recitation expired on my lips. Did I know more than Ankhuemhesut about such matters? And what I was reciting, did either of us believe it anymore?

"So I was taught, too," Ankhuemhesut said. "So were we all. But we know better now, don't we? Maybe what we were taught about Sekhet-Aaru is a description of some place a soul might go, under some circumstances, sometimes. But what I am telling you now I heard from the Leyvie, who have received it from Mohsheh. And all this past year, from the day Mohsheh returned to the Black Land, has his word ever failed?"

"So Yoseyf could see a person's soul and know what it was meant to do," I conceded. "Fine. So because of this he moved them from the Lower Kingdom to the Upper? That's the deep secret he saw in a soul? That it needed to live in a different town?"

"Yoseyf saw that there were souls among us who shared a common ancestor, a common father, with the Iebiru. He saw that those who possessed these souls were, in fact, distant and estranged brothers of the Iebiru, though they had no awareness of this. He knew a day would come when those souls would long to be with their Iebiri ka-brothers.

"And he understood that when that day came and the Iebiru would be redeemed and go off to the worship of the Eternal One, these souls would want to go too. So Yoseyf identified them, one by one. It was just as the master of a garden chooses cuttings that share a trait and sets them aside in their own plant-bed to be with others who are like them."

"He moved people around because of their souls?"

"Yes, though no one could guess it. And we, Mereyamun, have within us sparks of those very souls. You, myself and Khenut, Harkuhotep, Neferet and Setka, Inyotef and Adjedaa, we, and all those who feel as we do, we all somehow received parts of those souls.

"That is why we long to go out to the worship. And that is why, in your heart, you long to come too. For you surely are descended from those who Yoseyf set aside in the Upper Kingdom, if only to keep them a little more distanced from the cruelty and violence to the Iebiru who, in the end, we would come to know as our brothers."

"What about Okpara, then? How can his father and sister possess such a soul and he not?"

"It is not a matter of kinship. A brother and sister may share the same blood but possess very different souls," Ankhuemhesut said with some confidence. "Or it may be that Okpara's soul does share in this, but he rejects these feelings as unworthy. Or perhaps he wrestles with it, even now, not sure of what to do. As you do, Mereyamun."

Khenut guided me through the twisting branching alleys of the Southwest District until I was at the Street of The Potters and could find my own way. As we went she pointed out oddities that might help me remember the way back should I seek to come to them again.

A bricked-up window here, a crack in the face of a mudbrick wall there, a spot where the alley was eroded from sewage and someone bridged the flow with a splintered board and a few flat stones. She spoke of these landmarks and nothing else, determined that the way back be made memorable to me.

"In case you want to join us," she said. "Before nightfall, this coming Full Moon."

"Say I do decide to go out to the worship in the Red Land," I said. "Why would I join you here? We would have to get to Goshen anyhow, wouldn't we? That's where the journey to the worship will begin. Harkuhotep thinks so. Inyotef does too."

"It's true, the journey will begin from there."

"Then why are you and Ankhuemhesut still here in The City? And if here, why have you forsaken your home for a poor room in the Southwest District?"

"Because before we go out to the worship, we must join the Iebiru to eat of the offering on the night of the Full Moon."

"You could join them in Gohshen, that's where most of them are."

"Yes, we could," she conceded.

We walked in silence for a few steps while she considered sharing what she had not yet said. She stopped, and did.

"You see, it is said that Mohsheh will leave Gohshen and come here, to the Southwest District where many Iebiru live. To eat of his own offering, here. If he does, Ankhuemhesut and I hope to see him. And maybe he will teach or speak, and we will be able to hear him."

"But why would he come here? Why would he not make his offering in his own village, in Gohshen, among his own nation?"

"Because The Eternal One has decreed that four nights from now a great cry will go up from every household in the Two Kingdoms. And Pahroh will come down from his Throne and go out into the screams of the night desperately seeking Mohsheh. And when he finds him he will bow to him, Merey, and say to him: 'Go! You and all your People. Leave! Go to your worship.' And Mohsheh will do nothing that might delay that moment."

I looked at her, still not getting the sense of this.

"Mohsheh," she explained, "wants to be where Pahroh can find him."

∾

It was the time of the year in which the hours of daylight and of darkness are nearly equal, so there was no chance of using night to slip past the mobs gathered on every corner. Some were declaiming loudly that they would stop the Iebiru from leaving. If the life of a single firstborn of Kehmeht was taken, they blustered, "they would slay the Iebiru, every one!" Had they learned nothing this past year?

Other crowds were declaring that they would march on the Great House and remove the traitors who were keeping our Father Pahroh from sending the Iebiru to their worship.

These crowds interested me more, for it could be that there were among them men who were more than just talk. Men who could be moved to action if the right spark were lit. And I believed that Okpara meant to ignite that spark. And I had hope that Harkuhotep might help.

But I learned quickly to avoid those crowds because they would invariably take me for one of their lordly enemies. I had some narrow escapes. These cleared my head and made me determined to find Okpara as soon as possible. I had no more leads left for this day, but surely I would find him tomorrow at the procession for his mother out of the Houses of the Dead, just as Herit had said.

Herit! She trusted me with the most desperate question of her life, and I had let it slip my mind! But I knew very well what Ankhuemhesut would have answered. I knew it when Herit asked it. But I didn't have the heart to tell her.

We Children of the Black Land, with our thousand gods governing a thousand facets of the world, we were used to maneuvering around their contradictory wills. If you didn't like what one god decreed, you could always steer things into the lap of another. If a vengeful god sought the life of your child, you could appeal to the protection of a kindly one. Throw in a bribe to the first god, just to insure the bargain, and that would be that.

But if the Power of the Iebiru made a decree, where could you go for help? There is no other Power, Mohsheh taught. The only place to go for mercy was to Him. But could I have explained that to Herit?

"Herit," I might have said, "you cannot fool the Power with a trick. Putting your firstborn child into a bed with a child of the Iebiru will not foil his decree."

"Then I am lost," she would have said, choked with tears.

"No," I would have said. "There is still a way."

"Tell me, Mereyamun," she would have pleaded. "Anything."

"What you must do," I would have to have said, "is find a place where you are alone and speak to the Power. Tell Him what you fear. Admit to Him that you and all our People have done great evil. You must tell him that you are pained over the Iebiri babies who were drowned in The River, and that you weep over the ones buried alive in the walls of Pi-Thohm and Rahmessu. You must tell him that you are sorry for your part in making the lives of the Iebiru so bitter, for breaking their bodies, and breaking their hearts."

"Then you must run to one of the Elders of the Iebiru, the disciples of Mohsheh or, better, to Mohsheh himself. You must tell him that you realize now how everything you lived was a lie and that you want to leave it all behind. You must tell him that you want to join the Iebiru and go out to the worship in the Red Land and follow only the ways of The Eternal One all the days of your life."

"Then you must immerse yourself in a natural spring or in The River and emerge a new person, perhaps with a new name. And your little sons must immerse too, and you must ask Mohsheh or one of the Elders to take a sharp blade and remove their foreskins. And all this you must do with complete sincerity, for The Eternal knows what's in your heart. And you must do it before the new moon. You have four days."

What would Herit have done then? Laughed nervously in my face? Wondered at my cruelty to tell jokes at the time of her desperation? Fled from me, as one does from a crazy man? Rebuked me for my betrayal of all that is revered in

Kehmeht? The only certainty is what she could not have said.

"Yes," she could not have said. "Yes, this is true, I will do as you describe. And with a full heart."

I could not know how many souls clothed in the bodies of Children of Kehmeht were as Ankhuemhesut told, destined to find their way to the Iebiru and join them. The ones I knew, whether high-born as Neferet or as humble as Adjedaa, all had one thing in common. Their minds were restless and their hearts were open, and they had all spent this last tumultuous year wondering and changing.

I was like them in that way, I think. Were I to look in a mirror of the most burnished copper I would not be able to find the boy I was just twelve months ago.

But I did not emerge at the end of this year like the others. They wanted only their new "King," the Eternal One that no eye had ever seen. Their greatest hope was to be there in the Red Land when, for the first time since the world began, The Eternal One would show Himself to the Children of Men. Was this not enticing? Was this not something I wanted too? It was. But it came at a price I could not pay.

How could I look in that mirror if I abandoned my People to the misery of a death in every home? From Herit, for all her high birth, to the mob brawling on the Street of the Potters, was there one in a hundred who could understand what my friends were doing? And could any possibly conceive of joining them?

"Kill all the Iebiru!" some were saying.

"Send them on their pilgrimage with flutes and song!" others countered.

These were the only two paths now.

"Can you not see how their Power favors them?" the Send-Them partisans argued. "Hasn't He protected them this past year? While we suffered blow after blow? Doesn't that tell you we dare not touch a hair on their heads?"

"No!" the Slay-Them-All crowd would say. "Their Power abandoned them to servitude, torture, and death these last eighty-six years! Their Power is as disgusted by them as we are. And, if not disgusted, completely indifferent. Surely we could kill them all and it would be no different to Him than stamping out insects." So Hesera argued months ago, and he was counted among the Wise.

In this way my thoughts turned to Hesera even as I encountered him standing, rather oddly, outside the threshold of our house.

"I knew you would be coming," he said. "I have something to tell you. I have found a way to avoid being slain with the firstborn."

"What?"

"Have you grown even more stupid than the last time we spoke?"

"Less patient, maybe."

"Less patient *is* more stupid, Young Vagabond. But I will ignore your insolence and tell you how I will avoid the death of the firstborn on the night of the Full Moon."

"How?"

"Oh, that got your interest, did it?" he chuckled. Then he waited.

"Yes," I sighed. "You have won my interest."

"Good! Well first I must declare that I still believe Bilahm will return in time to wipe out the Iebiru and rid us of the problem. He is powerful, Young Vagabond. You never understood how powerful he is. His teachings are from the Fallen Ones, learned from them in the East in the Mountains of Darkness. It is to them Bilahm has gone to learn the secrets he needs to choke the life out of every man, woman, and runt of the Iebiru. And all in the blink of an eye, too."

He paused here again, eyeing me to see if I fully appreciated the wisdom he was imparting. All I could think was how wrong I was when I thought, just a few days earlier, that his madness had abated.

"I see that it beggars your weak mind," he said. "Perhaps you will see it happen, and then you will believe me."

"Perhaps," I offered, just to get past this.

"But should Bilahm fail to return by the New Moon," Hesera went on, "I have a way to avoid being slain with the firstborn. I will set my water-clock at noon tomorrow, just to be certain that it is precise. And I will recheck it at each of the three noontimes we have left after that. Thus I will be quite certain when midnight of the New Moon is about to arrive, for that is the hour that the Slaying is supposed to begin."

He seemed so satisfied with this detail that he stopped his explanation of just what he was going to do to save himself.

"So?" I encouraged him. "You will know when midnight is about to arrive... and?"

"And the sorcery of Mohsheh and the curse of the Iebiri Power will never touch me. I will already be dead."

"What?"

"I will not die at the hand of an Iebiri sorcerer," he said. "I will not die at the hand of some Shasu god."

I just blinked.

"I have already prepared two potions," he elaborated. "One a solution of metals that is unpleasant to the bowels but never fails. That's just a precaution and I don't expect to suffer from it at all because first I will down a tincture of venom from a brown viper of The River grass. Death comes in thirty breaths."

CHAPTER 8
THE SECOND WEEK OF IPT-ḤMT, THE THIRD MONTH OF SHEMU, SEASON OF THE RIVER RUNNING LOW

SEVENTY-FIRST OF THE SEVENTY-FIVE DAYS

S unrise completed the tally of seventy days since The Princess Esemkhebe Ta-Sherit was brought with sorrow into the Houses of the Dead. Who could forget how the entire City came out to weep for her that day?

Pahroh joined the mourners then, as did citizens from every layer of The City. For she was wounded in the same attack as we were, in the Curse of the Soot, which every son and daughter of The Two Kingdoms suffered in their own flesh.

But we survived and she did not, though she was the beauty of Kehmeht itself. This haunted us. So we poured out of our homes that day and we mourned for her, as we mourned for our own lives that would never be whole again.

Now, on this morning, The Princess Esemkhebe Ta-Sherit left the Houses of the Dead with nothing like the spontaneous mass escort that had brought her there. A few priests of high rank proceeded her coffin. One was dressed as the jackal-headed god Anubis to perform the rituals at the entombment. Another read from a scroll of incantations as he walked. His voice was high-pitched and beautiful and could be heard above the wails of the mourning women. These were professionals, the best in The City. Their blue eye makeup ran down their faces in streams of tears as they wept and tore at the hearts of those who were near the procession as it passed.

But where were the great crowds of citizens today? There were so few joined to the procession that I was reluctant to step in among them, a handful of the poor and the lost. They were neither presentable nor numerous enough to serve as cover for me. For I was not there to mourn. I was there to find Okpara and do what I could to overthrow the counselors to The Throne and save Kehmeht.

Okpara was not to be found, but that didn't worry me. He would surely join the funeral where the family of mourners usually joined, at the home of the deceased. This was always the first station of the procession from the Houses of the Dead to the Tombs.

But the "home" of the deceased in this case was The Great House itself. And The Great House, on this morning, was hemmed in by competing mobs calling, alternately, for "Death to the Iebiru!" or "Death to the Wicked Counselors!" I didn't see how the Royal Guards could risk opening any of the gates to let mourners out to join the procession. But then, who was in there who would want to join?

Harkuhotep, if anywhere in The City, was surely at Neferet's house, and she already said she would not join the funeral. Okpara might have been anywhere, but surely not inside the Great House which, after all, was going to be the fortress he would have to storm with armed men. And neither Pahroh nor any of his counselors who had honored

The Princess Esemkhebe Ta-Sherit when she was first taken out to the Houses of the Dead, would dare show themselves to the swollen mobs practically besieging the place.

So the procession skirted the edge of the crowds, making its orbit of the Great House take some time. But this was well-suited to Okpara's appearance which seemed to come out of nowhere.

He slipped into the procession at his proper place, just in front of the mourning women directly behind the casket. He was dressed in blue, as is proper and expected. And some of his tunic was rent and he wore no kohl around his eyes. He was alone among the close-blood relatives of the deceased. But anyone who cared to really look could see, he was not really alone. Far from it.

I counted about a dozen men who seemed to flank him, unevenly, as if they were simple citizens joining the procession. But they were all of a kind, strong men, grim and unaffected by the mourning.

They looked ahead steadily but, occasionally, swept a glance over the crowds of onlookers and the mobs besieging the Great House. If anyone cared to look closely enough, they would notice lumps under their tunics: knives or short swords. And once you read them for what they were, you could see many more of them at the rear of the procession, perhaps a hundred or so. So that's what Okpara had been doing. Assembling an army.

I wondered how the ones flanking Okpara would react if I tried to slide into the procession to get near him. But Okpara, though his head was drooped in the way of mourners, noticed me, and quietly sent one of his bodyguards to bring me in. I fell in beside him.

"Thank you for coming, Mereyamun" he said as we went.

"May your loved one find favor in the eyes of Wsir and delight in Sekhet-Aaru."

Okpara gave me one quick nod, and with that we ended the formalities of the funeral and moved on to the business at hand.

"Have you seen my father?"

"Neferet told me he was undecided about coming," I said. "But that was two days ago."

"He will not come. Go to Neferet's house, Merey, and find him for me there. Tell him that I have fighters, more than the ones you see here now. But we need his name. We need his authority."

"But you can persuade him better than me, you're his son!"

"And he is my father and that still runs deep, and he may, in the end, persuade *me*. No Merey, you go to him. Speak in my name. From this point on I will not leave the company of my fighters. Tell him he can find me at home tomorrow. But the next day, or the day after that we will move, with or without him. Tell him that."

It should have been just minutes to Neferet and Setka's house, but it took the better part of an hour. There were too many crowds and they were volatile, surging up one avenue and back down another for what exact purpose I could only guess. Whenever I saw one coming, I did a quick turn and got out at the nearest cross-street.

Some of these ended without exits and I had no choice but to wait in the shadows until the avenue seemed tranquil again. Then I would venture back out on my way until more unrest drove me into another alley.

In one of these I heard the bleating of lambs. No one in The City raised lambs, except perhaps sacred ones in the precincts of a temple to Khnum-Khufwy. But the hovel producing these sounds was no temple. It was a back-alley living quarter for several families who had to be Iebiru. Who else would have lambs in their houses? They might as well have hung out a banner emblazoned with the words "We Are Iebiri."

Every man in the blustering mobs proclaiming "Death to the Iebiru!" could surely find Iebiru like these living among us. But no one dared touch them.

This, more than anything, proved to me that either we compel The Throne to bend to the Power of the Iebiru, or we surrender to the death that was three days off. There were no other choices. So I doubled my speed and halved my worries about the mobs and made my way to Neferet's home in search of Harkuhotep.

Once again I found restless throngs in the street facing the house, still hoping that the great Harkuhotep would emerge with news and a plan that would save them. But they kept a respectful distance from the entrance now. It was flanked by soldiers, fully armored with helmets, lances and shields. My heart leapt at the sight, for what would Harkuhotep be doing with regular troops here in The City if he did not mean to use them in an uprising?

The people in the street shouted questions at me as I strode up to the door. It was opened by a soldier and closed quickly behind me once I was admitted. Setka's servant brought me into the great room. There I found Setka sitting not with his father-in-law, but with his father, Djedhor Hordedef, General of the Army of the Upper Kingdom. Gone to fat and decline, but still, General of the Army. He gave me a nod.

"You went to the funeral, Merey?" Setka asked, gesturing for me to take the seat across from his father.

"I did," I said.

"Okpara sent me here to see if I could find your father-in-law."

"He has gone from The City," Djedhor Hordedef volunteered flatly, without any real hint of opinion if this was a good thing or not. "We have no Vizier among us today."

"My father-in-law took Neferet and the baby and set out for Gohshen this morning," Setka added. "They will meet Inyotef and Adjedaa there."

My face must have questioned what made Setka stay behind, because Djedhor Hordedef leveled an answer at me.

"My son delays his own departure because he wants to try, one more time, to persuade me," he said.

This was awkward. I gave a half nod just to acknowledge that I had been spoken to. But if Djedhor Hordedef felt that I should excuse myself from a private conversation, he certainly didn't show it.

"But I do not wish to be persuaded," he went on. "I am of no faction in the Court. I am of no opinion. Not even about this new worship in the Red Land. So there is nothing about which I can be persuaded. Or need to be."

Was Djedhor Hordedef himself a firstborn? If so, he was offering a powerful display of equanimity in the face of certain death.

"Mereyamun is a scribe," Setka said at that point, as if this clumsy change of subject was just small talk at a boring party.

"Ah, then you must be thinking about the ports," he said.

I wasn't thinking about ports. But I struggled to look at least a little this side of stupid.

"The ports in the Crescent," Djedhor Hordedef explained. "They bring us tin, tar, olive oil, wine. They allow us to send wheat and barley to foreign markets across the Great Green, though this has been sadly reversed since the hail and the locusts.

"The Sea Kings covet those ports. They lurk in their ships out where the Great Green turns wine-dark and dream of taking them from us and growing rich on taxes and control of our sea trade."

I nodded politely at the lesson, though I had no idea why he was offering it.

"Well, in three days every home in Kehmeht will suffer a death. Every soldier who survives, every officer who remains will feel the pain of a brother or sister or father or mother or son or daughter struck dead. Would that not be the perfect moment for the Sea Kings to invade our Crescent?"

It would.

"Then, say the Raiders out in the western Deshret hear of it, as surely they must. Wouldn't they strike fast and hard at the rich oases they have wished to take from us for many long years? Would we be able to mobilize men and rush them both north to the Crescent and west to the desert towns to counter those attacks?"

It would be difficult.

"And wouldn't the Lords of the South..." Djedhor Hordedef turned to Setka, "you've fought them many times. You know they look upon our Upper Kingdom as a wolf does a plump sheep. Won't they tear at Kehmeht from the south as it is bleeding and prostrate from the ravages of the north and west?"

So this was what a General of the Army thinks about when he is about to die. Strategic threats. And nothing for the preservation of his own life.

"But do you know what makes this unique and awful without precedent?"

It already sounded unique and awful enough for me, but Djedhor Hordedef meant to answer that question of his own asking.

"A soldier always enters a battle with some fear, knowing he may die," he went on. "But he finds courage in the simple fact that perhaps, with luck, or skill, or the favor of his gods, he will live.

"But imagine, if you can, what would happen if before a battle, the soldiers who were destined to die in it were informed of their destiny? Each one. By name. With no room for doubt. And with all those destined to survive knowing who was to die. Can you imagine what would result?"

"Those who knew they were to die would fight fearlessly," Setka asserted. "They would rejoice in the certainty and fight with abandon. They would be terrible and unstoppable!"

"Maybe some," Djedhor Hordedef said with a rueful smile. "Maybe the very few who have hearts like yours, my son. But most would abandon the fight to spend their last hours in whatever, to each of them, mattered most. A few might join the line of battle but in despair that would make them the first to fall —though not before infecting those destined to survive with broken spirits. It would be no army at all."

We sat in silence for a few moments digesting this.

"Well this is what Mohsheh or his Power will bring upon us in three days' time, isn't it? A battle that cannot be won. It can only be faced. No one has an answer for it. So they run around in the streets brawling. Or they sit at home crying. It makes no difference. What is coming at the Full Moon is already decided. Those who will die already know who they are. And everyone else does too."

"But why must this be?" I protested. "Why can't men of courage rise up before it's too late? Why can't we force the Throne to send the Iebiru to their worship?"

There was a flicker of fire in Djedhor Hordedef's hooded eyes, and I understood that, beneath the rolls of fat on his no longer warrior body, he would still be a terrible opponent in a fight.

"It must be," he said leveling those eyes at mine, "because there are still men in Kehmeht who will fight to the death before allowing anyone to raise a hand against Our Father Pahroh. And we are men who know how to die. And how to kill."

"My Father..." Setka started deferentially, but faltered when Djedhor Hordedef raised a palm to stop him, turning again towards me.

"Mereyamun, do not believe that I think it dishonorable to go out to this new worship. Setka is going and he is the bravest young man I know. You have heard how he saved my life in fierce battle with the Lords of the South?"

"I have," I replied.

"He declines to join me this time because he wants to follow the new god. I have no quarrel with that. It is the choice of a brave and honorable young man. And it is no treason against The Throne."

"Standing up against the Court and freeing Our Father

Pahroh to send the Iebiru to their worship is no treason either," I said.

"Oh but it is. Until such time as Our Father Pahroh asks for such a thing, it most certainly is. Why spill your blood for such evil?"

"I do not intend to spill my blood," I protested. "I intend to save Kehmeht."

"But you will spill your blood. Or to be more precise, I will. I or one of my men. And I would regret that."

He watched me for a moment to see if the threat sunk in, then went on.

"Setka is going to spill a little bit of his own blood too, you know. He is going to cut off his foreskin, like the Leyvie. In order to join the Iebiru in their offering. If you want to spill your blood, Mereyamun, why don't you go with Setka and do as he does?"

"I will be leaving for Gohshen at first light, day after tomorrow," Setka said to me. "Meet me here, if you will come. Bring Okpara if you can persuade him. With his wife and his little ones. This is our hope. There's still time."

~

"Helping yourself to my stores again, Young Vagabond?"

Hesera found me seated alone in the kitchen working at a dried-out chunk of date and barley cake I found abandoned on the table, my first food of the day. My mouth was full so I just grunted something Hesera could take as an affirmation, or as an apology, if he preferred.

"But why admit to the lesser crime, eh?" he continued.

My eyebrows were enough to say I had no idea what he

was talking about, though even stale cake was an expensive luxury now after the hailstorm took the barley and the locusts took the spelt.

"What insolence! I know what you have been up to, Young Beggar. Treason, is it now? Treachery? Rebellion? Against the Throne of the Two Kingdoms?"

At this I swallowed hard, if only to avoid choking on what was in my mouth and on what had popped out of his. Did Hesera really know where I had been these days and with whom I had spoken? Did he really have that much sorcery left in him?

"You are amazed. Ha! Your wonder is more insolent than your lies. You think I am no longer among the Wise?"

I had never worked out how my Uncle's madness could coexist with his wisdom. But with all Kehmeht now thrown into madness, why not? While I thought on this, Hesera plunged ahead.

"There was little need for my farsight to know this, once you ensnared the simple heart of our good man in your evil plans. Don't look at me like a stunned calf, I am not fooled by it. I mean poor Kheruef, as you well know."

"Kheruef?!" I sputtered in genuine surprise. "Kheruef thinks I want to kill Iebiru, not send them out to their worship! He understands nothing of what we mean to do. He is too dull for us to make use of him!"

"Kheruef is no student of the Wise as you were...once," Hesera retorted. "But his failure to understand is not due to his simplicity but to his good heart. He cannot imagine raising a hand against the Throne!"

"It is not against the Throne that we will act," I argued, losing whatever patience I had left about this distinction. "It is against the Court. It is to *save* the Throne."

"The Throne does not wish to be saved!" Hesera hissed

at me. "Dolt that you have become! Pahroh is not beguiled by the Court. They race in their counsel and still cannot keep up *with him!*

"It is Our Father Pahroh, The Life of The River, The Soul of the Two Kingdoms who is more adamant than all of the Court put together. It is *he* who will not send the Iebiru. It is *he* who rejects all strategies of restraint. It is *he* who had your Mohsheh sent away from the Great House and charged never to return on pain of death!"

Now I really did look at him like a stunned calf.

"Have you spoken a single word with any who have actually stood before the Throne these past weeks?" Hesera asked. "Have you passed a conversation with any of the servants? Or even a few words with one of the Sister-Wives? You know nothing! And yet you will conspire in an uprising? Ha!"

"It doesn't matter," I replied in a voice so low and cold that I barely recognized it as my own. "If the uprising is against the Throne itself, so be it. We will save the life of Kehmeht. Even if it means taking the life of her King."

∽

"Bring a cup of spiced wine for Mereyamun," Okpara said brightly to no one in particular. "To wash away his hard conversations with difficult men."

It was supposed to amuse us, so we all acted amused. Even me. But I avoided catching Herit's eyes and I believe she was trying to avoid mine. We both shared the memory of our sad conversation of two days earlier, the one in which she let slip her gnawing terror of the death that was stalking her oldest child.

Had our glances met we would have had to nod or dim our faces. And that would dampen the optimism Okpara was nurturing for his guests, the men who would lead his uprising. Attentive servants did bring us spiced wine. So we managed to make a celebration out of the depressing report I delivered.

"It's true," I confirmed, "Harkuhotep will not be with us and in fact has abandoned The City. And Djedhor Hordedef," I reported, "is threatening to fight us with his best troops." I closed with Hesera's assertion that it is Pahroh himself, not his courtiers, who opposes us. A shadow of quiet blanketed the room.

"Well, better this way, then," Okpara said brightly. "Much better. It's time the masks were removed. High time." Then men nodded, a bit encouraged though no one could say exactly why.

"First, it means that they are afraid," he went on. "Afraid of the people surging in the streets, like flood waters probing their way over an embankment. Second, it means they are afraid of us, men of their own class and blood, who are ready to show the mobs the way."

At that point Okpara made some witty quips about General of the Army Djedhor Hordedef, centering around the fat figure he had become. He carefully avoided any reference to his father and moved on to some jokes about Hesera which made people nervous. You don't make fun of a sorcerer lightly, even a disgraced and deranged one.

So he winked at me as if to signal that at least we two, being within the family, knew the inside story. I had forgotten that Hesera was, in distant way, his great uncle, too. That's when Okpara joked that I needed some cheering up because of my verbal combats with these two difficult men. That's when the spiced wine came out.

The conversation then turned to practical talk of tactics. Tomorrow, it was decided, would be about moving around The City with three objectives. We'd try to meet up with the common mobs and get them to coordinate with us. We'd drive off any mobs threatening the Iebiru, since left intact they might rally to the defense of the Throne. And we would seek out members of the Court to persuade them to join us, or failing that, intimidate them to stand down when when we made our move. That was to be in two more mornings.

I tracked all this with one ear, but couldn't help but watch as Herit's oldest boy tugged his younger brother away from her lap and led him out to their courtyard where all the excitement was. It was an armed camp out there now, with perhaps two hundred men doing what men do before combat.

Some napped. Some sharpened spearheads and swords. Some sat in circles and played at dice. Some ate or drank. One sang quietly to himself.

But for these two little ones it was a life-sized toybox of soldiers. They skipped between the men who offered them sweets or overly hearty greetings. These made the boys laugh out loud and so encouraged the men to clown for them some more.

And their mother, sitting across this room, gazed out the window at them. And she held her gaze steady and did not weep. Though she had to know that if we failed, the littlest one, skipping so happily now through this garden of brave warriors, would never see his big brother again.

∾

We might have waited for more light, but the tension was too great. The few who had managed to fall asleep were woken by the rustling of the others strapping on sandals or sword belts. I had no sword as I did not think I would need it to deliver my report to Okpara the previous day and never expected that he would prevail upon me to spend the night.

"Why go back to the bitter persuasions of a disgraced sorcerer?" Okpara argued as night came on. "You know it will just make you lose heart. We should stay here together tonight, all of us."

"But I'll need my sword."

"We'll send someone for it," he promised reasonably.

We hadn't, and now as we were drinking morning cups of warmed wine mixed with cinnamon water and belting on weapons, Okpara assured me he had not forgotten.

"When we pass near your house, I'll send Bakenmut ahead to fetch your sword. Where will he find it?"

"Let him go around to the kitchens in back and seek entrance there," I said, hoping that he could avoid running into Hesera. "Let him tell Sartuma or Kheruef that I sent him. It's in my room, in the carved chest under the window."

With that settled I went out into the courtyard among the men who had risen long before and were standing in ragged ranks.

This was no army. A band of men at arms, maybe, with some veterans of the armies among them. But there was no notion of who belonged with whom or who precisely was to command which bunch of them.

The leaders, with whom I had spent the night, were simply their social betters. Men of higher standing or greater wealth, Okpara's associates. But what did that have to do with winning a fight? Especially if Djedhor Hordedef's idle threats weren't idle at all? Then it would be a real soldiers we would be facing.

But as we moved out of the narrow gate into the streets, the footsteps of two hundred determined men echoed proudly in the hollow dawn. It emboldened us and we began to stand tall as we went. We weren't a trained army, no. But we were armed (except for me) and it would not be a simple thing to stop us.

One of Okpara's friends, a noble youth named Qenpakheqa, began to call out a cadence. To my untrained ear it sounded like he knew what he was doing and I learned that he had indeed served in the army.

With his sharp and steady call he managed to get the twenty or so men around him to actually fall into step. And the steady beating of their feet on the paving stones began to pull the rest of us into its relentless rhythm. Some of the men added their own voices to the cadence, quietly at first but swelling as the first light shot over the buildings and warmed our faces.

"Kehmeht is eternal" someone called out, though it didn't really work as a chant.

"Kehmeht will live!" another offered and that worked a little better.

"We are Kehmeht!" someone else added and that sounded more like something an army would sing out. Other's picked it up, but in a ragged uneven way, though stiffened by the now steady drumming of our feet.

"Down with the Court!" someone bellowed and everyone broke loose with cheers. The thrill of shouting out loud what was forbidden to even think was too great to contain. "Down with the Court!" echoed through the canyons of stone that was The City. Our little army had found its voice. And now the whole city knew what about it too.

≈

Okpara must have sensed that at this peak of enthusiasm he had better do something before it cooled and slipped away. Or perhaps he was caught up in it himself. So he led us down some wide avenues to one of the largest and most splendid of houses, that of Rhamschosi, who held the title of Fan Bearer to The Right of the King.

Rhamschosi's wealth was legendary, inherited from generations of progenitors who always seemed to end up on the right side of every power-struggle. His home was a palace in its own right, so it would be natural for it to have men at arms among the regular servants. But none of us expected what we found there.

The servants were standing before the door, each with a club or a long knife or some other implement, looking less than comfortable at our coming. But between them and us there was a formidable double rank of soldiers, sixty or seventy at first glance, and in full armor with long spears. And off to the side there was a group of horsemen, also armored, about ten or fifteen of them.

We came to a halt across the avenue. The sudden cessation of our marching feet brought a stillness to the moment, punctured only by the snorts of the horses and the restless pawing of their hooves on the paving stones. We had no tactics prepared or practiced to face a coordinated unit of spearmen, and no way to deal with a charge of cavalry, no matter how small. But before these doubts could chill our resolve, Okpara stepped forward into the silence and spoke.

"Good morning, men of Kehmeht," he called out. "I am Okpara, Son of Harkuhotep, Seal Bearer of Upper and Lower Kehmeht, Unique Friend of Pahroh, Trusted of All His House. I bring greetings to Rhamschosi, Fan Bearer to The Right of the King. I would speak with him a little."

Okpara never stopped striding forward as he spoke, so that by the time he got to the "...speak with him a little" part he was maybe two handbreadths away from the soldier directly in his path to the door. The soldier stepped aside, and Okpara reached the entrance. He knocked but once. The Steward of the House opened it and Okpara disappeared inside.

Our men stood their ragged ground, facing down the soldiers who redoubled the implied threat of their formation, just to let us know that showing deference to a prince of a Vizier was one thing, but dealing with us was another. It grew tense.

The cavalry mounts were restless and had to be reined in by their riders. If just one of them lost control of his warhorse, by accident or purpose, the avenue would have exploded into a bloody battle.

But then the door opened, and out came Okpara. The steward of the house gave a polite bow from the waist, the line of soldiers looking back over their shoulders quickly parted for him as he strode back to us.

"It seems The Fan Bearer to The Right of the King is not at home."

"Could be Rhamschosi is in there somewhere, hiding," one of our company said.

"Well, I didn't search under his bed," Okpara answered, earning some chuckles from the men.

"Probably passed out in his wine cellar," someone else called out, earning bigger laughs. None of this was particularly funny but we were lightheaded from the face-off with the Lord Rhamschosi's soldiers, so it seemed like the height of comedy.

We turned our backs on those soldiers and moved down the avenue. The whole incident played out not far from Hesera's house, so by the time it was over, Bakenmut was back with my sword.

"Your man Kheruef fetched it for me," he reported as he handed it over. "And I saw no sign of the Master of the House."

"Then you've done well, Bakenmut," I said as I strapped on the weapon.

"And your house-matron, Sartuma," he went on as we resumed walking with the others, "asks me to tell you to be careful. And to please forgive Kheruef for not coming to assist you, but she needs him. She said that you, in your good heart, would understand."

Five minutes of marching brought us to the house of Nofrerenpe, Sandal Bearer to the Divine Pahroh. It was not as massive as Rhamschosi's house, but equal in elegance. Most notable was the complete absence of men-at-arms to protect it. Was this an ambush?

The door opened and out came a well-jeweled man who could only be Nofrerenpe himself.

"Okpara, isn't it?" he called as he strode towards us. "Harkuhotep's boy?"

I expected Okpara to bristle at being called "boy" in front of his men. But it was hard to take offense with

Nofrerenpe's easy manner and any question of insult was erased by the half bow he made, followed by nods to the assembled fighters.

"How is your father?"

"He is well," Okpara answered. "But he is not in The City. And he has left me in charge of the Chamber of Judgements."

Nofrerenpe considered this for a moment, looking just a little puzzled about how it explained our early morning show of force.

"Keeping the peace, then?" he said. "From the mobs?"

"Helping them, actually," Okpara answered. "Leading them. If they can be led."

"To what end?"

"To see the Iebiru sent to their worship. Before it is too late."

"So why have you come to me?"

"To persuade those who advise the Throne to give better advice," Okpara said. "And, if they will not be persuaded, to remove them from our way."

Servants filed out from the entrance of Nofrerenpe's home, some of them fingering household implements that could double as weapons. We outnumbered them ten to one and they looked scared. This appearance was obviously their own idea, out of concern for their master. It was no ambush.

Nofrerenpe caught our eyes looking past him and he turned to see the servants gathering tentatively at his door. "Go back inside," he called to them in an everyday way. "I am well."

"Okpara," he said as he turned back to the conversation, "are you thinking that I can somehow have the Iebiru sent to their worship?"

"You and the other courtiers, yes," Okpara said. "You can return to Pahroh this very day and tell him there is no other way to save Kehmeht. Our Father Pahroh will not reject the advice of his own picked companions and advisors."

"But he has. He does."

Okpara, usually quick to retort in any dialogue, paused here. What was Rhamschosi saying?

"You have been in mourning for your mother," Nofrerenpe reminded him gently. "Have you stood before Our Father Pahroh since then? Since the Curse of the Soot that took her life?"

Okpara shook his head "no" slowly and only once.

"That was when everything changed. Until then, the sufferings of Kehmeht were never visited on his Royal Person. When Kehmeht drank blood, he drank sweet water. The frogs were a nuisance to him, but never dangerous as they were to us. None of the rampaging animals ever found their way to him. The plague on the livestock was distant and just a matter of some wealth lost. It was the Curse of the Soot that first touched his sacred body."

"So he shared our pain," Okpara responded. "But he does not act to save us."

"No," Nofrerenpe said. "He does not. But why not? You would think that running sores and bloody ravages on his own skin would have made him consider compromise, wouldn't you? But it was just the opposite. He found some new fortitude in his own burning flesh. He dismissed any notion of compromise with Mohsheh."

"That is not as I have heard," Okpara said. "Everyone knows how after The Fire and Ice he called for Mohsheh and Aaharohn and confessed that he was wrong. And promised to send the Iebiru to their worship."

"Yes, it was as you say," Nofrerenpe agreed. "And yet he did not send them. Why?"

"Because his counselors persuaded him not to!" Okpara argued. "I do not know if you were among them Nofrerenpe, but our Father Pahroh was swayed by evil counselors!"

"You do not understand Okpara!" Nofrerenpe blurted out and then, looked around at who surrounded him and thought better of his tone.

"Forgive me. Had you been there you surely would have understood. But you were not there. True, once Mohsheh made an end of the thunder and the ice, and flames, we all dug in our heels. But none of us had to persuade Pahroh. He was as adamant as we were. More, maybe.

"Then, when Mohsheh and his brother returned and threatened the locust swarm all the fight went out of us. We knew it would be as Mohsheh said. Pahroh alone fought it."

"Surely by then Pahroh knew whatever Mohsheh warned of would come," Okpara said.

"Oh, he knew," Nofrerenpe agreed. "But he did not care! Believe me, Okpara, by this point we were begging him, we were arguing with him, we came very near to insulting him! 'How much longer is this man Mohsheh going to menace us?' we demanded. 'Send the Iebiru to worship their Power! Do you not realize that Kehmeht is being destroyed?' All this, we said to him. And he was unmoved."

"But then there were negotiations," Okpara insisted.

"They were a joke! Pahroh offers to send the Iebiru men. Mohsheh insists on the women and children too. Pahroh refuses. The locust swarm comes and, in a week, half the villagers in Kehmeht are boiling tree bark for soup and baking bread from seeds picked out of animal dung kneaded with sawdust! Men such as you and I spend our family fortunes to buy imports of the food our own black soil once gave us in abundance.

"Then the Darkness Curse comes and Pahroh offers Mohsheh to take the children to the worship. Fine, but the Iebiru flocks and herds must stay behind. The Iebiru will need their animals, Mohsheh says, for offerings to their Eternal One. 'So many?!' Pahroh counters. And Mohsheh answers that no one knows how many will be required. 'Not a single hoof can remain,' he says.

"And with that Pahroh dismisses Mohsheh. And Pahroh tells him that should he appear again before the throne, he will die."

Here Nofrerenpe paused for breath. Or for effect.

"And that, my dear boy, is where we are today."

"Are you not a firstborn, Nofrerenpe?" Okpara asked.

"I am," he answered.

"Do you not believe that, unless the Iebiru are sent to their worship, that you will die tomorrow night?"

"I do not doubt it."

"Then why don't you join us?"

"I am no warrior. I'd be of no use to you."

"Not wielding a sword perhaps," Okpara answered. "But wielding words. Escorting us through the gates of the Great House. Persuading the Sister Wives, the Priests, whoever else lingers in the Court, maybe even your old companion Rhamschosi. You two could help us ease Pahroh down from his Throne, until he sees reason."

"It is treason, Okpara. Let me die tomorrow night without that stain."

"It is treason to let Kehmeht die when you could save it," Okpara said, transforming before my eyes to something very like his father. "Walk with me,

Nofrerenpe, at the front of these men. Or I will have them drag you."

With that he turned to march again and we followed him with the now very miserable Nofrerenpe at his side.

~

A real army sends scouts ahead of its march. But we were no real army and thought nothing of turning blind corners, never knowing who or what we would encounter. But we could hear shouts and cries of clashes as we got closer to the Great House and these only quickened our steps into the unknown.

So, at a near run, we turned one blind corner too fast and found a mass of armed men hurtling towards us. I froze where I stood, which was shameful but better than turning and running away. They were perhaps two hundred paces from us and time seemed to stand still as they grew closer.

"Form a line!"

It was Qenpakheqa, calling out first to his own group of men and then to all. He shoved some of us this way and that, and then ran back and forth across the breadth of the street pointing with his sword, pushing one man back here and pulling another forward there until, miraculously, we were indeed a line, three ranks deep and braced to repel an attack. Or launch one.

The men hurtling towards us slowed to a walk, still menacing but cautious now. There were several hundred of them, but they looked tired and uncertain. Some were bleeding from fresh wounds. They came to a halt twenty paces from us, beaten from their last fight and desperate to move in our direction, even if it meant a bloody melee.

Off in the distance behind them, down at the end of the

long avenue, a new mass of men appeared, shouting at the top of their lungs and charging down the street towards the rear of the men facing off against us. Attacking them? Or reinforcing them for a fight against us? Okpara stepped forward out of our first rank and spoke to the men facing us.

"Are you fighting to have the Iebiru sent to their worship? Or to prevent their going?"

These men could have said anything. But they could not know what our cause was and, having already bled today, they spoke their truth.

"Sent to their worship."

"Then we are with you," Okpara said and then turned to us and shouted, "Come on!"

We let out a cry without thinking, a cry that was no word, a cry of battle as we rushed forward to join the men who had been facing us. They, finally believing their good fortune, turned around and together we rushed towards the force closing on us from down the avenue.

It was foolhardy to rush at them when we might have done better reforming a line and holding our ground. We would have been eight ranks deep with the addition of these men and the lines would have been anchored by stone buildings at both ends so no force could flank us.

Yet fortune favored us in this too, because as we charged forward, a murderous hail of stones flew in over our heads. There were slingers among our attackers, a good number of them, and they knew their business. Their aim was accurate and deadly to the place where we had been, and we would have been decimated had we remained there. As it was, a few of ours went down with pitiful groans leaving bloody pools on the paving stones.

Our charge combined with the charge of the attacking

force closed the gap between us in seconds so there was no more time for their slingers to unleash another round. Now everything was the crash of bodies against bodies and men punching and kicking because there was no room to wield swords.

The curved blade of Kehmeht, excellently balanced, makes a powerful warrior out of any man who can raise it and bring it down to slash his enemy from above. Used this way it can smash through a helmet and the skull within, or take off a sword arm at the shoulder.

But it was near useless in very close quarters where there was no room to raise it and bring it down again. So we, who were armed with the best weapons Kehmeht can forge, were at a disadvantage compared to both our enemies and our new comrades who held knives and foreign blades fit for stabbing.

Everyone was so close and crushed together that I could barely make out faces. And even if I could, how would I recognize friend or foe from the two hundred or so new men who were now our allies or the several hundred who were our enemies?

In the middle of trying to work that out, someone got his hands around my throat and was pressing in with his thumbs. I grew dizzy and my sword arm fell. I tried to pry his hands loose, which was the worse tactic I could have chosen, but I could not breath and so could not think.

My vision was going gray into darkness as he throttled me when, it seems, some other man or men knocked into my attacker from behind and he fell towards me and I fell backwards and was down on the pavement. I hit hard, but a forward tilt of my head saved me from smashing it.

Meanwhile my attacker let go of my throat, using his hands to break his fall, and that gave me a split second to squirm away from him, putting my throat just out of his reach. He recovered and lurched forward on top of me but this time I was able to catch one of his wrists in one hand, while trying to push his head backwards and away from me with the other.

But the man was heavy and had me pinned. I could not have held even his dead weight above me, and he was enraged and pushing down with all his might. My hand slipped off his sweaty forehead and he crushed my other arm as he came down on me and went for my throat again.

With only one free hand to resist I was soon gasping for air and blacking out when a splash of hot wetness hit my face. The hands on my throat loosened and the pounding weight of my attacker came to rest on me.

I never found out who my savior was, but he had hit my attacker's neck from the rear, smashing though bone to sever the blood vessel that gives sight to the eyes and life to the heart. I pushed the hated carcass off of me enough to squirm free and scramble to my feet.

The air was fresher now, as the melee had thinned and moved down the street a bit. I found my sword and picked it up, but then felt sick from the effort. I stood there, taking in gulps of fresh air and, before I needed to figure out what to try next, the fight was over.

Our attackers retreated back down the avenue towards the Great House. We and our new allies were left in possession of the street, but at a cost. There were men groaning on the ground, or crying out in pain or for help. There were others who did not move.

Men improvised litters out of spear shafts and cloaks for those who could not walk or, in some cases, to carry the dead. Some men kicked in the door of a home on the street and emerged with beds that could be used as stretchers.

Among those moving back towards where I stood, I spied Qenpakheqa and Bakenmut on either side of Okpara who could walk only with their support. His left side was bloody and his clothes were rent there, but whether by an enemy sword or by his comrades seeing to his wound, I could not tell. Both, probably. I hurried towards him, unsteadily.

"Okpara," I said. "Are you well?" Which was a stupid thing to say, but of course it meant, "I hope your wound is not fatal." He was in pain, but determined to be in good spirits.

"You don't look that well yourself, Mereyamun" he said, scanning my blood caked face and tunic.

"It's not my blood," I said and instantly regretted my choice of words because it sounded like a claim to some heroic deed proved by the gore of my enemy. Okpara smiled a bit, but then his knees gave way and had he not been caught by Bakenmut, he would have collapsed to the pavement.

"We must carry you, my friend," Qenpakheqa said. "No more arguments."

And so I helped them place Okpara onto one of the looted beds, despite his protests, and walked with him as he was borne back to his home.

~

"Father is calling for you," a small voice chirped. "Father wants you to come to him."

I opened my eyes on to see the older of Okpara's sons, his firstborn, standing over me in the darkened room. I blinked at him until the tide of memory rushed back in.

We had returned, after the fight, to Okpara's house. Our fighters, their numbers swelled by the men who had joined us, filled the courtyard and spilled into the street. They made cook-fires and settled places to bed down for the night there, the new men meaning to stick with us for what would be the decisive battle in the morning. The wounded filled the first floor of Okpara's house.

I did what I could to help the physicians who had been called. This became difficult as it was that time of year when the hours of day and night are equal, and the light faded in the middle of our work. The servants lit oil lamps that cast shadows here and there. I settled down into one of those dark spots against the far wall and let the heaviness of my eyelids lead me into a dreamless sleep. Until now.

"Father needs you to come to him."

I felt heavy and not yet rested, but awake now to the bruises on my back and the pains in my throat where I had been throttled. I imagined I had slept only a few moments but I saw that lamps were guttering and smoking so it must have been a few hours since I passed out. It hurt to stand up and it was painful to walk. But I went as quickly as I could, for the child was insistent and I was full of dread about Okpara's wounds.

"Mereyamun has come," Herit said quietly into the ear of her husband who was laying absolutely still, save for the shallow rising and falling of his chest.

Okpara opened his eyes and lifted a hand in a wan greeting, as if I had arrived at some late hour supper. He gestured for me to come closer. Qenpakheqa and a few others seated on low stools around the bed made room for me at its head opposite Herit. Bakenmut slid a stool under me. I had to lean in to hear what Okpara was saying.

"Where is Nofrerenpe?" he asked me. "Do you know what happened with him?"

It took me a minute to remember The Sandal Bearer to the Divine Pahroh, with all that had happened since we took him into our custody.

"I lost sight of him at the street fight," I said.

"We all did," Okpara admitted. "He probably saw his chance and took off for the Great House."

"To visit his old friend Rhamschosi," Qenpakheqa said, adding the title "Fan Bearer to The Right of the King" but uttering each word with more contempt than I thought those words could hold.

"So, it's good then," Okpara said. "We have them cooped up in the place to which we are going in the morning."

Did Okpara think he would heal by dawn and lead us in an assault on the Great House? I exchanged a glance with Qenpakheqa. Okpara caught it.

"Is there anything else worth doing in this one day that is left to us?" Okpara challenged.

"No," Qenpakheqa answered evenly. "No, we must reach the Throne tomorrow and have the Iebiru sent away. Or we must die trying."

Okpara nodded his assent and then looked at me.

"You don't agree Mereyamun?"

"I know it is what must be done," I said. "But I do not think you are in any condition to lead such a battle. Or even to be there when it's over to see our purpose through. You must heal first."

Herit's red eyes were beyond tears at this point, but a small light of gratitude and hope flashed in them.

"Anything less than complete victory, and this time tomorrow I will be dead," Okpara said, "along with all the other firstborn. If we are to be defeated, better to fall in the battle than to stay here waiting for a midnight execution by the Power of the Iebiru."

"But we will not be defeated," I said without reflection or thought. "This time tomorrow we will be celebrating the salvation of Kehmeht. Here. With you."

Where in the world did those words come from? I could hardly believe I was saying them. Yet, at that moment, I meant them with perfect certainty.

Not certainty that we would win the battle tomorrow, for who could know that? But certainty that we could not lose, whether we won the day or bled out the last of our lives onto the marble of the courtyards and corridors of The Great House. Either way, we would not be defeated, even if we would have to enjoy our victory in the Happy Land of Reeds.

"We were magnificent today, weren't we?" Okpara said.

I nodded. We all did.

"I wonder what my Father would have thought," Okpara said. "I wonder what he would have thought of us I mean, if he had seen us today? If he could see us tomorrow? He would be very proud of you, Merey."

"But he does not agree with us," I said.

"No, but he would still be proud of you."

"He would be most proud of you, Okpara" I said, for what else could I say? But I meant it.

"Surprised, maybe," Okpara smiled. "Very surprised about me."

And his eyes fell closed and we left him to sleep with Herit at her bedside vigil and Bakenmut stationed faithfully outside their door.

～

I t was a different band of fighters that lined up in the street at first light. We had fought. We had bled. We had lost friends and comrades. There were fewer quips and mutterings as we fell into place. But more joy, a quiet joy you could taste. For we were all desperate men now, with nothing to lose and so, nothing to fear.

Self-pity over my own fate was gone. If I had any pity at all, it was for those who were not with us, those who would do nothing but wait for death through this last day of their doomed lives.

"Ready," Qenpakheqa called out as the first command to start our march. "By your ranks... at the sign from your commanders..." And he should have finished with "March!" But he stopped, his attention turned to the open gate of the courtyard where Okpara appeared.

Okpara walked with difficulty, with pain even, but without hesitation. And he did not allow Bakenmut to support him, though Bakenmut hovered close by, ready to catch him if he fell.

He had some sort of exterior bandage wrapped very tightly around his ribs, stomach and the small of his back, girding him, holding him together really. It was painful to see. But it was also a thing of joy, his courage and his faithfulness. The men started cheering as he walked past them towards Qenpakheqa. Cheering and calling his name.

"You are insane," Qenpakheqa said when Okpara reached him.

"Probably," Okpara agreed. He was radiant and I was proud to be with him this day.

We made a great deal of noise as we moved through the streets, walking so quickly that the whole mass of us threatened to break into a gallop like a warhorse who must be reined-in against the drumbeat of his own heart. But breaking into a run would mean leaving Okpara behind. As it was, he struggled to keep up and in the front, though he was trying his best to hide it.

It was still first light but The City was awake to us. People appeared in windows. Some shouted praise, some called out curses. But all seemed to be done with sleep, if they had had any at all.

Who would sleep away their last morning of life if they were firstborn? Or their last chance to share some life in this world with brothers, sisters, parents and children who were? For some, we were a hope. Maybe, just maybe, we would win our battle and the Iebiru would be sent away this day and their Power would spare us.

Small groups of men with weapons, genuine or improvised, joined us. Others ran away from us, making it clear that they were not on our side. Either way it meant that we would have no element of surprise when we reached the Great House. Turning down the last avenue we saw it looming up in the distance.

The Great House was the largest structure in The City and the tallest, though a few temples came close. It had a number of gates on different sides, and it would have made sense to learn which ones were the most guarded and which the least defensible against us. But no such reconnaissance was possible because it was surrounded by such a thickness of crowds, pushing, arguing, shouting, chanting, wailing.

It would have been clever of Djedhor Hordedef to situate these crowds on purpose, just to impede any move we would make against his troops ready for action inside those gates. And if he hadn't thought to arrange it, no doubt he saw the advantage once he found those crowds there. That was why he had not ordered his troops to disperse them.

Rhamschosi and Nofrerenpe and the other counselors, and perhaps even Pahroh himself, would surely look out from high windows this morning and find delight in the crowds. For whether they were clamoring for an audience or begging for salvation, they reinforced the only thing that mattered to The Throne: That Pahroh alone was King and there would be no replacing him with any invisible Power.

"The Sun Gate," Okpara said as we closed in on the place.

Of course. Not the First Gate through which supplicants to the Throne would be vetted. No, it would have to be the gate that faced the rising sun on the first and last day of its yearly journey though the sky this very month.

This was the gate used by the Lords and Counselors who lived and worked in the Great House. The gate that Okpara, son of Harkuhotep, Seal Bearer of the King of Upper and Lower Kehmeht, Unique Friend of Pahroh, Trusted of All His House used, always. He would be known there. His name would mean everything to those who guarded it.

"Of course we know you, My Lord," their captain said from his side of the entrance. "But we may not admit anyone today unless they are named by the Throne."

"That is for strangers," Okpara said evenly. "That is for guests. Do you think the One Who Sits in The Chamber of Judgements is a guest?"

This made the captain uncomfortable, to be sure. His eyes flitted from Okpara to Qenpakheqa and me, we three being the ones with rank that could intimidate the guards. He also seemed to wonder at Bakenmut who was wearing enough of his kit as a Great House Guardsman to make the Captain wonder if he was missing something here.

But the Captain's glance also took in our men. They stood off at a discrete distance, having parted the crowd and deployed to keep them parted. But he had to wonder if that what was all they had been brought here for.

I wondered if the Captain was himself a firstborn who would be dead this night? Probably not, because he feared what punishment the Chamber of Judgements could mete out to him, and though the arm of its justice was long, it could not reach unto the dead.

The Captain made a curt half bow to Okpara and gestured to his men to open the gate and admit us. This they did, opening the gate wide, for it would have been impertinent to make one of Okpara's rank slip through a less than gracious opening.

Qenpakheqa gestured for me to follow and then, surprisingly, for Bakenmut to follow me, which was a departure from all protocol. Bakenmut, who knew his station in life, hesitated for just a second, perplexed. But Qenpakheqa caught his eye and he understood and entered, with Qenpakheqa falling in behind him in the unhurried assurance of nobility.

The Guards, meanwhile, were only waiting for all this to be over so they could close the gate against our armed men. But Qenpakheqa was insouciant, actually stopping to look up and around as if he wanted to admire the architecture.

Had he drawn his right foot up to his left, the Guards could have gingerly closed the gate and let loose a sigh of relief. But there he was, his foot in the way, and who among these men would dare to ask him to move it?

It was not for nothing that the Iebiru called Kehmeht the House of Slaves, for they long understood that although they were the lowliest, they were far from the only slaves in the Black Land. We were all slaves to our betters, even though some of us wore collars of gold.

Okpara, Bakenmut, and I turned to wait for our noble companion who seemed given over to some flight of thought or observation. The Captain took this in and his eyes went from us to our men outside the gate who had seemed to have lost interest in their crowd-control and were looking toward us.

"Your Honor..." the Captain said with a bit of a head bow to Qenpakheqa, "if His Honor does not mind..." and decided to finish the sentence with courtly gestures indicating that he would be very grateful if Qenpakheqa would move just a bit and allow his men to close the gate.

Qenpakheqa looked him up and down as if he were an insect, and in the eternity of seconds this transpired, our men started moving toward the gate. They were just walking, but there was a great number of them and something in the Captain decided that this new threat was greater than any offense he might give his betters.

"Close the gate," the Captain commanded his men. "Close it, close it now!"

And so they would have, even though it meant sweeping Qenpakheqa's noble foot aside. But they never got that far. Qenpakheqa's strong left arm stopped the gate with the flat of his hand, and he drew his sword with his right. At this our men let out a roar and charged with all speed.

More Guards poured out of the Great House and battle was joined just inside the gateway. Qenpakheqa was surrounded at first and much put upon. But his blade rose and fell at deadly speed and then slashed sideways as he spun and brought down death from above again. Blood splattered, and his attackers backed off only to be pursued by our men now through the bottleneck of the gateway.

Until this point Okpara, Bakenmut, and I were largely ignored. Having not drawn our weapons and standing apart made us seem like legitimate visitors to the Great House caught up in something we had no part in. An officer of the Guard running past us even shouted to Bakenmut (who he read as a guardsman) to move us in and away from the trouble.

It took only a few moments for this fight to end. We had passed the gateway and now possessed the courtyard inside it. The guards fled, leaving their wounded and dead on the pavement. We formed up behind Okpara and began moving through the garden and towards the bronze doors of the building. I wondered if they were bolted and how we would deal with that, but they obliged us by suddenly opening.

Men emerged, armored and helmeted, with spears so long that they would not clear the lintel of even this massive doorway until lowered half-way into attack position. These were regular soldiers, disciplined and drilled, hand-picked by Djedhor Hordedef probably, trusted enough to be stationed with weapons inside the Great House itself.

We slowed some in our course toward the entrance, but these soldiers did not rush out to engage us. Instead they formed up two ranks deep, arrayed across the breadth of the garden, with one row of spears leveled at our belts and the second row angled at our faces. We came to a stop, of course. What good would it have done to charge now and impale ourselves on those iron-tipped shafts?

"I am Okpara, son of Harkuhotep, Seal Bearer of the King of Upper and Lower Kehmeht, Unique Friend of

Pahroh, Trusted of All His House," Okpara said. "And I am entrusted with the Chamber of Judgements in my Father's absence," he added. "Part now, and let me enter."

At another time this might have been very funny. In my panic at that moment it was all I could do to stop myself from laughing. Okpara's pronouncement was true, yes. He just forgot to mention the several hundred armed men he brought with him or the dead and wounded we left littering the courtyard beyond us.

No officer answered Okpara. No officer even appeared, though even with the morning sun in our eyes we could make out the figure of a man inside the doorway. He was surely in command. But this was no battlefield and the protocols of war were not going to be honored today. This was civil insurrection. This was the desperate last throw of the dice to decide if Kehmeht would live through the night.

From within the dark rectangle of that double doorway, the man called a command, and the soldiers began to march in place. He called a cadence and the doubled ranks of soldiers lifted and stamped their feet to it, a drumbeat of their soles on the pavement.

It was a strange thing to see and made me want to laugh again, looking so much like a silly dance at some harvest festival. But the men I was with knew what this was and they were not laughing. They stiffened and shifted their weight on their feet, ready for flight or perhaps a hopeless last stand. A few more drumbeats of those pumping feet and the ranks began to advance on us.

It was no wild charge, it was rhythmic and perfectly in cadence as when they were marching in place. But now the deadly purpose of that comic sight was clear. Marching on us, slowly but relentlessly, their line would never break, there would be no street fight. There would be only those iron spearheads pressing us back until we were pinned bloodily against the wall of the very courtyard we had taken.

Some men turned to look for the gate, half-opened, the way to it littered with the wounded and dead of the Guard. Some broke and went for it. It was soon jammed with too many men tripping over too many fallen, desperate to exit, but squeezed aside and forced back into the crush. Qenpakheqa took this in and understood that, in seconds, the spears closing in would mean slaughter for those trapped at the gate... unless something were done to hold those spears for a time.

Qenpakheqa let out some battle cry, a command that I couldn't understand for all the yelling. Bakenmut was shouting into my ear to help him take Okpara who, until now, had not budged from his place, and drag him toward the gate. I backed up with them, not wanting to turn my back on those spears and saw Qenpakheqa and the group of men who were closest to him charge at the advancing spearmen.

Those soldiers held their ranks as they moved forward, thrusting their spears forward a foot or two then retracting them and then thrusting again, doing whatever an arm's length could do while still holding their ranks. This was what Qenpakheqa was counting on.

He and the men still with him charged up to the spears, then stopped and feinted with their heads and upper bodies like boxers. And when a spear point had just missed their faces or torsos, they would grab the shaft of the spear and use it against their opponent.

Some pushed back on the shafts, making the soldier wielding it stumble backwards into the man behind him. Qenpakheqa pulled hard on the spear he grabbed, using the thrust of the man who held onto it to his demise. The man tripped forward, righted himself just in time for Qenpakheqa's blade to slash his throat.

This counterattack broke the line of spearmen at its center, for a few moments at least. I believe that had Qenpakheqa and his group not done it, we would all have been trapped and impaled. It gave time for the chaos at the gate to sort itself out, for the gate doors to be pulled open wide, and an escape to the street begun in earnest.

Okpara was balking at leaving and I turned my attention to him and begged him and pushed him and supported him as Bakenmut pulled us through to the street. So I did not see Qenpakheqa's end, though I know it was glorious.

All I saw, as we left, was the line of spearmen closing its ranks, reforming, and marching again towards us. Qenpakheqa and his men had gone down and disappeared under their feet. The points of those spears were wet with their blood.

～

Our men were now mixed into the mobs in the street, in part because those mobs did not know what was happening inside the gate and were still surging towards it. This made it very difficult to move against the human tide while supporting Okpara, who was stumbling now.

I saw that the outer bandage wrapped around his tunic was stained with blood from his wounds of yesterday. Bakenmut saw too and looked to me, but dared not speak of it. Instead he began pushing and throwing people out of our way, whether they were coming or going, allies or opponents.

He took blows and gave them back and he disarmed a man waving a long knife too near to us. I took some punches too, one strong one to the side of my head that left me blacked out for a moment, though I never knew who gave it or even if it was intended for me.

I stole a glance back towards the gate to see if the soldiers were coming out to pursue us. But whether by order of their commanders or the fact of the mobs that crowded the area, they stopped with their reconquest of the courtyard. I turned my attention back to supporting Okpara and following Bakenmut to whatever safety we could find.

We needed to rest Okpara and look to his reopened wounds. But there was no safe place to stop. Swollen crowds of people, lowborn or high, were pushing and shoving and falling into fist fights and beatings. It made no sense, there was no way to tell what cause anyone believed in. For all I knew, I was punched by men who were fighting for the very thing I was.

Bakenmut used the flat of his sword to beat off attackers and keep us moving, but some had clubs or blades of their own. More than once they would have been the end of us, if not for the fact that others started brawling with them.

Then there was a great roar from down the avenue. Something had happened at the First Gate and a good number of the people near us turned and started moving toward it. Those who, a moment ago, sought our blood with death in their eyes, were now the first to turn and sprint towards whatever was unfolding down there. We could get some air again.

"We should have gone with them," Okpara said.

"You need to rest," I told him, fearing that he would insist on us helping him down the avenue into whatever was erupting there.

"I mean this morning," Okpara said. "We should have found more allies, we should have acted with a bigger force. It's my fault."

I told him whatever words of reassurance came to mind. I told him how courageous he had been and how, who knows?... Maybe our engaging those soldiers was the spark that ignited whatever was happening now down at the First Gate. I'm not sure what I said exactly because I was distracted by the amount of fresh blood soaking through Okpara's garments.

I silently gestured to Bakenmut that we should get Okpara across the broad avenue into the shade where he could rest. And so we moved off in that direction haltingly, not wanting to rush Okpara's steps beyond what he could bear.

We made only a few paces when, with another great roar, a torrent of men began surging back from the First Gate and down the avenue towards us. There was a clang of arms and an inchoate shouting from innumerable throats, all of it coming at us like a stormwave off the Great Green. They were coming on fast and would trample us for sure if we did not get out of their way.

There was no time to continue across the avenue, the best we could do was turn back toward the Great House and hope that by pressing ourselves against its courtyard wall we would avoid the crush. Okpara could not move fast enough so we dragged him, Bakenmut almost lifting him off his feet, as we rushed for the wall.

We were not alone in this, many had scattered to the edge of the avenue. But we found a piece of wall just beyond a slight bend that seemed to offer shelter from what was coming. We crouched down there. Our view was of feet and legs, running, stumbling, turning at times to look behind, and turning again to break and flee.

Trumpets sounded and there was a thunder of hoofbeats on the stones of the avenue. The swirling dust thickened, and with cries and the rumble of their bronze-banded wheels, chariots appeared.

There were tens and tens of them, each with a driver at the reins and a fighter standing in the car, wielding lances they plunged again and again into the backs of the fleeing mob. Their thunder went with them as they passed, and the street became strangely quiet, punctuated only by groans of the wounded and the cries of men calling for missing comrades.

"Senwosret," Bakenmut said quietly, perhaps to himself, perhaps to me. "I saw Senwosret."

It was possible. I had asked Setka to find Senwosret a place with the charioteers. But it seemed to matter so little at this moment, I wondered why Bakenmut would care.

He was pale and listless, exhausted as he sat with his back against the wall. I saw blood pooling beneath his thigh. It was lifeblood, the pool was expanding with each heartbeat.

"You are wounded, Bakenmut," I said. "We have to staunch that."

Okpara seemed to recover some at the emergency and managed to rip off a piece of his outer tunic for me to apply to Bakenmut's leg. "Hurry, Merey," he said.

I reached over to tie off the bleeding, but Bakenmut hardly paid any notice.

"I saw Senwosret," he said again, as if this was terribly important to him. "He was our friend, Your Honor."

"He was," I agreed just to say something to keep him from passing out altogether.

"Listen," Okpara said urgently. "They're coming back."

It was the thunder of the chariots, off in the distance down the avenue where they had disappeared. But it was growing louder. They were indeed coming back. But for us? If so, we were trapped there against the wall.

Their dust preceded them and we were enveloped in a choking cloud even before they reached us. The hoofbeats and bronze hoops of the wheels made a racket against the paving stones and it was hard to speak or be heard. I closed my mouth against the dust and squinted my eyes, leaving me just enough vision to finish knotting off the bandage around Bakenmut's thigh.

It looked like they were going to ignore us, off to the side as we were. They were rushing towards a bigger fight back outside the First Gate. Good. When they were gone I would try, somehow, to move Okpara and Bakenmut across the avenue into quieter streets and get help for them from the first physician I could find.

"It's Senwosret," Bakenmut said again, which was completely without sense. Who could make out anyone in the swirling dust and the speed of the chariots? And what would it matter?

But Bakenmut pulled himself up onto his feet and stumbled out into the avenue. I reached for him from where I crouched and my fingers caught a bit of his tunic, but not enough. He became another silhouette in the cloud of dust alive with horses and drivers and fighting men.

I do not know if they stabbed him or if he simply collapsed beneath the hooves and bronze wheels. He was dragged a great distance from the spot where he fell. When the dust settled, his broken body seemed halfway to the

First Gate. I threw up then, though there was little in me to come out. Okpara put his hand on my shoulder to steady me and I caught my breath.

"Can you walk now?" I asked Okpara. "If you lean on me? We need to get out of here."

"Yes," he agreed to both my question and my plan. "Yes, let's try now."

He raised himself up, using the wall for support. I put my arm around him to steady him for our move across the avenue and away from the Great House.

We were a few steps into our crossing when a new mob, armed and angry and fresh with purpose came out of the street feeding into the avenue across from us. We stood and looked for an escape since they had cut us off from the refuge we were aiming for.

To our left other mobs were returning at a run, coming back now from where the chariots had chased them off earlier. And to our right, soldiers from the First Gate were moving on us.

These were not the disciplined spearmen we had encountered, those were still inside the Sun Gate. These were simply men at arms, without any particular order I could discern. They were another mob really, but armored and experienced at killing.

It was Okpara who tugged at me and broke my frozen despair so that we made our way back, once again, to the wall where we had been. There we crouched down all over again and watched for another chance to get away.

I cannot tell you how long we were trapped there. I do remember noticing that the sun above us had somehow reached noon and a bit more and we were still there, burning with thirst, watching for a path of escape. But every time things seemed to quiet a bit, a new wave of street brawling or mob combat surged onto the avenue again.

Okpara's bleeding was intermittent but it was not stopped and he would fall silent for long stretches. This, I knew, was dangerous, so I kept up conversations with him whenever I could think of something to say. I searched for things to talk about, words that might engage him to keep him from a helpless sleep in which he would bleed out his life.

"Remember the last time we were here?" I asked him.

He looked at me with glassy eyes and probably wondered if I had lost my mind, for we had never been here, sitting against this wall like two beggars. Unless I meant a half an hour ago, which would make my words inane.

"Not in this spot exactly," I clarified hoping I could keep him interested. "I was right next to the gate itself, looking in. And you were inside the gate. At the procession to the Houses of the Dead. For your mother."

Light came back into his eyes and he nodded a little. "It was the twenty-ninth day of Renwet," Okpara said.

Two and half months ago. But enough time for our world to flip upside down and die.

"You stood at the gate with Uncle Hesera," Okpara noted.

I remembered the tracks of tears ruining the kohl around his eyes as he followed his mother. And how his glance fell on us at the gate and how he gave a small nod and smile thinking I had reconciled with our Uncle Hesera as he wished. But I had not and, at this moment, there was none more in opposition to Hesera and all he stood for than Okpara.

"He will think this is all some sort of victory, you know,"

Okpara said. "Uncle Hesera will rejoice in how we have been bloodied. And how Pahroh has stood against us."

"Until midnight," I added.

"Until midnight," Okpara agreed. "Still, it galls me that he will go to his death feeling like he has won something."

"It won't matter," I said. "He'll be as dead as we'll be."

"He'll die in shame, Mereyamun."

"He won't feel any shame at all," I said.

"Then that will be his shame," Okpara responded. "It will be his disgrace in the Happy Land of Reeds."

A few moments passed without talk. Okpara's eyes closed and his breathing slowed and I thought he had fallen into sleep or worse. But I found nothing to say to enliven him. Then he spoke.

"I won't make it to midnight."

"You will!" I insisted. "We'll make a break for it soon, we'll get you patched up. And then who knows what might still happen before midnight? There's still plenty of fighting, who knows?"

Okpara looked serenely unconvinced. He fingered at his bandages a little, as if trying to see underneath without actually loosening them. They were not just stained with blood now, but actually wet to the touch. He looked at his own fingertips, reddened with the effusion his saturated bandages could no longer hold, and confirmed his thoughts.

"I will die here, Merey."

"No. You won't."

"This is one debate you cannot win."

We were paying no attention to the sword fights and brawls and charges and retreats going on before our eyes. We were done with them.

"You should have gone with my father," Okpara said.

"With my sister and Setka and the others. You would have lived through this."

"You could have gone too," I reasoned. "But you stayed to fight for the life of our People."

"I could *not* have gone," Okpara insisted. "Not at all. I wanted the Iebiru to be sent to their worship, yes. But I could never have joined them. I cannot believe the things they believe. I do not care for the things they care for."

"But I do?"

"Don't you?"

"I believe the Eternal One of the Iebiru will not be denied," I conceded. "I believe that in the end it will be as Mohsheh says. Pahroh and all the Children of the Black Land, will say that the Eternal One is the lord of us all."

"So go now," Okpara said. "Go join them before it's too late. There's still time."

"I won't leave you."

"But I will leave you, Mereyamun. I will go to the Happy Land of Reeds and you will still be in this world. So go. Save yourself."

Okpara's eyes closed again, but he continued in a sleepy voice. "There's still time."

How long did I wait there with him, watching the rising and falling of his chest in shallow breaths? Until there were no breaths. I took his wrist and felt for the echo of his beating heart, but there was none. His arm became heavy in my grasp. I felt for pulsing in his neck, but there was none there to find.

I got up onto my feet and stood there, looking this way and that, down at Okpara and back up to the street. But I saw nothing.

～

I walked out into the avenue, past fighting men, through the midst of them too. I was jostled and pushed this way and that but I saw nothing. I just kept walking and somehow I found myself on the other side of the avenue.

The shadows there had grown longer, with the sun on its dip into the west. I walked into half-shaded streets, away from the Great House, away from the noise and the blood.

I did not realize how tired I was, or how battered. I had bloody wounds on my left arm, though I did not remember being cut there. And my right leg shot with pain from the ankle to the knee whenever I placed any weight on it. And I was very thirsty.

My throat was parched and burning and I would collapse if I did not drink soon. But I feared to collapse where someone might come along and slay me if it pleased him.

I knocked on a door to beg for some water. But no one answered. I could hear people inside but no one would come. And so it went for several doors. I moved down the street, using the walls between the doors for support. Finally one opened a crack.

"Wait," someone beyond that crack said to me and resealed the door. I put my back to the wall next to the entrance and waited. And the door opened again and a maidservant stepped out with a clay jug. She thrust it into my gasp wordlessly and disappeared behind the door again. I heard the latch close.

I slid down the wall into a crouch holding on to the jug for dear life. I emptied it into my mouth in quick gulps until I choked and sputtered. I then let myself collapse completely on to the floor, looking, I imagined, like a drunk who could not make it home. Which, in a way, was not all that far from what I was. Then the aroma came to me.

The best poet cannot describe an aroma, not really. They choose fine words, yes, but those words can only dance around it, gesture towards it, point to it. But in the end they fail. The aroma alone speaks for itself. Such an aroma came to me then. And I knew, without knowing why I knew, what it was. The Iebiru were roasting their offerings.

I never tasted meat in my life, at least not knowingly. And even if Mayati and her father had fed me meat during my stay in Gohshen, it was disguised in soups and stews. The thought of consuming meat had always made me ill. But now this aroma of freshly killed lamb roasting somewhere in The City came to me and it was sweet beyond description and desirable beyond understanding.

"I could go there," I thought to myself. "I could go to the Lower Market and then through to the Street of the Potters. I could go to the bottom where the Southwest District begins. The Iebiru there are roasting their offerings now. I could find Ankhuemhesut and he would help me.

I would need to have my foreskin removed but Ankhuemhesut would know an Iebiri who would help with that. It would be painful. But I had already endured cuts and wounds these past days, this would be just one more. I would surrender to The Eternal One of the Iebiru, and He would accept me. I would be there at the offering to Him and be fully one of his children." And with this I lifted myself up.

I noticed the jug was still in my hand. I knelt and set it down carefully next to the door. Then I walked off in the direction of the Lower Market.

I did not know the best route to take. My memory ran down big streets and avenues, but those were still bursting with brawls and stampedes that came without warning. So I tried smaller streets and the alleys that crisscrossed them, trusting to a general southern direction.

I became confused at times, unable to decide with confidence which way to move next. In those pauses I would feel how tired I was and how battered. I wanted nothing more than to collapse onto the pavement. But then the aroma would call me, and I would move off again in search of the roasting fires that spawned it.

The pain shooting up my right ankle warned that I could not run fast enough to get away from any mob that might come upon me. So I slowed as I came to cross streets and listened for who or what might be coming. If it seemed quiet enough I would peek around the corner. If I spied danger coming, I would flit back and try to move along the walls into whatever entranceway or crevice between buildings could conceal me.

But this made slow going, and the sun was racing west toward the close of the day and the end of my chance at joining the Iebiru. I decided to take more risks. What would happen, would happen.

As the way began to curve gently downhill, I gave only a quick glance at the side streets without slackening my already pathetic pace. Downhill had to mean towards the Street of the Potters and from there I thought I would recognize the way Khenut had shown me to where she and Ankhuemhesut were staying.

Lost in that thought, I limped toward the next cross street and exposed myself before I realized that I hadn't given even a glance to see what was coming. It was a crowd, walking briskly and with purpose. And, strangely, they were singing as they went. Iebiru.

They were cloaked in too many garments, too much wool. There were bearded men with women wrapped in embroidered shawls, and old ones and young ones, children skipping along, babies carried in arms. One man bore a lamb on his shoulders.

They saw me, but paid no attention. They just continued on their way, passing quite close, singing. But instead of continuing on what I thought was the path, they turned left onto a cross street. Surely they were going to the Southwest District to join the other Iebiru.

Didn't Khenut tell me that Mohsheh and Aaharohn themselves would bring their offerings there so that Pahroh could find them and send the Iebiru to their worship? These Iebiru had to be headed there. And they knew a shorter way! So I turned into the street they had taken. I would follow them and get there in time after all!

But this street narrowed, it was soon reduced to an alley that bent and curved this way and that. Limping as I was, I lost sight of them. I knew they had to be ahead of me, I could still hear their singing. But as I came to branching alleys and unpaved paths between buildings I realized that their song could be coming from almost anywhere.

I had to make decisions about forks in the path, any one of which could have been wrong enough to get me lost. The sound of their singing seemed to be coming from off to my right when it should have been ahead of me, so I turned and retraced my steps uphill on a path with broken cobbles, treacherous for my damaged leg.

More than once I turned that ankle or wrenched that knee and had to hold on to a filthy wall to keep from being knocked down by shooting pain. In time the ring of their song faded. But it was replaced by the murmur of many voices, a great many people outside in the streets.

The Iebiru would be roasting their offerings outdoors, in open lots or in the streets, this had to be them. And the aroma became incessant and called to me saying, "yes, yes, you are almost there... but hurry! Hurry before it is too late!"

I rushed ahead on the dusty path. It pitched downward sharply so that I fell into a hobbled run and then found myself delivered into a garbage strewn dead end. Windowless walls on three sides left the steep path behind me the only way to climb back out. I used my hands and my one good leg to scramble onto the path again, and traced it back uphill until it intersected another alley.

I turned into that and moved as quickly as I could, though by now I was heaving for breath. This opened onto a paved street which I took, trusting that it would surely not betray my steps as an unpaved alley would. And in the relative airiness of this street, I could hear the sounds of the Iebiru again and receive the aroma of their roasting offerings.

The sun was low, but I could not be far now. Then, from down a larger street that angled into this one, a crowd of men and women appeared. They were shouting and whooping about nothing that seemed intelligible to me, except that it told me they were Children of Kehmeht.

Some were staggering, others held flagons and clay bottles that they swigged from and passed around. They came up to me, all of them talking at once, and one of them extended a small vessel of pungent wine to my face.

I was short of breath and needed to lean on a wall to get the weight off my injured leg. I declined the offer of their wine with a shake of my head and a few polite words. They reeked of the wine and shouted incoherent things to one another incessantly so I doubt they heard or understood what I said. The vessel was thrust in my face again, too hard this time, bloodying my lip. I pushed it away with annoyance and someone punched me in the side of my head.

I blacked out for an instant and then when the light returned to my eyes I found myself on the pavement, up against the wall, being kicked in the groin. Someone stomped on my good leg, then stomped again on the bad one, and the pain rang through me. I passed into darkness.

∽

I woke without understanding where I was or when. But memory trickled in and slowly spoke the sad truth. The full moon had risen. The sick feeling in my stomach had nothing to do with kicks or blows. It was the voice of profound failure and impending dread.

"You have not saved Kehmeht," it said to me. "You have not even saved yourself. Listen. The Iebiru have gone inside to eat their offering and sing songs to their Eternal One. And you are not there. It is too late now!"

I closed my eyes against this knowledge, but it was inside me and could not be blotted out.

"Harkuhotep, Neferet, and Setka," it said. "Inyotef, Adjedaa, Mayati, they are all at the eating of the offering now. They will live. They will go out to the worship in the Red Land. They will be there when the Eternal One reveals Himself. But you will not."

There was no answer to this and I remained silent in my thoughts. But this voice wished to be heard and would not stop.

"You are not even with Okpara," it continued, "on his

way to the Happy Land of Reeds, rejoicing in his sacrifice. You will just die an ignoble death in fewer hours than you can count on one hand. Midnight will come for you. You needn't bother to go home. What difference will it make? You can wait here in this filthy gutter and die in it just as well."

"I want to go home," I thought to myself. "I should go home."

I got up and turned back up that street, away from the Southwest Quarter, somewhere behind me. It was surely full of bearded men and wool-wrapped women eating roasted meat in the certain expectation that sometime after midnight the Father of Kehmeht would come to them. He would come down from his Throne of the Two Kingdoms to send them into the Red Land for seven days. But I would not live to see it.

The walk back into the part of The City in which I lived became more familiar as I went. Soon the mudbrick filth was behind me and I was among the limestone houses with their fine carvings and courtyards. The full moon illuminated them, and they looked so prosperous and peaceful.

"Kehmeht, the Land That Makes Her Children Happy!" they announced. I laughed at that. Then a cool breeze of the night fanned my face and settled my thoughts. There was stillness inside me, and all I heard was my own footsteps and, here and there, snatches of conversations. A man and a woman quarreling. Someone sobbing. At one point I heard the clash of blades and shouts of fighters a street or two away. It meant nothing to me now.

I found the door to our house bolted and felt very impatient about that, though it made no difference. I had only a few hours left to live, what did it matter on which side of the door I passed them? Still, I pounded on the door until, in time, I heard the bolt thrown and it was opened to me by Kheruef.

"Good evening Your..." but he trailed off, mumbling something about "not being allowed to call you that anymore."

He took in the filth and dried blood on my clothes, the wounds on my arm, the bruises on my face. Sartuma was standing some paces behind him, her eyes reddened from weeping, but dry now with no more tears to offer. She started to speak to me but also checked herself with some mumbled excuse. Looking around I realized what I had interrupted.

They were making offerings to Behs, burning incense on the small alter we had made for the golden statue. There were bowls of dried fruit and some parched grain placed before it. These were scarce now, after the hail and the locusts. I hoped Behs appreciated that.

I went back to the kitchens and found some watery date beer and drank. With that in me I realized I had not eaten since before first light. I found some remains of spelt cakes and few dried figs and sat down on the servant's bench and chewed on them.

What a strange thing it was that I wanted to eat now. The food I took in would not have the time to be even half digested before the life it was supposed to sustain would be taken from me. Yet I wanted these scraps of food. I delighted in them.

"I like life," I thought to myself, as if it was a secret newly discovered. "I want to live," I added. It was inane. But it seemed profound to me.

I was just fourteen days out from my birthday. Fourteen days and it would be a year since I saw Mohsheh and his brother for the first time before the Throne of the Two Kingdoms. Could all this have happened in a single year?

Without really deciding to do it, I stood up and went over to the cistern to wash my face and hands. This was a foul thing to do, since I was filthy and this was the water we filtered through sand and gravel to drink and prepare food. But I was too tired to draw washing-water for myself and I thought it a kindness not to disturb Sartuma and Kheruef in their supplications before Behs, as useless and wrong-headed as they were.

Maybe the Eternal One of the Iebiru would consider their ignorance and the fact that they were simple people. Maybe He would forgive them for their loyalties to a useless god of metal and to a stubborn king of flesh and blood.

Were the other servants still around? There was little sign of them. I guessed that some went home to their villages to see the firstborns of their families one last time, to witness their final moments and, after their deaths, to tend to their remains in the Old Ways of the Black Land. Or maybe, knowingly or not, some went off to die themselves as firstborns. The Children of Kehmeht were so steeped in the secrets men and women keep close, who could be sure of the circumstances of their own birth?

The water comforted me and I began to use the dipper more liberally, pouring it over my head and wounded arm, letting it sting and chill and warm me all at once, making me feel alive. I left a great puddle on the floor. I floated the dipper back into the cistern and went off to my room.

There, I released the finely tooled leather sword-belt I still wore, wondering where my sword had gone. I had no memory of losing it, leaving it, or tossing it away. I tore off my soiled and bloodied clothes and pulled fresh garments from my chest. Clean clothes, beautiful clothes, to die in.

I laid down on my bed, exhausted. I felt my lids growing heavy and wondered if I could just sleep through my execution by the Power of the Iebiru.

I heard a tale once from a courtier who had been hunting with the Old Pahroh, the father of our current king. This Pahroh had put two arrows into an exceptionally huge lion but the animal endured and turned on the King where he stood in his chariot. His driver whipped the team frantically to pull away but the horses, rearing in terror, were useless. The man who told the story leapt from his own chariot with a lance but before he could use it, the lion turned on him and he was taken up at into its jaws.

The beast shook the courtier by his torso. Its jaws gripped like a vise, and its sharp teeth stabbed so that it seemed the courtier would die from the tearing and shaking. But Pahroh loosed a third arrow, it struck home and the lion collapsed into itself and died.

The courtier, released, was bleeding and broken but miraculously alive. Upon recovering he was asked to describe those dreadful moments. Was it not a great terror, he was asked?

"No," he answered. Once he was in the lion's jaw and he felt the teeth pierce him and his bones break and his organs shook loose, a great calm came over him.

"More than a calm," he said. "A great peace. A great serenity and quiet such as I have never known before or since."

I let my eyelids close over the thought that perhaps I too might feel a great serenity like that. Maybe it will not hurt at all. Maybe it will not trouble me at all. Maybe I will be at peace..."

The door slammed against the wall with a bang and I bolted upright.

"They let you in?" Hesera demanded. "Kheruef? Sartuma? They admitted you?"

"Obviously," I said, having very little patience for this.

"I warned them. I reminded them that you have no rights to this house," he said. "I was very explicit about that."

"I imagine you were." I said.

"Did you beg to be admitted?" he asked. "Did you request hospitality? Or shelter?"

"I guess you could call it shelter," I said. "We didn't talk much. But they could see I needed shelter."

"Ha! What did you think would happen with your swordplay and brawling and who knows what?"

"We fought to make Pahroh send the Iebiru to their worship. There was a chance to save Kehmeht. We took it."

"You took shame. You took treason. You dragged the good children of The Black Land down into dishonor. You led them into suicide."

"So? What's wrong with suicide? You've chosen suicide for yourself haven't you? All prepared with two tinctures ready to go, right? At least I offered my life to save Kehmeht. You will take your own out of pride and spite without trying to do any good for anybody."

"I will not take my own life."

"What?"

"I will not drink those poisons. I have already discarded them."

"What?"

"Do your ears fail you now along with your wit? I threw them out yesterday."

"Why?"

"Upon reflection I realized that they would doom *you*, Young Ingrate."

"What are you talking about?"

"What is a firstborn? He is first among siblings, is he not?"

I nodded, just so he'd move beyond long pauses and get on with whatever he was trying to say.

"In a family of wealth he inherits everything and leaves the second sons to find their own way in life. Among the great of Kehmeht he takes the offices of power. In the highest family, he takes the Throne itself."

He paused for a moment looking for some glimmer of understanding from me. Finding none, he soldiered on.

"But even in a brood of the poorest villagers, he or she is the one the others look to. He or she is the one who understands what father and mother are doing, where they have gone, what they will expect, what they want.

"The firstborn in every household is the god of the other children, the one who must be acknowledged, the one who knows, the one who must be obeyed. From a mud hut in the meanest village of the floodplain to the Great House itself, the firstborns are the gods of everyday life. That is why the Power of the Iebiru will slay them. To put to rest forever any question that there can be any lord but Himself!"

Hesera spat out these words in his voice of madness, spittle spraying, voice cracking. But the thought behind them was lucid. And terrible.

"So? Why does this make you forego taking your own life? Before the Power can take it from you? Wasn't that the whole idea?"

"Have you always been this stupid, Little Vagabond? Was I mistaken all these years about what scarce wit you actually have?" He took a breath and went on.

"There will be a god cut down in every household, your

own Mohsheh has said so! There must be a firstborn thrown down to death in each and every home. If I escape by taking my own life, who will He have left here to kill? Are you really too stupid to see?"

"He will have me to kill," I said. "Me. I am a firstborn."

"You..." Hesera spat out, "are..." and he paused to give space between his words "...*not*... a... firstborn!"

I searched his eyes for some sign that this was just more of his hateful madness.

"You are not a firstborn," he repeated. "Not of your mother. And not of her husband. And not of your father."

I could not speak. I could not think. I stood there, blinking at him.

"This is why I took such pains to be sure that you had no portion in this House, Mereyamun," he said. "This is why I stripped you of all rights and all authority. This is why I ordered the servants to cease obeying you. I wanted to be certain that nothing of the status of a firstborn stuck to you, not in the minds of the servants, not in my mind, and most important of all, not in your own."

And with this, his bizarre lesson on the nature of the firstborn and my own genealogy was ended. There was only quiet between us now. I saw wet in his eyes. And I realized that, in all his madness, he never stopped loving me.

"I still hate them, you know," he said simply. "I hate the Iebiru for what they have done to our Happy Land. I hate the two Brothers for what they are doing to the whole world. Oh, they are riding a whirlwind! Sooner or later they will bring on their own destruction. And if not, Bilahm will return from the East and will vanquish them. You'll see, Mereyamun. I will not live to see it. I will be dead by morning. But you will be among the living."

"What must I do?" I said, not knowing what I was really asking. What must I do to save him? To save myself? To go on in the world that will be when this night of death has passed?

"Live," Hesera answered. "Live as best you can, in whatever way you think you should. Cleave to that ape Harkuhotep and his band of traitors if you like. Or wait for the day of vengeance that will surely come against them and their Iebiru comrades."

I nodded, just to say that I heard him.

"Now we must say goodbye, Merey. And there is no good way, so let it at least be quick."

Tears were pooling in my eyes now. He saw.

"Instructions, then Mereyamun," he said curtly. "I will go to my chamber. I will close the door. You are not to dare to open it until full sunrise. Is that clear? Say that it is."

"Yes."

"No matter what you hear coming from my chamber. Cries, curses, moaning, even pleas for help, no matter what comes out of my mouth, you are not to enter. Is that clear? Say that it is."

"Yes," I whispered. "It is."

"Swear," he commanded. "I want an oath on it. Swear."

"By whom?"

"By whatever Power still avenges oaths unkept," he said. "By whatever name you call it."

I took an oath by the Power of the Iebiru, though I said it in a barely audible whisper.

"Good," he said. "It is done. Farewell then."

I opened my mouth to bid him farewell in return, but I froze.

"I see a question on your face. It stains it, like the face of a boy who has eaten too greedily of Sartuma's honey pudding. A boy like you were once, Merrimu..." his voice trailed off. He recovered.

"One short question, and then, a good night forever."

I swallowed. I spoke.

"Are you my father?"

Hesera looked at me, really looked at me for the first time in a very long time, as if I was some strange new thing that he had never beheld before. My breathing slowed to near nothing in the long silence. Finally he released his own pent-up breath in a snort.

"You, Mereyamun," he said, slowly, deliberately, giving each syllable its due. "You are no firstborn of mine."

And with that he closed the door.

~

The room grew darker even though the moon was up and whole. Its beam angled through my window but it was a cold light and illuminated little.

I turned to the shelf where a solitary lamp was guttering and replenished it with olive oil from a filigreed vessel, a gift from Hesera back when things like that mattered. Sated with the replenished oil, the lamp tried its best to dispel the gloom but succeeded only in adding some faint gold to the silvery moonbeam. The room remained murky.

I gravitated to the window to look out on the orchard, the place where I could always settle my thoughts. But there was no orchard.

The animals came and uprooted the trees and trampled them into the earth, hadn't they? Huge beasts pushed them over and furry demon-like things of the jungle tore out their branches and despoiled their fruit. Then the hailstorm came in barrages of ice and fire and destroyed what was left. Then the locusts. No, there was no orchard anymore. It was a walled-in wasteland, no longer a place to settle any thoughts.

Unsettled thoughts, then. They turned on Hesera, of course. On his claims, his revelations, his plots, his cabals. If what he said was the simple truth, then I might live through this night. But since when did Hesera deal in simple truth? He dealt in arcane wisdom, he dealt in whatever manipulated things to his will. What else does a sorcerer do? He wields wisdom only to bend the world and all of us in it to his own ends.

So Hesera had me in one last grand manipulation. What was unknown was its purpose. It could be that he pitied me, his failed apprentice. It could be he wanted to calm me with a false hope so that I would not suffer too much until midnight when I would be struck dead.

But it also could be that he loved me and wished to see me find a life in the new world that would be born this night. A world in which he wanted no part. But why did he hint so darkly at who I am and what I might be?

Was I child who needed a fable to explain how I came to be born? Whoever my father was, he was gone before I could know what a father is. My mother was only a memory of soft linen and the scent of myrrh, cardamom, and cassia. Why not just tell me who they were, these two who conceived me? If there was shame in it, it was not my shame.

But that is the way of the sorcerer, isn't it? To siphon the life out of women and men, demons and animals, plants and metals, and bend them all to his own purposes.

In the ordinary way of things, I did not have to stand

still for this. Our Black Land, the Land That Makes Her Children Happy, did not leave me without recourse. Where sorcerers fail to help (or refuse to) there are courts.

I could petition a high servant of the Throne to look into my case, take testimonies from the living, search into the papyrus annals of the dead. The Chamber of Judgments could rule on who I was, and what was mine, and where I fit in the weave of things. Wasn't I a familiar of Harkuhotep, Seal Bearer of the King of Upper and Lower Kehmeht, Unique Friend of Pahroh, Trusted of All His House? Would he not adjudicate my case?

But Harkuhotep had abandoned his Chamber. He was, this night, in a crowded mudbrick house of Iebiru, sharing in their destiny. He was tasting with them, for the first time in his life, the flesh of an animal, a young one of the sacred Ram, the star sign of this month at the turning of spring. It took little imagination to see him there. Harkuhotep and all the others.

I could see him sitting with Avishamah and his family, relieved of his greatness, delivered of the burden of being anything other than a plain man who had known, in his youth, mudbrick houses not so different than this one. I could see him glance over at Inyotef, his true firstborn son, who would live now because he had become Iebiri and a servant of their Eternal One.

Was Harkuhotep thinking also of his other firstborn, Inyotef's half-brother, Okpara? Lying dead in the shadow of the Great House among so many others who bled out their lives there to save Kehmeht? We Sons of the Black Land slew one another because we could not agree on what "save Kehmeht" meant. Now it turned out we were, all of us, wrong.

My thoughts turned to Herit. Did she know now that

her husband was already gone? Did she go out into the night, slipping past final clashes of fighters, picking her way among the slain outside the Great House, searching for Okpara?

Or was she bound to stay near her children, waiting for the firstborn one to join his father in the Happy Land of Reeds at midnight, while comforting his little brother who would wake to find both his father and his big brother gone?

And Herit herself, was she a firstborn? If she was, how terribly and truly alone that little brother would be. It was terrible to think about, and my thoughts turned away from it and back to Gohshen.

Adjedaa would be happy this night. She would find warm welcome with Avishamah's family. They would see in her villager's simplicity something not so foreign. And they would feel in her fire for her new King something of what was in their own hearts.

Setka, to whom loyalty always mattered more than life itself, would be saying little. Few in that house would understand the courage he was summoning to do this thing, to eat of the meat of the offering, to turn his back on the Throne of the Two Kingdoms, to go out in the morning into the Red Land, there to accept from this day and forever, the Eternal One of the Iebiru as his King.

And Neferet. She would be taking it all in, missing nothing, her mind racing, her heart swelling with what they were doing, the bunch of them being born into a new life. She would be holding her baby son the whole time, full of happiness that this second birth of his was granted so near his first one.

He would grow up a servant of the Eternal One. He would never know the pain and confusion of we who had mistaken flesh and blood for a true King. He would grow up to be a man of a kind the world had not yet seen.

And then there was the only person in that house who, at this moment as I thought of her, might be reaching out in her mind with thoughts of me. Mayati would wonder, first of all, if I was safe.

She saw me last that night before the locusts came, and had no way of knowing if I made it back to The City or what had happened to me during the Six Days of Darkness. She might have been relieved of doubt when Inyotef and Adjedaa arrived, if they told her I was well. Stubborn, foolish, but well.

Setka could have confirmed it when he arrived, the part about being stubborn and foolish too. Being without guile, Setka would have told how I intended to force the Throne to send away the Iebiru.

This surely would have frightened Mayati on two counts. First, because she knew I was no warrior. She considered me more than a little naïve about how unyielding and cruel the servants of the Throne, once challenged, would be. And second, because she "knew" in her understanding-without-knowledge that what Mohsheh said would happen this night would, indeed, happen.

The fighting I would join would be bloody and futile. Pahroh would not yield until the firstborn were slain. The very thing we were fighting to avoid would inevitably happen. And what was the chance of me surviving such a conflict? Or, if I did, then surviving the slaying by the Power?

So while Mayati was eating unleavened bread and bitter herbs and roasted offering that was their worship this night, some part of her would be really angry with me.

She'd be mad at me for being so stubborn and dooming myself and never returning to her.

And then she would sigh and turn her attention back to this new thing. She was going to go out on the journey tomorrow, take the three day walk into the Red Land where The Eternal One would show Himself to her.

And then, she thinks, everything will be alright. She takes comfort in that. And in the hope that maybe, in all that goodness, somehow, I too might be saved.

~

There was singing in the night outside my window. Iebiru certainly. With the orchard flattened I had a line of sight from my window all the way to their dwellings down by the irrigation canal. Those poor mudbrick hovels were cheerful now, lit up and happier than our limestone palaces that would soon hold a mix of the living and the dead. How soon?

Midnight had to be close. But how would I know it when it came? I very much wanted to consult the water clock in Hesera's chambers. The tension of not knowing whether I would live or die was unbearable, enough to make me consider breaking my oath. But how could I be so faithless?

Hadn't I taken that oath in the name of the Eternal One of The Iebiru? He who would either take my life or spare it, any moment now? No, I would do nothing, not even think. I would quiet my thoughts and wait for what would come... Crack!

Lightening scalded my eyes. I squeezed them shut in pain. I took hold of the window to steady myself and then, slowly, cautiously, opened my eyes to soothe them in the dark. But there was no dark.

It had become bright day, the light was the light of noon. But there was no sun in this night sky, just the illumination of daytime, everywhere. I heard a great crash from downstairs followed by screams, one after the other, terrible and full of desperate dread. Sartuma.

I ran down to the great room and found her in full-mouthed hysteria, short screams, one after the other, again and again without pause. She was standing though, clearly not struck dead. But she was inconsolable, despite Kheruef's attempts to say something, anything, to calm her.

Nothing coherent was coming out of his mouth either, just noises as he shifted his weight in a bizarre dance from foot to foot, gesturing wildly with his hands trying to say something for which he could find no words, only sounds.

And there, spilled out on the floor stones between them, a steaming pool of molten gold. And at its source, the lead shards of the fallen and shattered form of what had been Behs.

It never occurred to me that you could slay a statue. But Behs was *slain*, there was no other word for it. He was cast down with great force, his skin of gold flayed and melted off, his body of lead broken, decapitated, limbs amputated, torso fractured. His altar was smashed, his offerings cast down and scattered. He was vanquished, an object of wrath and vengeance.

I was frozen by the sight, and by the rhythmic screams of Sartuma and the bizarre pantomime of Kheruef. I might have gone on standing there, a gaping statue myself, were it not for the storm of noises that came in through the windows from all sides. Men, women, yelling, crying out, the pounding of running feet, shouts and the calling of names.

I moved toward the door to see what was happening but thought better of it. The door would best stay bolted for now. Still, I needed to know what was going on. So I turned back up the stairs and ran down the corridor to the narrow steps that would take me up to the roof.

The City, visible from up there, was lit up as if midday. I saw men dead or dying all over the streets, still grasping swords and knives. These were the last of them, the fighters in the civil war that was supposed to make the Throne surrender to the Power and spare us all this.

Many showed no wounds. Yet they writhed on the ground, strangled and choking for air that would not fill their lungs. They made dreadful sounds, gasping, sputtering, wheezing, until life was choked out of them. Some found their end in a few moments. Others went on in long agony.

Then there were the cries from the houses up and down the street, cries of the suddenly bereaved calling out the names of their loved ones again and again. "No, no!" they cried out helplessly against the death that had come into their chambers.

Doors burst open and husbands and wives and parents and children called out into The City, as if help might come. As if there was anyone who could do anything.

There were other piteous screams. These were the cries of the dying who could not die. They were being tormented with an end that was nowhere near enough to give any hope of relief. Their cries were the most chilling, for they went on relentlessly, and anyone who heard them became sick at heart and crushed with despair. I went from one side of the roof to the other to escape those cries. But there was no escape, they came from every quarter.

On the street below I saw a horse collapse and die under its rider who managed to roll away and avoid being crushed. The animal was a firstborn, surely, and the rider I guessed was not. He must have been bruised by the fall, he moved so slowly getting back to his feet. Then a pack of dogs turned the corner, snarling and barking and the man found his legs and fled.

The pack pursued him but broke off their hunt at a patch of land tucked away behind a home, marked off by a low wall of white stone. The dogs took the low wall easily and fell to scratching at the earth, digging furiously with their forepaws. Clods flew until they were able to lean into their excavations and emerge with the bones and, in one case, the not-yet-decomposed arm, of corpses buried there.

Sometimes in Kehmeht, when a family would suffer the loss of a beloved firstborn child, they would bury him close to the foundation of their home and take comfort in an image of their precious one painted skillfully on the wall nearest the grave. They would bring offerings of fruits and grains and pour out libations of wine and sing and dance before it, so that their lost one, now a kind of minor god, would watch over them.

But from this night onward there were to be no gods, only the Eternal One. Living men and women, beasts and birds, statues of stone, silver, or gold, even corpses, it did not matter –if they were ever thought to be gods they were to be destroyed this night.

I saw more than one dog ravaging the corpse of an infant or small child and making any who would interrupt them pay dearly in blood. I don't know why it was so harrowing to behold, these tiny corpses were, after all, already dead and there was much worse suffering of the still living all around me.

Yet I could not turn away from the sight. It evoked the Iebiru babies bricked up alive into walls. Or the ones who were born only to suffocate helplessly in the muck of the clay pits where their mothers were forced to slave while giving birth. Or the untold numbers of newborns drowned in The River and disappeared from all memory and guilt.

Was this what I was being kept alive for? To witness this? To admit to all the evil that was done in my name and in the name of my Land and my People? And only then to be struck dead as a firstborn, just as a condemned man is forced to listen to his crimes before his execution?

I let the screams and cries and snarls and curses and thunder and lightning and barking and baying wash over me, standing there in this night that was bright as day. I thought then that death would not be so bad if all this would just end. But I did not die. I waited for it, but it did not come.

I was done with this roof and let my feet lead me back down the steps into the house. Sartuma's screams had become more muted but they were relentless, like a drumbeat and I wondered, if she was meant to live, would it not be with a diminished mind? I thought to go down to her when I heard cries from Hesera.

He was old and his lungs were no longer powerful, and perhaps in ordinary times the sound would not have been heard behind the oaken door of his chambers. But this was no ordinary time and what he was voicing was no ordinary sound.

It was raspy and gurgled as one would expect from a man in his condition. But it was sustained in a way I could not explain, as if it were not breath coming out of him but life-force itself. It was the sound of not only a body being tortured but its ka itself in torment.

I went to his door, remembering my oath all the while. I knew I would not violate it. But I could not stay away. I stood there, just outside the door, taking his cries into my own soul until I wished for either his life to end or mine.

I think I might have fainted there at some point. I could not be sure. I do not have a clear memory of how I came to be back in my own room, huddled on my bed, the door closed tightly against everything. But that was where I found myself when the sunrise came.

I t was a real sunrise. The unforgiving noon-like bright of the terrible night was gone. This light was warm and familiar and gentle. The disk of the sun had just began to appear in the East. There were birdsongs, as befits a morning near the closing of Ipt-Hmt, the third Month of Shemu.

I found Kheruef and Sartuma in the great room still, seated on stools they had drawn as far away from the remains of slain Behs as space would allow. They were calm. The night of horrors had passed and they were both alive.

"It is over now," Sartuma said to me.

"And we are alive," I responded as if this was the way the Children of Kehmeht would greet one another from now on.

"We must do honor for our Master Hesera," I said.

Sartuma nodded her agreement and Kheruef rose immediately to the task. Sartuma took his offered hand and he led her the long way around the perimeter of the room rather than tread on what had been Behs. I started to lead the way to Hesera's chamber, but Sartuma called me back.

"Let us do it," she said.

It was a great kindness, as I did not at all want to look upon the remains of what had been Hesera, wrap him in linen and transport him to the Houses of the Dead. So they made their way around me and up the stairs while I stood and contemplated the mess on the floor. I realized that at least part of their generosity was that they feared the shattered pieces of a god more than the corpse of a man.

No matter. I went to the kitchens and returned with a cleaning shovel and a copper refuse box and went to work on removing what had so offended the Power of the Iebiru. It was strange that I had once thought that this statue would help in some way. I never thought it was the god himself, but I did feel that somehow the image would enable us to find help from his powers.

But, of course, there were no powers and there was no god and this image was a lie. As of this morning, there were to be no more lies.

So I threw the head and arms and the larger chunks into the bin like the rubbish they were. It took some scraping with the shovel to get the molten and then congealed lead and gold unstuck from the floor. I paused about the thin slivers of gold, knowing they still had value. But it was repulsive and I let them fall from my shovel into the bin.

This clean-up took some time and just as I finished I heard a clattering from the flight above me. Kheruef descended with a light bed which he manhandled down the steps and set down off to the side of the great room. He nodded to me that everything was in order as he sprinted smartly up the steps and disappeared into Hesera's chambers, only to appear a moment later his hands firmly under the arms of a white form wrapped in white linens, Sartuma holding up the feet.

They laid Hesera down gently on the bed. The perfumes they used were extensive and the room filled with their aroma so boldly that they just about announced how unbearable the unconcealed odor of this corpse must actually be.

As I looked at the white form, so clean now in its linens with no trace of corruption, I wondered who was inside? Was this the vengeful cackling enemy of the Iebiru and their Power? Or was this my great uncle, the kind master who raised me and, in his way, loved me? And could one man be both?

A knocking on the door gently broke my reverie. It was a polite knocking, quiet and with long patient breaks between repetitions. Sartuma opened the door to reveal a small group of Iebiru.

I recognized them immediately, for they had been here once before. They were the ones who came when I was encased in The Darkness and they had moved through my room with a light that emanated from themselves.

"Excuse me," a man of them said tentatively. "I know this is a hard day...a harsh day for you..." and he gestured very slightly with his head toward the wrapped corpse on the bed behind us.

"It is no trouble," Sartuma responded to him in a mixture of deference and fear. She stepped back from the door allowing them to enter. Two men, a woman, and a girl-child, just as I remembered from that night. Especially the girl-child, who knew exactly where secret treasures were concealed in my wall.

"With your permission," the Iebiri woman explained,

"we would like to borrow some things for the worship. Some things of value."

"Yes, yes," Sartuma agreed readily and turned to Kheruef who was already off to Sartuma's room. He returned with a bag of silver coins and a tiny spoon of gold with lapis lazuli in the handle. He handed them to Sartuma who thrust them into the Iebiri woman's hands as if they were too hot to hold.

"Thank you," the Iebiri woman said, and the little girl and the men added thanks of their own.

But Sartuma, still fearful, looked here and there for more things of value, things for the Iebiru to just take and go. I saw her gaze rest for a moment on the bin with the remains of Behs inside, but she shied away from it, and said to Kheruef, "The Master's chamber." No sooner did she say it then a look of shame and a new fear came over her as she glanced sideways at me, wondering if she had gone too far.

"It is good, Sartuma," I said to her. "It is what is meant to be."

The relief on her face was palpable, and Kheruef went and returned with an armload of instruments of polished brass and silver whose purpose he could not even guess. These he forced upon the Iebiri man who was nearest.

"Take these, please," he said.

"Please," Sartuma added hopefully, wanting nothing more than to see these Iebiru sated and gone.

But the Iebiru did not go. They stood there, awkwardly, but stolidly and turned to look towards me.

"Is there nothing you can add?" Sartuma pleaded to me in a small voice.

"May we borrow from your treasury?" the girl-child asked me, confident that we both knew very well what she was talking about.

"Of course," I said and led the way up to my room.

All four Iebiru followed, trailed by Sartuma and Kheruef who were curious about what I had been concealing and terrified that some fault might be found in us by these Iebiru. What would happen if they complained to their Power about us? Would He not blot out our lives as He did those of so many this past night?

I stepped aside to allow everyone into my room. As a result, the little girl arrived at the exact spot on the wall before I did and waited there.

But she did not reach out her hand to do anything regarding the false stone covering. This I did, much to Kheruef's genuine surprise. (As for Sartuma, I couldn't be sure if her face revealed some prior knowledge of this secret.) I used a blade from the chest under my window and worked my way around the concealing stone until I had enough of an edge to grip and remove it, revealing my vault.

I reached in and pulled out each of the two bronze chests hidden within, laying them on my bed one at a time. I stood aside to let the Iebiru open them until I realized that they were not going to do that. So I opened each of them myself and then, frustrated by the Iebiru just standing and waiting, I sunk my two hands into a chest and pulled out fistfuls of treasure.

I placed two handfuls of earrings, nose rings, necklaces bracelets, and coins into the hands of one of the men, then returned for two more handfuls. But there was no one to hand them to, as the woman had only one hand free and the other man was loaded down with Hesera's instruments. I thrust what I had into the hands of the little girl who cradled all of it with her two arms against her robe.

"Thank you," the second man, nodded.

"This is most generous."

"Thank you," the girl-child chirped with a nod of her head and the agreement of all the others.

An awkward moment followed with all of us just looking at one another and Sartuma so frightened that she looked as if she was about to burst into tears.

"Here," I said taking the near empty chest. "Put everything in here."

I relieved them of their burdens by holding up the chest and when it was full, I gave it to the larger of the two Iebiru men. I then picked up the other chest and thrust it into the now empty hands of the other.

"Thank you again, thank you," the Iebiru were saying as they left.

"This is very generous, thank you."

The thanks continued down the steps right to the door and there, the Iebiri woman with moist eyes turned to Sartuma who was weeping openly. They regarded each other for moment. Then they embraced. And then the Iebiru were gone.

"It is over now," Sartuma said to me. "It is over."

～

It was not quite entirely over. Out on the street several near-slain of the Black Land still moaned and writhed in their agonies. Some bystanders and loved ones remained with them. But none were able to do anything that helped.

The three of us watched from our open doorway. We stood there, letting all the pity and terror of it wash over us, along with the generous waves of relief we guiltily enjoyed. It was awkward. Finally, mercifully, Kheruef spoke up.

"Should I hire some men?" he asked. "And maybe a cart and driver?"

"Yes, of course," I said. "The Houses of the Dead will be overwhelmed, the sooner the better."

Grateful to have something to do with himself, Kheruef jogged out into the scene and disappeared around a corner. Left alone in silence with Sartuma, I finally said the simplest and truest thing there was to say.

"I am happy that you are alive."

"I am no firstborn, it seems," she said.

"Nor am I," I said.

She teared up again and, unable to find any more words, bustled off to the kitchens to take up once again what she could of the busy and useful life she had once known.

~

I wandered out into the Spring morning for no reason other than that I could. I was alive and this was a morning that just a few hours ago I was not sure I would ever see.

Knots of people were gathered up and down the avenue. Some were busy moving bodies off to one side. These were laid out in orderly rows to wait for carts that would come for them. The still-dying were moved too, though placed at a decent distance from the corpses. The general effect was to clear one side of the avenue for travelers.

These included heralds, some mounted on horseback, delivering the official words for what everyone already knew:

"So says Pahroh to the Nations of the Iebiru!" they

called out. "You are no longer under my dominion! You are servants of the Eternal One! Go now on your journey to His service in the Red Land!"

Soon, almost as if in answer to the proclamation, the cleared side of the avenue began to fill with Iebiru. They led donkeys, whole trains of them, laden with all the good things of Black Land.

Innumerable chests, much like the ones I had loaned our Iebiru visitors, appeared on every donkey's load. If the value of their contents was anything like the elegance of their containers, great fortunes were passing before my eyes. But what caught my attention most was the Iebiru themselves.

They passed before us, large families of them, white bearded elders, venerable matriarchs, youths and maidens, men and their wives cradling infants in their arms while herding uncountable flocks of children. Nothing remarkable about that. Iebiru loved nothing so much as their families and breeding children in abundance. But this day, at this moment, there was *something* remarkable about it.

Most of my life I thought of Iebiru as indolent and sullen, as is the way of slaves. They labored when forced to and avoided it when they could get away with it. They swarmed over our land but never with any purpose of their own. It was our purposes that defined them. So who, then, were these moving through our streets this morning?

Like soldiers on a march, these were full of a single purpose. It was in their step, in the set of their faces and in the light of their eyes. Their too many cloaks rustled in the breeze like banners of triumph.

I was not alone in seeing them as if for the first time. Children of the Black Land, highborn and low, lined the street to see for themselves. A great many wanted to engage the Iebiru as they passed.

Some called out blessings of "Go in good fortune!" and "An easy road!" as if this was just another merchant caravan heading out to a trading city beyond the Two Rivers. Others broke ranks to press a few more small treasures into their hands, a few extra coins, a cunningly crafted arm bracelet or a necklace of silver and lapis lazuli. Some patted backs or squeezed grips of encouragement onto shoulders or upper arms. But what they all meant was: "Please, go! Go quickly, with no delay! For if you stay, we will surely die!"

If those Iebiru had chosen to still their skipping children and stop their donkey trains for even a moment, if they had simply called a brief rest to their progress, I believe not a few Sons of Kehmeht on that street would have fainted in terror. We were, this morning, survivors of a massacre that was barely over. Every single house had its slain, there were no exceptions. And all because their Eternal One came, in the end, to claim His Iebiru.

What if His thirst for vengeance on their behalf was not yet slaked? What if we did anything to suggest that we were not yet chastened? I wondered if the fact that I had taken up arms to force the Throne to send the Iebiru protected me from further wrath?

Would the Eternal One of the Iebiru show favor to those of us who had failed, but at least tried, to have His Iebiru sent to Him? Or would He know that what we did we did for ourselves, to save our own lives, to save our own nation from destruction?

And what about those of us who had the opportunity to come to His full moon feast and eat of His offering, and yet did not go? Was that an insult to the Power of the Iebiru, that we preferred to kill and die in a revolt against the Throne, rather than accept the grace He offered us? Would there be a reckoning for that too?

Those who did accept that invitation were rewarded with their lives this past terrible night. And now they were going to be rewarded again. They were going to be taken out to the Red Land to see Him, The Eternal One who none had seen before. He would reveal himself to them, just four days from now. And I would not be there to see it.

And then came an even darker thought: Was it known in the Great House that I had been part of the bloody days of insurrection? Was I noticed and identified? Was my name on some list? Would I be sought out? Would there be a knock on my door late some night, grim officers come to take me in chains? Or worse?

"There you are!"

I jumped as a hand clapped down hard on my shoulder, and spun around to fight or fly or face my doom.

"Inyotef."

"I've been looking for you everywhere."

"How did you get here?"

"Horses, chariot, the usual way," he said. "Though never so quickly as this morning."

"But you were in Goshen."

"Until daylight, yes. And now I'm here."

"Why?"

"I left someone behind here. Someone I care about. I came back to get him," he said. "But we have very little time. Let's go?"

He rushed me back down the street, past where his chariot and horses were tied, and into the open door of the house.

"Just grab a traveling cloak," he said. "And a nemes."

"Are we dressing for court?" I asked incredulously as I ran up the stairs to my room.

"We're in for a scorching in the Deshret," he called up. "You'll need more than that wig."

"Should we fill some water skins?" I asked as I bounded back down the steps two at a time with a cloak and a headdress in my hands.

"I helped myself when I got here. Jugs in the chariot."

I followed Inyotef out the door, then came to a halt just behind him.

"What?"

"Uncle Hesera," I said.

Inyotef nodded, having understood who it was lying wrapped on the bed in the great room.

"There is nothing you can do for him," Inyotef said kindly.

"I sent Kheruef to fetch a cart and some men to bring him to the Houses of the Dead. But I don't have any coins to leave for him to pay. I lent what I had to Iebiru this morning."

Inyotef nodded as he took the bridle of his team. He knew about the Iebiru borrowing things for the worship.

"But I have money stored with the priests at the Temple of Djehuti." I told him. "We could stop off there."

"There is no time, Merey. As it is we will need a blessing of speed, even more than I had this morning, to get back to Gohshen before the departure."

I looked back through the open door to where Hesera lay, as if somehow this would tell me what to do.

"Besides, the Priests of Djehuti have most-likely already loaned your money to the Iebiru," Inyotef said. "And the temple itself is probably half-destroyed."

Given what happened to our homely Behs, I could only

imagine what the wrath of the night had wrought on the giant golden image of Djehuti. I envisioned his ibis head torn from his human body, staved-in or melted over the flag stones of his own temple.

"Kheruef will find something around the house to pay the carter and the hired men," Inyotef said. "And no one at the Houses of the Dead will turn away a Royal Sorcerer. They'll take their payment later from what Hesera has left behind."

Inyotef gave me a moment to consider this. It troubled me, though I could see no better way.

"Alright, then?" he asked.

"Alright."

With that we jumped into the car of his chariot. Inyotef walked the horses round in a wide circle, putting us out onto the cleared side of the avenue. He clicked the team into a fast walk, a near trot, and people jumped aside as we sped our way out of The City.

But strangely, whenever we came up on a family of Iebiru, Inyotef did not look for a way around them to pass at speed. Instead, he would pull up on his team and bring us to a slow walk, a plodding pace behind the long trains of donkeys led by Iebiru on foot ahead of us.

And yet, looking around at the familiar buildings as we passed them, landmarks of The City I had lived in all my life, I realized they were rushing by us, as if we were racing at a breakneck gallop. It was an impossible thing. But so was the noon light at midnight. So was the precision slaying of the firstborn by an executioner who knew the secrets of every coupling in the Black Land. This was a time of impossible things.

I wanted to ask Inyotef about this strange bending of time. I wanted to tell him what I had seen these last days. I wanted to hear what he saw in Gohshen and what he knew. But the clatter of the bronze hooped wheels sparking against the hard city streets was too great. Then, just at the northern boundary of The City, we turned into a stable. The horses needed to be watered before we pushed further.

The stable owner hurried over to serve us, but faltered in his steps as he took us in. You could see him stealing worried glances at the Iebiru passing by on the road, while trying to puzzle out who or what we were.

I appeared a well-born Son of Kehmeht. But Inyotef was a puzzling sight. His dress said he was a Royal Herald and he drove a team out of the King's stock. But he was bearded now, not quite like the Iebiru, but no longer appearing a son of the Black Land.

The poor man seemed to puzzle over the possibilities. Were Iebiri to be heralds now? He could barely speak as he offered Inyotef a small pouch of silver coins, all he had left probably, to lend to this royal Iebiri.

Inyotef gently pushed the pouch back into the man's hand and produced a coin of his own for the water and the bit of feed we were taking. The man watered our horses, still casting uneasy glances now and then at both us and at the Iebiru on the road moving steadily northward. Inyotef and I watched them too.

"Are we a blur to them now?" I asked Inyotef, trusting that he had experienced what I had when we were moving with them.

"Probably."

"But when we get back on the road with them, then we will see this place as a blur too? As we speed away from it?"

"I believe so," he said. "Yes."

"It is very strange."

"The Eternal One is hurrying things," Inyotef said.

"There is an appointed time and it may not be delayed." He shrugged. "Come."

Inyotef drove the team out from the stable yard at a quick trot onto a stretch of open road and then released them into a run. At that speed it was barely a moment or two until we caught up, once again, to a long train of laden donkeys led by Iebiru. Once again we reined in and slowed to their pace. And once again the world around us whipped by as if we had broken into a gallop. But we were just walking.

And so it went, the villages, The River, the slightly sloping plains of Gohshen, they were all there. We traveled through them all, nothing was skipped, nothing was missed. Yet you only had to look up at the sky to see that the sun had run but very little of its course and our journey was almost done. There, in the distance I could see the abandoned towers of Rahmessu.

So this was the chosen assembly point. This place in which Iebiru were scourged and maimed by labors that had no purpose and no end. This place where infants choked out their lives in its walls and hope was murdered in the hearts of the survivors. This was the place to which the Iebiru were called today. They were to see it and remember it this one last time. Then turn their backs on it and follow their Power out into the Red Land.

As we drew closer the roads choked and became impassable. The Iebiru with their trains of laden donkeys alone were sufficient for that. But add to them the flocks and herds, massed in numbers none had ever seen or counted.

These were all the animals the Iebiru had plus all the sheep, goats, and cattle of Kehmeht. All sent to be available at need for the worship festival, just as Mohsheh had said they must be. Then add to them the many sons and daughters of The Black Land mixing into the press of the Iebiru.

They had surely taken part in the offering last night, for they jostled to stay with the families they had joined. The sheer number of them was astounding, matching the count of the Iebiru themselves.

Their number was not hard to estimate because they did not blend in very well. Their dress was not quite Iebiri – though they no longer looked like sons and daughters of Kehmeht either. Too much hair on the faces of the men, too much cloth wrapping the women. All surging forward to be as close to the Iebiru as they could, and to be, themselves, as Iebiri as possible.

Add to this the many, many, ordinary people of Kehmeht who arrived for the send-off. They came from The City and from the towns and villages too, for no reason other than to see the Iebiru off and on their way.

It was a relief and a festival for them, the great celebration of the end of a year of destruction and death. Now it was time to be happy again. Now it was time for reconciliation. So they cheered and applauded the Iebiru. In this they were joined by companies of dancers and singers, the finest and most famous in The Black Land.

Only the Throne could have sent such performers here. Inyotef said it was so and that Pahroh himself was seeing the Iebiru off, though looking around I could not spot his chariot and entourage. But with all notion of roads obscured and people and beasts flooded onto the plain before Rahmessu, who could find anything?

I had never conceived of so many people in a single place. If I had ever imagined an assembly even a tenth of this scale, it might have been in a great migratory hoard out of legend. Now it stood before me in the clear light of morning, as if some ancient epic had come to life. Come to life, and, I noticed, armed.

The Iebiru wore swords on their belts or carried lances. Some had shields strapped to their backs or bows and quivers crossed over their shoulders. Some wore no arms at all, but had spears and shields strapped to their donkeys, plentiful and close at hand. Armed Iebiru. Hundreds of thousands of them.

I tasted, for just an eye-blink, something of the dread that must have gripped The Black Land some two centuries ago. Here was the sight that so troubled the imaginations of our forbearers. It was fear of this that brought the Iebiru into cruel bondage. But all in vain. Because for all that had been done to them, here were the Iebiru this morning, their yoke broken, very much alive, and armed to the teeth.

We were still burying our slain of just a few hours ago. We had lost at least one dead in every household, an outcome that dwarfed the most catastrophic defeats in military history. And the entire battle was fought *for* the Iebiru by their Power. The Iebiru themselves never lifted a finger. Not one of those blades they were wearing had tasted blood.

But what if they turned on us now? Could they not easily finish what their Power started last night? Couldn't the Iebiru seize this moment and become masters of the Black Land? We would become their slaves. Or be driven out into the howling deserts forever. Or simply exterminated.

A calmer mind might have noted that, although they were armed, none of these Iebiru had ever been in combat. Kehmeht had never relied on Iebiru as slave-warriors, they were never trusted and trained with weapons and could know nothing of the arts of war. But what, then, was all this armament for?

Were the Iebiru afraid of brigands out in the Red Land? Were there enough brigands in the whole world for a multitude like this to fear? Or had some nation from the East threatened to attack them? Or could it be that these bows and blades played some part in their worship? Did their Power crave dances with swords and lances?

It was puzzling if you thought about it. But what reason was there to think about it? This roiling mix of men, women, and children, old and just-born, had nothing of conquest or struggle about it. It was like nothing so much as the gathering of the first guests at a celebration.

They are full of anticipation. They are happy. They cannot suppress their smiles, they cannot quite stop their feet from dancing just a little as they speak with one another. They laugh a bit and break out, sometimes, in snatches of song, while some, with closed eyes, sway gently at thoughts of the good that is coming. These Iebiru were not now as we had ever seen them.

Was this joy of theirs a secret kept from us all these centuries? Or had we stifled it in them so thoroughly that now, as it overflowed, they were as surprised by it as we were?

～

Inyotef had been given to understand that the Iebiru would group themselves by their nations. Each nation would take the position that their ancestor, one of the twelve sons of Yisraale, took around their father's death bed some two centuries ago.

This meant that the nation of the Dahnii would be on

the north side of this great assembly. It was there that Avishamah and his family would be found. And with them we would find Harkuhotep, Setka and Neferet, Adjedaa, and Mayati, who had all spent the Night of the Offering in their household.

So Inyotef turned the team to the left, westward to make a great circle around the gathering and bring us around to the north. This took us away from the crowding and up to a small rise from which I could see the shape of the assembly.

I could see three nations to each of the four winds, east, south, west, and north. I could see sons and daughters of Kehmeht mixed in among them and wrapped around them too, mostly to the west. Behind them, the herds and flocks stretched out so thick they looked like a new layer of undulating earth.

Then a soft tremor went through the assembly. Just a feeling at first, fueled by a whispered rumor. Reports flew from mouth to ear, then cries of recognition. People parted like a broken wave rushing back out to the Great Green, then returned again to press up against the edges of the pathway they had just cleared. Everyone wished to see the one who was passing through. Mohsheh.

Some said his name quietly, as if the sight of him so near had to be confirmed and sealed with a spoken word. Some called out to him as he walked, as one calls to a father, a friend, a captain.

Families of the Nation of Leyvie followed after him. They were all so unnaturally tall, every eye would have gone to them at any appearance. But nearest Mohsheh, closer perhaps than Aaharohn and his sons, was a party of men bearing a coffin. They carried it on their shoulders and a hush fell on the onlookers as it passed, all eyes upon it.

I wondered what it meant. Whose remains were being carried in such state out to the Red Land? And why? The Iebiru did not worship their dead. And if some had taken on this practice, so foreign to them, would they dare perform it in front of their Power now, just days before He was going to reveal Himself?

"Inyotef!" a voice called, breaking my thoughts. Adjedaa squeezed her way uphill toward us through the crowd. Inyotef thrust the reins into my hands, leapt off the chariot, and jostled his way to her.

Adjedaa told breathlessly how she had been watching for us at the edges on the north side of the assembly but had found it impossible to see much of anything at all, as she was not particularly tall. Uncertain, she sprinted after royal chariots several times, but as she closed in on each one of them, found it to be not her husband but rather officers of the Throne sent to escort the Iebiru.

"I ran *miles*, this way and that," she panted. "It could have been that we were to leave at any moment and I didn't know if you were going to make it back in time. And then I saw your chariot halted on this rise! If you hadn't paused here, how would I ever have found you?"

She caught another breath and continued.

"I thank The Eternal One that we have found each other in time."

Inyotef murmured some kind of assent to this, as if it was a totally normal thing to assume that the Eternal One of the Iebiru busied Himself with details such as where our chariot would pause at a given moment, all for the sake of a young wife worried about her husband. I found this strange. But touching.

I was gawking at them, then realized this was a private moment. So I disguised it by shifting my gaze beyond, looking out again at the strange sight of the men bearing the coffin. They followed Mohsheh into what appeared to be the center of the assembly.

"It is Tzaphnaht Pahnayakh." Adjedaa told us. "Yoseyf, son of Yisraale."

Inyotef nodded his understanding. Adjedaa was surely reciting lore she must have heard from Avishamah last night.

"On his last day he revealed that a Redeemer would come and take the Iebiru out from Kehmeht," she said. "He bound them in an oath that, when that day came, he would be taken out him with them."

Why? I wondered. What role could he play in the worship in the Deshret? Would he be brought back to life and rise from his coffin? If he did, what would be when the worship was concluded and we all returned to The Black Land?

Would Pahroh make him Viceroy again, as he had been at the time of the Great Hunger? Yoseyf had virtually ruled Kehmeht then. Would he do so again now, but in our present Pahroh's name?

And then, for that matter, what would Mohsheh be when we returned? He was the uncrowned king of the Iebiru and, looking around me, a kind of king to countless Children of Kehmeht too. Would Mohsheh ascend to the Throne of the Two Kingdoms? Would Kehmeht, eight days from now, wake up to three Kings? Would they rule together? Would they war on one another?

Mohsheh had never acted like a king. He always showed courtesy toward the Throne. Even now, you could see that he did not take up a place at the head of this great gathering. Instead he and the men bearing Tzaphnaht Pahnayakh halted at its center. If we were to walk eastward, the nation of the Yehudiim and two others flanking them would all be going ahead of Mohsheh.

I was absorbed in this and barely registered Inyotef telling me he was going to get the chariot and horses taken care of by some of the grooms with the royal escort. Adjedaa jumped into the car with him and they were swallowed up by the crowd.

And so I found myself alone, though I was at the edge of a greater mass of people than I, or perhaps anyone, had ever counted. So many voices, so many faces, so many clutches of friends, so many families, Iebiru and Children of Kehmeht, all together now, as if this easy, happy, moment was always meant to be.

∾

I thought if I could find just one face, one face that knew me, all would be well. Neferet and Setka were here somewhere. So was Harkuhotep. Mayati would surely be watching for me. Maybe one of them would lay eyes on me before I spotted them.

But to do that they would have to turn around and look outwards when all eyes were inward now, toward Mohsheh. This was best. I didn't have any heart left to tell Okpara's father and sister how he died, though there was much in the tale to comfort them. There was courage, more than any of them might have guessed. Courage and tragedy.

And with that thought, all thoughts flew from me. I stood there, empty and desolate despite this great human sea of peace and friendship lapping up around me.

I opened my mouth to say something, but there was nothing particular to say and no one in particular to say it to. A cry, then. Some cry should rise up from deep within me and burst into this morning. But none came. What came, instead, was a tear. So the year ended the way it had begun. A single hot tear escaping onto my face.

"Tears?" said a man I discovered glancing at me as he passed. "On this happiest of days?" he said to his companion as they jostled past me.

He looked back at me over his shoulder as he pushed forward.

"Everything is good now, my brother," he said to me. "From now on, all will be well."

Was he Iebiri or a Son of Kehmeht? His words were brief and I could not tell. But that was the point, wasn't it? We all had one father now, the Eternal One. So we were all brothers and sisters, children of one father, weren't we?

"Yes," something said within me. "Yes," I smiled to myself.

A surge rippled through the assembly. There were gasps and expressions of wonder. And in front of the place where the Nation of the Yehudiim gathered, stood a thing for which I had no name.

It was a pillar, in form. But a pillar that stood on the earth and extended skyward without end, disappearing from sight at a height no one could guess. And it was made not of stone or anything of this world, but rather of cloud.

It was a sort of blue in color, yet I could see it against the sky. And it seemed to me, somehow, a kind of living thing, a creature of ka perhaps, appearing out of nowhere only because the Eternal One wished it to be so. And then, it moved. And the assembly began to follow it.

I started walking. We all did. I was moving as everyone was, at a comfortable pace. But if I looked out beyond the edges of the assembly I could see things that stood in their place vanishing from sight as if we were moving faster than racing stallions. The musicians and dancers from The City, the crowds of people who had come to see us off, they were, in seconds, left far behind, vanished from our view.

We turned southeast after the Cloud Pillar. I saw mountains of the Red Land off to my left but they were blurred by our speed. Yet our walking was measured and at a pace that both the very old and their little great grandchildren could keep.

Once again time was mysteriously changed, distance shrank. All was at the wish of The Eternal One. I was filled with the desire to see Him. If I had to walk like this for three days for that to happen, then I would.

All will be well now, I thought as we went. In three more days, our new king will reveal Himself to us. Then we will know happiness as we have never known before. We will return to the Black Land soaked in happiness!

We will live together with our Iebiru before Him. We'll be as brothers and sisters. We'll rejoice together at the happy conclusion of our pilgrimage. We will laugh together in relief and amazement at all that has happened in just twelve months, a single journey of the sun.

We will mark the day as the same one last year when Mohsheh first appeared before the Throne. All will be well. Seven more days then, and Kehmeht will be again the Land That Makes Her Children Happy. All her children. Sorrow and suffering will be over.

Just seven more days.

EPILOGUE

SEVENTY-FIFTH OF THE
SEVENTY-FIVE DAYS

B
ut it was not to be.

I was not to return to The Black Land in seven days. I would not set foot in Kehmeht again for all of the coming year. And it was to be a year in which I would see wonders and terrors beyond imagining.

A war would find me. A war with a nation of shapeshifters and sorcerers who hated the Iebiru and those of us who were joined to them more than they loved their own lives.

I would see the sky torn open and learn what was beyond. I would hear a voice that has no echo because it penetrates even rock. I would *hear* lightening with my ears and *see* thunder with my eyes. I would die and be brought back to life.

I would see civil war again and bloodshed. People I loved would be lost. And the Eternal One would speak to us. And we would finally come to know what all of this was for.

But these are matters for another scroll. I will set them

down there, a tale of another year and twenty-five days in The Red Land. As for this part of the story, it is ended now, at the closing of the tale of Seventy-Five Days to the Red Land.

THE STORY CONTINUES!
FREE OFFER

Visit
cityofagreatking.com
to sign up for news and previews of
A Year and Twenty-Five Days in the Red Land,
Book Three of the City of a Great King series!

Want to Talk With the Author?

QUESTIONS? COMMENTS? SOMETHING TO SHARE?

or
Just say hi!
You can reach Y. G. Shoresh at
https://www.cityofagreatking.com/contact/
or at
ygshoresh@gmail.com

CAN YOU TAKE A MOMENT TO LEAVE A REVIEW?

Thank you for reading this volume of the City Of A Great King series. It took many years to shape through lots of research in a couple of languages and lots of doubts about whether I could tell the story I hoped to tell.

Whether you liked it or if you found fault with it (or both!) it would be a great kindness to me and to other readers if you would leave a review on Amazon.

I read every word of every review posted, so you can be sure that whatever you want to share about this series will shape the new releases (and maybe even a reworking of some of what's already published!)

And through your review, new readers will discover that there's something here for them, something they would not want to miss but might never have known about without the awakening of their interest because of your thoughts, feelings, and ideas shared in your review.

Here's a link to the Review page:

amazon.com/review/create-review?&asin=B0B5PXSP9N

Many Thanks,

-Y. G. Shoresh

Dedication

Akiva, Ayelet, Eliana, Bentzi, Dovid, Talia, Sruli, Orah, Roni, Chesky, Yakira, Tzivia Chaya, Nachman, Ahuva, Yishai,
Akiva Shalom, Dovid

This was written for you.